# The Carriers

Kristina Caffrey

# PART ONE

## *Chapter One*

***Now***

Through the window she gazed at him sitting inside. She did not bother to glance away every few seconds to avoid drawing his attention. No—he had never seemed to possess that uniquely human awareness of being watched. Or perhaps his obliviousness merely proved that old habits die hard: perhaps long ago he had grown accustomed to her gaze, and perhaps years later he still conceded to her eyes like second nature.

After all this time, it had all led to this, to standing outside a Midtown Manhattan outlet of a ubiquitous café chain. Here she was, contemplating the spectacularly special thing that had happened to her, and yet here she stood, at the most mundane location possible, one which managed to silence the profundity stirring within her. How obviously and even pitifully ironic that the most momentous event of her life would occur in a nondescript numbered franchise of this multi-national corporate conglomerate.

She could have accepted the clichéd nature of a coffee shop meeting if it had at least been a locally-owned-and-operated coffee shop, but this café chain's snooty Italian vocabulary, its iconic logo, and the yuppies clacking away at laptops inside all mocked her need for a singular existence.

Of course, he had chosen the meeting place, and so she had not been able to location-scout or set-decorate this episode of her life. While she would have chosen a grand and romantic landmark for this conversation, he had sought refuge in the absolutely impersonal, as if he hoped the coffee shop's very public nature would moderate the intimacy of the discussions he expected to occur within it. Or maybe deferring to the coffee bar was just laziness on his part. Of course, pondering what his choice of meeting place said about his mental state was likely a futile task. He had been as impervious to psychology as he had been to her gaze. But then, as she reminded herself yet again, she had not seen him in a while. Things might have changed.

She would also not be able to write each snippet of dialogue for this scene, although in a moment of weakness she had allowed herself the small fantasy of walking in and hearing him say, "Of all the gin joints in all the towns in all the world, she walks into mine," quoting movies to each other as they once did long ago. But she knew he would not follow her script. He never had.

A rush of adrenaline flooded her system and sent tsunamis of nausea across her stomach. Classic flight-or-fight signals, but a misplaced reaction, considering she was the hunter, not the hunted. She had spent the last five minutes studying her target and preparing herself for the strike. He, on the other hand, had no inkling of what the next few minutes held in store for him.

She moved to the door and grasped the handle, but did not open it. She had thought so much about this moment—rehearsed it, and even dreamed it, both in sleep and in waking. In the visions she was assertive, brave, relentless. But now that she actually had to live this moment, of course she ended up stuck on the threshold. The hand holding the door may have belonged to a twenty-six-year-old woman, ready to greet a former childhood acquaintance, but the blood pumping hard through that hand belonged to a scared and vulnerable girl who wanted nothing more than a kind word from the elusive creature who now sat inside.

But then she heard the unmistakable sound of a fabricated throat-clearing. A harried-looking woman stood behind her waiting to enter the coffee shop. Rather than her own internal drive, as she had hoped, it was the caffeine withdrawal of the stranger behind her which propelled her through the door and toward the figure waiting inside.

As she approached his table, she saw that a New York Giants beanie cap obscured the most tell-tale sign of the chemotherapy. Apparently he had abandoned the Chicago Bears he had favored in his school days. His left hand rested on a page of an open magazine over which his head was bent. God how she remembered those hands: the long fingers, the close cropped nails, and the narrow wrist with its prominent ulna bone protruding at the joint. Strong, masculine hands, but with such a delicate wrist. She had never held that hand. Its callused fingertips had brushed hers once as they both moved to retrieve a dropped coin. She had paused; he had not. But now she did not pause.

"Hello, Jason." The reviewers chattering inside her head were favorable: remarkably even voice, not too much giddiness, no tone of dripping sympathy.

He looked up.

And there were those blue eyes. They widened with curiosity. He blinked several times, cocked his head, and then the blue eyes in their steel frames narrowed.

"Hadley?"

His voice rose on the second syllable of her name, and that slight inflection immediately torpedoed her ego. He had double-taken, he had questioned her identity. He had not remembered her; he had not thought about her in years. She should not have come here. She had fallen into the exact same trap into which she had fallen so many times before. She had convinced herself once more to reach out, but again she came face to face with the unwanted conclusion. He had forgotten her.

Then again, she had cut her hair and her curves had filled out. She wore makeup now. It was entirely natural for him to turn the simple fact of her name into a question. She used these excuses to swallow the catch in her throat.

"Yes. Hadley."

Jason rose now from his chair but offered neither a hand nor a hug. Jason and Hadley stood facing one another. How much distance separated them? One part of Hadley's brain measured the distance at twenty-four inches. Another part measured it in metaphors.

Jason looked at her silently for a few seconds. "What are you doing here?" he finally asked, although he did not need to. He knew the answer. Her. Here. Now. Jason's analytic, statistical mind was trained not to jump to the conclusion of causation, but instead to stay safely at correlation until further data became available. Here, however, he needed no further data to prove his hypothesis. Despite so many variables—the number of coffee shop franchises, the day, the hour, the May weather outside, this city, this street—he could see only one inevitable conclusion. She was there for him.

"Well," Hadley began.

Jason interrupted. "I'm waiting to meet someone here, someone…important. And you coming at the exact same time—it can't be a coincidence."

He spoke it as a scientific fact: a near lifetime of accumulated evidence indicated that she had entered *this* coffee shop because she knew *he* would be there at *that* exact moment. Jason did not dabble in such nonsense as fate or destiny or higher powers. He lived on logic, observation, and analysis, and those skills told him that Hadley's apparently ad-libbed appearance here was not spontaneous at all.

Jason's last sentence rang in Hadley's ears. Although it had been subtle, she still caught the inflection, the slight stress on the word "you," and she understood the exact connotation that the emphasis carried. If anybody else—friend, acquaintance, celebrity—had walked through the coffee shop door at the very moment he sat waiting, Jason might pass it off as mere happenstance, but he would never be able to regard *her* presence as anything other than deliberate.

And yet, an unanticipated smile came to Hadley's lips, along with recollections of adolescent flirting. Remembering distant days of one-upping, double entendres, and snarky comebacks, she asked, "Why can't it be a coincidence?"

"There is no such thing as coincidence. I suppose it's just —" His eyebrows rose in a sarcastic sneer—"meant to be."

Hadley's cheek flushed with sudden cold, as if Jason had torn a mask off of her face. He had exposed her, like in spy movies where the secret agents use a special code phrase to identify one another. He had used those very same code words—meant to be—that had hovered on her lips so much the past few days and robbed her of so many hours of sleep. Perhaps this was evidence that she and Jason still shared…something. Of course, this commonality revealed all the differences between them. She had spent days philosophically grappling with it, while he had spat it out for sarcastic effect.

"Aren't they the same? Every coincidence just a step toward fate?" Hadley asked with raised eyebrows and a pursed-lip grin. She did not seriously intend to proffer this as an intellectual position. Her rhetorical question merely continued the game.

Jason did not smile back. Hadley obviously had the

advantage, and he would not let her play it by answering the question.

The espionage had petered out, the shock of the opening gambit had evaporated, and Hadley sensed Jason would not deign to steer the conversation to the current factual dilemma: how she knew he would be sitting in this coffee shop.

"Relax, okay? I'll tell you." Her left hand reached out and touched his right arm. His navy blue knit shirt set off the light blue of the eyes into which she now gazed steadily. As she made contact, another wave of adrenaline lurched through her stomach and discharged tremors through her hands. The fingertips rubbing the ribbed texture of Jason's shirt quivered.

Hadley could not hold her position without shaking, so she dropped her arm. The entire orbit of her hand—from dangling at her side to Jason's arm and then back down again—had consummated two decades of longing in five short seconds.

Jason nodded and sat down. Hadley busied herself pulling out the chair opposite him and sitting down. At least he had made the sensible selection of conventional wooden table and chairs, rather than floppy armchairs. The structure of the laminated wood would securely contain the tension of the occupants. When they both were safely seated, Hadley placed her hands on the table, then lowered them to her lap, then replaced them on the table, physically unsure of how to proceed.

Finally, she took a deep breath and calmly said, "I know."

For Hadley, this simple statement rang with triumph. For so many years she had simply wanted access to his life. She wanted security clearance from him, and he had resisted so vehemently, leaving her clinging to scraps of second-hand information and vague I-can-neither-confirm-nor-denials. At this moment she did not deny herself a tiny piece of vindication, like the arrogant satisfaction of detectives on cop shows when they interrogate the prime suspect after already collecting the vital piece of evidence.

Jason leaned forward. Hadley was still speaking in riddles and euphemisms, still mistaken that he had an inclination for subtlety or sensitivity.

"Exactly how much do you know? And you can say the word, by the way. It doesn't bother me anymore, hearing the word. We're adults now, after all" Jason responded. It was only half true—they had become adults so long ago.

"I know your leukemia has recurred."

The lack of sympathy in her voice actually relieved him. He had never played the role of Noble Suffering Hero particularly well, even going so far as to walk out of rooms when people wilted into tears around him.

This by itself was unremarkable. Hadley could have found out about the recurrence via the rumor mill of the internet, before he successfully begged his sister to take down that infantile website page on which she chronicled his "journey"—using the altogether accurate excuse that it made him vomit even more than usual. That Hadley cared about the recurrence was the more puzzling component. Hadley had never even responded five years ago when he wrote to her about the first relapse. That had been during their senior year of college…when had she stopped her correspondence? She had to have stopped contact right around then.

"I would prefer it wasn't *my* leukemia. But I see your point. Go on."

"I know you need a stem cell transplant."

This tightened the social network considerably. Nothing on the internet about that. Jason considered whom he had told and the avenues by which the news could have traveled to Hadley. Mentally he started drawing telephone trees and counting degrees of separation.

"I know your sister is not a good match," Hadley

continued.

At this Jason went into a defensive posture, folding his arms against his chest. She had now crossed the line—this was inside information. Even she, with all her nosiness—she would not have done something so desperate as to contact his doctors, his parents, his sister. It was not a question of could, but would. She had always had the self-discipline of a skilled prosecutor, always playing by the rules so he never had grounds to raise an objection.

Hadley surveyed Jason's face for any responsive quakes that might register through muscle and skin. Although she saw no outward manifestations, she guessed at the tectonic shifts disrupting his mind. He would mentally flip through his address book, trying to determine with which old mutual acquaintances she still enjoyed regular contact, trying to remember when he last talked to that former friend in that distant state. Then he would wonder whether she would ever be so foolish as to tunnel down into his private life by dubious routes.

"Hadley?" His voice again rose on the second syllable, this time out of accusation.

She continued without answering the implied question of how she had discovered this tidbit of information. She had to lay out each inference, each step in the evidentiary foundation, until she snapped the last link in the chain. No time to waste imagining his cut-away reaction shots.

"I know Parker Holmes is a much better match. I know he is your biological brother. I know he was adopted as a baby. I know he's agreed to donate stem cells to you. And"—here she drew a quick breath—"I know you are supposed to meet him here this afternoon. Right now, actually."

Jason's eyes widened and he leaned forward a few more inches. She had check-mated him. But as she sat there, satisfied, almost gloating, he knew the grand denouement would not come quickly. She would make him ask for it.

"How do you know this?" Jason did not speak in a whisper, as a man confronted with some profound and religious truth might have. A whisper may have suited the acoustics of ancient stone temples or musty medieval libraries. And whispers are fine for enlightenment, for drawing back upon oneself in the face of awe and inspiration. The modern coffee shop did not accommodate whispers, though, and so he spoke with the tone of a skeptic, not a believer.

"I saw the letter you sent him. And the emails. Parker's waiting around the corner. We thought it would be better for me to come in first. He's pretty nervous about meeting his brother for the first time in his life, understandably." She now took her hands from the table, where they had rested loosely—for once in her life she had managed to keep them somewhat still—and fingered the zipper on her purse, inside of which a copy of the letter rested.

She had really included the "understandably" for herself. She needed Jason to understand, and beyond understanding, to appreciate, the bravery required for her to walk through the coffee shop door after so many years carrying the emotional equivalent of a loaded gun.

Parker's nervousness was objectively understandable. An adoptee meeting the brother he never knew he had to discuss a stem cell transplant would be forgiven some level of anxiety from any corner. Hadley, though, had never managed to make anyone, least of all herself, understand why her body sent shots of adrenaline coursing through her veins at the mere thought of seeing Jason.

"Understandably. But that doesn't explain how you know him, or how he told you I would be waiting for him here. I'm guessing you're his…" Jason searched for a plausible relationship between Hadley and Parker. "I suppose you're his shrink?" Jason asked with raised eyebrows.

A faint shadow of a smile glimmered on Hadley's lips. At least Jason had remembered her college major. She glanced away from his face for a selfish second, just long enough to lord it over him, and then back.

"No. I'm his wife."

# *Chapter Two*

## ***Then***

Yellow autumn sunlight filtered through the windows of a Philadelphia coffee shop as Hadley wove her way to a cushy armchair. A gift card in the harvest-themed care package from her mother and a rare absence of projects immediately due had lured her off campus for a precious Saturday afternoon of reading-for-pleasure.

Hadley sank into the cushions, took a tentative sip of coffee, and pulled out an obviously loved copy of *The Great Gatsby*. The care package from her mother had also included the current New York Times #1 bestseller, but she had callously abandoned it in favor of the soda-stained, spinal-injured old friend. She did have an excuse for revisiting *Gatsby,* though. A week ago she had woken from a particularly vivid dream of Jason with green lights blinking in her eyes and lines from the book ringing in her ears. Her psych classes had not entirely dispelled the notion that dreams were unconscious expressions of desire, so she grabbed *Gatsby* and went.

She felt a pang of guilt as she opened the book—guilt for the long list of unread books waiting next to her computer. But a week ago her subconscious had told her to read *Gatsby*, and some things, she thought with a touch of sarcasm, were just meant to be.

Ten minutes later she reached for her coffee, and as her eyes glanced up, she caught sight of the door. A man—no, a guy really, not old enough to be a man—had just entered.

*He looks like Jason.*

The association rose unbidden to the top of her mind. One small glance and her neurons had gone to work comparing the new image to the pictures of Jason already on file in her brain. With the subconscious connection already formed, she consciously studied the guy now. Yes, she could see a resemblance.

She pretended to go back to her book, but continued to watch furtively over the paper's edge. Tan corduroys, fleece jacket, brown leather shoes. She could not yet determine the sub-species—mature college student or weekend young professional. She looked over a few paragraphs without actually reading them as he waited for his drink. She then watched him move away from the counter. She eyed the empty armchair straight across from her, but he sat down at a table against the window.

Oh well. Coffee shop meetings were cliché anyway.

Two minutes further into *The Great Gatsby* she paused in the middle of a page. She sensed eyes on her.

Her eyes fluttered up and into his. They were blue.

He grinned.

*His teeth are like Jason's.* Again she freely made the association before noting the evenness and squareness revealed by his smile.

Then he held up a copy of *The Great Gatsby.*

A person's entire past is supposed to flash before her eyes in the moment before death, but now, a whole future flashed before Hadley's eyes in the single moment after she registered the title on the book's cover. She saw an old woman telling her grandchildren how she and Grandpa met. And then passionate kisses, close embraces, whispered confessions under starlit skies. She saw mapped out before her romance, intimacy, and fulfillment. She saw love.

This was it. It would happen this time. It was all hers, all for the taking. When only a few minutes before, his choice of seating had doomed her to a life of solitude, a book title now made her life bloom and blossom with possibility. It was—she saw with perfect clarity that her entire life had logically led up to this very moment—meant to be.

Hadley smiled shyly.

The guy—although if he decided to talk to her he might have the confidence to be called a man—got up from his spot and sat down again in the armchair opposite her.

*God, he looks just like Jason.* The words flashed in her brain like a blinking neon sign.

"Is this your first time with Mr. Gatsby?" he asked, and nodded toward her book.

Yes, he was definitely a 'man;' he had the boldness to connote sex on the very first volley.

And Hadley played along, responding, "Oh no, I know *Gatsby* intimately. We spend many afternoons together." She smiled more broadly now, with her teeth showing.

Continuing the theme, he replied, "I have so many others demanding my attention, I sometimes feel like I'm cheating when I go back to *Gatsby*. But you've got to do what makes you feel good, right?"

"It's the only way to live," she deadpanned. She did not really believe that, of course. In fact, she believed firmly in regularly doing things which terrified her. It was this belief that led her to venture into real life with her next statement: "I know exactly what you mean about the cheating."

"You do?" His eyebrows scrunched, not in flirtation, but in genuine surprise that someone would know exactly what he meant.

"There are so many books that you haven't read, that you should read. You have a list of books a mile long to get to"

"Actually, they're collecting dust on my nightstand."

"Exactly. And you feel bad for these bits of paper—these inanimate objects. You feel bad for going back to your favorites."

He laughed and her heart dissolved into a quivering puddle. Laughter on any occasion is one of the most beautiful sounds in the world, but it takes on a symphonic splendor when pouring forth from a person who may, in fact, like you.

"I don't think I've ever met anyone else who shares my sympathy for poor, neglected books." Actually, he was *sure* he had never met someone else who shared that sympathy. He had never even revealed to anyone the bizarre guilt he felt for the stack of unread, rejected books on his bedside table. Perhaps she also shared the particular neurosis that led him in his childhood to rotate his stuffed animal sleeping companions so no one would feel left out. He held out his hand. "I'm Parker, by the way."

"Hadley." She took his hand and then felt them. Sparks. A million points of bright light shot into her head and an electric current bolted through her body as her skin touched his.

"So Hadley, what keeps you coming back to *Gatsby*?"

"I drift here and there trying to forget the sad thing that happened to me. *Gatsby* seems to help." Hadley veiled this personal exposure in a quotation from the book, even though her previous attempt at intimacy—the shared knowledge and experience of readerly guilt—had gone remarkably well. She relied heavily on this particular novel to numb some of the sting of the sad thing that happened to her, but she could not reveal that sad thing yet. "What about you?"

Parker responded in kind, with another quotation from the book: "An extraordinary gift for hope, a romantic readiness. I keep thinking if I just read it one more time the ending will change."

"You know that's the definition of insanity, right? Doing the same thing over and over and expecting a different result." With this question Hadley retreated back into flirtation. The few dips into close confidences, successful as they were, had been enough for now.

"Oh really? You know this for sure?" This time his eyebrows squinched in mock incredulity.

"Of course. I'm a psychology major." She widened her eyes in feigned sincerity.

"Well if you ever become the head of a psych ward, I suppose you'll have to admit me."

He smiled at her again. A new variety of smile, it began at the corners of his eyes and spread down his face to his mouth. His grin left her dumb for several seconds. The only word that came to mind as an appropriate response was "Jason."

What she actually said next was, "I'm sorry. I forgot what I wanted to say."

Parker laughed again, and Hadley seemed to feel happiness physically filling her, starting in her chest and spreading deep down into her toes. She thought she could even feel the happiness coming out of her pores.

"That's okay. So what year are you?"

"I'm a senior at Penn. But you're not a student, are you?" She thought she could see just a touch of grey at his otherwise dark brown temples.

"No. I'm a chemical engineer. Usually it's pretty boring: a lot of equations and planning and meetings, but occasionally I get to wear safety goggles at work. But psychology. Wow. Exploring the mind. That's brave."

Brave? No one had ever before called her brave, although she had long ago assigned that epithet to herself.

"I guess. I'm actually here taking a break from my senior

project."

"What's it on?" Parker may have asked it merely to move the conversation along, but the way he asked it, his earnest but light tone, made Hadley feel he actually cared about her project. Parker's posture—leaning back into his chair, left ankle on right knee, hands grasped around coffee cup—gave her an implicit invitation to talk as much as she wanted.

"Psycholinguistic differences in cross-cultural adoption. It's a kind of nature versus nurture thing. How do adopted kids from other countries use language differently, and what does that say about their psychological development? There's already a lot of material out there on the psychology of adoption, but I'm looking at it from a different angle. This grad student in the Chinese language department is helping me with some Mandarin." She paused when she saw Parker's brows furrow inward and his eyes narrow.

"That is so interesting." Parker said it almost at a whisper—definitely breathless. He placed his coffee on the table beside his chair, uncrossed his legs, and put both hands under his chin with his elbows resting on his knees. He leaned forward and peered at her. First *Gatsby*, then she agreed to joke with him, and now this. The elephant in Parker's room had disappeared mere minutes into the conversation, and for the first time in his life, Parker felt the delicate touch of something he much later decided to call fate.

Hadley understood from his change of position and searching eyes that he did not find Mandarin linguistics all that interesting. As she tried to remember making some silly slip in language and made sure her cardigan had not suddenly become unbuttoned, she saw the cuff of Parker's right shirt sleeve slip down his arm, revealing an inch or two of forearm: a sharp, prominent ulna bone, a delicate wrist, large hands now cupped around his chin. Like Jason's.

"What is so interesting?" She was now breathless too.

"I'm adopted. Not cross-culturally, just…domestically I guess you'd call it. You kind of surprised me by mentioning it. I don't make a big deal of it normally, but…" He trailed off, unable to articulate that for the very first time he thought that maybe, just maybe, the universe had given him a sign, a signal, a go-for-launch.

"I understand." Her voice embodied the very essence of understanding. She understood he would not want to make a big deal of his adoption, she understood his relief at not having to awkwardly explain, and she understood even what he had not said. She had felt the fingertips of fate brush against her before, and now she thought she could see the hazy figure of destiny darting in and out of her field of vision. Perhaps this time it would not be a case of mistaken identity.

In the days, months, and years that would follow, Hadley would try to convince herself that her first reaction upon hearing of Parker's adoption had not been hope. Simple curiosity—yes, she had seen his face, his hands, and considered the vague possibility of relation between Jason and Parker. Curiosity was surely not a sin. But hope? She did not want hope. And anyway, after a while she could not remember her immediate emotional response to the revelation of Parker's origins. She did not want to remember.

Their paths to the coffee shop took relatively little time to retrace. They needed only one more cup of coffee to relate how they ended up at this particular outlet overlooking the Schuylkill River and downtown Philadelphia. He bought her second latte—the first time any man besides her father had ever bought her a drink without discussing cost-splitting beforehand.

Parker had arrived there via the suburbs of Chicago. He grew up on leafy streets in the kind of suburban landscape that

Hollywood movies used to signify regularity and prosperity. His own upbringing had been startlingly normal, with a split-level house, a father who commuted into the city to do something involving "business," an interior decorator mother, and a high school career spent mostly holed up in a spare chemistry lab. He regularly performed well at science fairs and bowls and competitions. Without his stylish mother's influence, he would still have been wearing shirts with the periodic table on them, which some of his friends still embarrassingly did. Those were the friends with whom he spent elementary school playing the strategic fantasy game *Magic: The Gathering*. Despite his obvious scientific talent, his parents also encouraged his interests in art and literature, funding drawing classes and discussing his latest English assignment around the dinner table.

That scientific talent drew him to college in Philly, a degree in chemical engineering, and a job with one of the major corporations centered within the metropolitan area. To avoid feeling too much like an evil corporate sell-out, he liked to come back into the heart of the city's academic quarter, put on his university corduroys, and read exuberantly impractical books.

Now twenty-eight, Parker did not physically show signs of youthful days spent meticulously copying dragons from the ones on the cards in his *Magic* game deck. His lean, almost gangly limbs had finally filled out with muscle, and his sloping jawline, cleft chin, thick brows, and very square, even teeth had led many girls and women over the years to call him handsome some of the more creative ones had even gone so far as dashing.

Hadley arrived via the dusty roads of Albuquerque. Her financial planner father and math teacher mother had somehow produced a daughter obsessed with words instead of numbers. Her high school English teachers had begged her to major in English, and Hadley had gamely tried a few courses, but she could not tolerate the endless round-and-round of maybes that constituted college lit classes. She publicly declared that it was the presence of too many pajama-clad slackers which prevented her from devoting herself to Lit studies, but her reluctance really came from an instinct toward overprotection of her favorite novels and poetry.

Although she loved her books, she had long ago realized that the world she lived in did not appreciate them as she did. She had decided on psychology as a relative practicality, but she had found that the discipline's more scientific aspects complemented her unflagging need for answers and explanations.

Despite her own categorization of herself as a "smart girl," Hadley could have passed for the "interestingly attractive artistic girl." She had a slim-bordering-on-skinny body with long limbs that made her appear much taller than she actually was. Dark brown hair and fair skin that never tanned set off deep-set green eyes. Her more than a decade of violin playing still showed in her extremely short fingernails and strong, flexible hands.

Parker and Hadley had swallowed the last of their coffee and exchanged their votes for best cheese steak shack in the city when Parker checked his watch and announced the time as five o'clock at night. Hadley glanced out the window and saw the short October day already retreating into the coming evening, the pink sunset fading into the hidden waves of farmland that rolled out to the west. When she again sensed Parker's eyes on her, she turned back.

According to her own perception, Hadley did not attract too many male stares. She neither bemoaned the lack of whistles nor wished for more. She knew she would never be model or movie star material, and awkward teenage years had left her bereft of the charisma many of her college classmates used to reel men in.

And yet, when she turned back to Parker and saw him

studying her, saw his head tilted to one side with a faint smile flirting at the corners of his eyes, Hadley instantly understood the vulnerability of being desired and the fundamental insecurity of beauty. She sensed the thirst in his eyes, but simultaneously she already feared that he would not always lean forward with mouth open, as he did now. Already she wondered whether the consummation of his desire would satiate it forever.

In Parker's gaze Hadley realized the courage required by desire—not the courage of the watcher, but the courage of the watched. She could sense already the assumed perfection that Parker's eyes thrust upon her. How could she ever surpass the memory Parker would carry with him of this moment?

This was the courage on which love depended—the endeavor to make a dream come true, to match in reality the idealized perfection of a world seen through the refracting kaleidoscope of fascination. She had always credited herself with the bravery brought out by love, but until this moment she had only considered the bravery of the giver, not the recipient. Now she counted herself brave for not collapsing under Parker's eyes, brave for not turning away.

As Hadley met Parker's gaze, she saw the eureka erupting in his blue eyes. It was an expression she knew well, because she had worn it so many times before: a selfish bask in the endlessly new and unceasingly surprising revelation of another person's existence.

Hadley now remembered how all her precious memories lost degrees of meaning whenever love came upon her, not because of its strength, but because of its newness. How astonished she had been, each and every day, that love welled up inside her yet again, whenever she saw that one person. It was as if she was a scientist who went to sleep each night and forgot the existence of plutonium, but then awakened to a ripe morning and discovered anew the power, the explosiveness, and the danger of that element. Every time she had taken a few moments to simply watch that one person, she thought she knew how Columbus must have felt as he first glimpsed the shores of the new world.

Before today, though, she had never considered the perspective of those brave new worlds themselves. They had to hold wonders; every grain of their sand had to sparkle and every space had to manifest destiny itself. It was an impossible task.

Parker leaned back to study Hadley. Even with her face hardened in concentration, she was definitely attractive, but he could see a certain sadness that came and went like waves on her face. When she lifted the corners of her lips into a bright smile, the sadness would retreat away under her brow, but it would then drip back down into her eyes.

"You're beautiful." As soon as he said it they both blushed.

Hadley almost blurted out, "Really?" but caught herself. Was she really beautiful, and if so, would a guy—a man—ever actually tell her that? The fact that she had dreamed in both waking and sleeping of hearing this statement did not lessen its weight or cool the warmth that now spread across her face.

"You look skeptical," Parker said. "You don't believe you're beautiful?"

"I just…I mean, no one has ever really told me that before." She had heard "you look beautiful" a few precious times from family members, but that concerned her physical appearance, not her essence. "You are beautiful" was an unqualified existential pronouncement.

"Well, you've been hanging around the wrong people if no one's ever told you that."

"So I suppose you're going to suggest I start hanging out more with you." Hadley's flirtatious smirk returned to her face. She had to ascend from the depths she and Parker had reached—she had to breathe—and so she breached the surface of their conversation.

"Absolutely. Starting with dinner tonight. Right now." He grinned the same grin with which he had first greeted her two hours before—a rakish, almost lustful grin.

"All right then. Just give me a few minutes." She eased herself out of the armchair, slung her purse over her shoulder, and walked to the bathroom at the back of the café.

If this was a movie, this would be the moment for face splashing and a pep talk in front of the mirror. Because this was not a movie, though, all she did was lean on the basin, close her eyes, and take deep breaths to keep the room from spinning.

Disconnected, disjointed images and memories flowed from her like a surrealist movie. Sounds, too, burst like revolution in her ears.

For a few moments, an almost bodily confusion jerked Hadley's mind back and forth, past and present and future, like a rickety amusement park ride. She did not know when she was. One second she was alone with Jason in the orchestra room at school. The next second she was with Parker in the coffee shop, then with Parker at a wedding which might have been her own. And then she had a glimpse of Parker and Jason next to each other, maybe even talking to each other, and then straight back to the hospital with Jason.

From these hazy flashes of memories and futures, of sounds and visions, a phrase emerged: "Billy Pilgrim has become unstuck in time." Ah yes, *Slaughterhouse Five*.

"I have become unstuck in time," Hadley told her reflection in the mirror.

The face, the hands, the wrist bone, the teeth, Chicago, the blue eyes and *Magic* cards and math skills. And the right age too.

And then there was that voice. The voice was the eeriest part of the whole thing, because she could not articulate exactly why it sounded so familiar. She could break down facial features and biography as easily as she could break down the mechanics of a poem, but the voice defied analysis. Like the mystery of why a particular song moved her, or why a passage of music miraculously lifted her heart, the voice resisted solving.

Maybe it was the pitch—at the higher end of the spectrum for a guy. Maybe the nasally, pinched sound. Maybe it was the slight mumble, or the very distinctive phrasing. Maybe it was all these factors, but matching these qualities to what she remembered of *his* voice was like trying to remember a dream.

She could still hear so many phrases in her mind, replaying those notes as easily as she replayed a song on the stereo. And yet, more than hearing them, she felt them. The memory of his voice had been saved in her mind not merely as frequencies and hertz, but as emotion. She remembered that voice not as high or nasal or mumbly. She remembered that voice which had held her like a stream melting through the high mountains in the last days of winter: cold, quiet, and small, but vital and imperative.

Parker's voice raised the hairs on Hadley's arm, because that voice spoke to her from some intersection of memory and dream. It was not merely similar; it was evocative. And that evocation touched her in ways that her sight never could. Faces could be similar, but the music of voices belonged to a world beyond.

"Jason," she whispered at the mirror.

And then, in a fortified and louder voice, "It's just a coincidence. Totally unrelated people can look like each other. Even sound like each other. The internet has tons of examples of doppelgangers. Strangers look like each other all the time."

Hadley knew that if her reflection in the mirror could speak out loud it would say, "But they're not adopted all the time. And they don't ask you out on a date all the time."

"A date," Hadley repeated aloud. "A date," she said a second time.

A man had just asked her to dinner, and she could count on one hand the number of times guys had "asked her out," and none of those were to actual dinner. Dinner itself was no harm. Dinner meant only that—a meal. Dinner was not destiny.

Just then Hadley's stomach rumbled, and the handle on the door jiggled, as if someone outside had tried to enter and found it locked. She would have to get out soon.

And so Hadley freshened her lip gloss, turned, and walked out of the bathroom. She walked to where Parker stood waiting at the front door of the café.

"Are you ready?" Parker asked.

"Yes," said Hadley, entirely truthfully. "I'm ready."

## *Chapter Three*

***Now***

"His wife?" Jason almost shouted it, then goggled side to side, with eyes a-bug, as if waiting for hidden cameras to pop out of the walls and announce that it was all a joke.

"Calm down and lower your voice. Yes, Parker Holmes is my husband. Okay, I married your brother. It was an accident."

"Really? So you went to the county clerk's office and signed a marriage certificate accidentally." Twenty-six years, a high stress, competitive job, and round after round of cytotoxic chemotherapy had honed Jason's natural wit into keen, caustic sarcasm. He had cackled so hard at the news of his last blood count that the oncologist filled out half a psychiatric referral form before Jason sobered up.

"Come on, Jason. You know what I mean. I married him on purpose, but I didn't know he was your brother," Hadley protested. In the years since she had seen Jason, her debate skills had atrophied. She had forgotten how clinically he could pick apart any inexact or overbroad statement.

"Did you know he was adopted?" Jason demanded.

"Yes, in fact he told me five minutes after we met." Parker had told her, she reminded herself. She had not asked.

Jason leaned back in his chair in exasperation. He did

note Hadley's use of the word "we." In some of their final conversations, he had heard her gasp almost inaudibly when he used that word to refer to a duet in which she did not play. Now *he* had to experience the exclusionary push of a "we" to which he did not belong. "When did you meet him?" he interrogated.

"Five years ago this coming October. It was my last year of college. I went to get coffee in Philadelphia and he was there too, and we just…met. No internet matching, no planning, no… nothing. Just two people randomly in the same place at the same time." She shrugged.

Five years ago this October. The date rang in Jason's ears as the anniversary of when the first leukemia recurrence was diagnosed. He had sent Hadley an email with the announcement about a week after he got the news. She had never responded.

"What's he like? Anything like me?" Jason blurted out. And then, to cover the purpose of his question, he added, "I mean, it's an interesting nature versus nurture thing, biological siblings who don't grow up with each other." Jason's curiosity was not really piqued by the basic sociological question of nature versus nurture, but by the revelation that this mystery man's entrance into Hadley's life had coincided so closely with his own exit.

This was where Hadley's defense of "it was an accident" got harder to prove. To be sure, some siblings looked and acted nothing like each other—Hadley and her own sister shared very little resemblance—but Jason's first glimpse of Parker would defeat any defense of plausible deniability.

"There are some similarities between you and him. You certainly look very similar. Similar bodies. He's great with numbers and figures—you know, good mathematical reasoning. He's a really amazing artist. He draws beautiful pictures. He loves to laugh. I can always make him laugh." Hadley paused momentarily, unsure whether her last sentence was a stand-alone description of Parker himself or a memorial to the old days Hadley and Jason spent giggling together in the backs of carpools and classrooms. "And he played Magic: Tthe Gathering when he was a kid."

Jason could not help but grin, either from happiness at the reminder of his dorky middle school habit or out of self-deprecating shame that he would have partaken in such a pastime.

"That face you just made! Parker—" She stopped on the cusp of self-incrimination.

"Parker what?" Jason asked even though he already knew the answer.

"Parker smiles exactly like that." Damn it. She still could not lie to him.

"He doesn't still play *Magic* does he? I hope he didn't teach you to play and make you play it with him." Jason retreated back into a façade of coolness in order to bury his nerdy youth.

"No, he didn't do that." Hadley took a few seconds to indulge in the recollection of a lunch period in sixth grade spent squeezed onto a cafeteria bench with Jason and all his boys as they explained the rules of the game, each pitching in a few cards so she could play. It had only happened once, but for the rest of middle school she carried some measure of pride at being the only girl the boys had even considered welcoming into the fold.

The memory was bittersweet: the fresh recollection of the joy of sitting on that cafeteria bench was now mired in all the pain and adult knowledge which had accumulated since then. At the time, the game and Jason's invitation to play it had carried great significance for her, but fifteen years later, she saw with the disillusionment of hindsight that the moment had made no difference. It had never really mattered at all.

Hadley carried many memories like this, memories

whose value had diminished instead of appreciating over the years. She had deposited so many moments of time into the vault of her mind, but many of them had never collected any interest—they had never compounded or increased from the added value of years of pleasant reminiscence. They were now worth only the joy of the moment.

Back in the real world, Jason pressed on. “So if I look like him and smile like him and played the same games as him and he’s adopted and he’s from Chicago and I didn’t show up at your wedding wearing a nametag that said ‘Cousin Jason,’ didn’t you put two and two together and figure it out?” For Jason, this was an essentially intellectual matter—Hadley should have looked at the available data and come to the obvious conclusion. She certainly had the brains to do that. Of course, Jason knew that despite her considerable intelligence, there was still one person she could be fooled by: herself.

This time, Hadley was prepared for the tough question. “First of all, we really only ever talked about his being adopted one time. He knew nothing about his birth parents. He never tried to look for them and he didn’t want to know anything about them. And second, I could never have imagined *your* parents having any kind of life before they had you.”

Jason did the eyebrows-raised, shoulders up, half-shrug to the left that meant, “You do have a point there.” Very few people would ever be able to imagine that his parents’ pasts included a secret love child. His parents, he liked to tell people, were the personification of mini-vans: safe, reliable, and determined to raise happy, healthy, overscheduled children.

Hadley continued, “His adoption was never an issue until now, and there was no reason to believe you and Parker had any kind of relationship.”

“But you had to suspect some kind of connection. You’re

way too smart not to see how everything fit together."

"God, Jason, you make it sound so sinister! So he looks like you and has some similarities? There are also some very big differences between you and Parker."

"Like what?" Jason raised his hedge-like eyebrows.

"He doesn't get off on arguing, he trusts people, and he genuinely cares about other human beings." As soon as Hadley said it she regretted it. She did not regret the actual things she said—they were all true—but she regretted that once again she had risen—or rather, descended—to Jason's argumentative bait. It was one of his most effective rhetorical techniques: he pushed and pushed until she folded and ended up looking like the insensitive one—the one who stooped to ad hominem insults to make her point.

"I see." Jason's eyebrows fell. He had goaded Hadley into insulting him before, but this time her attacks stung particularly sharply: although they had not heard from each other in five years, she still listed his faults completely accurately. Apparently he hadn't changed much.

But Hadley had changed. Jason could plainly see that. She seemed controlled and calm. She carried herself with confidence, although he could not tell if it was a constant confidence from within or only a consequential confidence from holding all the cards. There was something else, too, something else that had changed in her. He sensed a lightness in her, a lightness of both weight and luminosity, emanating from the places where before she had been heavy and dark. Her face shone brightly, and her shoulders did not seem to bear their past loads.

Hadley paused now. She still clutched the upper hand, still controlled the narrative of the conversation, but she would soon have to move on to questions—and specifically, the question to which she did not know if she wanted a "yes" or "no" in response. "Yes" would mercifully hold those springs of hope at bay, while "no" would send those springs gushing out a dangerous torrent. "Yes" would give Jason an incentive to cooperate in keeping secrets, but "no" would leave Jason a free agent. "Yes" would close that door once again. "No" would give her another shot at the stars. Going back and forth over the past week while the curiosity slowly killed her, she had come no closer to a decision as to which answer would serve her better.

Hadley looked Jason straight in the eyes and asked, "So are you with anybody? Wife? Girlfriend? Partner, I think the term is now?"

Jason could measure Hadley's transformation in the tone of voice with which she asked the question. She used to ask that type of question in a small, scared, nervous little voice, but now she spoke in a purely reporting, fact-finding tone. He gave her a once-over to see if any particular desire motivated her question, but he could not detect any. Maybe—stunningly—he could not accurately attune to her desire because she might be wishing for a "yes" rather than a "no."

"No," he answered with as little tone as possible.

With that little word "no," buoyant jets of bubbles flushed up into Hadley's head, and she instantly knew she would have been better off with "yes." The froth of hope rippled through her like a bath bomb plunged into a full tub. "Yes" would have been so much simpler, so much cleaner and easier and grounded than the effervescent aspirations fighting and fizzing their way into her brain. She swallowed hard—her mouth still tasted like nervousness and adrenaline—to tamp them down.

"I see. What happened to Elena?"

"Elena? We moved on years ago. I had a few temporary people, but nothing too serious. Recurrent cancer is not a very useful thing to put in a dating profile."

Hadley briefly thought of winning, of measuring victory

on this point, but this was not the time for score-keeping. Instead, she tilted her head a few sympathetic inches and asked, "Then who's going to take care of you? After the transplant?"

Hadley's expression achieved just the right level of genuine concern—and with no pity—that Jason knew she did not intend a sideways putdown. And so he answered honestly, "My parents, initially. And who knows, maybe I'll end up at one of those resort ranches in Northern New Mexico. You know, hippie places."

"That doesn't sound like you at all."

"No, but I'll need all the help I can get."

"Is it that bad?" Hadley asked quietly.

"It could get that bad. They caught this one early, and I'm still healthy enough to get through the transplant, but it could get pretty ugly."

Jason's last words presented Hadley with an open door through which she could pass one of the messages she finally felt ready to deliver—the words perfected years after the original opportunities to say them flustered her into silence. Hadley looked steadily into Jason's blue eyes for several seconds. He did not look away.

"Jason, I know you don't like when people say they're 'sorry' about your health. But I want you to know that you have my sympathy and support. I care about you, I genuinely do."

Jason's eyes fluttered down to the table. He did not look at her as he said, "Thank you. I genuinely appreciate that."

"And Parker cares too, of course," she added.

Jason's head shot up, suddenly alerted back to Parker and the impending disaster. "Hadley, what have you told Parker about…" he chose his words carefully. "your history with me? I hope you're not expecting me to pretend not to know you."

The swelling satisfaction which only moments before had filled Hadley now shrunk to nothing. She swallowed and set her jaw. Not "us." Not "our." Never together. Always "you" and "me." Always separate.

"No. I don't think it's very realistic to expect either one of us to pretend we don't know each other. That's why I came in here ahead of time. To get this straight. I told Parker we went to the same schools and had a few classes together. I told him you moved away before junior year of high school and I lost contact with you. That's all I told him."

Here came the bargain: the request Jason could easily refuse, if only for the curiosity of dropping a smoking grenade of chaos into her life. "I ask that you keep it that way and not say anything further." Jason looked skeptical, as she thought he might, and so she added the hook for his self-interest to hang on. "And that's not just to protect me. It's to protect you, too. If Parker knew about…anything… he might think differently about the transplant." She pursed her lips.

Jason could tell Hadley had worked out the angles beforehand. She knew him well enough to recognize that he could never and would never count on the pure selflessness of someone else. Therefore, Jason would never believe that Parker would go through the donation under all circumstances—Jason would never rely on that hope in human kindness. And so Hadley sweetened the deal by slipping in the threat that Parker might change his mind about donating stem cells. All correct assumptions, and perfect prey for Jason's cynicism.

"Of course. That's fine with me," Jason said and nodded several times. "So how did you get him to wait outside?"

"I told him that if I chatted with you for a few minutes, you would be less nervous, which would in turn make him less nervous, and the whole thing would go more smoothly." Hadley's voice had assumed a professional air; she had taken control of the psychological situation.

She continued as if lecturing a class of undergrads, "You

have to understand, Jason, that Parker never dreamed about meeting his biological family. He's never thought of anyone except his parents—his adoptive parents. He's felt totally fulfilled his whole life. This is not automatically a happy reunion, okay? It's not automatically traumatic, either; it's just very, very confusing for him. Please do not upset him."

"Point taken and message understood. I want this process to be as straightforward as possible."

"Should I call him to come in now?"

Jason nodded, smarting from Hadley's implication that he would upset someone.

Hadley spoke into her phone, "You should come in now…Yeah, he remembered me…Yes, he knows you're nervous…Do you want a coffee?…Okay…I love you too."

She transferred her phone back to her bag and her attention back to Jason. "He's coming. Do you want something to drink?"

"Sure. Anything's fine, really. Whatever you guys are having."

"All right." Hadley got up from the table and went to the counter.

## *Chapter Four*

***Then***

Hadley and Parker's first dinner went remarkably well. It went as movies and television always portrayed dates as going, but as Hadley had hitherto not experienced: Parker drove, they both had wine, and Parker paid. They arrived at the restaurant by six but talked and laughed until well after ten.

The conversation came easily and quickly, but neither Hadley nor Parker dared comment on the immediate comfort each felt with the other. Calling attention to the process of falling in love would be as illusion-shattering as a magician revealing the mechanics of his conjurings. And so neither Hadley nor Parker drew the curtains back by saying, "I can't believe I'm talking to you so easily" or "I'm usually kind of quiet." Instead, they made a nonverbal contract, maybe even a telepathic one, that they would both believe in the version of themselves they showcased to each other. The secrecy of this faith gave it its strength.

And so Hadley presented herself as pretty yet quirky, witty but kind, and accomplished but modest. Parker accepted that presentation without question. Parker, meanwhile, marketed himself as masculine *and* gentle, intellectual *and* artistic, and confident throughout. Hadley obligingly recognized and complimented all these qualities.

At last they exited the restaurant, but they stopped for a moment under the damp yellow leaves of an undernourished city tree. Parker put his arm around Hadley's shoulders and tugged her close. And then he kissed her.

She had never before been kissed as Parker kissed her now. It was a kiss like strong coffee at dawn: rich, bold, and awakening. When their lips parted after a few seconds, Parker grinned.

And then it was Hadley who lunged forward. Like a swimmer in distress who breaks through a wall of water to gulp down precious air, Hadley inhaled Parker's kiss. It was the oxygen that flowed into her nostrils that suffocated her, but it was the air which rushed from Parker's body into hers which was her relief from drowning, the air that would save her. When he finally paused and drew back, he took her breath away.

Parker put his arms around her again. She curled hers around his abdomen and lower back and rested her head on his shoulder. They stood entwined for a full minute.

"What should we do now?" Parker asked.

"I don't know, whatever you want," she murmured.

Parker knew exactly what he wanted to do. He had done moderately well with girls over the years, had his fair share of one-night-stands, and definitely wanted to sleep with Hadley. But he also desired something else, something he had never wanted before: not only did he want to wake up tomorrow with Hadley in his bed and in his arms, he wanted to wake up like that on every other tomorrow. Which meant he would have to sacrifice tonight for many more mornings.

"I'll drive you back to your dorm."

Hadley and Parker kissed again before she eased herself out of his car. As she slid her key card through the slot at the dormitory door, she could sense him still watching her, and so after she pushed the door open, she turned around to look at him one more time. Through the car window he waved and smiled. This smile had warmth and affection and also self-consciousness, as if he was embarrassed at smiling so broadly.

Hadley's three roommates in the on-campus apartment were all out, presumably at the kind of party that made her too nervous to stay more than ten minutes. She sat down at her desk and pushed aside the journal and pen which always occupied it. Recounting the day's events in longhand would take far too long; she would laptop this one.

Simple, pure, irrepressible joy—joy at meeting a wonderful guy who called her beautiful and kissed her and had great taste in books—contended against another emotion she struggled to identify.

"What did I just do?" she said aloud.

Guilt. Not guilt for the kissing and embracing and softly running her fingers through his hair, but guilt for doing those things with someone who might be—

When Parker had taken her hand, she imagined Jason's hand. And when Parker had spoken, she heard samples of Jason's voice playing on a loop at low volume in her head. As tame as Parker's advances had been, they had already spoiled Hadley's virtue. As soon as he embraced her, she had understood that her own desire was as guilty as his was innocent, as corrupt as his was pure.

"It's just a coincidence." She had to say it aloud to force the thought.

Hadley opened her laptop. She journaled almost compulsively, motivated by a sense that unless she recorded and recounted the seminal moments of her life, they would disappear. Like the proverbial tree in the forest, she questioned whether certain events had really happened if she did not have evidence of their happening. Plus, the value of time rose and fell in relation to how well she could remember it. Merely recalling happiness or sadness was not sufficient; she needed a replica of that precise interval of time, set down in as detailed a description as she could make. Mere moments in time had little worth themselves; what counted was the memory.

And so she spent two hours tapping away at the keyboard, actively remembering every little thing he had said and noting the exact progression of events. She added notes about how she had reacted to or felt about various things, like an actor scribbling motivations next to every scripted line. In an act of editorial discretion, however, she did not include the internal debates she had held within herself in the bathroom of the coffee shop, or here in her dorm room. Instead, she ended her account with Parker's last smile seen through the car window. With that, Hadley finally climbed into bed.

There, she undammed the river of fantasies that flowed every night between the moment she closed her eyes and that mysterious, liminal threshold when waves of sleep finally washed the day away. Years ago she had started doing it purposely, using the time—she never knew if it took seconds or minutes—to imagine...a life...maybe even her life. She did not believe in the principle that if she visualized a particular course of events, they would miraculously happen, but she had discovered that her flights of fancy invited sleep much more easily than worrying or weeping did. Her depictions of the future, done with exceptionally detailed set decoration, lighting, dialogue, tone, and even music, assured her of the mutability of reality: that whatever occurred during the day was but one "cut," one edit, one version of life. She might have tallied down the day's events in a journal, but this did not guarantee any particular conclusion, did not mandate any particular consequence. As long as she could close her eyes, she could change the future.

Tomorrow would not actually happen until tomorrow; in the meantime, she could live any life she wanted. Every night behind her eyelids, she could construct a much different reality, carved into the grey matter of her brain like sculptors carved their marble gods.

What had begun long ago as a deliberate exercise to welcome sleep had over the years become an involuntary ritual. So now, as Hadley sailed off on the soft undulations of coming slumber, she saw herself clad in a white gown dancing with Parker to the Beach Boys' "Don't Worry Baby;" looking up at a New Mexico sky confettied with hot-air balloons and hugging Parker in the autumn morning cold; and on a ferry returning to shore from the sea, Parker whispering, "I love you" in her ear.

Hadley did not see Parker on Sunday, but they met for breakfast Monday morning, visited the art museum Thursday afternoon, and paid their respects to Independence Hall on Saturday. Hadley then spent a week preemptively completing homework so she and Parker could drive out to Lancaster County the following weekend.

When she was not walking around with Parker, Hadley walked around in a state of disbelief. She could not so easily accept that the universe would suddenly start being so nice to her. Hadley knew enough about the world that she would not dare call her life "hard," but she also never predicted that she would describe it as "easy." Yet Parker was so inconceivably *easy*. He made it all so clear. He actually telephoned her, he kissed her, and he called her "beautiful" at least once during all their dates.

Parker really did seem like a Prince Charming, and Hadley really did want to be rescued, although certainly not physically or financially. She needed, as the old song went, an emotional rescue: someone to save her from herself. She was not imprisoned in a tower, a dungeon, or even a poisoned sleep, but she still she saw the bars of a cage all around her. She had built that cage herself: the over-analyzing, ceaselessly whirring brain that pined and agonized and yearned endlessly. Hadley had ensnared herself on a sticky web of self-doubt and sadness, and she had waited patiently for someone to come along and cut away the ropes binding her to unhappy contemplations.

Parker freed her, but not from a dragon or a witch or an enchanted slumber. He freed her from herself and all her useless ruminations. With Parker there was no play-by-play commentary inside her own head. With Parker she could just *be*. This freedom was even physical; Hadley felt warmer, lighter, and airier, and even thought that maybe, just maybe, if she ran fast enough and stretched her arms far enough, a wind might come along and sweep her up in flight.

Parker, for his part, felt more grounded and steady than ever before. Hadley just seemed to get him. She appreciated his juvenile nerdiness, she sensed exactly which jokes and observations would make him laugh, and she constantly wanted to hold the hands he considered his best feature. Parker had never had the chip on his shoulder of the "misunderstood" intellectual, but he had also never experienced the pleasure of having someone catch on so quickly to his non sequiturs and tangential connections. And she even literally understood him. Parker had been a mumbler in childhood and still sometimes lacked clear diction. Hadley, though, never asked "What?" or "Sorry?" She caught every syllable.

That was not to say he understood her. Some aspects of Hadley still puzzled him. For one, she seemed so unused to affection. She behaved like a starving person who cannot comprehend the sudden presence of food. She gorged herself on his hugs and kisses. When he pulled away even a few inches from her, he saw in her face a faint wisp of hunger, like the unshakeable voracity of one delivered from famine. The speed at which Parker's devotion had grown would have turned off many modern women, but he had not yet satisfied Hadley's appetite for endearment. Parker had called her "beautiful" several times now, but she still responded with widened, skeptical eyes. She appeared ravenous for warmth and tenderness, and as their dates went on, and as Hadley remained amazed each and every time he asked her out again, the idea began to grow inside Parker's mind. He would fill her—he *had* to fill her. He would open his heart to her. He would let her inside and wrap her up. He would make it —whatever the sad thing was that had happened to her—he would make it better.

Two weeks after they met in the coffee shop, Parker and Hadley drove through yellowing and reddening foliage out to peaceful Amish farmland. They admired handmade furniture in quaint shops, bought fresh apples from a roadside stand, and picnicked as horses and buggies went by. During the drive back, one of Parker's hands remained on the steering wheel, while the other rested on Hadley's thigh. He brought the car to rest outside a pleasant apartment block in a recently gentrified neighborhood.

"So this is it. Should we go inside?" He gave her the friendly, welcome-wagon smile.

They walked up one flight of stairs and Parker unlocked his apartment door. Hadley had seen no other bachelor pads, so she could not judge Parker's on comparison, but it looked generally organized and neat.

But then she stepped in further and gasped.

"Oh my God," she said breathlessly.

"What's wrong?" Parker rushed to Hadley's side, but she was staring at the opposite wall.

"That picture." As if responding to some siren song only

she could hear, Hadley glided right up to the frame. If Parker could have seen her face, he would have seen the same expression of hunger he saw when he pulled away after a kiss. But Parker saw only Hadley's back as she stood before the picture.

A red fox tentatively dipped one paw into a rippling pond. Beside the fox, tall pine trees bent in an invisible wind. A full white moon and tiny diamond stars watched overhead. The fox looked directly out of the picture with a gaze sharp enough to break the glass of the frame.

Hadley could see the technique of the picture: the careful and distinct lines, the subtle shading, and how the slightly irregular ovals of the fox's irises gave them realistic life. Hadley had seen these eyes before, staring at her from the margins of Jason's vocabulary exercise book and from the walls of the elementary school art room. Jason liked to do more mythical creatures—griffins or dragons—but no matter the species, the eyes always remained the same; always concentric circles of progressively darker pigmentation rippling out from the pupil. The eyes of the fox on Parker's wall had a subtler ombre, growing from a light yellow at the center to a deep brown at the edge, but the effect was unmistakable.

"Where did you get this?" Hadley did not turn her head as she asked the question.

"I actually drew it myself."

Now she turned her head toward Parker. "You drew this?" she asked sharply.

"Yeah." He bit his lip as if it pained him to say the next thing. "But I can take it down if you don't like it."

She did not turn back to the drawing, but continued to look at him. "I love it. It's perfect."

Then she came over to him, kissed him, took his hands in hers, and studied them.

"I'm sorry I scared you like that. It shocked me…it reminded me of someone." For the very first and very last time, she told Parker, "You reminded me of someone."

Hadley held tight to Parker's hands and continued, "I used to know a guy who drew exactly like that. He always showed me his pictures, and I hadn't seen anything like it in a long time. It threw me off."

"Well, is that guy as wonderful as I am?" His flirtatious, half-cocked grin appeared again.

She had asked herself that question repeatedly over the past two weeks, but had consciously avoided coming to a definitive answer. Now, though, Parker's verbalization of the question forced her into an answer. A few seconds of silence went by, and then Hadley's instincts jumped to fill that silence, as they always did.

"Definitely not."

Her leather jacket fell to the floor. Within minutes they were tangled on the couch. Parker deftly lifted Hadley's shirt over her head and ran his fingers down her back so lightly she shivered. His hand then came around to the front and unbuttoned her jeans.

She grabbed his hand with hers, not to guide it below the waistband, but to push it away.

"Wait." She sat up abruptly. "I don't…I don't know."

"What's wrong?" He attempted to stroke her almost bare back, but she flinched.

"I don't know how…I've never…" She stood up, retrieved her shirt from the floor, and carried it in her twisting hands toward the door.

"What? Hadley, come back." Parker sprinted to the door and reached it before she did. She squirmed away from him, but he got hold of her shoulders. "What's wrong? Did I go too fast?" Again he bit his lip before he said, "If you don't want to, we can wait."

She stared down at the floor. "No, I want to. I just…"

"Hadley, are you a virgin?" he asked gently.

She nodded. "I'm sorry," she whispered.

The apology took Parker so completely off guard that he said, in a much harsher voice than he would ever have intended, "What do you mean you're sorry?"

She said nothing.

Anger flared in Parker—certainly not anger at Hadley's virginity, but anger that she felt compelled to apologize for such a thing. At her age and sophistication, virginity was certainly unusual, but still not something to feel shame over.

A phrase rang in Parker's ears—"trying to forget the sad thing that happened to me." The line from *The Great Gatsby* Hadley had lobbed at him that day they met. Over the past two weeks, Parker had decided it was not just a book quotation; it was also a true line from Hadley's life. Looking down at the top of her downcast head, he realized again how famished for affection she was, and again he sensed some compulsion from within that moved to supply it to her, to step into that void and fill it.

Maybe someday he would press her to reveal the sad thing, but tonight he saw no need to drag the past out into the light. Right now he would simply hold her, simply try to get inside that hard little heart of hers. Tonight, whatever that sad thing was, he would make it better.

Parker tightened his arms around Hadley's waist.

He whispered into her ear. "Hadley, you have absolutely no reason to be sorry. You do not need to apologize for anything." He kissed her lovely white neck and released his grip.

It was the kindest thing anybody had ever said to her.

She still did not look up, but she did slowly unfasten all the buttons of his shirt. Then she kissed the spot where his collarbones met. When she looked up at him again, he softly kissed her forehead.

She desperately did not want to talk or explain herself or analyze the reasons why. She ached to go to a place without words, and Parker understood. They melted slowly into each other and into a warm cloak of intensely pleasurable oblivion.

Then they lay unclothed in the blackened bedroom with their fingertips lightly touching. It had gone as well as Hadley could possibly have hoped. She smiled in the darkness.

Having now passed a crucial test of intimacy, Hadley concentrated on the dusky ceiling and broached the subject she had waited two weeks to address.

"Parker, tell me about your adoption."

"What do you want to know?" His voice was dozy, disinterested.

"Well, whenhow did it happen?"

"It happened right away. My parents took me home from the hospital the day I was born, so there's not much to tell. Apparently my biological—or, you know, the lady who gave birth to me—she was in college and didn't feel she could raise a kid."

"Do you…" She cleared her throat to cover a stutter. "Do you know her name?"

"No." The response came on the cusp of the question. Parker put no inflection into his voice, but the speed of his answer gave it all the meaning it needed.

"When did you learn you were adopted?"

"Let me put it this way I never knew I *wasn't* adopted. I grew up knowing. My parents were very open about it. There was no big revelation or announcement or…anything. Anyway, being adopted is not the defining characteristic of me. It's a fact of my life, not…an issue."

"I see." She tried to make her voice as light as possible

for the next question. "Have you ever tried to find your biological parents, or contact them?"

"Nope." His answer was also a fact, not an issue.

Hadley mentally counted to twenty, waiting for the silence to become awkward enough so that Parker would have to continue.

And sure enough, the silence dragged on and Parker finally sighed. "Honestly, I just don't feel the need. Or the desire, I guess. I love my parents and they love me. I've never needed anything else. I've never felt like I lacked anything. Look at it this way—when I say 'I love you' to my mom or dad, they always say it back. Now, I could go out and find my biological parents, and I could tell them, 'I've thought about you a lot.' I could even tell them 'I love you,' but I have no guarantee they'd say the same thing back. They could tell me to get lost. Why would I take such a big risk? I wouldn't take that chance, you know?"

She did *not* know. She thought back to the time when she had taken that risk, when she said "I love you" with no guarantee she would hear the same thing back. And all those times when she had wanted so desperately to say it, despite that risk of silence. She had never regretted saying it. After all, it was a thing which deserved to be said.

Hadley was grateful for the darkness as she blinked away tears. She had not said it in quite a few years. As the time had stretched on from that first silence, she had lost the muscle memory of those words in her mouth. And as the memory had faded, as the custom had grown dusty, so had the desire to say those words.

But she was not like Parker. She would take that risk. She would take that chance.

"I love you."

Parker rose onto his elbow and looked at her. She turned

her head on the pillow to face him.

"I love you too."

He lay back down and intertwined the fingers of his right hand with her left.

She closed her eyes briefly, and then opened them to an entirely new world. Parker's response acted like a time machine on Hadley. It had taken her back to that first moment when she had *not* gotten an "I love you too," and changed it, fixed it. From then on the entire trajectory of her life shifted, like how Marty McFly altered the past and then returned *Back to the Future* to find the world, and himself, transformed.

Hadley immediately tried to replay Parker's words in her mind, not for the meaning, but for the sound of them. She wanted to remember that sound exactly, because it was as important as the words themselves. The sound came from that voice, that voice with its strange familiarity, that voice whose fluctuations played like the melody of some lost song. Not only had she always wanted to hear those words, she had wanted to hear them said in that tight and bracing murmur.

Hadley did not tell Parker how much she had longed for the response, because it did not matter now. Parker's "I love you too" opened up a parallel, alternative timeline, one where all the remorse and regret and righteous indignation never happened, and had never needed to happen. Instead, on this parallel timeline, Hadley was, and had a*lways been,* loved. In this parallel universe, she had always gotten an "I love you too" from the boy with the blue eyes.

"So, do you believe in any kind of fate or destiny?" Hadley searched for some hook to add on so she could turn it into a question for Parker. "I mean, that you ended up with the parents you did and you fit with them so well?"

"The thing that's always confused me about fate is whether people deserve what they get. I didn't do anything to *deserve* great parents; I was just a baby. Life just happened. I guess I don't know whether or not to call that fate."

"Well, I've been wondering what I could have possibly done to deserve you." She had given serious thought to this problem, but Parker took it jokingly and replied by tickling her belly button.

"Hadley." He used the same tone as Hadley had used when she broached the subject of his adoption. It implied that he too had a series of Serious Questions in store. He sat up.

"Why were you a virgin? You don't have any religious objection and I mean"—he spread out his arms over her naked body to indicate that she presented a desirable display—"you could have found plenty of guys."

She did not look at him as she answered, "For a really long time…there was this one guy. I only ever wanted him…but he never wanted me. And I never met anyone who remotely compared to him. Before you, anyway."

Parker placed a finger on Hadley's chin and turned her face toward his. "Well," he said, "I want you. And"—Hadley could actually *hear* the smile on his face as he said, "I love you."

This time she did not look away. "I love you too."

As Hadley heard herself say those four words, bursts of warmth started deep inside her core and diffused through her limbs. It was not adrenaline. Adrenaline made her shaky; this calmed and stilled her. It felt just like those childhood mornings in autumn when she stood in the early chill beside an inflating hot-air balloon as it prepared to lift off into the turquoise New Mexican sky. The stark, crisp air of the high desert glowed with the pale fire of hundreds of propane tanks sending their blue and yellow flames up into silken canopies. She squealed with delight at every flare, and then stepped back in fright from loud crackling of the fuse and the sudden heat which radiated from it. And then she leaned in again, eager for the sensation of the next blaze. The warmed air inside the balloon was lighter than the cool air outside of it, and so the warm air rose above the cold of the dawn. It floated above the city and the mountains, and it carried with it the silk balloon and the gaze of the child standing below it.

Hadley did not modify her life in significant ways after that first night with Parker. Nor did she change anything after the second time she slept with him. Only after the third time, which happened on the first Monday of November, did she decide. That Tuesday morning, she checked her email the way she always did.

She had a new message from Jason.

The first thought which came to her mind was the astonishing absence of thought itself: she had not thought of Jason in days. For many years Hadley had listened for his life, as a young mother listens even in sleep for sounds of breath from her child and rises in terror after only a few seconds of quiet. Yet for the past two weeks, Hadley had slept peacefully through Jason's silence, and waking this morning to his presence did not comfort her as the sounds of a waking child would comfort that young mother.

To open or not to open. That was the question.

Opening it would start the vicious cycle again. He would give her a glimpse into his life—maybe one or two scenes, or a short collection of snippets, like the movie previews on the coming attractions reel. He never let her see the entire thing, and the snapshots he did show her would remind her again of how much still lay hidden.

But not opening it—the benefit there would be…

She clicked Jason's message to highlight it and then waited.

If she opened it, she would once again start filling in the rest of the movie herself, extrapolating from the few tiny clips she got to see. As she spliced in all of Jason's inevitably gorgeous friends and associates and his inevitably fabulous adventures, she would realize again that all her scenes had been edited out.

The benefit to not opening it was fidelity. Her fidelity to Parker. He had loved her, after all, had welcomed her into his bed and into his heart. She appraised his generosity and knew it was worth far, far more than her faithfulness. And every time he touched her, he seemed to push her shame further and further away. Now she could do some pushing of her own, sending Jason back into the shadows, sending the email back into the deep corners of cyberspace from which it had come, and carrying her shame with it.

And anyway, did she even need the peep show of Jason's life anymore? A firm, real man had made love to her last night; she could still feel the redness on her cheek from where Parker's stubble had brushed it. Her skin still smelled of the ocean-breeze-scented detergent Parker used on his sheets. She could never touch what Jason showed to her. She could never be there herself; she could only imagine him. Why bare her warm world to the cold gust of uncertainty which would blow in from the opened email?

The mouse's arrow point hit "delete." Jason's message disappeared.

Next she contemplated whether to take the far more drastic step of banishing Jason's email address to the junk mail category. She did that, too. Finally, she scrolled through her music files and found the "Jason" playlist. She had not listened to it in a while; in the last few weeks she had had no need for such sad songs. She deleted that, too.

And just like that, with a few clicks, he was gone. Deleted as Jason was from Hadley's technological life, he did still exist in twentieth century form, in journals stacked in boxes in her parents' garage back in Albuquerque.

And he still existed in her dreams. Two nights after the deletion, sleep found Hadley unloading pickup trucks full of camping equipment in the parking lot of her old middle school. She carried an armful of sleeping bags into the main hallway of the school, and there stood Jason. He wore a posh, three-piece gray suit. Hadley tried to hide; she covered her face with her hands and tried to rush out without Jason seeing her. But Jason recognized her and ran after her.

He chased her through dream-land all the way to a museum atrium. Columns ran along a long room with a vaulted, carved ceiling; in between the columns, potted plants and statutes stood in alcoves. Little wicker tables and chairs were scattered throughout the enormous hall. Hadley and Jason sat down side-by-side at one of the circular tables. A wrinkled old woman came to take their order. Jason asked for a latte and Hadley ordered iced tea. Before the gnarled waitress could return, Jason leaned in close to Hadley. He cupped his hands around her ear and whispered something.

When she awoke the next morning, Hadley retained the vivid images of Jason in his dignified gray suit and the great length of the marbled hallway. She also recalled the exact angle of his body as he bent forward to share his secret. But she could not remember, or perhaps she had never even heard, what he whispered in her ear.

## *Chapter Five*

***Now***

Parker strode briskly through the coffee shop door just as Hadley returned to the table, back from ordering what were likely utterly superfluous coffees. Once Parker crossed the threshold, Hadley's view of the scene switched to bullet-time mode. Everything moved frame-by-frame, inch-by-inch, with all the speed of fists flying in a slo-mo, kung-fu sequence.

Parker's legs pedaled languidly across the floor, his face melting from one expression to another as he recognized Hadley and the man who must be Jason. As Parker swam near, his right hand was already raised in the kind of premature handshake with which overeager salesman greet prospects. The confident smile, which Hadley knew concealed impossible-to-describe anxiety crawled across his face as he crept forward through the delayed shot. In the foreground of the scene, Jason gradually rose from his chair, each muscle movement articulated in its own filmic cell, and extended his own arm. The two hands fastened around each other.

Freeze frame on the hands. Orbital shot.

Like the cameras whirling and spinning around a recumbent Neo in *The Matrix*, Hadley seemed to revolvearound the two figures now standing before her with their right hands entwined together. Her eyes orbited an entire circuit around them. She zoomed in on the point of connection, squinted to correct the focus, and lingered on the chapped skin of Jason's knuckles, the white flakes melting off them, the veins popping on the back of his hand, the blood running through them saturated with uncontrollable, unstoppable mitosis.

Cut from bullet-time. Back to normal frame rate. Dolly zoom on the facial profiles.

"It's great to finally meet you," Parker said.

Hadley recalled an old LP her parents had, one whose cover had made her pause as she flipped through their old boxes of records. Pink Floyd's *Wish You Were Here*. The cover had two men shaking hands. That was what Jason and Parker looked like. But…no—not quite, Hadley thought. Neither Jason nor Parker was on fire. Yet.

She ran through other famous pictures of handshakes. Maybe they looked like Elvis and Nixon? Mao and Nixon? Begin and Sadat?

A stentorian, documentarian voice boomed inside Hadley's head, describing the great importance of this handshake in history. And certainly, in the context of Hadley's personal history, it carried as much significance, and as much formalized awkwardness, as the signing of miraculous peace accords, as the unprecedented opening of diplomatic channels, as the forging of bizarre and unparalleled alliances carried in the history of the world. A flash of permanence for the annals of time, over in the mere shake of a hand.

She vaguely heard Jason respond, "I say this without any irony, but the pleasure is all mine."

Parker contrived a laugh. The sound jolted Hadley back into to the coffee shop.

Parker and Jason released hands and sat down. Just then, the teenager working the counter called out their coffee order.

Hadley jerked her head toward him and was halfway there before either Parker or Jason reacted. She returned to the table carrying three carefully balanced iced coffees and three straws. The mechanics of withdrawing straws from paper wrappers and inserting them into plastic caps occupied the trio for a few seconds. Then they each took a sip.

Hadley had an especially low tolerance for conversation lags; whether in class or in a social setting, she usually broke the lull first. Only with Parker could she let spaces fill with silence. He had taught her that just because they sometimes did not speak to each other in the car for ten minutes, they had not run out of things to say and had not become fundamentally boring people. He had led her to associate such hushed moments with easy comfort, rather than with nervous dread. Plus, she and Parker had become fluent in a much more intimate form of communication, one that did not depend on constant verbalization. She loved their language of small glances across crowded rooms, lingering gazes under bed sheets in the early morning, brief strokes on the small of her back, and deep, slow thrusts. Sometimes it seemed like the less she and Parker talked, the more they said.

Here, however, the old discomfort came back vengefully. The silence quickly became heavy and unwieldy, and the awkwardness grew unbearable. Hadley felt it almost as a corporeal form—an invisible ball of malevolence looming over the table. If someone did not attempt a rescue maneuver soon, the ship would sink before it even set sail. And yet Hadley literally could not think of a single thing to say.

"So Parker, is this your first time in New York City?" The chit-chat came from, of all people, Jason.

Parker smiled rigidly, obviously grateful for this bit of grounding minutiae. "Oh no. I lived in Philadelphia for ten years, so it was always easy to come in. I remember the first month or two Hadley and I dated, we came in for the evening to see

*Cabaret*." He flashed a quick look at his wife, expecting to see a grateful smile as an acknowledgement of his generous courtship, but she stared fixedly down at the table.

When another few seconds crawled by without a word, Parker clutched for some stream of sensical conversation, even if it was a non sequitur. "I'm from Chicago, of course, so I do look down on New York in some areas. You know…pizza…hot dogs…" he reached desperately for a third item… "skyscrapers." He finished with a lackluster attempt at a smile, and Jason and Hadley chuckled charitably.

Jason turned to Hadley. "Didn't we get pizza here once? When we met up here? I was here from Boston and you came in from Philly. How many years ago was that?" Jason did not even glance at Parker.

Hadley's stomach lurched in horror. How could she have forgotten to cover this? Overlooked details, a minor inconsistency in the story—these small mistakes were what got spies hauled in from the cold.

Hadley's nails dug trenches into the skin of her thigh as she attempted a quizzical expression. Parker's eyebrows narrowed together like the bars of a jail cell slamming shut.

"Oh my god, I totally forgot about that. I remember now—Jason and I ran into each other, here in New York, of all places. We were both on spring break."

She drew a shaky breath and could not avoid smiling at the memory she actually had never forgotten. "Must have been seven or eight years ago. And we did get pizza." She focused determinedly out the window.

Parker's jaw tightened as he turned to his wife. Her words said this pizza meeting was so insignificant as to not even be worth remembering, but her face said that pizza was the most significant pizza she had ever eaten. She wore the same expression as she did when she, to use her own description, daydreamed. Parker would come home to find her at the kitchen table, her papers and books spread around her, staring into space —but not in concentration. Instead, a secret smile danced on her lips, like the hidden beauty of a still-unopened rose. Parker would stand in the kitchen doorway and imagine what phenomenon compelled Hadley's smile. And then he would whistle, tap his fingers, or clap to get her attention. She would turn and her smile would change—it would swell outward like a time-lapse video of a flower blooming. Sometimes Parker would ask what she had been thinking of. She always had the same answer: "You."

The memory of getting pizza with Jason in New York City brought that same secretive smile and that same contemplative, almost lost look to Hadley's face. It was enough to make Parker wonder whether she had told the truth all the times she had answered, "You."

Hadley continued to peer out the window, apparently unaware of Parker's questioning eyes or unwilling to answer them.

Jason's voice broke through as he tried, once again, to jump the conversation's engine. "I'm sure Hadley's taken you to New Mexico right?"

Parker turned back to Jason's awkward expression, which was pained and twisted not from nausea, but from the unfamiliar steps of the chit-chat minuet. "Yeah, New Mexico. It's amazing. I've gotten addicted to green chile, obviously, but…you know, it truly is different." His forehead wrinkled in deeper thought. "I can't get over the space, how big the sky is, how explicit the horizons are. You can see forever there." He slipped back into the superficial. "New York must have been quite a shock for you, Jason, after growing up out there."

"Well, we moved to the suburbs of Boston when I was sixteen, and I went to college there, so I got a good transition to the urban jungle. Oh, speaking of Boston, my parents—uh, I mean *your* parents, sorry…*our* parents are coming in tonight and I thought we'd all have dinner together." Jason gulped gratefully at his coffee.

Hadley had watched the last few exchanges the way she watched horror movies: clenching her fists and biting her tongue to avoid shouting, "Don't open that door" at the screen, as if that would ward off the heroine's certain confrontation with the ax-wielding maniac or the demonic child. But at this mention of parents, she knew that unlike those horror movie heroines, she had no chance of outrunning the monster which lurked inside this haunted house.

The word "parents" thundered in her chest like the pulsing bass lines of an ominous film score accompaniment. Again she had overlooked an obvious and critical detail. It was almost like she wanted to be caught.

Parker cleared his throat several times, stuttered, changed direction, and cleared his throat again. Finally, he mustered the courage and nonchalance to ask, "Speaking of the parents—did you know before this that they had another kid…I mean, had…me?"

"No, they never mentioned it. They don't say much about themselves. They have that Midwestern tendency where they hold back from talking openly about certain things." Jason paused and glanced at Hadley. "I unfortunately have developed the New York tendency of having no tact and no restraint."

Out of the corner of his eye, Parker saw Hadley wince.

"I don't think you can blame that one on New York. It might be a preexisting condition with you." Hadley could not keep a small shard of sharpness from her otherwise joking tone.

"She's right," Jason raised his eyebrows in Parker's direction and grinned. Parker did not quite like the knowing-ness of Jason's grin.

"She usually is." Parker glanced fondly and possessively at his wife and draped his arm around Hadley's shoulders.

Jason's grin fell, but he continued looking at Parker. His eyes narrowed ever so slightly, and he coolly asked, "Did she tell you about the time she beat me in the geography bee? She got first and I got second."

Hadley felt a tearing inside her. Jason had finally remembered something of their shared history, but he still had not directed his memory toward her. He had acknowledged their past, but he still refused to share it with her in the present. At the same time as Hadley smiled at the recollection of the geography bee, her nostrils flared in anger.

Without looking at Hadley, and without glancing away from Jason, Parker made his territory-marking overt: he slid his palm up Hadley's thigh, letting his fingertips dangle just above the crevice of her legs. It was the twenty-first-century, passive-aggressive version of a gorilla pounding his chest to guard his harem against intrusion from a rival. "No, she didn't. So what was the winning question?" He turned to face Hadley. "What didn't Jason know?"

Hadley jumped in. "Oh, it happened a million years ago. I'm surprised Jason remembers it at all; he usually never remembers things that happened in eighth grade."

Jason quietly said, "Which river carries more water to the ocean than any other?"

"The Amazon," Hadley automatically responded, and as explorers once struggled to discover the origin of that great river, she struggled again to discover the origins of memory. Did Jason remember the question simply because his steel-trap brain was wired to remember everything? Or did he remember the question because the geography bee stood out in his mind as a significant event? Because she was there? Did he remember because of her or in spite of her?

"I said the Mississippi. Oops."

Hadley recovered her smirk and said, "You were obviously in denial," confident that Jason would correctly provide a proper punchline.

"Actually, the Nile is the *longest* river in the world. I do know that."

"So does that knowledge come in handy in the stock market?" Parker snatched the wheel of the conversation again. Despite his careful steering, the topics kept drifting into Jason's lane.

"No. My job is mostly concerned with numbers which are only important in someone else's imagination. It's pretty boring. In fact, I think maybe after this whole transplant thing, I'll look for something else. Maybe try to help the world instead of bleeding it dry."

Hadley's eyes opened in exaggerated surprise. "Well, well, well, I'm impressed Jason. I thought cynicism was an incurable disease."

Jason turned toward Parker. "I have a reputation for, as I prefer to think of it, realism. And I don't consider that a bad thing."

Parker replied, "I guess that shows biology only goes so far. I'm probably the least cynical person I know."

Jason's eyes stayed on Parker as he said, "We can't all live in fantasy worlds and always expect a happy ending." He did not smile.

"You don't think this whole transplant process will have a happy ending?" Parker's eyebrows narrowed.

"I want it to have a happy ending, of course I do. But I can't ignore the possibility of other outcomes. I can't blind myself to the true facts, the statistics I've seen. I can't go on without some respect for the vagaries of chance or human frailty. That would only hurt me, and it would hurt people around me."

Hadley's hands squeezed her coffee cup so that the plastic buckled. Although addressed to Parker, Jason's last two comments were meant for her. Just as he had not praised her directly about her geography bee victory, he would not even insult her directly either.

Jason squinted at Hadley's hands as they gripped the cup.

"You still play." Jason said it softly, almost to himself.

Hadley released her grip and examined the skin flaking on her left-hand fingertips.

"Yes. Of course, not nearly as much as I used to." She grimaced a little as she asked, "Do you?"

"I haven't picked up my violin in six months, I'm afraid. I just don't have the energy." He also grimaced.

Parker took Hadley's hand in his and kissed it rather ostentatiously. "What was that piece you were playing the other day? That new one I'd never heard before?"

"Mozart's fifth violin concerto."

Now Jason smiled fondly and said, "Ah, Mozart five. Still my favorite."

Before Parker could inquire why Hadley had suddenly start playing Jason's favorite violin concerto, Jason's cell phone buzzed. Jason reached into his pants pocket and glanced at the message on the screen.

"The parents will be here in about half an hour. Should we get going? We can walk back to my apartment. I can show you some of my neighborhood."

"Maybe I should just let you two go on alone. So you can have this time alone with Jason's—I mean, yours—everyone's—parents." Hadley thought this excuse, improvised as it was, had a legitimate chance of success.

"You should come," Jason and Parker said at the same time. Then they both carefully avoided the other's eyes.

"I'd really like you to be there," Parker said.

"And I'm sure they'd like to see you," Jason added.

Hadley briefly thought of claiming a sudden onset of bubonic plague, but this would only delay the inevitable. And so she nodded.

"Are you up to walking?" Parker asked as Jason gingerly rose from his seat.

"It'll be good for me."

Jason got to the door first, pushed it open, and remained on the inside as Hadley passed him. She did not make eye contact with him and did not linger in the doorway. Once outside, Parker took her hand.

Walking in New York City as a threesome did not accommodate conversation very well, so Jason assumed the role of tour guide, and Parker assumed an expression of polite, mild interest. Hadley shuffled along hand-in-hand with Parker, consumed with her own thoughts and oblivious to the trivia of which obscure poet had lived in which building.

Hadley's mind flopped around like a slinky. She could feel herself…unraveling. The anticipation of seeing Jason had wound her tighter than a spring, and during those first few minutes alone with him, she had bounced up and down with the strain. But when Parker entered the coffee shop, it was like the spring had uncoiled and lost all of its taut tension. Now, the helixes and loops of her mind lay unspiraled on the floor, and the memories and emotions she had kept so tightly scrolled for so many years were all falling open.

Over all that, a layer of metacognition added more confusion. Her reactions to the meeting seemed all wrong, somehow. Of course she had felt great anxiety and great awkwardness, which had even given way to a sharp sensation of fear, yet this was not what she had expected. As she had prepared to meet Jason, she anticipated the meeting would provoke mostly sadness and pain.

Hadley supposed the expectation of agony had something to do with authenticity. She could fabricate happiness no problem, could imbue her voice with false cheerfulness with ease. However, there was something in pain that could not be faked. She was not such a gifted actress that she could forge misery or counterfeit despair. Pain belonged in the province of absolute reality: even in dreams, pleasure can be perfectly replicated, but when confronted with pain, the dreamer always wakes.

And the obsession with authenticity arose because as the days and years A.J. (After Jason) grew, Hadley sometimes wondered if she could entirely trust her memory—whether everything with Jason had really every happened at all, or if she had simply made it all up. Had he really made her feel all those feelings, or had she felt them only because she wanted to? Were all of those movements, those crosses left and right, merely the manifestation of a role? Were all those bathroom mirror soliloquies simply a script she had purposefully written? Was she merely a player, and all the world a stage?

Hadley remembered learning about unreliable narrators in high school English classes, with the teacher using Edgar Allan Poe's *The Tell-Tale Heart* as an example of a narrator whose version of events could not be trusted. That concept had utility even now, as Hadley wondered whether she was an unreliable narrator of her own life. It was so hard to tell whether her perceptions were correct—whether she accurately picked up the right signals. And then there was the possibility that she had left some things out, or had changed details to flatter her side of the story.

But somehow, if she collapsed in agony now, somehow it would prove that she had not made it all up, that she had not been wrong, that she had correctly caught on to some essential truth. Today's pain would legitimize and validate the pain of years ago.

It would prove that the past—or her past, rather—had been real. That she was real. And that she would not simply disappear into the shifting shadows of her own imagination.

Consumed by these thoughts, Hadley collided with Parker and looked up. They had stopped in front of some building of some interest. Jason pointed and gestured as he talked. Parker dropped Hadley's hand. He evidently needed both of his own to illustrate some architectural concept.

She watched the two men—brothers, she reminded herself. They both gestured so elaborately one could have mistaken them for Italians. Hadley noted the fluidity and grace with which the four hands moved through the air almost like a small flock of birds. Four thin wrists, four rounded prominences where the ulna bone ended, twenty long fingers, twenty close-cut nails.

Hadley let out a musical, childlike laugh.

"What?" They both said it at once and both turned toward her.

They would have been easily recognizable as brothers if not for the effects of Jason's condition and treatment, which canceled out much of the resemblance: his skin an even whiter shade of pale next to Parker's fair cheeks, his blue cap no match for Parker's brown whorls, and his frame gaunt next to Parker's well-tended build.

And yet both sets of eyes looked at her with an expression of the exact same sadness. After walking such different roads, they had reached the same end. Both sets of eyes begged for explanation, both sets teased an exchange of apologies and forgiveness, and both sets promised that she could dive deep, deep down and drown herself in their blue.

Two roads diverged in the blue. And sorry she could not travel both, long she stood, looked down one as far as she could to where it bent…and then to the other, just as fair, because it was fresh and wanted wear. And both that afternoon equally lay in depths no step had trodden back. Yet knowing how way leads on to way, she would be telling this with a sigh somewhere ages and ages hence. Two roads diverged and she chose…?

Jason's blue orbs considered her through steel-framed glasses, while Parker studied her with his own Lasik-corrected ones. Despite Parker's 20/20 vision, she knew it was Jason's near lifelong myopia that more correctly read her.

Jason granted her a brief reprieve from the choice. "Let's go," he said. "It's just a few more blocks." He turned away and began heading down the street.

Parker took Hadley's hand again, and they walked on behind.

# *Chapter Six*

***Then***

On a lush evening in May, Hadley climbed the stairs of the apartment building at a pace slightly faster than a trudge, weighed down by a backpack full of books, a laptop case, and a lunch bag. Living in a lovingly restored, Prohibition-era Chicago building had its perks, but a consistently working elevator was not one of them.

She had one year left on a Ph.D. in psychology at the University of Chicago. At first she insisted she would never get in to the prestigious program, but Parker had encouraged her to apply. When she received the acceptance letter, she rushed to greet Parker in person at his office in Philadelphia, jumping into his arms and announcing, "You get to go home!"

They moved into an apartment in the revitalized Woodlawn neighborhood. Parker found an engineering job he loved at an environmentally progressive firm that helped companies "green" their systems. They drove out to his parents' home in the suburbs every week for Sunday dinner, visited a different ethnic restaurant every Thursday, and gradually decorated their little home with pieces from the funky independent shops nearby. They made love several times a week in a century-old ponderosa pine bed Hadley inherited from a grandmother.

Hadley pushed open the door and squeezed her baggage through the narrow doorway. She dumped her things underneath her workstation in the living room and glanced, as she did every day, at the wedding picture sitting on the desk. It showed a candid moment at the reception: they sat with their heads resting against each other and their hands embraced on the table. Both bride and groom wore wide smiles; Hadley also had the slightest glint of a happy tear in her eye.

Hadley headed into the kitchen expecting to find Parker starting dinner. She was hungry and thirsty and bustled to the cabinet for a glass. She noted Parker sitting at the kitchen table, but she did not notice the smaller details: the piece of paper resting on the scrubbed table beside a sliced-open envelope, Parker's normally active hands resting on his knees, and how he appeared to be mentally computing some complicated chemical equation.

"What's up?" she asked absent-mindedly and carried her glass to the refrigerator.

"My brother needs a bone marrow transplant."

"Parker, you don't have a brother." She opened the refrigerator door and reached for a pitcher of iced tea.

"Apparently I do. A biological brother. He has leukemia and needs a bone marrow transplant."

Hadley's fist clutched at the handle of the iced tea pitcher. She closed her eyes as adrenaline scoured her veins and arteries. The adrenaline jacked up the volume of her heart and sucked the oxygen out of her chest.

She had the sudden urge to jump straight out the kitchen window, but instead, she forced her lungs to expand south into her diaphragm.

When had she last thought of him? It happened less and less frequently as time went by.

Hadley's stomach spasmed and she tasted bitter bile.

It might not be him. Plenty of people came down with leukemia.

In the early years with Parker, she had considered the possibility that Jason would turn up, or that the connection between Jason and Parker would be discovered. However, when she thought about the possibility, it always seemed only a theoretical chance, like the calculable odds of an asteroid slamming into Earth, or the odds of getting sliced in half by a shark: a possibility, yes, but one only articulable in mathematical terms. And when she imagined the discovery, it always played out like a scene from a movie, like it could never really happen to *her*. It always seemed to be happening to someone else. And so, she could not act like those supremely cool James Bond supervillains who calmly pronounced, "I've been expecting you," when 007 showed up at their lairs.

Hadley turned from the fridge and set her unfilled glass on the table. Parker silently handed her the letter. She took it in her shaky fingers and skipped straight to the bottom.

The signature was illegible, but she knew immediately and instinctively that it was Jason's. She could picture his right hand with a pen tightly clutched between his fingers. He always held his pens with his thumb coiled around the top of his index finger.

Above the signature, a typed "Sincerely, Jason Snyder," and below the signature, an email address and the phone numbers and addresses of a lawyer and a doctor, both in New York City.

Hadley's stomach heaved again. All of the air inside her suddenly swooshed out of her open mouth in one swift tidal wave. She felt herself hurtling through a pitch-black tunnel as wind whipped her face. A shattering crack split through her ears, like the sonic boom of a lately departed supersonic jet.

She flipped her eyes back up to the top of the letter.

Dear Parker,

There is no code of etiquette that governs how I should broach the subject which I must address, so I will hold true to my normally blunt manner of communicating and just say it. You and I are biological brothers. My parents, Rick and Linda Snyder, recently revealed to me that when they attended the University of Illinois, they experienced an unplanned pregnancy. They mutually agreed to put the baby up for adoption. That baby grew up to be you. They felt they did not have the resources or maturity to raise a child. They are very responsible people. Ironically, the pregnancy and adoption process brought them much closer together. They decided to marry, and about seven years after your birth, I came along. (I also have a three-years-younger sister). My parents assure me that you and I are full-blooded biological brothers. I located you through the help of a private detective. He was able to track you down based on your birth date and the hospital where you were born. The original adoption agency also provided the initials of the persons who adopted you.

I have leukemia. I first got it during my sophomore year of high school. I went into remission after chemotherapy treatments. Four years after that, I had a recurrence during my final year of college. I again responded fairly well to treatment and seemed to be in the clear. But it came back again last year, and it has stopped responding to chemotherapy. My doctors tell me that my best, and perhaps only, option for long-term survival is a bone marrow transplant (they are officially 'stem cell' transplants these days, but most people understand the term 'bone marrow' better).

Bone marrow transplants work best when the donor material comes from someone who is genetically similar. My sister has been tested and is only a mediocre match. We have also scoured the transplant databases but have not found an optimal match. Faced with this news, my parents suggested we search for you.

I write you now to ask you to submit to testing to determine if you would qualify as an optimal donor. If it turns out that we do match well, I must then ask you to donate peripheral blood stem cells. This is much less complicated than a full bone marrow extraction but still very effective. Of course, we will only cross that bridge if you turn out to be a good match.

I therefore ask that you get tested for leukocyte antigens. This requires only a blood test. I hate to beg, but my prognosis does not look especially rosy. Time is of the essence. Most hospital laboratories can do this test. If and when you have your results, please have your healthcare provider forward them to my doctor at the fax number listed below. The test typically takes up to one week, so again I must ask that you act with all due speed. If you decide to get tested, you can inform me by email at the address below.

If you do this, I will be eternally grateful. I admit I do not have a great belief in the kindness of strangers, or for that matter, even the kindness

> of blood relations. I hope you can change my mind.

So he was sick again.

And apparently he had a recurrence in their final year of college. Hadley tried to remember. Their last year of college. She had met Parker that year…she had deleted Jason's email that year…

"I don't know what to say." Hadley looked up from the letter.

"You're crying." Parker got up from his chair and brushed a tear off Hadley's face.

"Well, having leukemia three times, that's…objectively tragic."

Parker laughed. Hadley never tired of hearing that sound.

"You think I should do it?" Parker wrapped his arms around his wife's back. She pressed her face into his chest so she would not have to look at him.

"Of course. You have to."

"Yeah. I know I have to. But…the tone of his letter…it kind of pissed me off. Don't you think it's awfully cold?"

She agreed that the letter was awfully cold, but she pulled out an old excuse, one she had long ago used on herself. "Sure, it's a bit formal, but honey, the man has cancer. Maybe he's depressed…or something like that."

"Maybe. You know, even though I never wanted to meet them, I did used to imagine what my biological parents were like. But I never considered a brother or sister. It's so weird—the brother I never knew I had suddenly turning up and asking me to save his life. He's a perfect stranger to me."

"But people save the lives of strangers all the time. I've never had the opportunity to do that, but if I could save Jason's life myself, I would."

"Oh Hadley." He backed away from her and nudged her chin so that she had to face him. He again wiped a tear from her still wet cheeks. "You're so good." Parker kissed his wife.

Hadley's quiet sobs redoubled. He called her "good" and she did nothing to dispute it. She let him believe that she was just a disinterested bystander motivated by a sense of general humanity, rather than by profound, personal prejudices.

Parker turned back to the letter on the table. He picked it up again and stared at it.

"I wonder what he's like."

Hadley remained silent. She certainly would not answer that question now, not yet, but even if there came a time that she *would* answer it, she questioned whether she *could.*

Hadley unbuckled the violin case. She unhooked the bow from its slot and tightened the hair. She slipped on the shoulder rest and perched the violin under her chin. She set the bow upon the string and allowed the weight of her shoulder—the weight of the world, really—to sink into the string. And then she drew the bow rapidly back.

The Chaconne from Bach's Partita #2 for unaccompanied violin. Unlike the histrionics of the Romantic composers, the chief difficulty of this piece was in its exposure. There was simply no way to hide along the steep ridge of melody. If playing Tchaikovsky or Sibelius was like juggling four flaming torches while being chased by wild bulls at a dead sprint, this was like climbing a mountain while meditating.

It was the piece she reached for whenever she felt…too much. When she needed to transfer something away, to lessen the load upon herself. She could let the weight of her body meld with the violin, let the tension relieve itself into the bow, and the heaviness of her heart would transform into music. The waves of emotion would become sound waves, drifting away and taking her tears with them. Even if she could not form it into words, the violin carried the message for her.

She had not played this piece in a while, but it still lived in her fingers, in her hands and her arms and her shoulders and deep down into her core. Her muscles held the memory of it like a living thing. The music awakened under her fingertips, grew conscious and vital. And as the music stirred, so did a part of Hadley that had slept dormant for years. As her fingers found their old patterns and her right arm settled into the familiar dance, she began remembering. It was as if her personal memories were located in a locked vault, the passcode of which was a particular sequence of musical notes. Only when she played them could she access the recollection; in the association between the violin and herself, the memory had become music.

Two hours later, Hadley roped her arms around Parker's neck as he sat in front of his computer. She reached down to his stomach, slid her fingers under his shirt, and tickled him. He giggled and pointed at the computer.

"Look at this. Jason Snyder is an investment analyst at a Wall Street firm in New York. He went to Harvard and has written a few articles for economics magazines. Do you think I should pay for the background check?"

"Parker, no." Hadley quickly drew her arms back.

"I was joking. He doesn't have a huge internet profile. Of course, I had to limit the search to 'Jason Snyder New York,' otherwise I just get endless stuff about an Australian rugby player. He doesn't have any social media, but it looks like some friends of his made a bone marrow match profile. You know, with pictures of him and explanations of how he's such a great guy. To convince people to get tested and matched."

He twisted in his seat toward Hadley. "You want to see it?"

Hadley reflexively flinched backward. She could not yet face evidence of him, let alone possible happiness, friends, all the people who loved him…knowing the pictures would not include her.

"I'll look at it later," she lied. "Have you emailed him yet? To tell him that you're going to get tested?"

"Not yet." Parker continued to scroll through the internet search results.

"How much information about yourself are you going to include?"

"What, you think this is some kind of scam? I won't tell him my social security number, okay?" Parker swiveled his chair to face her.

"I didn't mean it like that." She toyed with the buttons on his shirt as she said sheepishly, "I just wondered if you were going to mention my name."

"Your name? Are you suddenly shy? That's not like you."

"I just don't want you to get hurt by revealing your life to this guy, only to find out in a week that you're not a match and he doesn't want any more contact with you. I don't want you to open yourself up to him and then have him slam the door. He might just want stem cells, not a complete brother."

Parker's jaw tightened. "You're probably right. We will proceed with optimistic caution. I'll just tell him I will get tested as soon as possible and we'll cross any other bridges when we come to them. And I won't track him down all over the internet." He paused. "I guess I got my hopes up about having a brother for the first time. I guess I never admitted to myself that I wanted to see my biological family so much." Saying these words seemed to drastically change his mood. His hands tightened around Hadley's hips.

Hadley, in her most therapeutic voice, asked, "Do you want to talk about it?"

"Not yet." He lifted up the hem of her T-shirt and began kissing her stomach. Over his shoulder Hadley could still see the website of Jason's Wall Street employer and his very short biography. She reached over Parker's head and closed the laptop.

Later, Hadley lay awake next to an already sleeping Parker. He rested on his side facing her. She watched him sleep, saw the covers slowly balloon outwards and then collapse back inwards.

She would tell Parker if she absolutely had to—but only if they actually had to go to New York and see Jason in person. If Parker was a match, she would have to tell him something, if only because it was unrealistic to demand that Jason pretend he had never met her. She also knew she could not simply wait for Jason to recognize her without warning and have Parker ask, "Do you know each other?" But she would not tell him unless she had to. She would not take the risk without utmost necessity.

And to get Jason to play along, to get their stories straight, she would have to find some way of reaching Jason before Parker got to him. She could not rely on the possibility that Jason had awoken from his fog of extreme emotional density and would recognize the sensitivity of her predicament. He might very well say something to give her away.

Hadley got up off the bed, closed the door softly, and went out to the living room. She approached her desk and ran one finger along the edge of her closed laptop. It would be so easy to open the computer, to do a simple search, to see him. Several times in the early years of her relationship with Parker, she would begin typing Jason's name into the search bar—just a peek, she would tell herself. Just to find out where he was living, to ensure she would not run into him. She always managed to resist, however. She quickly deleted the half name, changed it to an innocent and plausible search.

Hadley opened the computer. She did not bring up the

internet search program, but instead opened a word-processing program. She put her fingertips on the keyboard. Just like her memories lived within music, within the remembered sensation of fingerings, bowings, in the pittering and pattering of her fingertips on the violin's ebony fingerboard, Jason also lived in the keystrokes she knew so well. She closed her eyes and typed his name.

Hadley opened her eyes. She would not do it unless she had to…unless Parker really was a match, unless they had to go to New York, unless Hadley had to gird herself to face a wife, a girlfriend, a lover.

Hadley reached for the ipod next to her computer. She lay on her back on the couch, put her earphones in, and scrolled to Bob Dylan's *Blood on the Tracks.* She started "Tangled Up in Blue," and for the first time in many years, worried herself to sleep.

Five nights later Hadley had managed to fall asleep, but a shot of adrenaline opened her eyes at five in the morning. Over the past few days Parker had mostly managed to sustain his normal, almost catatonic sleep, but he did notice a few of his wife's absences from their bed. She blamed it on her dissertation, which seemed to satisfy him. Meanwhile, the lab had fast-tracked Parker's test and yesterday sent the results off to New York. That meant today they would get an email—or worse, a phone call.

Both Parker and Hadley largely avoided the subject. They retreated to separate corners of the apartment and manifested their angst in different forms. Parker's was visual; immediately after he came home from his blood draw, he went to work on a large, heavily geometric drawing of intersecting and diverging lines.

In her corner, Hadley tapped away at her dissertation, but like Penelope at her weaving, she deleted the material she wrote every night. Penelope's trick forestalled an undesirable event, but no matter how much Hadley typed and deleted, her fingers could do nothing to prevent or guarantee anything happening. It was out of her hands and into the hands of tiny proteins sitting on the outside of Parker's cell membranes.

Hadley rubbed her eyes as she looked at the beside clock. The last moments of a dream had woken her. Since Jason's letter, her mind had been running wild as she slept. She usually recalled her dreams with a high degree of detail, but these were different; although she sensed Jason's presence and knew for certain that he played some role, upon opening her eyes the exact circumstances of the dream would slip away and vanish just beyond her field of remembrance. She would wake out of breath, feeling as if she had escaped some dangerous specter just in time. Parker also followed her in sleep, but when he drifted onto the scene, he appeared strangely blurry: his physical boundaries blending into his surroundings as if she looked at him through a curtain of mist.

And then there was the one dream in which Hadley seriously suspected Parker had morphed into Jason. She and Parker sat next to each other in an old-fashioned red leather booth at a schmaltzy restaurant. A cloth napkin fell off the table. Hadley reached down to retrieve the napkin, and when she emerged from under the table, she found Jason sitting next to her.

Hadley watched the sun rise through the kitchen window. She missed the sunrises and sunsets of Albuquerque. Up until this morning she had simply missed the astonishing palette of colors, from the dusky violet to the creamy salmon pink. This morning, though, she missed the clear horizons of Albuquerque—there the sun came up behind mountains and went down behind a sharp mesa. Somehow, that clear demarcation of the mountains as the day began and the mesa as it ended made the world comprehensible.

Her own personal horizons badly needed that kind of clarification. She needed the steady bulwark of mountain and mesa now—the boundaries and borders of an understandable world. Her dreams were slippery enough; she could not also handle a sunrise that slithered and slid unsteadily through skyscrapers and along asphalt.

Through the thin walls of the apartment, Hadley heard Parker getting up. She heard him in the bathroom and then at his laptop in the living room. She poured another cup of tea and set it on the table for him.

Parker paused in the doorframe. The morning sunlight streaming in from behind outlined his form like a full-length halo.

"Six out of six."

"That's good, right?"

"It means I'm a perfect match. For full siblings, there's only a one in four chance of being a perfect match."

Hadley felt like she was on an elevator—she wanted to go down, but her stomach wanted to go up. It was not surprising, of course. Shocking, but not surprising.

"Hadley, you look like someone just killed your puppy." Parker stepped out of his halo and emerged, flesh and blood, boxers and bedhead, into the kitchen. "What's wrong?"

"I'm just worried for you. It might be…" She searched for a word that would not be a lie. "Dangerous."

"I've looked into the new procedures they have. It's practically just giving blood. In fact, the doctor said I could do the donation here and they'd ship it to New York. But I really feel I have to go there." Parker collected his tea and hopped up on the counter. "And you have to come with me. Hadley, I want you to meet him."

"Why do you need me? You said yourself it's practically just giving blood. I have finals and term papers to grade and summer syllabi to assemble." She hoped this would lead Parker to mistake her pained expression for work stress.

"Hadley, this is one of the hugest events of my life. This is…it's just…huge for me. I need your support."

Again Hadley tried to talk herself out of what must have been an expression of extreme nausea. "Parker, you've never expressed any interest in your biological relatives. You said you didn't need it. And now you say you do. Do you genuinely want to meet these people or does it just seem like the right thing to do?"

Parker sprang off the countertop. "Why are you so against it? Okay, maybe I had a fear of rejection back then, but they can't reject me now, can they?" He stared down into his mug of tea. "I know it sounds selfish, but I kind of like the idea of going in there as the hero. And besides, my parents taught me that families care about each other no matter what. Well, I care about my brother no matter what—even though we've never even met each other."

Parker took a gulp of tea and then continued, "And I'll personally call up the dean of the entire University and insist you come with me. I have to take this stem-cell boosting treatment for a week, so we'll fly out next Sunday morning and come back the following Friday. Your grading can wait."

Hadley mustered up a smile and said, "All right."

"Good. I'll start looking at flights."

Hadley had it all planned. She would look at the internet first, but she would have her violin and a large glass of wine at the ready. She pulled out her laptop and searched for "Jason Snyder leukemia." The first result was a profile on a charitable website devoted to people searching for transplant matches. She clicked on it.

Pictures of Jason flooded the screen. Jason and several

other young men, all in boots and shorts, standing in front of a rock formation. Jason in his cap and gown, graduating college and grinning next to male and female classmates. A candid shot of Jason holding a red Solo cup at a college party. Jason writing a complicated equation on a chalkboard and smiling sideways at the camera. Jason on a bicycle beside what looked like a dike in the Netherlands, smirking. Jason with friend after friend after friend, hiking and drinking and attending seminars. Jason in a lei and a Hawaiian shirt. Jason laughing. Jason smiling.

None of the pictures seemed to pre-date college. None included anybody from the old crowd—nobody from Jason's previous life, except his family.

She read the messages posted next to the pictures. The "profile" section had been written by a "Melissa M.:" "We made this site for our friend Jason, who won't do it himself! He's brilliant and talented and needs a bone marrow transplant! Please leave a message of encouragement for Jason, and please get tested and registered on transplant databases!"

The messages of encouragement littered the screen space in and around the pictures. "Jason's a great guy, hope he can overcome this!" "For my bro Jason, wishing you the best!" "I know you hate prayers, dude, but we're all thinking of you."

Hadley's stomach lurched before she could read them all. And then her head was in her hands, the heels of her palms crunched against her eyes as she tried to black out the images swimming before her. Teardrops rained down on her knees.

Of course he had a life of his own. She had always known he would have developed a life. She did not expect, however, that it would look to be such a good life, or such a happy one.

No evidence of a wife, though, or any steady lover.

Hadley clutched at the violin which lay at the ready. She also pulled out the stained, tattered copy of Mozart's Fifth Violin Concerto she had checked out of the college music library on her lunch break. She would do as she had done so often before: bury herself in the music, let the endless unfolding of notes occupy her mind. Exhaust herself on four strings until she could momentarily forget the images which still glared behind her eyes.

She had escaped learning the piece during her school days. Her lush, robust sound was much better suited to Romantic music than to the polite, but to her mind soulless, compositions of the Austrian master.

Jason, though, had a superb spicatto and a tight vibrato perfectly matched for Mozart. Always looking for a challenge, or perhaps just an opportunity to show off, he had dived into Mozart's fifth concerto in eighth grade, bypassing more age-appropriate repertoire. Hadley, of course, had to compete, but she chose the moody, intense Bruch concerto as her show piece.

Hadley's fingers found the trills, turns, runs, and flourishes easily enough. As she picked her way through the first movement, the sadness overwhelmed her. It was not the music itself—the music was charming, although aloof. No, it had nothing to do with the quality of the notes.

It was because the music…it was him. The brilliance of the high E-string trills, the ambitious rush of the sixteenth-note passages, the faultless logic of the rhythm, the brusqueness of the spicatto on the G-string…it was all so overwhelmingly him, truer than any photograph could ever be. He may as well have stood right there in the room beside her, so evocative was the manifestation.

She had thought about him during the last five years, of course, but only as a character in a book, or a historical figure. At some point, he had ceased to be real. Flesh and blood had become concept. But as she played, Jason became real for her for the first time in years. His existence again became a definitive reality.

The otherwise haughty lines of Mozart reanimated the concept. The effect of the pictures on the website came nowhere near to the effect of the refined, restrained melodies. As she felt the vibrations of the violin in her neck and shoulders, she felt him. He was there. He was real.

At last she popped the joint in her neck and turned to put her violin away. That was when she saw Parker standing in the doorway. He clapped in applause.

"Bravo! That was nice! Is that something new? I don't recognize it."

"Yes and no. It was written in 1775, but I've never played it before."

"Well, it's lovely." He turned to go back down the hallway, but then halted. "Oh, I got us a flight to New York for Sunday morning. We'll meet up with Jason Sunday afternoon. He suggested a coffee shop, which I'm fine with." He attempted a smile. "You know, in case he's an ax murderer."

Hadley chuckled and turned back to wipe the rosin dust off the strings.

On Saturday morning Parker returned from getting his stem-cell-booster shot to find Hadley sitting on the living room floor with a large book in her lap. A cardboard banker's box sat beside her with several journals scattered around it. One of Hadley's old hippie songs played on the iPod dock—it was Bob Dylan's "If You See Her, Say Hello," although Parker did not recognize it. He turned the volume down.

Hadley twisted around. She had tears in her eyes again.

Parker eased himself onto the floor and crossed his legs.

"Is that one of your high school yearbooks?" He nodded toward the glossy pages of tiny black-and-white portraits.

"Yes. Freshman year." She took a deep breath and looked

steadily into her husband's blue eyes. She hated how perfectly innocent they were. "I have to show you something." She passed the thick yearbook to his lap and put her index finger on a picture.

Parker immediately recognized the resemblance. His eyes ran over to the column of names and then back to the face. He blinked several times but continued looking at the picture.

"You knew Jason?" he asked in a hushed voice. He sounded afraid, but not suspicious or accusatory at all—not what Hadley had feared.

"Kind of. He was a hard person to really know." She swallowed the catch that threatened to break her voice. "We went to the same elementary, middle, and high schools and had some classes together. He moved away after our sophomore year of high school."

When Parker turned his face to Hadley's, she saw that he now had tears in his eyes too. She also saw something in his eyes she had never seen before: hunger. It was as if she had shown him a photograph of someone long dead but terribly missed. Perhaps Parker had viewed that part of his past as dead and buried, doing by accident, Hadley realized, what she had once tried to do on purpose.

"What was he like?" Parker even asked about him in the past tense.

"Aggravatingly perfect, and perfectly aggravating. Brilliant, first of all. And very arrogant about that brilliance."

"So not like me, then." Although the fourteen-year-old Jason wore no medals in his yearbook picture, Parker spoke with the awe and reverence due to some decorated and honorable soldier, as well as with disappointment that he did not share the best attributes of the great man.

"Which part, the brilliance or the arrogance?"

"The brilliance."

"Parker, you are brilliant. I mean that."

The thirst in his eyes subsided and his expression changed to one Hadley knew well. He had fallen in love with the tiny black-and-white picture.

Parker remained silent. Hadley caved and nervously said, "I really didn't know him that well." An odd statement considering she had spent so much time insisting to anyone who would listen that in fact, she did know him well, and trying to prove to herself that she knew him better than anyone else did.

Whether her statement was or was not a "lie" in the objective sense of the word did not really matter, because she could never determine a standard version of the "truth" where Jason was concerned. Her psychology studies led her to intellectually understand that every individual creates his or her world as it goes by, and that perception and perspective color everything, even whether a traffic light says stop or go. And emotionally, it had been her experience that whenever she felt herself sinking, the particular life raft called "truth" never stopped for her. She was left to filter from the surging waves a few precious grains of honesty which she could call her own.

"So, why didn't you tell me before that you went to school with him?"

"I didn't automatically make the connection between the name and the face. Now I see the physical resemblance, but I didn't make that connection before. It took a while for all the wires in my brain to get sorted out. My dissertation has really messed up my mind, I think."

"Wow…I…I just…"

After a few more lurches forward and a few more hard brakes, he finally said, "I'm trying to think of the odds of this—you going to school with my biological brother. I almost want to say the whole thing is..."

Hadley waited for the inevitable words.

"…meant to be," Parker finished.

He paused and gazed back down at the headshot of Jason. "…like the world threw me and you together just to prepare for this experience, like you and Jason and I are all on the same trajectory of destiny. Triple soul mates." His forearms flew through the air, intersected, and then fell back to the yearbook. Hadley thought back to the carefully constructed model airplanes still flying through Parker's bedroom at his parents' house. Intersecting arcs of flight was not the most comforting metaphor for this situation. While airplanes with different flight paths and different trajectories did sometimes collide in midair, they tended to fall out of the sky when that happened. Hadley would have preferred the image of ships passing in the night.

"I know exactly what you mean." She said it so quietly that Parker seemed not to hear.

"Do you believe it could happen that way? That fate or destiny guided us both to that coffee shop in Philadelphia at the same time?" He had not said God. Hadley and Parker had never actually discussed the place of a god in their relationship; neither had gone to church as a child, a judge performed their marriage ceremony, and they had made out living wills at the behest of Parker's exceptionally practical father. The question, "Do you believe in God" had tempted Hadley a few times as she stared into the veil of darkness after making love. Now Parker was finally endeavoring to pierce that veil.

"And with the same book, no less." Hadley looked down at Jason's picture in the yearbook. "I don't know what I believe anymore. I don't even know what I want to believe. Fate seems to have left its fingerprints all over this, but what if you weren't a perfect match? What would you say then? Fate doesn't control leukocyte antigens. That's random biology."

"I think I want to believe."

Hadley watched her husband's hunger for the picture in

the yearbook. She knew that up to this moment, Parker had honestly never questioned his path in life. He never questioned what led him to that coffee shop that October day. It was not because of denial or fear. It was simply that nothing in Parker's life had obligated him to consider his fate; nothing until now had mandated this level of rigorous soul-searching.

That was not to say that Parker was a simple or shallow person; on the contrary—Hadley had sounded down into the depths of her husband, and while not unfathomable, Parker did have quite a few layers to him. However, in her explorations Hadley found no evidence of any emotional earthquakes which would disrupt the strata. Parker had never experienced any kind of tragedy beyond grandparents' natural deaths. No poverty, no major depressive episodes, no traumatic disruptions, and no serious heartbreak. By all accounts, including Parker's own, he had lived a rather charmed life.

Now Hadley witnessed Parker undergoing the upheaval she herself had experienced several times. Unlike him, she had crashed up against uncertainty early and often. From the age of six she had not been able to simply sleep under a blanket of blissful ignorance.

Parker had just lost his innocence, Hadley realized. That innocence was not necessarily *belief* in fate or god or Santa Claus. Loss of innocence did not necessarily mean loss of a specific belief. Rather, innocence was a state of certainty, and Parker had just slipped from it.

"I know what you mean again," Hadley said. "I used to want to believe so badly. If I believed that something greater than myself and greater than random coincidence controlled the universe, then I could explain away every sad thing that ever happened to me. Whether I called it fate or destiny or even god, I could explain Romeo and Juliet or Gatsby and Daisy and why love doesn't work out the way it should."

"I know one thing I believe in." Parker looked at her.

"What's that?"

"You." Parker got up from the floor.

"So. Tomorrow we'll see him. There'll be some check-ups on Monday, and the donation will be Tuesday. Jason's already started his pre-transplant chemotherapy and I've gotten most of my stem-cell boosting treatments." Hadley looked up from the floor at Parker. The late morning sun illuminated him as he stretched his arms back. It turned the hairs sticking up at the back of his head all golden. He turned to go.

"What are you doing?" Hadley asked.

"Going to shoot Jason an email about you."

Hadley tried desperately to keep her voice nonchalant. "Oh, you don't need to do that. He'll see me tomorrow. No reason to clog his inbox with any extra information. He shouldn't have to worry about anything but his health. And tomorrow, let me go in first and reintroduce myself. I think it'll be better for everyone's mental state."

"Whatever you say. You're the psychologist." Crisis averted, Hadley got to her knees, scooched over to her husband, and untied the string at the waist of his jogging shorts.

Within only a few seconds Parker did not care why his wife did not want to immediately tell his brother they had once gone to school together.

## *Chapter Seven*

***Now***

Hadley, Parker, and Jason milled about in Jason's apartment. He had lived there almost four years, he told them, although it remained undecorated and spartan, except for the books cramming the shelves and overflowing onto stacks on the floor. While Jason and Parker discussed the relatively safe topic of politics, Hadley perused the spines running along the bookshelves. She ran her finger down the edge of one faded orange paperback. She recognized it as one installment of a middle-school fantasy series. Jason had read the first book in the series and raved about it, so of course Hadley had to see what the fuss was about. She quickly devoured all the entries in the series, and Jason had actually borrowed one of the later books from her, and he even unexpectedly biked to her house on Memorial Day afternoon to return it—

"Hadley." She whirled around. Jason stood at the doorway talking into the intercom. Parker sat on the couch and looked at her with pleading eyes. It was Parker who had called to her.

She rushed to the couch and smiled at her husband's blanched face. She took one of his hands in hers.

"Are you ready?" she asked.

"No, but I never will be."

"I love you," she whispered in his ear.

He said nothing back.

Hadley heard knocking. Parker rose from the couch. Jason opened the door and ushered in two well-dressed but non-descript…parents. There was no other word to describe them.

The parents made their way into the room, and they and Parker stood motionless for a few awkward seconds. Then, wordlessly, Parker threw his arms around his equally dumbstruck mother. Father wrapped mother and son in a silent embrace.

Hadley watched the threesome and smiled in…what was it? It was pride she felt. How proud she was of Parker, at his ability to throw open his arms, and his heart, to these strangers. How extraordinary it was to see him, without blame or bitterness, envelop himself in the promise of love.

She felt a gaze on her and turned her wet, green eyes to Jason. His face was inscrutable. Sadness? Anger? Jealousy? She continued to silently question Jason as her tears welled up. Did they have the strength to throw away all the old fears as Parker and his parents had done? Could they too shed the baggage of so many years? Or would they wait, standing here like shell-shocked soldiers watching helplessly as comrades went down?

Jason pulled off his cap to reveal a perfectly hairless, perfectly white, and perfectly round head. He rubbed a spot just above his ear, and Hadley winced at the way she could see the bones of his skull as his scalp moved over them. Without the cap he was pitiful, naked, and defenseless, like a warrior who has thrown aside his sword and shield. It was both a surrender and a provocation, allowing her see his fragility and sickness and daring her to offer him the comfort of her arms.

Hadley stood up from the couch.

The voice of Jason and Parker's father shocked her back to the room.

"And are you Parker's wife?" She turned to see Parker and both his parents dabbing at their streaming eyes with tissues. At least her own smudged cheeks would not seem out of place.

Before Parker himself could answer, Jason broke in. "This is quite the little coincidence. Remember when I was in eighth grade and we carpooled to orchestra on Saturdays? Remember the girl you drove, the other violinist? This is her. Hadley. Parker's married to her."

Linda, the mother, clutched at Hadley incredulously. "What? That's impossible!" Linda leaned forward to peer at her. "Hadley! Of course I remember you. You organized that lovely Christmas concert at the hospital when Jason was an inpatient!"

Over the woman's shoulder, Hadley saw Parker collapse. It was like the human version of the World Trade Center towers falling. He seemed to disintegrate from the inside out.

Rick, the father, was saying "Wow. Just think of the odds" over and over again. Linda had released Hadley and was blowing her nose loudly. Jason had gone in search of more tissues.

Hadley scrunched into a corner of the suddenly suffocating apartment. Her lungs seemed unable to find enough oxygen in the room; she consciously breathed in and out, willing her diaphragm to expand and contract, but the only things that flowed in were the suspicions and secrets that had gone unsaid. Surely the others noticed it too, as if the standard carbon dioxide fumes of each exhaled breath carried with them the poisonous fumes of unspoken uncertainties.

No wonder libraries full of old books smelled so musty and moldy. All those words just rotting away, pages and pages of language decaying in the dull air. The cold pieces of cellulose fiber sitting and waiting instead of going back to the earth and fertilizing new flowers. All those words and ideas dead and shriveled like buried bones.

Hadley's shoulders sagged with the weight of her own invisible library full of untold stories. For years she had secretly checked out memories, confident that no one saw her running through the aisles and delving again and again into the same heavy volumes. No one could make sense of the catalog but her; no one even knew of its existence but her. Until now. She saw it taking shape in Parker's mind. He could see the white marble structure with its elegant columns. He could see the door. Now he only had to open it.

The whole group went to dinner at a Thai place a few blocks from Jason's apartment. Linda insisted on walking arm-in-arm with both her sons, one on each side. With Rick strolling alongside, they looked like quite the happy family. The third child, a daughter, would arrive tomorrow morning from college in California.

Hadley hung back, an unnecessary and potentially disruptive fifth wheel on an otherwise functioning vehicle. Maybe not a spare tire—no, more like a large boulder lying in wait behind a hairpin turn, waiting to rend the newly welded bonds of fraternity. She gratefully accepted the opportunity to be silent.

At dinner, the parents quizzed Parker for two hours about his life, his adoptive family, his jobs and friends and travels. Jason listened politely, and Hadley purposefully kept her eyes on her husband and off of Jason.

Although she successfully controlled her eyes, the rest of her was a different story. Her stomach growled, but she could not tell whether from hunger or fullness. She could touch the wetness beneath her arms and yet involuntarily shivered. Her eyelids sagged with sleepiness and yet her ears pricked up at strange words spoken at a neighboring table. And for all the obsession with the past swarming around her, she herself wanted to think only of the future; the future, that is, in the form of a runway at La Guardia.

Parker was telling an apparently very funny story about dressing up as Albert Einstein for a middle school biography project. Jason interjected, "See, when I had to choose someone for my middle school biography project, I chose Stephen Hawking. I had a hell of a time finding a wheelchair to borrow on the day we had to dress up."

Everyone laughed politely, and then Jason turned toward Hadley. "And you were Edmund Hillary, right?"

She paused before responding. She slowly and deliberately turned her head to face him. She tried to keep her face as passive and expressionless as possible, but a purse of her lips and a glare probably escaped.

"Yep, that was me. I admired that he did something everyone said was impossible. But tell me honestly, did you ever actually finish *A Brief History of Time*?"

Jason answered, "Absolutely! Of course I finished it. I can't say the same about *War and Peace* unfortunately."

"Well, I can say from all my psychology studies that all that space talk is overrated. It's not nearly as important as exploring the human brain. There are still so many things we can't explain about how humans behave, how they think, what drives their actions. Why worry about a unified theory of space when we have so many issues down here on Earth?" Indeed, Hadley knew that the real mysteries of the universe pulsed not at the heart of some black hole ten thousand light years away, but at the heart of a human being mere feet away from her.

Even as Hadley decried Jason's focus on the stars, she had to admit to herself that scientific theories did better explain her current feelings than any psychological manual ever could. According to the theory of relativity, a stationary observer experiences time at a glacially slow pace, while a moving observer experiences time as zooming by. Perhaps that was why the spaces between the ticks of her watch seemed to stretch out forever: she had gotten stuck at some stationary point. And that immovable vantage point was in the past, deep within distant memories, where time had grown unbearably slow. Perhaps if she could get moving—if she get out the past and into the future—the inevitable would pass by more quickly.

And maybe gravitational time dilation, another of Einstein's postulates, explained why the clock beating in Hadley's chest had also stuttered to a standstill. As a clock moves closer to the gravitational pull of a massive object, time passes more and more slowly. Likewise, as both Jason and Parker exerted their gravity against Hadley, their giant masses left her feeling like a tiny little speck of space dust caught in a tug-of-war between two exploding supernovas.

"What's your psychology practice like?" Rick asked.

"Actually, right now I'm working on a Ph.D., so I don't see a full slate of clients yet. I'm researching the psychology of love, basically what influences whether a person can or can't attach to someone, whether they can process the reception of affection. It actually has some application to autism, even though I've mostly been concentrating on what laypeople call romantic love." She paused. "I think most people take for granted that everybody just accepts love, but that's really not true." She briefly caught sight of Jason's blue eyes.

"Well," Linda began, "I want you to know that we accept and appreciate the love that Parker has shown to this family. And I hope that both of you," she indicated Parker and Hadley, "accept the love we'll give back to you." She started tearing up again. Rick suggested calling it a night and motioned for the check.

They said their goodbyes on the pavement outside the restaurant. After Linda and Rick took turns wrapping Parker and

Hadley tightly in their arms, Jason stepped up. When Parker did not immediately leap forward, Jason reached out and lightly, almost carelessly, flung his arms around his brother. Parker's chest shrank inward, as if he was once more deflating from the inside out. They parted quickly, and then Jason turned expectantly to Hadley. He held out his arms.

She sank in to her first hug from Jason Snyder. Though the entire process couldn't have taken more than five seconds, she noted every detail about it. Both of their chins moved to the left. Her right arm went over his left shoulder, while her left arm went below his right armpit. Thanks to her cork wedges, her chin easily rested on his shoulder. She felt him exhale and hot breath gently dusting the bare neck under her ponytailed hair. Her arms reached all the way around his frighteningly thin frame. He seemed so child-like and helpless, like he might blow away on the wind like a wisp of a feather. His hands, splayed across her back, had no strength in them. They did not grip or squeeze her; they simply rested faintly on her shoulder blades, more like the shadow of a touch than touch itself.

Jason drew back from her like a trick of the light.

Parker insisted on hailing a taxi to return to the hotel, although Hadley would have preferred to walk. If this stretch of New York City street actually had beds for flowers, the buds would have bloomed in the balmy May evening. It was such a womb-like atmosphere—dark, pleasantly warm, and with constant white noise in the background. Hadley wanted to remain in the city's placental saturation as long as possible, because she knew that very soon she would be expelled from the present comfortable stickiness. Like babies being born, she would open her eyes to the severe light of an uncovered bulb, and she would try to blink away the harsh light jolting her from the amniotic darkness.

Newborn babies survived the trauma of being born all the

time. If such small defenseless creatures could survive their first freefall into the world without even a parachute, she could survive the freefall that awaited her at the end of the taxi ride.

During the drive back to the hotel, Hadley stared out the window while Parker made small talk with the Pakistani driver. The hotel stood on the edge of Times Square, and as she stepped from the taxi, the theatrical billboards and neon lights made her crave darkness. They seemed to say, in a threateningly seductive voice, "Run away. Just run away and we won't bother you again."

Parker paid the driver, and they walked in silence through the lobby and rode the elevator quietly up. They made it all the way to the room without a word. She sat on the edge of the bed, waiting for—well, waiting for whatever would come. As she faced forward toward the blank television screen, the bed sunk beside her.

"So do you want to tell me the truth?"

Yes. She so very desperately wanted to tell the truth, but even more than that, she desperately wanted someone to understand it. Whenever she had previously tried to tell this truth to someone, they either could not or would not grasp it. No one had ever before held her truth to be self-evident.

"I just want the real story. Whatever happened. I mean, I know you didn't fuck him." He chuckled, although there was no pleasure in it. "That first night when I had you, when you were so nervous. When you came as soon as I touched you." His voice dropped dangerously. "You couldn't fake that."

Hadley's cheeks stung. Parker had never insulted her in bed or belittled her sexual inexperience. The only purpose of the reference to her virginity was pure humiliation.

"But you carpooled with him. You visited him in the goddamn hospital. You met. His. Fucking. Parents. *My* parents."

Hadley continued to stare straight forward.

The traffic outside hummed in the otherwise silent room. Ever since Parker had left the coffee shop a few hours before, he had been plugging variables into permutations and equations, trying to arrange them into a sequence, shape, or ratio that made sense. But no matter how many combinations he tried, the figures never added up and the reactions never balanced. It just didn't make sense.

"So what did you do, date him? Hold his hand? Go to prom? I don't understand and I need you to tell me."

"I never got to hold his hand." She took a breath. "I loved him. I was in love with him for…for so long." A small tear escaped her eyelashes.

Hadley evidently thought her confession was a cataclysmic earthquake and that Parker would be overcome by the resulting tsunami. He could tell by her hunched shoulders, strangled voice, and persistent refusal to look at him that it had taken everything she had to get it out.

But to Parker it was absolutely anticlimactic. He could not say exactly what he had expected, but it certainly was not something as childish as this.

"So you loved him? That's all?"

The tip of Hadley's tongue pressed against the back of her front teeth as rage marshaled itself, almost as if Bruce Banner had morphed into the Hulk somewhere inside her. The nerve. The stupidity. The density, the lack of vision, the emotional shallowness.

"No. That is not all." Hadley chewed the n's and bit off the t's.

"That is…" her mouth worked silently, "everything. I loved him. I mean, I *loved* him. And that means something. It matters. Loving someone the way I loved Jason, it's something you carry with you for the rest of your life. It creates obligations and…and…" She could not complete the thought.

She hovered just above hysteria. Her fingers clawed at her thighs and her eyes had flushed red. She had accelerated from zero to sixty in under ten seconds. Parker had personally never seen someone throw a switch so fast. In Parker's world, everyone acted like old pickup trucks without power steering, not like Ferraris. He had no concept of how someone might move like a sports car, how she might shift and maneuver in response to mere fingertips on the wheel, how she could turn on a dime and whip around hairpin curves.

Just when Parker was going to say he had never seen Hadley like this before, he remembered the tortured, bumbling Hadley who tried to run out of his apartment when he first slipped his hand under the waistband of her pants, when her eloquence deserted her and she withered to a stuttering fool.

"Hadley," he said quietly, "I don't understand."

"Why?" With a yelping sound, she finally turned to face him. The tears came flooding now, in sobs. "Why can't you understand? Why can't anyone understand? He didn't understand either. He never understood! He was the love of my life. I was supposed to be with him. I was supposed to spend my life with him!"

"What?" Parker felt a bullet penetrate his gut, felt hot blood seeping from him, and futilely looked around for the unknown assailant who had crept upon him so silently. He had never even contemplated that such a bullet existed with his name on it. Now all he could feel was a hole expanding rapidly in his torso and pain spiking in his head.

"I loved Jason. My entire life revolved around him. So much of what I am is because of him. And he didn't…" Her voice dropped in both volume and pitch. "He didn't love me. And then he left. I missed him so much. I missed him even though…" She sank to a whisper and her eyes fell to the floor, "even though he didn't want me."

Silence flooded the room again. As the rush of adrenaline dissolved, Parker grasped for the only hand in reach. His mathematical, logical brain took over and reviewed the equation as it now stood with all the variables plugged in. Something still didn't make sense. He studied it for a few seconds and then spotted the essential miscalculation.

"But, Hadley," he spoke slowly and softly, "you were in high school when he moved away. You were too young to feel that way."

She answered with a mixture of disdain and righteous indignation: "That didn't matter. I felt what I felt and I will not allow someone to tell me otherwise. It doesn't matter if I was six or sixteen or sixty. It was real. It was absolutely real."

Hadley then began to recite in a mournful intonation. "But my love it was stronger by far than the love of those who were older than me, of many far wiser than me."

Parker recognized the cadences of Edgar Allan Poe's "Annabel Lee," which Hadley had once recited to him one evening as they lay in bed. But he did not know the poem well enough to note that she had changed the pronouns.

So apparently it was not only real, but also poetic.

"Start at the beginning."

# PART TWO

# *Chapter Eight*

I met Jason on the first day of first grade. We were both in Ms. Cummings' class at Aspen Elementary School in Albuquerque. I remember it exactly. All of us little kids had found our classroom, and our mothers and fathers were waving goodbye. We all stood around not talking, too nervous to say anything or sit down, god forbid we sat in the wrong seat or said the wrong thing. Kids at that age can't easily hide their motives, and we all knew we were sizing each other up, evaluating who would become friends or enemies. I looked around the whole classroom, but only one kid caught my attention. He was the only one bold enough to sit down, but he wasn't talking to anybody or showing off a rollie pollie he had snuck into school. He was reading. And it was a chapter book, not a picture book. It wasn't that thick of a chapter book, but it still caught my attention. *Fantastic Mr. Fox,* by Roald Dahl. It fascinated me.

I already knew how to read and I liked to do it. I had graduated to reading the harder picture books—like *Berlioz the Bear*. But I had never read a chapter book before, and looking at Jason with his paperback, I saw a challenge. The audacity of him—the balls to come to the first day of first grade with a chapter book and just sit down like he owned the place. It kind of pissed me off. Both fascinated and pissed off, from that very first moment, I wanted to know him.

And I've had that same mixed reaction ever since that day. He pissed me off a lot. He made me laugh a lot. But no matter what, he always fascinated me, and I always felt a constant compulsion to get close to him. Maybe that's because he always seemed far away—like I had to travel much further to get right beside him than I had to with other people.

Jason was not popular in first grade. He didn't quite fit in, but in the beginning it did not bother him. It bothered most of our classmates, though. They didn't trust him. Even at the age of six, he was already so…himself. So in control and secure in his own superiority. If the first graders had known the word, they would have called him arrogant. He apparently had it all figured out. And since any kind of abnormal knowledge in elementary school is automatically suspicious, his attitude didn't win him any points with other kids.

That very afternoon, I came home from first grade and demanded my mother take me to the bookstore to get a proper chapter book. I got *Matilda*, by Roald Dahl. It had a lot more pages than Jason's book did. And so began the great competition between Jason and me. The competition between us excited and stimulated me, but it also eventually destroyed a significant part of our relationship.

I don't mean to sound arrogant myself, but from the very beginning, everybody—the teachers, the other children—everybody saw that really, it was only between Jason and me. No one else even came close. In first grade we had this chart for spelling tests. Anyone who got over a ninety percent would get a sticker. Jason and I got many more stickers than all the other kids. It went like that for years—in eighth grade we got gold stars on a poster on the wall for one hundred percent vocab tests. Again, Jason and I won. Sometimes it felt like we lived in a bubble together and everybody else had to watch us from outside.

All through first grade, you could have called Jason and me "friends." He didn't even try to fit in and play nicely with the other children, but I tried, although with limited success. Sometimes I would spend recess with a few other girls, swinging or jumping rope or even just walking around talking. But many days I would spend recess with Jason. If the other girls annoyed me, or worse, started teasing me, I knew where to find Jason. Our playground had a few huge rubber tires—like six feet in diameter. Not many people liked to play in them, so Jason made it his own spot. I would climb in there with him and we'd talk and make little jokes. Or sometimes I'd find him reading a book.

I would try to get Jason to play "pretend," as I called it. I would tell him, "Okay, now we'll pretend that we're orphans on the run from an evil businessman." Or I'd want to be secret agents. But Jason never wanted to play pretend with me. He called my little fantasies silly.

In his defense, my girl friends also called playing "pretend" silly. It did hurt to hear the girls I considered my friends tease me. It hurt a lot. But when Jason called me silly, it didn't hurt. In those early years I never took offense at Jason's comments. I took them as legitimate criticism of my childishness. Even at six years old he had a way of making it seem like he knew what he was talking about—that by giving me advice, like to stop playing pretend, he was doing me a favor. And I believed it, at least then.

I came into elementary school lagging behind in some measures of maturity, including understanding relationships between boys and girls and knowing what certain words meant. I had no idea that my hanging around Jason in the middle of a giant rubber tire would attract any attention. Toward the end of first grade, the girls on the playground started talking about Jason and me, inserting our names into little rhymes and songs. Jason and I would walk back to the classroom and hear squeals behind us. "Hadley and Jason, sitting in a tree!" or "Hadley and Jason like each other!"

Perhaps those girls first put the idea into my head. I mean, I do remember coming home from school during first grade and telling my parents that Jason did this or that at school today. I suppose I thought of Jason as someone I liked, but my vocabulary at that point did not include liking someone in the way that those girls articulated it, with high-pitched squeals.

There's a field of psychology that studies which comes first: the emotion or the language to describe it. Some theorists say that people cannot truly have emotions without the words to embody those emotions. I've often tried to apply that theory to my life. Looking back on it now, I don't know which came first: liking Jason or the suggestion from the playground girls that I liked him. Did I like Jason without knowing that I *could* like Jason? I don't know.

I did already know how to lie, though. I insisted to the girls that I did not like Jason and that I thought he had cooties, but even at six years old, I knew it was a lie. Maybe it was actually the guilt of lying that first made me realize I *did* like him. We can only define something by saying what it is not—and by claiming the negative, I defined the positive.

I didn't see Jason during the summer between first and second grades. I must have missed him, though, because I showed up on the first day of second grade with a list—an actual physical list in my hand—of things I wanted to tell him about my summer. By fortune, fate, or coincidence we had ended up in the same second grade class. And partway through that year, the school tested both Jason and me for the gifted program. He was very much aware of his intelligence in a way I was not. It was a big revelation for me that I had more intellectual and academic capacity than my classmates. It came as a complete surprise that I could read faster or that I knew more facts than they did. I just naturally assumed that everyone operated exactly like me. Jason, though, had a savvy about those things. He knew he had something special going on in his head.

And he knew I did, too. A few days before my test, he asked me if I was going to be in the gifted class. Throughout our school time together, I could always depend on Jason for an honest assessment of my intelligence. He would never try to prop himself up by putting me down, but he also would never inflate my abilities to make me feel better.

Being in the gifted class meant that Jason and I spent a significant portion of the day together, even in the years we had different regular teachers. During the years we had the same regular teacher—third and fifth—we would leave our classroom together every day and walk to the gifted room for language arts, reading, and math. Having Jason there to walk beside me, to offer me companionship in my outcast status, was enormously comforting. Any kind of difference automatically isolates a kid, but walking down the hallway with Jason made me feel like much less of a freak. Even though I felt labeled as "different," at least Jason and I could be different together.

I began to look forward to the walk more than any other feature of my school day. Distances always seem much larger to children, and I've gone back to that elementary school as an adult, and these days the hallway looks so short. But back then it seemed like Jason and I had to caravan across the Sahara, or trek the entire length of the Silk Road, or sled the route of the Iditarod. I relished those little moments when Jason and I ambled down the hallway together. It made me feel like I had a best friend—that I had any kind of friend, really.

Sometimes Jason would carry his textbooks—the miniature ones with grammar or spelling exercises in them—in his arms. He clutched them against his chest, and to this day, one of the overriding images I have of Jason is of him in elementary school, with a bowl haircut, before he got glasses, carrying a grammar textbook in his arms.

In the years we didn't walk together, I would look forward to meeting Jason in the gifted classroom. I would have a whole list—sometimes I literally wrote a list on paper—of things to tell him, little ideas I had thought up since the day before. Or an interesting fact I had learned. I wanted to impress him so much. A lot of the time, maybe even a majority of days, he would already know the particular information, or my view on the subject would not surprise him. But on those days when I did impress him, it felt amazing. No matter what Jason said, my mood would always lift when I saw him, but when he would bestow a smile upon me, or maybe even say "that's cool," it got me high. If you charted my happiness, the line would rise in anticipation of Jason and would peak when I first walked into the classroom and saw him waiting at the table for our chit-chat.

But the trouble with Jason throughout all the time I knew him was that I would always fall back down. I could never maintain that peak.

By third grade Jason had become the barometer of my life. I measured whether I had a good or bad day according to him. I remember coming home from school in third grade and my mother asking about my day. My answers invariably referenced Jason. "Jason hadn't heard about that new dinosaur they discovered" or "Jason drew an amazing picture of a cat today."

We began to see each other away from school as well. I suppose that at some school parent night, our parents realized that we got along and that we both needed friends. In the summers we ended up enrolled in the same art classes and soccer camps. And then there were the postcards. Our parents encouraged us to write to each other about our vacations as a kind of extracurricular learning opportunity. My parents took my sister and me on some pretty great vacations, and I got to see many different landscapes, but those faraway places never seemed as exciting to me as the places described in Jason's letters. My family went to the beach in Florida during spring break of third grade, but I didn't truly appreciate the thick, warm air or the soft sand until Jason mentioned it in a postcard a couple years later. Everything and everywhere appeared so much better, so much clearer and sharper, through Jason's eyes.

Childhood summers always take on a golden sheen when you look back at them, and I certainly remember mine as utterly blissful. And yet the days that shimmer the brightest are those long summer days I spent with Jason, or the days when I could rush back from the mailbox with a postcard from him.

We mostly saw each other in organized activities like camps or classes, but we did get together spontaneously sometimes. One of those times was a July night between third and fourth grades. He came over to my house in the afternoon, just before one of the thunderstorms that break in the early evening in the summer in New Mexico. I wanted to run out into the rain together, but he didn't want to get wet. Instead, we sat side by side at the piano, banging out "Chopsticks."

I tried to hug him. I reached out and put my arms around him, but he stood up and walked away. He didn't say anything and didn't run screaming out into the street. He just got up and went to look out the window at the sunset. I didn't say anything either. I stayed at the piano and continued fooling around on it. A little while later his father knocked on the door to pick him up.

I never tried to hug him again, and perhaps I've spent all the years since then just trying to get back to that piano bench. Sitting there with him, with our knees touching, it was so perfect. It just felt *right*. Even as a nine-year-old, I could tell that with Jason beside me on the piano bench, the world suddenly made sense. Everything in my childhood world, the clouds and the sun, the rain and the trees and cactuses soaking it up, the birds chirping outside, and even the keys on the piano, everything was in harmony. The whole universe vibrated in tune, with Jason and me at the center.

Someone had given me a cute little diary for my birthday, the kind with a tiny lock and a separate key. That night, after Jason had gone, I wrote down in the diary that I loved him.

One day in fourth grade, in our regular class, not our gifted class, we had to do a project about becoming a grown-up: what kind of job we wanted to have, if we wanted to become moms and dads, where we wanted to live. Every child then had to present his or her future life to the rest of the class.

When I thought about the future for that school project, I could not think of any life plan that did not involve Jason. See, I've never been able to imagine my life without Jason in it. When I was asked to look ahead and fantasize about my life as an adult, I could not do it without including Jason.

Love. Every poet and second rate screenwriter has a great catchphrase about what love is. For me, that fourth grade assignment provided the definition. If you really love someone, you cannot imagine your life without him. And that imagining—that love—can run absolutely contrary to any actual evidence from real life. I already knew Jason didn't even want to hug me, yet despite that evidence, I imagined growing old with him.

And even now, even after all the things that happened, when I imagine the rest of my life, I still cannot imagine it without Jason. Even after years apart, I've never counted him out completely. I've always imagined some kind of chance meeting, some coincidental encounter in an airport or hotel lobby.

I knew I could not say anything about Jason in front of all the other kids in the class. Like I said before, the elementary school girls already teased me about hanging around with Jason, and after the thing with the piano bench…I knew I had to stay silent about certain dreams. I knew the ridicule that would come of them.

But in the end it happened anyway. I stood in front of the blackboard in Mrs. Woodward's fourth-grade class in front of an audience of up-turned faces while I read out my plans for becoming an actress and moving to Hollywood.

And then little Sara Martinez yelled out to the entire class, "I know what Hadley really wants to do! She wants to marry Jason! She wants to kiss him!" The room erupted in laughter.

I stood there with my face burning as the class giggled. Within seconds I started to cry. I scrunched my eyes shut, so I did not see how Jason himself reacted. With the laughter still ringing in my ears, I did the walk of shame back to my desk. I don't remember whether the teacher chastised the class or not, because I was too busy drowning in humiliation.

Was Sara right? Did I want to marry him even then, even at nine years old? Maybe. To my nine-year-old mind, marrying Jason would simply mean seeing him and talking to him every day. I certainly wanted that. I still had no clue about sex at that point.

My parents were pretty conservative, but they did keep some old hippy records in the house and sometimes played them on Sunday mornings on an ancient turntable. The day of that presentation, I came home and asked my father to put on the record that had a song called "You've Got to Hide Your Love Away."

At the time, I didn't consider whether the incident had any consequences for Jason. Now I see that he faced serious social repercussions because of what Sara did. I'm sure he wanted to live his own life and make his own way just like any other kid on the verge of adolescence, and she screwed up that opportunity. His identity, his socially constructed identity at least, would always be bound to mine.

His social identity may have been tied to me, but I was connected to him at a much deeper level. As I grew up, I formed my self around Jason, like a pearl forming around a grain of sand inside an oyster. By accretion, Jason slowly built up inside me and around me, and I built myself around him.

At that point, I didn't have a choice. It just happened. I was a kid. I didn't start with any conscious plan. I opened myself like every child opens herself, and what came in was Jason.

The way it worked in Albuquerque, two or three elementary schools would feed into one middle school. In grade school Jason and I had a few other friends our age who were in gifted classes with us. We all got along well, but I still considered Jason a special sort of friend. And of course, everyone knew I liked him. When we got to Franklin Middle School, though, our social structure changed dramatically. Jason suddenly had classmates and potential friends who had no idea of his connection to Hadley Keane. For those children from the other grade schools, he was simply Jason Snyder, not part of "Jason and Hadley."

We suddenly could hang out with a lot of other kids like us: smart, interesting, vibrant. In this new talent pool, we split up. I found myself part of a group of girls and he found some boys who played the same fantasy card games. We still had a lot of classes together, most importantly our gifted language arts and literature class.

And of course we had orchestra together. This would become the source of so much hostility later on, but it started off perfectly innocently. The summer between fifth and sixth grades, I decided I wanted to join one of the musical groups at school instead of taking "exploratory arts," the standard sixth grade elective. I settled my sights on the violin. My parents welcomed any project that could hold my curiosity for more than a few hours, so they happily bought me a lovely new violin and arranged for private lessons.

On the first day of sixth grade I walked into Beginning Orchestra to find waiting in the classroom—who else?—Jason.

He had not yet chosen which instrument he wanted to play, but I helped to persuade him to go for the violin. I was always looking for ways to grow close to him, and I thought this could do it. I demonstrated a few songs I had already learned in private lessons and let him take a spin on my violin.

Just as I vividly remember seeing Jason on that first day of first grade, I have burned in my brain the image of eleven-year-old Jason with my violin under his chin and my bow in his hand. He had this awful bowl haircut, he had gotten glasses the previous year, and the early effects of puberty made him look like a newborn giraffe—all gangly limbs. But when I saw him take my violin in his hands—his perfect hands—he transformed into the most beautiful thing I had ever seen. That moment, I truly fell in love with him.

I mentioned my new group of friends. Two girls in that little clique deserve special attention: Katie and Lauren. I had known Katie for a long time because we played on the same soccer team, even though we didn't go to the same school. We became friends and invited each other over for slumber parties several times a year. She ended up at Franklin Middle School and we grew close. In contrast, I had never met Lauren before middle school. We became very fast friends and started spending a lot of time together.

As much as I enjoyed the opportunity to make new friends, I missed my special relationship with Jason. Back when I first met him, I could hold his undivided attention. Now I had to compete with new diversions, new interests, new friends, and, worst of all, new girls. Even though I was still kind of socially delayed, I could tell that some of the other girls liked Jason. I wanted him all for myself, though, and I knew in my bones that I liked him more than all the other girls did.

And even at that point, at eleven years old, it occurred to me that I also deserved him more than all the other girls did. I felt *entitled* to Jason. I felt like I had a right to him, a right more valid than anyone else's. By virtue of our history together, by virtue of all the trips down the hallway, the recesses spent hiding in an out-of-the-way corner of the playground, and all the shared anecdotes and jokes, I had a claim to him. I thought that history, that investment, meant something.

Of course there's a massive internal contradiction in my conceptualization of Jason. I had so much respect for him, for his intelligence and his belief in himself. I so admired the security he had in himself and wished I could have that security in myself. But despite my respect and admiration for Jason, I denied his autonomy. I denied him his free will in choosing how he wanted to grow up and mature.

I thought he owed me something. I figured that because he once sent me a few postcards and sat with me on a piano bench, he had an obligation to our relationship.

Hearing myself say this, I realize how ridiculous it sounds, but I can explain. To me, every interaction *meant* something. Every "hello" Jason ever gave me was significant. I assigned such value to every word he said to me. Whenever Jason spoke to me or sat beside me on the bus or did anything in relation to me, I gave it…weight—weight above and beyond that which I gave to every other personal interaction in my life. All that weight accumulated over the years, and I carried it with me. That weight affected every choice I made and every direction I went. I couldn't understand why he didn't feel that same weight…why it didn't affect him the way it affected me. I elevated Jason and expected him to do the same for me.

Now I see the error of my perception. Not every "hello"

means something. Not everything can or should be weighed like that.

In sixth grade I stopped saying "I love you" to my parents. How could I say it to them when I couldn't say it to Jason? I could not say "I love you" to my parents knowing it would carry far less weight than a mere "good morning" to Jason.

I walked, and even today I walk, with a burden on my shoulders. Actually, burden is the wrong word. Burden suggests I didn't want to carry it. In fact, I loved carrying the weight of Jason. I welcomed it and gladly would have taken on more. It gave me something to hang on to.

Even if Jason and I did not have as much quantity in sixth grade, we had a lot more quality. Our interactions became flirtatious and funny. As our vocabularies grew with weekly word sets and usage tests, we discovered the world of puns and double entendres. I began to notice his blue eyes and how much the fluidity of his hands pleased me aesthetically.

That's the thing about Jason and me. From the beginning to the end, despite everything that happened, we could always make each other laugh. But thinking of the way we laughed brings tears to my eyes. So much of it revolved around inside jokes, dropping references to movies we had both seen or facts we both knew. Most of our remarks sailed straight over our classmates' heads.

It wasn't just the humor itself that excited me. I lusted after the challenge. We chased each other through words and I loved chasing him. The exchanges would play out so perfectly, one coming after the other in splendid succession, each step building upon the last, and finally resolving itself.

Back in second grade, I had felt proud to tell Jason some new fact, but our middle school flirtations made me feel...*beautiful*. I've never liked myself so much as I liked myself joking around with Jason. Sarcastic or nonsensical exchanges actually made me feel gorgeous. Just like the world had so much more excitement and intrigue when seen through Jason's postcards and letters, I myself transformed under his eyes into something incredible and extraordinary. Every minute with him made me feel one-in-a-million.

Jason and I were like the unofficial King and Queen Nerd. All of our friends in our social circle sensed the connection between us. In the spring of sixth grade, our class took a field trip to the Santa Fe Folk Art Museum, and a few of my classmates conspired to get Jason and me into an elevator alone. By then I had finally learned the socially appropriate way of dealing with that kind of thing. I resisted all the efforts of my friends. I even physically struggled against them as they tried to push me into the elevator. Truthfully, of course, I had no greater wish than to step in that elevator with him, have the doors close, and ascend with him to the stars.

I had finally picked up on social signals and expectations of boy-girl middle school relationships. I accepted the prevailing system of communication, even though it seemed silly to my naive and trusting mind. According to that system, if I liked Jason I had to pretend I didn't. I had misgivings about this deeply flawed method, but I stuck to it. I let my friends convince me that Jason, a precociously intelligent boy who nevertheless remained hopelessly unaware of the vast majority of the mainstream, would somehow understand those signals.

Here was an eleven-year-old boy already obsessed with Stephen Hawking, who played *Magic: The Gathering* for hours. For god's sake, when a yo-yo craze hit our school in sixth grade, he won the school-wide contest with a yo-yo he made himself and which he labelled Yo-Yo Ma. How could I ever have expected him to understand this smoke screen, this doublespeak?

As a psychologist I am very aware of the field of social

semiotics—the study of how humans communicate in various social circumstances. Any group or subculture will always have its own unique set of signifiers, and if an individual doesn't learn the particular signifiers, that individual does not become part of the subculture. I've also studied the coercive power of peer pressure on adolescents. Adolescents are so malleable that they very quickly soak up new communicative systems.

With that knowledge, I can look back on myself with a little more compassion. As intelligent as I was, I was just as vulnerable to social coercion as any eleven-year-old, and because I wanted to fit in to the prevailing subculture, I bought into the whole set of social signifiers. In reality, everyone knew I liked Jason, but the rules of the game demanded that I claim otherwise.

Looking back on it now, I see that Jason may not have done the same. He never seemed to act contrary to his emotions. I mentioned how in elementary school he never attempted to fit in with normal kids. I mentioned his distance and how little he cared about it. And for the first couple of years of middle school, he completely resisted any social coercion. And because he resisted all that adolescent crap, he did not completely buy into set of social signifiers. He did not learn that language. Perhaps all our problems were just questions of semiotics. Perhaps we just got our signals crossed.

I had identified the rules of the game. I had convinced myself that if I played by those rules, I would eventually win. But unbeknownst to me, Jason was not playing by the rules. He had no idea that the game even existed.

This stupid trend went around sixth grade where you and a friend would have a notebook—a spiral notebook—in which you would write things to each other and pass it back and forth. I had a notebook with Katie, and in it she said repeatedly that she thought Jason liked me.

Then of course there was the objective evidence: he

laughed at seventy-five percent of what came out of my mouth. One time in the cafeteria at lunch, he walked over from the boys' table, where they played *Magic*, to my table to tell me, me specifically, that he had just won. Everything added up so nicely and all the variables led to one conclusion.

I suppose it was about this time that I started fantasizing. Wherever I went, I would imagine seeing Jason there. My parents would take my sister and me to shows of touring Broadway musicals, and I would picture seeing him across the crowded auditorium. The summer between sixth and seventh grades, I went to a release party for a Harry Potter book at a local bookstore. Before I went, I imagined bumping into him and him turning to face me with a lightning bolt drawn on his forehead.

I also catalogued every fact I could gather about Jason. When I found out he didn't like raisins in his carrot cake, I wrote that down so that when the day came, not *if*, but *when* I made him a carrot cake, I would not put raisins in it.

One of the facts I catalogued was that his parents were from Illinois. I organized a lot of my school work in an enclosed, zippered three-ring binder. Trapper Keepers, they were called. Mine happened to be blue with orange swirls. One day Jason complimented my choice of school supplies because the colors were "appropriate." When I probed further, Jason expressed disappointment that I was not a Chicago Bears fan. When I asked why he followed that team, he told me his parents had grown up in Illinois.

I catalogued that he wanted to be an astrophysicist when he grew up. That had changed from the fourth grade project, when he wanted to be an astronaut.

Although I admired Jason's interest in space and his knowledge of celestial bodies, I wished he would show a little more interest in the world immediately around him and develop knowledge of some bodies closer to his own. He dreamed big, and I loved that about him. But his dreams had no room for me. I wouldn't have fit into the space capsule with him, and he certainly did not need a telescope to see me.

I gazed at him as intently and often as some people gaze on stars. He never told me to stop, either because he didn't sense my eyes on him or he didn't care. I particularly enjoyed watching his hands. Jason's hands provoked my first sensations of warmth spreading in the region below my belly button. The lines of his hands, fingers, and wrists had such an elegant beauty, and he used them so eloquently when he spoke. I would also watch his hands when he played the violin. He didn't have perfect position —he didn't round the fingers of his left hand enough, so he played on the pads instead of the tips of his fingers. But the pronation of his wrist and the cupping of his palm made his forearm look strong and firm and refined.

We moved along into seventh grade, which played out similarly to sixth grade, with one change that will become relevant later on. I mentioned that during sixth grade I became friends with Lauren. For reasons I still cannot pin down, during seventh grade she broke up with me—I mean, broke our friendship. Of course, by the time she decided to stop talking to me, I had already confessed to her that I really liked Jason.

Jason and I moved into advanced orchestra. I did take private lessons, and I did practice, but up until the first days of seventh grade, I didn't put one hundred percent into the violin. Up until then, it was just a diversion for me, not a passion. Jason, though, must have spent the entire summer practicing, because when he returned to the orchestra room in August, his playing had grown by leaps and bounds.

He had become quite skilled. Of course, he wasn't playing Paganini Caprices yet, but he definitely had achieved greater proficiency than I had. And just like the sight of him with a chapter book on the first day of first grade had pissed me off, his showing off his new violin skills on the first day of seventh grade pissed me off.

I started practicing for an hour every day. I begged my teacher for harder material. I researched famous violin players and asked my parents to buy the best recordings. Calluses arose on my fingertips and neck and chin. Jason had caught me sleeping and there was no way in hell I was going down without a fight.

After that call to arms, Jason's behavior toward me did change. Sometimes he ignored me when I tried to talk to him, and our repartee started sinking into sarcastic insults. But on the other hand, he also frequently stole my lunchbox, and I cannot think of a clearer signal of significant affection in middle school semiotic structure than playing keep away with a girl's lunchbox.

He also challenged me to grow up a little. For example, I had gained an unwanted reputation as a good girl and teacher's pet, and one day at lunch, Jason and his friends teased me that I was too prissy to say a swear word. And so just to show him, I blurted out, "fuck." And then Jason said that hearing me say fuck made his day.

Making Jason's day made my day. I was so sensitive and receptive to changes in him, like mercury in a thermometer. If I could get Jason to laugh, I would feel a surge of happiness, but if he didn't laugh, or if he said something mean or didn't say anything at all, my mood would plummet.

But I liked it. In fact, I loved it. That is an essential part of this whole story. You have to understand, I loved the ups and downs. They made my life exciting. They made me feel like my life had some kind of meaning.

I can't quite explain this feeling I've had all my life. It comes and goes and I've never found the words to accurately describe it. Even as a child, and then growing stronger in my adolescence, I felt my life should mean something *more*. But more than what? *More* than ordinary, *more* than normal. I looked around at my classmates, my family, people I saw out in public. They all looked the same to me. They blurred together and faded into the background. But when I looked in the mirror, I saw myself as *marked* in a way, marked for something different. When I first read that poem "Alone," by Edgar Allan Poe, I knew exactly what he meant. I have not been as others were, have not seen as others saw. I could not awaken my heart to joy at the same tone.

I though Jason had the mark too. I know I'm weird and not like other people and I know sometimes people look at me like I just dropped here out of a spaceship from another planet. Jason, though, made me feel a little less alien. I thought we were together in our difference.

In our seventh grade language arts and literature class, we read the novel *The Giver*, which had just recently come out. It takes place in a dystopian future in which people can't see color. Their world is literally in black and white. The main character, though, can see in color. That describes how I interpreted my difference. I saw in color while the rest of the world only saw in black and white. And I thought Jason could also perceive, and not only perceive, but appreciate, the full spectrum of color. I thought he shared my vision.

How can I explain it better? I believed the events of my life should be significant, and...profound and...glorious. I needed to do something, to feel something, worthy of remembrance. The twentieth century simply could not accommodate my desires. I wanted blood and sweat and tears. I wanted quests and heroism and adventures. I could not accept that I might just be an ordinary American teenager at the tail end of the millennium.

Maybe that desire contributed to falling in love with Jason in a different sort of way. I absolutely know I first fell in love with Jason himself, with the actual flesh and blood creature I saw every day. Along the way, though, I admit I also fell in love with the idea of him.

The idea of Jason, and in fact the idea of love itself, satisfied my delusions of grandeur. You can blame it on being a bookworm. I was enchanted by stories of agonized affairs, the intertwining of two people against all odds, and love conquering all. If I had to fight for him, if I had to wait for him, if I had to overcome enormous obstacles in my pursuit, well, that was all the better. I liked the idea of a struggle. It made the world make sense, and it made the prospect of finally uniting with Jason seem all the more profound.

And certainly from eighth grade on it became harder to love Jason himself. I had served as Jason's apologist for many years, but once he reached eighth grade, I found it far more difficult to defend his quote-unquote self-confidence. I had to acknowledge that what I called security had crossed the line into arrogance and pretension. Socially, he devolved instead of progressing. For the first time in the seven years I knew him, he expressed a desire to become popular.

So he set out to achieve popularity. He never got that much, but he got more than I ever did. He showed up to the first day of eighth grade with a brand-new haircut. The bowl was gone, replaced by a short spiky style that made me go weak in the knees. He wore shirts with a very trendy brand name on them. Even with his glasses, he certainly looked the part of a popular thirteen-year-old. He looked completely fantastic, actually, and my insides began to tingle far more frequently.

I had two different reactions to Jason's pursuit of popularity. First was disillusionment. He had sold out and caved to social pressure. With his overpriced polo shirts with their pompous embroidered logos, he pandered to social forces far below his intellect. For the first time, I had to consider the possibility that Jason was weak, that he lacked some steely internal fiber.

My second reaction was mobilization for rescue. He had merely given in to pressure, and it was up to me to rescue him and show him the error of his ways.

But how could I catch him at the edge of the cliff when he spent fewer and fewer minutes with me? He abandoned his nerdy friends to chase more socially mobile companions. He started coming to class late and doing homework at the last minute. He even—this was before it became grounds for suspension to use the word 'gay' as an insult—joined in on calling his best friend Nate 'gay.'

Our repartee took on an additional dimension: a meta-level. By that, I mean Jason and I finally verbally acknowledged that a relationship existed between us, and we began to examine its contours. Again my faith in Jason fell. For years I automatically gave him credit for sensitivity and intuition, but in eighth grade, I discovered that as intellectually brilliant as he was, he was hopelessly dense when it came to emotion. He had no sensitivity and no intuition. Several times he told me, to my face, that our relationship consisted of nothing more than "mutual insults." And in the first couple months of eighth grade, he asked me several times whether I had ever liked him and whether I liked him now.

Back then, I couldn't express my true feelings. I know I don't do it very well now, either, but back then I couldn't say much more than, "fine." And because I could not answer him truthfully, because I could not force those words from my mouth, I flung back non-answers or asked rhetorical questions, like "Where have you been, under a rock?" That certainly didn't help matters.

I must clarify that in eighth grade there were actually two Jasons: the one I saw during regular school hours and then the other one, who only showed up twice a week. That second version, the old and good Jason with whom I fell in love, came out on Friday afternoons and Saturday mornings. On Friday afternoons we had rehearsal for a string quartet at school. Jason and I traded off on first and second violin parts. We laughed good-naturedly and share constructive criticism.

On Saturday mornings I—well, my mother or father driving the car—would pick up Jason at his house, violin case in hand, to take the two of us to All City Junior Orchestra. This group was audition-only—the best middle school players in Albuquerque. Jason and I both auditioned and both got in. Our parents then had the brilliant idea to carpool.

Jason would stand outside his front door clutching his violin case. That's another image that has stuck with me over the years: him against the stucco wall, brushing his sneakers against the cement, head down and thinking about who knows what. I'd have him all to myself for the twenty-minute drive to rehearsal. I'm surprised I never had a heart attack on those carpool mornings. My heart beat so fast! Although I'm a stickler for punctuality, sometimes I wished we'd get caught in a traffic jam just so I could have a few extra minutes with him. I felt very close to Jason on those Saturday mornings when we arrived together at rehearsal, both carrying our violins across the parking lot.

At the end of rehearsal, we'd pack up our instruments, and Jason and I would climb into one of his family's mini-vans. That's when I got to know his parents. Fitting in with Jason's family was very important to me, and I felt very confident when I contributed to his family's discussions from the back seat of the mini-van.

Those Saturday morning carpools reminded me that not only did I love Jason, I liked him too. Beneath the cool exterior he displayed to the world, in the backseats of those cars Jason allowed me to see a much different side of him—happier, less sarcastic, gentler, and even kind. Sometimes his little sister would ride with us on the return trip. He interacted with her so beautifully. It made me think that he would make a great father.

I would come home from rehearsal on Saturday afternoons exhilarated, absolutely positive that Jason and I really had a connection, and I would pledge to myself that if I just hung in there, Jason would eventually discover that connection.

And then I would get to school on Monday morning and find my sweet Jason transformed into an absolute asshole. In response, I told myself that only I knew the *real* Jason—that I saw the real him on Saturdays. It strengthened my resolve to rescue him from the stupefying effects of peer pressure.

In mid-October of eighth grade something very bad happened. I have to put this into perspective. When I say it out loud, it sounds like a typical piece of middle-school melodrama. But like I tried to explain earlier, I always saw the world at an epic scale. If you had cameras installed behind my eyes, the film would probably come out looking like *Lawrence of Arabia* or *Lord of the Rings*. I blew everything out of proportion, not consciously, but just because I seemed to experience every event harder, faster, stronger, deeper. It was as if the air itself was a drug and each breath got me high.

Jason started "going out" with Lauren, my ex-best-friend. I had grown used to serving as the butt of jokes, but now they took on a new tone. My classmates, who all had seen ample evidence of my affection for Jason, teased me mercilessly about how I couldn't have him now. Jason and I shared a circle of friends and acquaintances, and they all took sides, most of them choosing to ally themselves with Jason and Lauren, even my then-best friend Katie. I got the castoffs, including Jason's now ex-best friend Nate, but we turned ourselves into a tight group and spent more than a few lunchtimes plotting Jason's demise.

I rather naively thought I had a bond with both Jason and Lauren. Admittedly, Lauren had rejected my friendship, but some outdated notion of honor or a code of morals led me to believe that even if she had broken up with me, she would respect the secrets to which she had been privy and not move in on the boy she knew I loved.

I also thought I shared some kind of bond with Jason. I thought he cared about me. Even if he didn't want me to hug him, didn't want to ride in an elevator alone with me, and didn't want to "go out" with me, I still believed he cared about me. I expected him to care when he saw me alone, moping against the wall in an out-of-the-way corner of the lunch area at school. I expected him to care when he heard people teasing me.

I've skipped a step, though. For Jason to care about my sadness, he would have had to know that the source of my sadness traced back to him. Once I factor in that intermediate premise, I'm left with two unpleasant options to consider: one, Jason did not understand his centrality to my life, or two, Jason *did* know and just didn't care. At the time, I thought Jason and I had a level of trust that was susceptible to betrayal, but looking back on it now, I wonder whether Jason ever considered that the trust between us deserved protection.

If someone had read my journals from that period, they would think I was crazy. And I kind of was. I managed to mostly hold it together at school, but then I would go home, turn on some music, and cry into my pillows. Then I'd pull myself back together again and put on a normal face for my family. Although my parents drove Jason around town on Saturday mornings, they never grasped my true feelings for Jason.

I mentioned earlier that poem "Alone" by Edgar Allan Poe. It has a line, "All I loved, I loved alone." I loved Jason alone. I had no one to talk to, no one to whom I could reveal myself, no one who could or would understand. Obviously telling someone my own age was out.

Telling my parents was also out. I already knew they found me weird and silly. Sometime in sixth or seventh grade, I prattled on about Jason while sitting around the dinner table with my parents. My mother cut me off and asked, "Why do you always talk about Jason so much? It's not normal to talk so much about one person. People will think you're weird." I assumed I could trust my parents—after all, your parents are supposed to love and support you no matter what. Plus, they were grown-ups. I figured they would understand what it felt like to only want to talk about one other person, every day, all day.

So I told my parents, and my sister of course, right there at dinner, "Well, I love Jason, so I guess I talk about him a lot." My mother and father eyed each other across the table, you know, one of those parental discussions that occurs solely through eye contact. My mother's eyes said to my father, "What's wrong with our daughter? What did we do wrong? How did she become so weird and abnormal?" My father's eyes said back, "I wouldn't be too concerned about it. It's probably just a phase, but she definitely shouldn't talk like that in front of other people."

After they nonverbally agreed on a course of action, my mother leaned over to me and said, "Honey, don't be silly. You don't love Jason. I know he's your friend and you like him as a friend, but you can't say you love him."

From that moment on, I never discussed Jason with my parents again, never sought counsel from them, never let on the real reason for my fits of melancholy. And since my own parents called me silly, I sensed that any other adult would find me patently absurd. And so I just had to hide it all away.

Even within my group of fellow gifted students, I began to get stares that had only one possible meaning: you're weird. I shaved my legs and kept up with pop culture, so it wasn't just nerdiness that made me weird in their eyes. Maybe, despite my attempt to hide everything, it still showed through, and they didn't know how to respond to it. However, their judgment just increased my conviction that I stood apart, that something they could not even contemplate had taken over me. The disapproval in my classmates' eyes proved to me that what I felt was…real.

This idea of realness, of authenticity, is a very important point for me to emphasize. In the pages of my journal, I hammered home the idea that my love for Jason was not merely a schoolgirl crush, not only physical infatuation, and not a passing obsession. I don't know how else to say it—it was real, and it was important that it was real.

During the time Jason dated Lauren, I also wrote down in my journal for the first time that I hated Jason. And I did. I hated him for his spinelessness and the chinks I found in his armor. I hated his posing, his arrogance, and his lack of vision. But mostly I hated him for turning me into the girl moping alone at the edge of the schoolyard.

Despite all this, Jason still sent signals that sent me into a tailspin of confusion. One day Lauren was absent for some reason, and so I actually got to sit with Jason at lunch. He threw a Skittle down my shirt. In the semiotic system of pre-teen adolescence, that is a sure sign of affection. He accompanied the Skittle-throwing with a peace offering. He apologized for being mean and argued that if he wasn't mean, he would never become popular.

But then he had the nerve to ring my doorbell on Halloween. With Lauren. Trick-or-treating. I heard them downstairs making small-talk with my parents. I stayed barricaded in my room in protest, so I have no idea what kind of costume Jason wore.

I'm sure I had dreamed of Jason before eighth grade, but during that fall, the dreams began coming much more frequently, and I started recording them in my journal. In the first one I wrote down, in November of eighth grade, I dreamed Jason asked me to spend Thanksgiving with him. I remember he had on purple pants in the dream, and he had a helicopter waiting to take us to whatever relative of his was hosting Thanksgiving.

Jason and Lauren "broke up" in early December. Lauren actually dumped him. And flush with happiness and ready to shower Jason with tea and sympathy, what did I do the very next day? I beat him in the geography bee.

Why did the geography bee just have to happen on a day when I had a perfect opportunity to repair things with Jason? He had just been dumped and I had a great opening to counsel him and sooth over the hurt. But instead, the controllers of the universe scheduled another competition and as it inevitably did, it came down to Jason and me. I couldn't deny myself the satisfaction of winning, and specifically, the satisfaction of winning over Jason. I couldn't stop myself from saying "the Amazon." And then we had to walk back to class together. We had to enter the classroom, and he had to explain to everyone that I won and he got second.

It wasn't the first time professional problems —"professional" in the eighth grade sense of the word— obstructed things with Jason. In orchestra, we always vied for first chair, and whenever we would overtake each other for first chair, we would stop talking for a few days. He tried to show off by learning a Mozart concerto, and so to ensure he didn't hog the spotlight, I had to learn the Bruch. He bragged about sitting in on some master class at UNM, so I bragged about going to the dress rehearsal when Itzhak Perlman came to town.

We also constantly squabbled for dominance and attention in other classes. In the spring of eighth grade, Jason and I had drama class together, and in late spring it came time to put on a show. Our drama teacher appointed Jason director and assigned me the lead role in the play. So of course, Jason tried as hard as he could to wrangle me into the line readings he wanted, and I fought just as hard to do it my way. Even as I huffed and puffed around like the biggest diva of the middle school stage, inwardly I knew all our disagreements had made us better—he made my performance better, and I made his direction better, just like our constant competition in orchestra made us both far, far better than we would have been without each other.

But of course it was never all bad. Jason still did and said hilarious things all the time. One week in eighth grade, he and another boy—who was coincidentally also named Jason—decided to go vegan for a week. I know this might not sound overtly funny, but two thirteen-year-old boys eating nothing but Skittles and tortillas with hot sauce for a week, especially if one of those boys was Jason, made us all laugh hysterically. I remember he wrote this hilarious short story in eighth grade somehow involving a babushka, and when he read it aloud, he over-pronounced babushka to spectacular effect. I would often catch myself giggling at something he did, and then I would have to remember to stop laughing, because he made me sad.

We also argued so well together. Not arguing about each other—not fighting. Debate, discussion, the equal exchange of ideas, about books we read in class or history we studied or music we played. For example, Jason's drive toward popularity included abandoning Pink Floyd for Eminem, so we debated whether Eminem had real artistic merit or just shock value. It seems we could talk about anything, except each other. I learned as much, if not more, from arguing with Jason than I ever learned from any teacher. I learned how to articulate and defend my ideas just by standing in his line of fire. He tried to distract me from the real substance of the debate with all kinds of rhetorical maneuvers, so I developed focus and concentration. He was a worthy adversary. He challenged me. I liked it.

After Jason's empty facade of a relationship with Lauren blew over, I faced a much more serious problem. I began to suspect he had a real, substantial relationship with Katie, the girl who had been my best friend for the past year and a half. Jason's dalliance with Lauren had flown in from left field, but Jason's relationship with Katie evolved slowly and incrementally. At first it was just small glances between them. Then, when everyone had to choose rival camps between me and the dynamic duo of Jason and Lauren, Katie deserted me and defected to their side. I started seeing Jason and Katie walking between classes together, chuckling madly along the way. They passed notes to each other, even during class.

Jason and Katie definitely bonded over one thing: me. In me, they found an easy target for their whispered gossip and rolled eyes. Sometimes, when one of them would receive a note from the other or just before sending one off, they would sneak a peek at me and cackle away. I asked them once what could be so hysterical about the note, and they answered back that if I knew what it said, I would be hurt. I replied that I had been hurt a lot in my life. I intended it as a massive hint to Jason that he had hurt me before and was doing it again, but either he didn't understand or he just didn't care.

The banter and flirtations which used to flutter constantly back and forth between Jason and me gradually disappeared, replaced by secret references and furtive whispers from the backs of classrooms where Jason and Katie now sat.

I have a much stronger case of betrayal against Katie. Practically every kid at Franklin Middle School knew I liked Jason, even if they just thought it was a crush. But I confided in Katie much further. I confessed to her that I seriously loved Jason and that I had envisioned us getting together some day as adults. And then she told me right back to my face that Jason and I were perfect for each other!

I could have passed over the Lauren debacle as an anomaly—a deviation from the norm from which Jason would soon return. I had simply gotten fooled, and I did not anticipate getting fooled again. But when I saw Jason looking at Katie, when I heard their evil-genius cackling, I realized I was not being fooled. I was the fool myself. Jason had not deviated and he would not come boomeranging back to me.

It forced me to ask that basest and most pathetic of rhetorical questions: "why me?" Or more accurately in my case, "Why *not* me?" Why did Jason pass over me for Lauren and Katie? What about me so repulsed him? And what about them so enchanted him? Katie and Lauren were both intelligent girls, certainly. They had brains. But I had *more*. I knew I could give him more than they could. I was the only person who could handle Jason intellectually, emotionally, musically, or in any other way.

And I made him laugh! I repeated that statement over and over and I'm still repeating it now. I made him laugh.

True, Jason laughed with Katie, but it wasn't like it was with me. They didn't make each other laugh; they just laughed at other people.

I put my intelligence down in the pro column, but maybe Jason put it on the con side. The mental connection with Jason thrilled me. I absolutely adored arguing with him. I really did. I thrived on our verbal fencing bouts. For me it represented a kind of cerebral foreplay. Provoking and prodding Jason's mind aroused me, and I assumed our mental teases and twisting excited him too. Maybe they didn't. Maybe he didn't want a girl who confronted him and defied him.

Okay, I admit it: I got off on winning. I definitely liked to win; I will never apologize for saying that winning feels really fucking good. And I could not imagine Jason showing me any affection if I had not earned it. From my point of view, I earned his attention every time we argued. It took me a long time to wrap my head around the concept that not everyone needs to win. Maybe he didn't need to win. Maybe he didn't need to fight. Perhaps he wanted it easy.

I can't pinpoint the exact date or even the month when I first started persuading myself into sleep with reveries of Jason. Before, I would simply get into bed, put my head on the pillow, and close my eyes. On some particularly dark days in eighth grade, I admit I cried myself to sleep. The tears would leak out of my eyes and I would let them slowly roll down my cheek. Because I slept on my side, the tiny rivers would wind all the way down to the corner of my lips, when I would taste their saltiness for a fraction of a second.

I didn't enjoy the sensation of the moisture on my face or the salt on my tongue, but I never wiped the tears away. I squirreled away so many journals and so many facts and so many other things I could collect from Jason. Those tears came from him too. I had to store them away too, so I took them back into my body. I literally drank back the evidence of my love. Maybe that was a bad choice. Perhaps the saltiness festered inside and became bitterness.

Going back and forth over every detail of the saddening or maddening events of the day made it difficult to get to sleep, though. And crying plugged up my nose and upset my dog, who slept with me. I would wrap myself, or more like entangle myself, so tightly in yesterday that I could not extricate myself in time to face tomorrow. I needed something else to distract me from analyzing in circles and considering the connotations of every word Jason said to me.

So in order to prepare myself to face the future, I rehearsed it over and over in my head until the repetition eased me into sleep. I lived an additional life beneath my darkened eyelids. In the minutes between pulling the covers over my shoulders and the nebulous moment when waking becomes sleep, Jason and I shared French kisses under the Eiffel Tower, embraced each other in gardens and forests and on beaches and cliffs, comforted each other next to the beds of dying parents, opened presents around Christmas trees, had knock-down, drag-out fights and apologetic make-ups. In the moments before sleep, I made love to Jason and even, a few times, clasped his hands over my pregnant belly.

And sometimes I imagined seeing him somewhere after many years apart. Before I had even turned fourteen I already imagined reuniting with him at twenty-five, thirty, even sixty-five. I suppose it proves what I said earlier; I couldn't imagine my life without him. Even my senior citizen self wanted Jason somewhere in her life.

The dreams I let myself dream during the twilight minutes before sleep overtook me went on for a very long time. They continued even after Jason moved away. In fact, they became stronger and in a way, more real to me after he left. I had to keep Jason alive inside me; I had to preserve his memory. And strangely, the way I did it was to create entirely new memories. Even if I couldn't have Jason in the present, I could have him both in the past and the future. Two out of three was good enough for me.

I only stopped the fantasies when I found someone I could actually share a future with.

***

Hadley waited for Parker to say something, but he did not. Hadley pulled herself off the bed and walked over to her suitcase. She unzipped a compartment and took a folder from it. She opened the folder and slid something out from a pocket, then walked back to the bed. She sat down on the edge and placed a sheet of paper encased in a clear plastic sleeve between her and Parker, its long side just touching the bare thigh beneath her shorts.

***

One day in February of eighth grade, Jason was wallowing in a round of self-pity—he actually did that quite frequently, the whole woe-is-me self-deprecation act—and he said to the class at large, "Everybody in here hates me." Before I could even think, the words flew out of my mouth: "I don't hate you. How I feel about you is at the other end of the spectrum from hate." Some helpful classmate noted, "the other end of the spectrum from hate is love." We all just kind of looked at each other, dumbfounded by the implication. Neither he nor I said anything else.

It was the kind of wordplay Jason and I shared every day, the puns and hidden meanings and puzzles. It was only natural that the first time I said it, I would cloak it in a riddle. I don't know why I said it, other than it was true.

Before that, I had never contemplated telling Jason directly. It did not even occur to me. Prior to that point, I thought I could compel him to understand through action and innuendo. I thought the thing itself—my love—was enough; that if I lived it, if I imbued it with my own vitality and spirit, it would survive on its own. If I just believed enough, Jason would go through nothing short of a conversion experience, an almost religious epiphany when he would suddenly come to a revelatory understanding.

Fairy tales and epic romances, after all, are populated with exquisitely intuitive characters who can tell with the slightest glance from across a castle courtyard that their destinies lie along the same road. In the real world I had to contend with the density of a boy who was brilliant on paper, but who was also still only an emotionally stunted fourteen-year-old.

The day after the "spectrum" comment, Jason and I went to the geography bee for our school cluster. It would decide who went on to the city tournament. It seemed so representative of our entire relationship that a competition would immediately follow my confession. As it always and inevitably did, it came down to Jason and me. This time I let him win. I pretended I didn't know that Sherpas act as porters in the Himalayas. Of course I knew that. Sometimes I felt like a Sherpa myself—carrying thousands of pounds of gear up Mount Everest. I don't know if Jason realized I threw the competition on purpose. I now regret taking a dive, but I had to test my theory that Jason resented our rivalry. His minor victory, though, didn't result in any change in conduct or attitude, and neither did the spectrum comment.

It was not until April 20th that the moment of truth finally came. It was a Friday. The day had been a bad one, full of tension between Jason and me. We argued all day about a literary magazine our language arts class was putting together. The class had elected Jason and me the editors, inevitably, ensuring plenty of disagreement between us. Jason kept whispering to Katie during the entire language arts period as the rest of us tried to actually get some work done on our projects. I desperately wanted to know what they were talking about, and I, a little too obviously, kept finding excuses to wander to their corner of the room.

It happened in drama class, the last class of the day for Jason and me. Our teacher was absent and we were watching some documentary on Shakespeare.

Jason launched a paper airplane across the room at me. I unfolded it and found he had written a message. It said, "Are you angry with Katie and I?"

Whenever I have had to make big choices in my life, I've always been guided by whether or not I will regret the decision. I knew I would never regret telling this truth. I knew I could never regret telling someone I loved him. I knew I could never regret taking that chance, the chance that the entire trajectory of my life could shift. I decided, without almost any hesitation or any fear, to just tell him. I suddenly realized, quite easily and peacefully, that love was *not* enough. It could not survive on its own. It had to be carried by someone. It meant absolutely nothing until expressed. It was doing nothing just sitting there in my heart.

I thought if I could make him understand…it would make him happy. I thought knowing I loved him would make him happy. If I could just explain it to him, then everything would work out. That was another huge assumption I made on a regular basis: I naively believed people want to be loved and that they want to know it. I bought into that old Beatles song my parents played all the time—"yeah she loves you, and you know you should be glad!" I took for granted Jason would be glad I loved him. I thought he would be thankful, appreciative, that someone cared about him so much.

And so I wrote back, "No. Just confused. And jealous. I'm not angry with you. I love you." I refolded the paper airplane and sent it flying back to Jason. I watched him open it and read what I had written. I watched his pencil scrawl across the paper. To this day I can always recall to my mind the image of Jason writing.

Drama was the last class of the day, but Jason and I had string quartet rehearsal after school. I let him precede me to the orchestra room. I let him go in and come back out of the instrument storage room, and then I went in alone. The paper airplane awaited me on the shelf that held the violin cases. I pulled the paper apart a second time. Jason had written, "That is the problem, as I love Katie. I am sorry. I feel very bad, really."

***

Parker picked up the plastic sleeve lying between him and Hadley and looked at the rumpled notebook paper inside. It still showed the creases of the airplane's folds. He recognized

Hadley's round, bubbly handwriting, in pen here. Jason had scribbled jaggedly in pencil, which either time or tears had smudged slightly.

Parker said nothing. He reached forward from his perch on the bed and slid the plastic encased paper onto the bureau where the TV sat.

Hadley remained silent for several minutes.

***

That afternoon as I waited through drama class, waited for Jason to write back, I…saw something. Nothing supernatural, not that kind of seeing…just a…perspective of the world. I saw myself from the outside. And I saw Jason too. But I only saw us two. From my new vantage point, I saw a world with only two occupants: Jason and me. The regular world existed as it always had, but a parallel world existed alongside it. Jason and I revolved around each other in this place, almost as if some force had projected us—well, not our actual selves, but another version of ourselves. These projected iterations of Jason and Hadley floated out there, facing each other, oblivious to all other matters or people.

Once I read his reply, I took a minute for myself in the instrument storage closet clutching at my violin case. I thought, tomorrow I will wake up in the here and now. I will wake up in a tangible bed alone. But no matter how many tomorrows I wake up in no matter how many beds with no matter how many bodies beside me, Jason and I will always be together. Not in the traditional sense of being together, but I knew in that moment by the instrument shelves that Jason and I will always be together in a different way—in the place where I saw us floating, in that extra world. There, we would be together forever.

Without a single tear, I carried my violin out into the orchestra room, took my seat, unpacked, put my violin under my chin, and played as if nothing at all had happened.

But I left some of myself in that instrument room. Childhood, or maybe innocence. The flight path of that paper airplane carved a border in my life, demarcating Before and After. I became old in the time it takes a paper airplane to fly across a room.

Of course, he didn't *actually* say he didn't love me, but that was the message. I did not analyze the semantics of Jason's words in an attempt to extract any measure of hope. Before that day, I always held out hope…but the airplane robbed me of any hope I had left.

Along with sadness came a tremendous sense of relief. At least now I had an answer. It should have given me the freedom to get on with my life, but I did no such thing. I did not move on and in no way, shape, or form did I even begin the task of "getting over" him. I did not get over him because I could not get over him.

Five nights later, Jason and I attended the final concert of our all-city orchestra program. It was a festival concert, meaning other groups also performed. In the confusion of getting from the stage down to the audience to listen to the more senior orchestras, Jason and I ended up sitting right next to each other. If I had not known Jason did not love me, perhaps I would have laid my hand over his where it rested on his lap. Perhaps I would have gently and softly slipped my arm through his where it sat on our shared armrest. Maybe I would have let my bare knee fall against his. But knowing what I knew then, I did nothing. I simply sat beside him listening to the music. I don't remember what the orchestra played that night, probably something sweet and sad.

Despite the sea change that washed over me, little changed in the day-to-day interactions between Jason and me. We compromised through rehearsals for the drama class production and compiled a kick-ass class magazine as co-editors.

Some days we flirted and joked around like the days of old. Some days we argued. But we never acknowledged what happened on April 20th.

Finally the school year came to a close, and with it the last school orchestra concert of the year. Every year the director gave a special award to a departing eighth grader. That night, though, she gave the award to both Jason and me. She said, "Hadley and Jason's names will have to share a spot on the plaque." To me this seemed the epitome of our entire history. Together on some plaque, but not together anywhere else.

I started crying, right there on stage. My parents must have thought I cried because of sentimentality, but I really cried out of regret for everything that had passed that year.

As I reflect now, it seems like eighth grade took twenty years to transpire. And I bet it will go down as one of the most momentous years of my life. I say that very ambivalently, because although I feel oddly grateful to have experienced so much life fairly early on, I do hope my life did not peak at thirteen.

I realized it was infeasible and unhealthy to continue down a path with Jason always beside me, so before our first year of high school started, I requested a schedule change so I would only see him for two periods each day. My family had moved several streets away, which also eliminated the potential for carpooling with Jason.

A few weeks into freshman year, Nate asked me to the homecoming dance. Nate has waited in the wings for most of this story. Nate and Jason had known each other forever through their parents. Nate went to a different elementary school, but then he joined Jason and me in middle school. There, Nate served as Jason's main *Magic* partner and, for the first two years, his best friend. In eighth grade Nate mirrored all my frustration with Jason's fluctuations and fickleness. Nate got rejected just as I did, and we bonded over our evictions from Jason's world.

My mother bought me a beautiful dress and I got my hair and makeup done. Nate took me out to dinner and then to the high school gym for the dance. I had a fabulous time with him. He complimented my dress and hair and held me tight for the slow dances. He was kind and sweet and awkward.

And yet I could not help thinking about Jason and imagining his hand resting on my shoulder instead of Nate's. I still feel guilty because I thought of his best friend while we turned in circles to Eric Clapton's "Wonderful Tonight."

I wrote in my journal that Nate called me beautiful that night, but I cannot remember him saying it. I don't think at that point I even had the ability to hear what Nate said to me. Jason had struck me deaf. I only had ears for him, you might say. Any compliment or nice thing anybody said to me had no meaning, because it could not compare, could not come close, to anything Jason said to me.

I went out with Nate on and off during freshman year, but it fizzled out, not because I still had strong feelings for Jason, but just because we both were still far too timid and awkward.

The throbbing, acute pain of Jason's rejections subsided, replaced by a continuous, dull ache. We shared helloes and goodbyes and interacted in the context of our few shared classes, but that was it. I found a new social circle and finally abandoned trying to win back the friends Jason had usurped from me.

Katie moved away mid-way through freshman year, but even with my main rival conveniently eliminated, I did not move in again on Jason. I had already grown accustomed to my lot in life, and it would be entirely fair to say I indulged my melancholy. In those days before ipods, I burned a mixed CD full of songs that stung the vulnerable parts of my psyche in such a way as to flirt with both pleasure and pain, songs that sent shivers up my spine and at the same time brought tears to my eyes. On Friday afternoons after a long week at school, I would flop back on my bed and mope indolently, nudged along by my carefully selected soundtrack.

My journal entries became far sparser during freshman year. Why waste ink and paper on excruciating details of high school when I had already lived, and in a way died, a life infinitely more worthy of preservation? The candidates for student body president always included in their assembly speeches dry platitudes about making high school the best years of your life. And once the colleges received my PSAT scores, the nausea-inducing glossy pamphlets flooded the mailbox, promising that if I came to their campus, I would "find myself" and have "unique intellectual adventures" and "meet my best friends" and other sentimental nonsense.

As far as I was concerned, the best years of my life already lay behind me. At fifteen years old, I had already become cynical. I already saw my best days, my best self, slipping away into an unreachable, bygone era. I looked at them historically.

And then one day in October of sophomore year, I met Jason at the door to the orchestra room as we both headed in. I noticed his nose was bleeding. Although I still haven't decided whether I believe in destiny or fate, I do consider it pure coincidence that I was the person who first saw the bleeding.

Maybe the sight of blood on Jason's face awakened my maternal instincts, maybe it initiated the Florence Nightingale effect, or maybe it reminded me of brave heroes returning from the battlefield bloody to their princesses for care. Whatever the reason, I just knew I wanted to take care of him. I wanted to heal him. I would not have shied away if a drop of his blood had landed on my hand or left a stain on my shirt.

I told him to go sit down while I fetched paper towels. I knew I couldn't, or rather, shouldn't, touch him, so I contented myself with handing him the paper towels and alerting our orchestra teacher to the crisis. Jason insisted on not going to the school nurse, so I sat beside him for the entire five minutes it took to stop the bleeding.

The sight of blood suggests something absolutely primal and instinctual. That spot of red above his lip acted on me like a drop of blood in an ocean would send a shark on the prowl. My eyes sharpened, my ears pricked up, my muscles tightened in readiness to respond to this primordial signal of vulnerability.

I once again paid special attention to his every move and mentally noted any sniffle, yawn, or grimace. He started missing school. A couple of weeks after the nose bleed, he failed to win a spot in All State orchestra. I overheard some mutual acquaintances marvel at the sub-par job he did on a big science project. His lovely, slim forearms and hands became scarily bony as they coiled around his violin.

A few days after the nose bleed, I tentatively asked him if he was feeling all right. He answered, "Good. Just tired." Every couple of days I would try again, varying my sentence structure from "How are you doing?" to "Any more nosebleeds?" to "Are you feeling okay?" I did not lord over him the fact that I made All State orchestra and he had not. However, my consideration for his health apparently annoyed him just as much as my adversarial conquests against him did during middle school.

About a week before Thanksgiving, I innocently asked him how he was feeling. Right there in the hall at school, he snapped at me. That's the polite way of putting it. If I tell it truthfully, I have to say he screamed at me. I don't remember word-for-word what he said, partially because of my shock and partially because of his incoherence, but he basically said we weren't friends and I had no right to ask about his health. He went on about how he was so stressed and how my asking about it didn't make him feel any better.

We happened to be standing outside the classroom of one

of my favorite teachers. Ms. Goldstein came out of her classroom and raised her eyebrows, which was all it took to quiet Jason down. Then she ushered us to the administration office. Jason and I did not say one word to each other while Ms. Goldstein spoke privately to one of the vice principals. I didn't feel angry—not at all. I felt deeply righteous, like Joan of Arc. I had every confidence I would be proven right.

The principal called us in. Jason sat sulking while I calmly explained that Jason had recently suffered a nosebleed, had missed an unusual amount of school, and did not seem up to his usual self, all of which caused me to ask about his health. The principal then asked for Jason's side of the story. This I remember perfectly. Jason said, "You don't understand. You don't know her. She's been doing this for years." The principal asked, "What? Showing concern for a fellow human being?" Jason repeated, "You don't understand." The principal thanked me, sent me back to class, and said she would speak with Jason alone.

The principal might not have understood, but I did. I understood perfectly that Jason did not like my meddling in his life, no matter how kind-hearted my motivations.

The next day Jason did not show up to orchestra. Nor the next day. I asked Ms. Goldstein if I had gotten Jason suspended. I mean, he had verbally attacked me, but suspension seemed too harsh for a first offense. Ms. Goldstein told me Jason had definitely not been suspended, but otherwise she knew nothing about his whereabouts or his condition.

Jason did not return to school for a full week and remained absent after we returned from the Thanksgiving break. Finally, on the last day of November, my orchestra conductor ended rehearsal five minutes early and instructed us to pack away our instruments and come back for an announcement. He got very quiet and sat down in front of us all. Every instinct I had told me the news would involve Jason.

"You've all noticed Jason Snyder has been gone for a few days," he said. Then he said, "Jason has been diagnosed with acute lymphoblastic leukemia." He next revealed that Jason was already receiving treatment as an inpatient at the hospital. Then he rambled on for a few minutes about the tragedy, how Jason was so talented, and how we should rally around him.

My fellow students fell to gasping around me, but for me the news was strangely anticlimactic. In the weeks since the nosebleed, I had managed to avoid turning into an amateur oncologist, and I didn't spend hours on the internet researching his symptoms, but I did suspect and maybe even expected a potentially catastrophic problem. I never saw the cancer as some kind of karmic revenge for his assholery over the years. Rather, I saw it as an inevitable plot development. It was like something out of the Odyssey. The gods threw every obstacle they could think of at poor Odysseus—storms and Cyclopes and suitors. And seductive nymphs, too, just for good measure. In our young lives, Jason and I had already experienced so much—rivalry and romance and rejection. Of course the universe had to add cancer.

The news Jason had leukemia did not sadden me. Rather, I saw, not for the last time, a second chance—a way to start all over again, do things the right way with him, and fix all the mistakes I had made. His multiplying white blood cells meant I could show all the compassion and tenderness that immaturity had left me incapable of expressing before. I very selfishly planted in Jason's misfortune the seeds of my own happiness. I thought if I could be there for him, show him I cared about him in sickness and health, show him my love would survive and even go stronger in the storm, then all that had gone wrong would end up right. I thought if I could rise above all his fair-weather friends, the ones who wouldn't be able to bear the sight of him pale and emaciated, then he would finally realize how much I deserved his love. And through all those hopes and desires ran the old assumption I still could not shake—the assumption that people want love and that people in need will gladly accept it. Jason was clearly in need. How could he reject me now?

The next day I went to my orchestra conductor with the genius idea of playing a Christmas concert at the children's hospital. I knew if Jason was undergoing intensive chemotherapy as an inpatient, the only way I would get to see him was if I had the orchestra with me. No way in hell could I just show up as a general visitor with a bunch of balloons.

My conductor went gaga over the idea and immediately called up Jason's mother. I mean immediately. I had stayed after class, which conveniently dovetailed with the lunch period. I stood in the office listening to my conductor's cell phone conversation with Jason's mother. She initially said no. She said Jason would not want it, but my teacher begged and pleaded with her to allow the group to come play for all the cancer kids. I listened to him explain how it would be a spirit-building exercise and would show us the healing power of music. Jason's mother relented, and when my conductor hung up, he put me in charge of coordinating the project.

I threw myself into organizing the trip. I copied music and assigned parts and arranged rides to the hospital. I spoke to the head pediatric oncology nurse and booked two visits.

I still wonder if I crossed a line by getting into the hospital through that back door. Maybe I did, but I had to see him with my own eyes. I had to see his sickness, because I needed to make it better. I wanted so badly to…be there for him, to act as his confidant. I began fantasizing in earnest again: imagining walking into the hospital, him smiling at me, and grateful and appreciative words from him. If he needed a shoulder to cry on, I wanted it to be mine.

But maybe here I failed to give Jason due credit. He did always have such a will in him. Perhaps he found his strength. On the other hand, maybe his pride and arrogance ran so deep as to prevent him from asking for support. Either way, he didn't need my shoulder.

In the midst of all my planning, I called Jason's mother. Their phone number was still in my parents' address book from the days of coordinating carpools. When she answered the phone, I introduced myself as the girl whom she had once driven home from orchestra on Saturday mornings. Without any prodding she started spilling. She said Jason did not want anyone to know the specifics of his condition or his treatment, but because she knew I had a "special relationship" with him, she would make an exception. Luckily, I had already chosen to make the call sitting down, because that comment would have caused me to fall over.

She said she had seen me a lot over the years. And she said Jason used to talk about me a lot—back in elementary and middle school. He hadn't mentioned me much in the last couple of years and she wondered why. I told her kids inevitably grow up and grow apart, but I wanted to grow close to Jason again. And then she said she had suggested to Jason many times that he ask me over or invite me to do things outside of school. She never actually used the word date, but she did say she always thought Jason and I would make a "perfect match."

I didn't tell her what her son would have said to that. I abruptly changed the subject and asked whether she would come to the hospital for the orchestra performances. She said yes and told me if she had to, she'd drag Jason out of his room to say hello and listen to the music.

So one Saturday about two weeks before Christmas, I tied green and red ribbons around the pegs of my violin and went down to the hospital. I walked into the lobby-slash-playroom of the pediatric oncology wing fifteen minutes before any of the other students.

Across the room I saw my orchestra conductor, Mr. Sandoval, and Jason's mother. I walked quietly over to them, still carrying my violin case. As I progressed across the room, I could tell Mr. Sandoval and Jason's mother were talking to someone sitting down. I purposely avoided trying to peak at the seated figure as I brushed my conductor on the sleeve. He turned to face me, and as he did so he revealed a full view of Jason.

He didn't look as sick as I expected. Yes, his complexion had turned an even whiter shade of pale, and a Chicago Bears woolen skull cap covered his head. Through his glasses, I could see dark circles under his eyes. I could tell he had lost weight, but he wore normal clothes—jeans and a hoodie—and had no needles or tubing coming out of him.

Although I stood barely two feet from him, I held up my hand in a wave. He did glance up at me but then looked away. He didn't look angry, but he did look like he had just surrendered in an argument with his mother and was now resigned to enduring two hours of holiday cheer. From somewhere beside me I heard his mother say Jason shouldn't hug anybody because the chemotherapy had weakened his immune system. It was so sweet of her, so generous, to assume Jason would have hugged me.

I wanted to hug him, of course. I wanted to touch him more in that moment than I ever had before. I had to consciously restrain my nervous system from reaching out to him or from plopping myself down on the couch next to him. I rocked back and forth on the balls of my feet to keep them from taking the step forward which would bring me into contact with Jason.

A nurse or orderly or someone called out for Mr. Sandoval and Mrs. Snyder to come decide on furniture arrangements. They departed, leaving me alone with Jason. We had not spoken since the day we wound up in the principal's office. I asked him how the place was treating him. To his credit, he answered me in a surprisingly civil voice and only complained about the lack of high-speed internet. I then asked if he had met any other interesting people. And in his answer, Jason came very close to giving me an actual compliment. He said, "Everyone around here is alarmingly average. Not like you."

The comment took me so off guard, I couldn't immediately think of a comeback. I smiled, though, and said, "I'm glad we could come." Jason responded, "It'll be good for the younger kids." I then heard my own name called out from the other end of the room, summoned to double-check the set list.

As I walked away from Jason, my cheeks flushed at his quasi-compliment. He suggested I was not average. I was not like the boring, middling people with whom he had to spend his time in the hospital. I was different and special. I had always felt more-than-average and unique and apart from everyone else, and now the person whose opinion mattered most to me saw me that way too—he saw me as a singular presence in his life and in his world.

Walking away from him in that hospital playroom, I felt like some kind of fantastic, brightly-colored bird of paradise or a multi-hued striped butterfly. An exotic of some kind surrounded by plainness and color-blind eyes. I know I've made it seem like Jason always made me feel terrible about myself, but that's not at all true. A lot of the time he made me feel great…special, at the very least. He brought out many qualities I liked in myself. I liked how I became funny, intelligent, and ambitious in his presence. Of course, I did not like how I became obsessive, lonely, and angry under his influence.

I considered turning back to him and telling him he was not, never would be, and in fact never *could* be average. Remember in *The Great Gatsby* when Daisy says to Jay, "You always look so cool," and it really means "I love you?" When

Jason said I wasn't average, it felt kind of like that. I mean, I knew he didn't love me, and I knew he wasn't trying to tell me he did, but his words carried the same kind of weight for me.

I have always had difficulty wrapping my head around the idea of loving someone ordinary. I often looked at couples out around town and wondered, "Why do they love each other? Neither one is anything special." I still do that. Something in me cannot love the ordinary; something in me cannot conceive of being loved if I do not do something extraordinary or if I am not someone extraordinary.

Before that day in the hospital, I looked at Jason and saw extraordinary things and an extraordinary person. But sickness has a great power for leveling the playing field; sickness highlights our most basic and common vulnerabilities. Bodies are just bodies, after all, with similar susceptibilities. Disease can strike young or old, rich or poor, good or evil. Whether or not Jason had extraordinary qualities in him, his cell division could still go haywire. Whether or not I loved him, his blood could just as easily become cancerous.

In that hospital, for the first time, I looked at Jason and saw someone average and ordinary. The cancer did a very effective job of exposing him, of peeling away the facade. That day in the hospital, I saw him as more human, more concrete and palpable, than I had in a long time.

We played for a couple of hours and shared cookies with the kids whose nausea didn't make eating ill-advised. Jason did not move from his original spot at the far end of the room. After we played seemingly every Christmas song known to man, plus the two obligatory Hanukah songs, we moved to pack up instruments and gather coats. In the confusion Jason slipped away. As I moved toward the door, his mother told me in a small voice that Jason had become very tired and needed to take a nap.

About a week and a half later we returned to the hospital

to play again. Jason did come out to listen, but I was swarmed by grade-schoolers with hairless skulls who wanted to try out the violin, so I didn't get to talk to him.

I did, however, get a card from his mother in the mail the day before Christmas. It had an angel on it, which surprised me —I had never figured that family for angel people. Inside she wrote that Jason's prognosis was relatively good, he was responding well to chemo, and he would probably return to school part-time in March. And then at the bottom she included Jason's email address, a valuable bit of information I had never managed to acquire.

Christmastime brought constant TV commercials featuring cuddling couples in front of roaring fires, which sparked in me a heated desire for physical contact. Jason had looked so very cold in the hospital. I wanted to take him in my arms and warm him up. And then there are all those slogans about the "season of hope." I had never before bought into those sentiments, but now I had something very concrete and unselfish to hope for—for Jason to make a full and speedy recovery.

Jason and I still shared a few mutual acquaintances with whom I remained friendly. I called them to wish them Merry Christmas or suggested we reconnect over a gingerbread latte, but really I wanted information about Jason. No one had anything to report. Jason had gone cold turkey from any social contact. He hadn't just cut me off; he had cut everyone off. I endured a rather painful lunch with my old quasi-boyfriend Nate only to learn he had attempted to contact Jason several times to no avail.

I know it sounds voyeuristic and creepy and it even makes me slightly queasy just saying it, but I felt as if all the good scenes were playing out behind the curtain, that I was missing all the good action by my exclusion from Jason's life. Cancer! Not only objectively tragic, but also objectively dramatic. Some of the most tumultuous and challenging months of his young life, and I could not do anything to help him through them.

Nothing really changes on New Year's Day, but the resolutionary spirit swept me along anyway. A mere few minutes into the new year and emboldened by the sips of champagne my parents let me try, I grabbed the Christmas card collecting dust on my bureau. I composed an email wishing Jason a Happy New Year and promising the upcoming year would turn out better than the last one. No big confessions, no spilling of secrets. Just a friendly greeting.

To my great astonishment, I received a reply on January 2nd thanking me for the good vibes. It seems small and insignificant in retrospect, but at that point I looked at it as a major breakthrough. Finally! Finally he had let me in a tiny bit and accepted a small gesture of friendship. And had even thanked me for it! I thought that despite the bitter cold of that particular winter, Jason and I were at last thawing out a little bit.

I mentioned I started fantasizing about him again. I forgot to mention the oddest fantasy of all: sometimes I actually imagined Jason dying. Mostly I envisioned how, at his funeral, I would get up and tell everyone how much I had loved him.

I carried on these daydreams despite his mother's assurance that Jason had a good chance of recovery. I suppose I did it because in all the great romances I admired, death seemed to play a very large role: Romeo and Juliet, Gatsby and Daisy, Aragorn and Arwen, Edgar Allan Poe and Virginia, et cetera. Of course, the great difference between those stories and my real-life version was that in those examples, the girl and boy loved each other and outside forces worked against them: war, tuberculosis, family feuds. In my version, the girl and boy never loved each other. The phrase "star-crossed *lover*" doesn't work as well as "star-crossed *lovers*." I wanted so badly to compare my life, my love, and my loss to the great literary romances. But it would always be an imperfect, flawed comparison, because romances generally need two sides to the story.

The new semester started without Jason. At times I had certainly wished he would disappear and leave me in peace, but when I showed up on the first day of school knowing I wouldn't see him that day, I couldn't believe I had ever wished for his absence.

I wandered around school and wandered around home. I sent him a few emails with news and gossip from school and got back short replies saying, "Thanks for the news." January and February passed with no Jason. Finally, he returned the Monday after Easter. He must have pre-arranged it, because I walked into orchestra and found him occupying the second chair in the first violin section. Meaning he would sit next to me. I had held the first chair spot for a good six months, owing first to his fatigue and then his absence.

I probably could have chosen my first words to him a little more prudently. I said, "How long are you going to wait before you challenge me?" referring to the procedure for moving up in chair placements. I should have said something softer and gentler like, "Glad to have you back," or "You're looking good." But no. I had to stir the pot once again.

He only attended school three days a week for the first few weeks as he got his strength back. He still had chemo sessions, and thus had no hair. Of course, I only suspect he had no hair, since I never saw him without some type of head covering. Since hats were very explicitly not allowed in school, he wore a plain orange bandana over his head, orange being one of the school colors. It complemented his blue eyes nicely.

Jason put on a brave face for everyone. He declined any gesture of sympathy, from held doors to offers to put his chair up after rehearsal. I overheard the more academically inclined girls quietly ask him how he was feeling. He gave a very curt, "Fine, thank you" to every one of them. To the dumb cheerleaders who mostly valued his nicely cut cheekbones, he didn't even include the "thank you." He didn't tell horror stories of hospital life and didn't discuss the effects of narcotic painkillers with the skater druggie dudes in the Bob Marley t-shirts. With the daily highs still only in the fifties, he could easily hide his weight loss under loose jeans and layered sweatshirts. But when his dangling sleeve fell away from his wrist as it bent around the neck of his violin, I saw how much more pronounced the bones and tendons had become in his already lithe forearm and hand. The bags under his blue eyes had also not dissipated since the December day in the hospital.

Even though Jason had seemed receptive to my emails, I still kept my distance at school. We had achieved a very delicate balance of tolerance, and maybe even friendship, I suppose you could call it. As much as I yearned to reach out to him, both physically and emotionally, I knew I could not jeopardize the detente between us.

In real life I could not verbalize my sympathy and concern, could not even offer a hand on his shoulder. In my fantasy life, of course, I listened patiently to all his fears and absorbed all his pain, and in my daydreams I comforted him with kind words and gentle caresses.

The one time I tried to tell him…well… The April orchestra concert at school was always the biggest and most important of the year, because it served as a warm-up for our judged performance at the state competition. Now, I've gone back and forth about whether the event that comes next in this story qualifies as a simple coincidence or has some aspect of fate and destiny to it. The fact that it also takes place in an orchestra room is not especially extraordinary, given that Jason and I spent a great proportion of our lives in orchestra rooms together. And the fact that it also occurred in April—well, it wasn't the exact same date as last time. I suppose statistically I had a one in twelve chance of the timing lining up.

However, looking back at my life, I have noticed a tendency toward repetition and deja vu. Certain things seem to happen over and over again in similar ways. Perhaps that's the insanity of my life—it keeps doing the same thing over and over, trying to get a different result.

Or maybe I simply found him alone and took my chance.

On the evening of April 9th, I passed the crowd of parents, siblings, and friends gathered at the entrance to the Performing Arts Center. I carried my violin into the orchestra room, where we always unpacked before going onstage. As I unzipped my case I saw Jason slip into the room and venture off into a corner. I gathered my shoulder rest and music and walked over to the auditorium to warm up. More and more kids took their seats and made one last pass at the difficult runs. I was caught up in my preparations—I had a big solo that night—when my conductor turned to me and asked where Jason was. He looked at his watch and told me to find Jason. I set my violin down and made my way out of the auditorium, shivering in the now cool night air.

I walked into the orchestra room and found Jason sitting on a chair in the corner with his elbows on his knees. The bottom of his violin rested on the floor. He held the scroll in his hands and spun the body of the violin around and around. He had exchanged his orange bandana for a black one to match his concert dress. He had gained back some weight, and some color had come back into his cheeks, helped along by the constant springtime breezes sweeping in from the mesa beyond the city. He actually looked quite sexy in a starving-artist kind of way.

"What's wrong?" I asked. "We have to start in a few minutes."

Jason said, "I don't want anyone to make a fuss over me or make some kind of welcome-back speech. I don't want everyone to…know."

He did have a legitimate apprehension—our orchestra director definitely would draw attention to Jason and the cancer and the whole inspiring/tragic/dramatic aspect of it.

Although I wanted to say so much more, I answered him by saying, "It's okay if people know. It's not your fault you got cancer. And you're going to get better. You made it through. That's a good thing, isn't it?"

He looked at me with those big blue eyes. And I realized then that maybe he didn't see it as a good thing. Something in Jason's eyes pleaded with me. They begged me to keep their confession a secret.

Jason's gaze fell to the floor and he said, "I just don't want Mr. Sandoval to call me inspiring or anything. I'm not."

"What?" I said. "Of course you are." The words flew out of my mouth before I could even think.

"And besides," I continued, "Mr. Sandoval cares about you. We all care about you."

He looked back up at me again and asked in an unmistakably sarcastic tone, "Really? You care about me?"

And I answered, in an unmistakably genuine tone, "Absolutely…I…"

After I got the "I" out, I swallowed hard, and in that moment, Jason said softly but distinctly, "Please don't say it."

I've mentioned that certain visual memories of Jason stand out in my brain more than others. That was one of them. His blue eyes perfectly framed by his glasses and those caterpillar eyebrows. The chapped lips I wanted to wet with kisses. The feminine cheekbones and masculine jaw. And every feature showing the exact same thing: pity.

You would think I was the one who had cancer by the

way he looked at me. As if I had done something so incredibly stupid as to forfeit my life. Or like I had attempted something unbelievably heroic that turned out a disastrous folly.

He stood up, picked up his bow from his case, and walked past without looking at me. I continued to stare at his empty chair. I did not feel at all disappointed or sad or mad. I really didn't feel anything at all, actually. I mean, I don't even know what would have come out of my mouth had he not interrupted. I don't know if I would have said "it," but Jason cut off that possibility.

He must have paused at the door, or at least I envisioned him doing that when I replayed it in my mind later. I imagined him with his violin under one arm, his bow in the same hand, and the other hand on the door. I also imagined him kind of half turned around to face my back.

I heard his voice from behind me say, "I'm sorry." Then I heard the door swing shut.

The orchestra shared the room with the show choir, which had gone through monumental fund-raising to install mirrors along one wall. I turned to look at myself in those mirrors. I noticed my shoulders scrunched up somewhere around my ears. I watched my reflection as I slowly lowered my shoulders, both feeling and seeing the relaxation spreading down my arms and into my hands, which until then had been clenched.

I wish I could say I looked beautiful in that mirror, but I did not see anything beautiful. I used to believe quite strongly that pain and anguish carried with them a sheen of beauty. My love-struck heroines in the movies certainly always looked gorgeous—all creamy skin and luminous eyes and flowing hair.

But there in front of the orchestra room mirrors, heartbreak had absolutely no beauty to it—no captivating light emanated from me. My cheeks looked unnaturally white, and not in a porcelain or alabaster way. My dry eyes simply looked tired.

I looked old. When I stared back at my image, I did not see a sixteen-year-old. I saw an aging, jaded woman who had taken a few proverbial trips around the block.

I turned, walked out of the room, and back to my chair in the concert hall. I sat silently next to Jason as Mr. Sandoval described him as inspiring.

Later that night, anger overtook me. He could not even let me say it. And to say sorry? Sorry for what? Sorry he couldn't love me back? Sorry I found him inspiring? Sorry I cared about him? Sorry he disappointed me? Sorry he didn't even have the balls to tell me to my face?     He could not even let me say it. Not only did he reject me as a person, but he rejected every good vibration I tried to inject into the stream of the universe. I would have given him everything…and taken nothing in return. I already knew love doesn't cure cancer, but I figured I could at least make him peaceful or content or even happy.

I would have gladly lost myself so I could find him. Because one and one don't make two. They make one. Without him, I was missing a piece. I had no part of me, no piece of the fabric of my existence, that didn't have Jason woven in.

How ironic it is that it was cancer. Because what is cancer but life gone wrong? It's a unit of life, a cell, out of control. Jason might have been the one with off-the-charts white blood cell counts, but a figurative cancer certainly grew inside me. For ten years, Jason had enlarged and expanded inside me. He stole all the nourishment away from me before I could get to it. He used my own vitality to grow inside me.

Sometimes even the most skilled surgeons can't remove tumors because they so completely overtake an organ. The malignant cells enmesh themselves with the healthy tissue. They pirate away blood vessels and sabotage nutrients. Sometimes the tumor lays siege so effectively, there's not enough of the original organ to even save.

Maybe that is why I've never been able to move past Jason. He reached every cell in me. He tangled himself in every part of me. He mutated my DNA. I cannot cut him away.

The school year in Albuquerque finishes up at the end of May. A few days before the last day, a friend of mine delivered a choice morsel of gossip. Jason's father worked as a chemist at one of the big government research labs in Albuquerque. My friend told me Jason's father had received a fantastic offer to go work at a private pharmaceutical company in Massachusetts.

For the first time, I had to seriously consider the possibility of a future without Jason. If he moved away…Despite the incident in the orchestra room, I never stopped caring about him, including caring about him in the future. Talking to him or even looking at him in the present hurt and angered me, but envisioning some future version of Jason brought me great comfort. I definitely loved the ghost of Jason past, and I also loved the ghost of Jason future.

But I don't know if I loved the ghost Jason had become in the present. Because that's exactly the transformation he had undergone; he had transformed into the ghost of the boy with whom I fell in love. And it wasn't just the leukemia. The leukemia finished the job, but the life began draining from Jason's skin long before the white blood cells began to proliferate in his veins.

On the last day of school, I asked him point blank if he'd come back next year. He said his family would likely move at the beginning of August, so… He didn't finish the sentence. That "so" hung in the air, implicating, "So you'll never see me again." I looked at him for several seconds, just to preserve the visual memory, and then turned away.

At last I could see an end in sight. It would all pass away. It would all become just a memory. All good things have to end, right? And all bad things also must pass. At that point, I welcomed an ending. I yearned for an ending.

In that moment, I truly believed I would never see him again. But I had my memories, my journal entries, my preserved paper airplane. And in a way I had my own future with him, the future I made every night before I fell asleep.

A new emotion entered my life and my vocabulary shortly after Jason left: fear. I got very, very scared I would never recapture the sense of drama, of possibility, of vitality that had characterized my years with Jason. I feared my world would become just like everyone else's. I had lost the most special and extraordinary force in my life. The best and brightest stars in my galaxy had suddenly been extinguished, leaving me out in the cold and dark with no north star.

Soon enough, everything and anything reminded me of Jason. Anything would trigger a memory: Skittles, the word magic, the particular model of mini-van his parents had driven, and any mention of cancer on the news at night. I had dreamed of him fairly frequently during our ten years together, but after he moved away the dreams came more often. The pages of my journal recounted the details of the previous night's dream instead of the details of the events of the day. I won't use the old cliché "haunted my dreams" to describe the situation, because I enjoyed every second of those dreams. Rather, Jason haunted my mornings. He took away my sunrises. His taste lingered on my tongue as the sun rose, leaving me uninterested in the day.

After six months or so going cold turkey from any contact with Jason, I pulled out his email address, the one his mother gave me almost a year before. I of course knew his birthday, which is in early November. I sent him a short little message wishing him a happy birthday and asking about his new environment. That he responded at all astonished me, but his actual response flabbergasted me. I had sent a few lines; his reply filled the entire computer screen. He described his new school and town and how a tribe of very ill-mannered geese populated a pond near his house. His style was still not very warm, and his punctuation, vocabulary, and formatting were more business-like than friendly, but he sounded far healthier and happier than he'd come across in person for the last several years. And more importantly, he seemed far more open to conversing with me than he had since elementary school.

Of course, his messages still drove stakes of insecurity into my heart. He never told me about girls. Unless I prompted him, he never mentioned any of our old mutual friends or acquaintances. We talked mostly about school, music, and books. When I saw a message from Jason in my email inbox, adrenaline would instantaneously overload my system. I would have to take several deep breaths and calm myself down before reading it. The sight of a letter from Jason sent me into paroxysms of excitement every single time.

I did this weird thing where I would not immediately read it. I would see it there, tempting me from my inbox, waiting to be opened, but I could never open it without working up my fortitude for a few hours. I would flit in and out of the computer window, summoning up the stomach to actually read his words. Every click took a few degrees of courage.

His humor did come through the lines of written text. Reading silently to myself, I could hear Jason's voice in my head, all his characteristic phrasings and pronunciations. I could even hear him mumble, could hear the words jumble in his mouth.

From thousands of miles away, he could still make me laugh. The laughter that had diminished at the end came alive again. Even if he didn't give me access to much of his life, he let me laugh with him. And for that I am incredibly grateful. Through the humor—the jokes and puns and funny references—we rehabilitated our relationship.

But still, something seemed off about the whole thing. Here I was, carrying on a casual correspondence with someone whose importance to me was anything but casual. I loved Jason more than anyone, and I carried on with him as if he was nothing but a schoolyard friend.

How could I ask for his interest? How could I pretend to be *someone*—to be a presence—in his life? As much as Jason's emails boosted my badly flagging ego, at my core I still felt extremely humbled by them. Who was I to Jason? No one. I felt like I was nothing to him, and yet he consistently sent me messages every couple of weeks.

The summer between junior and senior years, Katie came into town. Remember Katie, the friend who stole Jason right out from under me and moved away after freshman year? She called me completely randomly, said she was visiting for a few days, and wanted to see me. Two years had healed some of the wounds she inflicted on me, so I said yes. She actually spent the night at my house. We caught up on our lives and chatted and goofed around just like old times. It felt incredibly wonderful to know that some part of our friendship had survived. We had fantastic chemistry as friends. That night we laughed as we had as eight-year-olds. Just like with Jason, despite all the hurt which had passed between Katie and me, we could still laugh together.

We decided to sleep outside in sleeping bags under the warm summer stars. And there, stretched out on the lawn of my backyard, Katie told me she and Jason had kissed twice, during freshman year before she moved away. I had suspected this, but Katie's religious background was conservative enough to make me doubt whether it actually happened.

If I had heard that news at fourteen, I would have burst into tears or stomped back into the house and locked the doors on Katie. At seventeen, though, I simply told her I had suspected it all along and that I couldn't blame her for anything.

"Blame" is an interesting word. It implies someone is at fault for something. In the past I definitely blamed Jason for choosing Katie and Lauren over me and blamed him for withholding the happiness I rightly deserved. I blamed Katie for betraying our friendship and my trust.

Under the blanket of soft black night sky, I could no longer blame anyone for anything. I couldn't blame Jason for doing something I could never do: acting on emotions. I couldn't blame Katie for accepting affection which, if I traded places with her, I would have gladly accepted. They did nothing wrong. He liked a girl, so he kissed her. And she kissed back.

I asked Katie if she still kept in touch with Jason, but did not reveal my own ongoing relationship. She told me they had random, hour-long phone conversations every few months. My uneasy, hibernating jealousy woke within me. I carefully probed for specifics while trying to seem disinterested. What had he told her that he hadn't told me? She mentioned a few girls' names and launched into a convoluted story about Jason asking a girl out whom he thought was two years older than she actually was. I muttered a "hm" or "wow" at appropriate times, but inside I ached. This news certainly hurt a lot less than seeing him in person with other girls, but even hearing about his activities on the other side of the country enflamed the old wounds.

I hugged Katie in genuine friendship when she left my house the next day, but that was the last time I ever saw her. We lost contact over the years, and when I finally got married later on, I knew I could never invite her to the wedding, because she would…know. She would realize.

High school is supposed to be a great time, right? When you start experimenting with sex, drugs, and rock and roll. When you have this carefree attitude to life and when you believe anything and everything can happen. When you have the utmost confidence that your dreams will all come true. Not for me. Jason

—well, to be fair, it wasn't just Jason; there were other factors, but it was mostly Jason—had destroyed my ability to function as a normal teenager. Remember how I said I looked old when I gazed into that mirror? I felt old inside, too.

But for all my internal age, I remained pitifully behind the times of my contemporaries. The only times I drank in high school were at home, with family, at holiday celebrations. I never got kissed. Junior and senior years, no one ever asked me out on a date. No one really asked me to do anything. No party invitations, no "let's hang out" invitations. On Saturday nights when kids my age went out to parties and games and other social activities, I stayed at home and watched movies with my parents.

I entered a kind of suspended animation. The day Jason moved away, I switched off. I stopped growing. My birthday kept coming around, but inside I remained a sixteen-year-old girl. I mean, I did mature academically and went off to college without a hitch. But some part of me was paralyzed, frozen in time. Some part of me will always be that girl holding a paper airplane. Some part will always be standing in front of those orchestra room mirrors.

College should have been a new start. I should have put everything behind me as I flew east. I should have flirted with all the new boys and embraced their advances. I did finally start getting asked to parties and waved over to sit at tables in the cafeteria. Everyone told me, "Just have fun. Get to know them and maybe something will develop." But how could I wait for Maybe when I had already felt Certainty? How could I go from fire and ice with Jason to "getting to know" a perfectly average coed out on the campus quad?

I made out with a few guys as we stretched out on the grass or pretended to work on group projects in library study rooms. But I could never let it go further than that. Jason would always creep into my mind and ruin the whole thing. I couldn't conceive of going to bed with a guy knowing I would likely wake up to dreams of Jason. Just as it had with Nate at the homecoming dance, guilt assaulted me at every touch of a guy's fingertips. Guilt for somehow betraying the dream, and also guilt for using those guys to try to forget. They probably wanted to use me too, but knowing that a single kiss from Jason would mean infinitely more than anything those guys could give me—I just couldn't do it.

And something still separated me from all my classmates. I again perceived that other-ness of which I had become aware way back in grade school. I didn't have to become vegan to prove my special status. I had an other-ing factor all my own. Back in childhood I felt the world had marked me in some way. In college I felt marked by my past—almost as if I wore a scarlet letter over my heart. But instead of an A, it would have been a B. For "broken."

I knew something very few of my college classmates knew. I understood how really loving someone, and really losing them, changes you. Once you understand that, you can't interact as well with people who haven't experienced it. We assign people to so many categories which supposedly affect how they communicate with each other: black and white, male and female, gay and straight. I found that all those characteristics never made much difference in my interactions. What most impacted my capacity to relate to another human being was whether or not the other person had touched the void—if they had endured the silence of an "I love you" with no return.

Jason went to college in Boston, which of course was just a train ride away. However, I had no friends or relatives in Boston and no reason to go there which might disguise my ulterior motive. I could not blatantly ask to come visit him without some kind of excuse or explanation. That would have been entirely too forward. I couldn't risk scaring him away with one too aggressive move.

But then spring break of our freshman year of college came around. A couple of weeks before his spring break started, Jason voluntarily told me he planned to spend several days of his break in New York City, the hometown of his roommate, and if I wasn't off on my own vacation, I should come into the city one day to catch up with him.

When I first read the email inviting me to come spend the day with him, I physically collapsed on the floor next to my desk. I just could not handle it. I giggled hysterically. It was a moment of pure, unadulterated joy. I had not experienced that kind of simple, innocent, concentrated happiness in several years. As we emailed about dates and details and possible plans, I would go wild at each message—almost screaming with nervous anticipation. The idea of seeing Jason again was so surreal and fantastic. It seemed like meeting a fictional character, like Harry Potter himself had suddenly invited me to Hogwarts for the day.

My spring break fell during a different week than Jason's, so I actually still had school that day. But I went to visit him anyway, of course. At six a.m. Thursday, I sent some emails telling my professors I had come down with terrible food poisoning, and then I climbed on the train to New York. As I passed through New Jersey, I pondered the question I needed to answer on that trip: whether I still loved him or not. Or maybe the question was whether I had ever loved him at all. I needed verification of the truth, of reality. Had it ever been…real?

The moment I saw him at Penn Station, I knew. It was not quite love at *first* sight, but definitely love at first sight after a separation of almost three years. It was instantaneous. Out of all the people gathered in the big hall at the Station, all coming or going or waiting for god knows what, he drew me in like a tractor beam. Like I had a homing device which led me straight back to him.

As soon as I looked into those blue eyes, I broke into a huge smile, and then he pulled one of those incredible grins of his—genuinely happy, but with a playful and mischievous glint in his eye. The fact that he looked happy to see me…that made me happier than I had ever felt.

Physically, my stomach flip-flopped like someone had just sucker-punched me. My knees wobbled and my heart thumped. Unfortunately, a smile was all I got from him. He didn't hug me.

Jason seemed both incredibly familiar to me and astonishingly fresh and new. I alternated between feeling as if we'd known each other for years and feeling like I had just met the most interesting and wonderful person ever. I completely forgot we were walking in New York City. The city meant nothing to me, totally absorbed as I was in Jason.

He wanted to go Downtown to Wall Street and kiss the Bull—that big statue down in front of the stock exchange. He had decided on economics as his new calling, throwing physics out the window to the mercy of gravity.

I raised my eyebrows as seductively as I could and asked, "That's who you want to kiss?" Even as I pouted flirtatiously, inside I screamed. Now he wasn't even choosing other girls to kiss instead of me; he preferred to kiss inanimate objects. Jason could grin at me and joke about kissing, but he would never actually kiss me. We went down to Wall Street and I took a snapshot of him as he took the bull by the horns. I could not do the same.

We got some giant slices at a pizza parlor filled with junior brokers scarfing down a hurried lunch. Jason struck up conversations with a few of them, introducing himself as an economics major, and incidentally saying the nicest thing he ever said about me. He introduced me as his "friend." As in, "This is my friend Hadley. She's from New Mexico and goes to Penn."

Knowing Jason considered me his friend made me feel as melty and gooey as the cheese on my pizza.

After lunch we took the subway up to the Metropolitan Museum of Art and spent several hours talking about the paintings and about ourselves. The conversation came as it had during our best days. We joked and bantered and discussed with no anger, no bitterness, no mention of the bad times. I think it was the happiest time I've ever had with Jason. After so many worries and so many hours spent wondering about his life, I finally got to experience some of it with him. We got along fabulously. It worked so incredibly well.

He had to meet the family of the roommate for a Broadway show, so we made our way back to the theater district and the train station. Along the way we stopped for dinner at some kind of Asian restaurant. I say "some kind of Asian" not because I think all Asian cultures are the same, but because Jason so completely captured my attention I didn't bother to note whether it was Chinese, Thai, or Vietnamese. Jason so enthralled me, I could have been physically transported to one of those countries and still would not have noticed.

The time came to split the bill. As we pondered paper and plastic, I let out a very Freudian slip. I said, "I can give you anything you want." Superficially, I meant I could give him a $10 or a $20 or my debit card. Subconsciously, I meant something quite different.

I walked with him all the way to the door of the theater where the roommate and the roommate's parents waited. There, Jason introduced me to as his "old friend Hadley from New Mexico." Then he shook my hand and I caught a train back to Philadelphia.

Back on the train heading west, I could vent freely. I don't think I've ever felt as giddy and hysterical—hysterical in a good way, of course—as I felt sitting there on that train. My mouth really did hurt from grinning so much, and my face vibrated from all the excitement passing between my body and my brain.

Jason had very lightly suggested we talk on the phone, but I didn't know if I could survive the heart palpitations a phone conversation with him would undoubtedly give me. Still, somehow I got up the courage to call him two or three times that summer and the next school semester. Our chemistry didn't work well on the phone—somehow the brief delay ruined our comedic timing.

I loved hearing his voice, though. He actually does not have a great voice; it's too high and nasal, and he mumbles, but to me it sounded like a deathless song, as F. Scott Fitzgerald would say. His voice was a part of him I could never replicate, never preserve. I could remember what he said, and I could write it down, but I could never hang on to the sound of him saying it. The only thing that ever came close to his voice was his playing. Just like his speaking, his violin tone lacked resonance, sounded tight and boxy, but just like his speaking voice, I would recognize it anywhere, anytime, so distinctively…him was it.

Jason studied abroad the spring semester of sophomore year, and I did my study abroad the fall semester of junior year. We still maintained our email correspondence through our respective times abroad. However, although our journeys to exotic places gave us fresh material to discuss, they also prevented us from meeting up in person or even talking on the phone.

In the fall of our junior year of college, as I sweltered in the Florentine sun, Jason started mentioning a particular girl's name in his emails: Elena. He used her name in the context of "Elena and I:" "Elena and I went to Cape Cod last weekend." "Elena and I saw the most interesting documentary." I suspect he was waiting for me to ask who Elena was, but I would not give in before he did; if he wanted me to know he had a girlfriend, he would have to tell me himself. I could go on officially unsure of Elena's status in Jason's life, and I could use that official uncertainty to console myself.

Toward the end of junior year, I even convinced myself that in the upcoming fall it might finally be safe to openly propose a visit to Boston, but then that summer during one of our phone conversations, Jason finally identified Elena as his "girlfriend."

I felt so pitiful. I don't know of another word to describe it. I could still vividly remember the expression Jason had given me in that orchestra room. It carried equal weight even now. I imagined him answering my messages out of pity. I imagined him talking to me out of pity. I pictured him describing me to Elena, "This crazy little girl from first grade who says she loves me." I had to ask myself, "Why would Jason, who has a girlfriend and who hated me with a passion at one point, continue to play this little game?" I could not shake the idea he was only humoring me, only taking pity on a sad, pathetic girl who still wouldn't take a hint. I almost wanted to apologize to him for occupying his time with such a thankless task.

The thought of his pity made me loathe myself. I did gain some insight as to why Jason never wanted attention for the leukemia. He knew everyone had pitied him. Every "welcome back" or "get well soon" suggested a "Poor Jason." I certainly did not want his pity, so I could understand why he didn't want mine, or anybody else's, back then.

The self-loathing in me begged to cut off contact with Jason, pleaded with me to take hold of my own dignity. But I had no choice in the matter. I could not just choose to "get over" him. I could not just clap my hands and not care about him. I tried to get over him. I wanted to get over him. But I could not just turn my love on and off like a light switch. If I could have found some way of letting him go, believe me, I would have taken it. I would have let him go.

Jason felt like a 100 hundred-pound pack on my back that I had to carry up a huge mountain. Why wouldn't I want to walk freely and lightly and jump through dewy meadows? I did, but something had welded all that weight to me. I couldn't take it off. Just like I couldn't imagine my life without Jason, I couldn't relieve myself of carrying him with me wherever I went.

As Jason continued to mention Elena as his girlfriend, I had to confront the truth: I would never win him. I would never get to be with him. He had a future; I was his past. I had to find my own future without him.

And so my mind turned to a new question: Would I ever meet a second Jason? Would I get a second shot at love? Would I ever meet a guy who excited me and enthralled me as Jason did? Would I ever find someone like him? For a few months I answered no to those questions. I doubted very strongly I would ever find someone like him.

# PART THREE

## *Chapter Nine*

***Now***

“And then I met you.”

Hadley looked into Parker’s blue eyes and said, “And then I fell in love with you.

“When you walked into that coffee shop, you looked so much like him. You sounded like him. Your hands…they looked so very much like his. I felt like the universe offered me another chance, a different kind of second chance, and this time I did everything right. You were so incredibly wonderful. I started believing that maybe I had spent all those years chasing after Jason only in preparation for meeting you.”

She watched and waited, her eyes pleading for a response from him.

Before he could react, however, his mind thrust him far, far back into a memory. He could not have been more than three or four years old. As he played with Legos, as he built a house from the blocks, his mother had said, “You know, Parker, you are adopted. That means you came out of the tummy of another lady, but everyone decided you would belong to us.”

She had repeated it often during his childhood, ever increasing the anatomical and legal sophistication of her explanations. As a consequence, he had never felt abandoned, never perceived himself as an orphan. Parker had known other adoptees, though, whose parents had not treated the subject with the sensitivity his parents had. Those parents sat the kid down one random teenaged birthday and dynamited the foundation of his identity.

Now he understood how they must have felt.

He had started off bewildered by Hadley's story, which quickly grew to outright disbelief. After he grudgingly accepted her honesty, however, quiet fury simmered and flickered at the surface, thickening to a rolling boil before ebbing away into what was, unmistakably, a stunning, gaping, yawning chasm of loss. As if something had exploded inside him and obliterated him from within. As if he had watched a loved one die within this very room, watched her struggling to breath, saw her twist in pain, and embraced her hand as she slipped away. Something had died in this room…in him. His chest ached with the effort of drawing breath against the oppressive, suffocating weight of such an engulfing, enshrouding sea of grief.

Parker tugged his feet from where they had rooted themselves into the floor. The cold, empty air of the hotel room held him back like thick syrup. His legs halted and stuttered against the burden of Hadley's secrets.

He made it to where Hadley stood in the corner. He watched Times Square buzzing below for a few seconds. He turned to face her. She gazed defiantly back at him. Then he raised his right hand.

In the split second before he brought his hand down, he looked down at her and saw that she was not going to try to stop him. She did not cower, did not cover her face to shield herself from the blow. She just looked back at him, her pure, sacrificial defiance taunting him and teasing him. Hit me, it seemed to cry. Make the martyr I am, it invited him.

The palm of his hand smacked hard against the wall right

next to her head. He had swerved in midair. He did not even feel the smarting pain.

"Please stop lying." He said it quietly, softly.

"I'm not lying," she sobbed.

"You can stop, Hadley. You knew minutes after you met me I was adopted, I was from Chicago. You figured it out. You knew within minutes. You've been lying for five years."

"No. That is not true. I fell in love with you. I love you."

Parker said sadly, "Only because I reminded you of him."

"Correlation does not necessarily equal causation!" Hadley pleaded.

Parker laughed now, a bitter, acidic laugh. "What the hell does that mean? You'll have to explain it to me." His voice became sour and sarcastic. "Because unfortunately I'm not as brilliant as Jason."

"It means that just because you and Jason are…it does not mean that is why I love you."

Parker turned his back to Hadley and violently ran his hands through his hair.

"Please, look at me." When he did not, she continued, "Maybe I fell in love with you because of something inherent in you, or maybe it was because I associated you with Jason. But that was all in the beginning. I grew to love you as *you.* I married you because I love Parker Holmes, not Jason Snyder. The things I love best about you—Jason doesn't have them. Maybe in the beginning I focused on the similarities, but I stayed with you because of the differences. And after I met you, I never had any contact with him, I swear."

"But you thought about him." It was not a question. "And you dreamed about him."

He turned. "Didn't you?"

She looked down at the floor like a guilty kindergartener and nodded.

The walls of the hotel room swam as Parker's eyes filled. He had held her after making love, had watched her fall asleep, had seen a smile play upon her lips in her sleep. And it had been him…him visiting her in her dreams, even as his own hand rested on her bare skin.

He purposely said nothing. He knew her so intimately, knew his silence pierced her more deeply than even the iciest blade ever could. The ticks of his watch boomed out into the room, and each one, he knew, would drive nails of fear into her more horrifying than the shrillest scream.

And then it came, the shaky voice, quavering with terror: "It doesn't matter. It shouldn't matter why. Parker, your parents chose to love you. They didn't just discover a baby on the street. They chose to love you but does that make it any less real, any less valuable?"

"And I suppose you think I should thank you for choosing to love me." He said each word slowly, deliberately.

"No, I didn't mean it like that. I'm the one who should thank you…" She trailed off as he moved to his suitcase.

"You don't know what's it like, Parker." He paused at the dresser drawer he had ripped open. Her voice had an entirely new growl in it, one he had never heard before. Like the snarl of a usually placid mother bear shielding her cub from some threat.

"You've never felt homeless. You've never felt like an orphan. You've fit in everywhere! Perfect Parker, who fits in wherever he goes! Who perfectly bonds with his adoptive parents. Who fits in at school, at work, in love.

"The first night we had sex, you told me you didn't need to search for your biological origins because your parents always say 'I love you too.' Do you have any idea how it feels to not have that? To not have that guarantee? To not hear it back? Do you have any idea how privileged you are? You have no idea what it feels like to not fit. To not even fit in with the people you were born to—"

Parker flung the clothes he held across the room in the direction of his suitcase.

"I'm not the one who should be apologizing here, Hadley," he spat.

He did not even bother collecting his things from the bathroom. He zipped the suitcase and hauled it to the door.

"Please."

His hand fell from the doorknob, which snapped back with a metallic clang. This last sound had not come from her throat. It had arisen from somewhere long buried, unfathomable, a subterranean place within her. In that one word she poured everything, all the desire and need which kept her forever hungry, forever thirsty. It rattled around her dry and hollow heart, a perpetual plea.

Parker whirled around to face her. He could see his own reflection in the picture windows, varying shades of neon floating over his body; one blinking red light even hovered on his chest.

Hadley stepped forward toward him. With the bags under her eyes, the tangled and twisted strands around her face, and the sunken shoulders, she looked sick, Parker thought: just like she had described her reflection in the orchestra room mirrors, aged beyond recognition.

But her eyes were the most beautiful he had ever seen them. She had begun crying again, and the tears shone like spotlights illuminating her irises. Their usually muted green color quickly grew lush and verdant, as desert plants will green under a few drops of rain. Though it was sadness that drew her skin tight and palled her cheeks, that sadness also transformed her eyes into vital, flourishing orbs.

"I feel awful about what I've done. I've hurt for the last five years. Goddammit, I've hurt almost my entire life. But let me remind you of something else you said to me that night we first made love." Now those vibrant, wet spheres overflowed, spilling and gushing over their brims. "You told me I had no reason to be sorry. You said I didn't have to apologize for anything." She brushed at her running nose; the ugliness of the gesture did nothing to diminish the gorgeous glow from her streaming eyes.

"I have no reason to say I'm sorry now. I have nothing for which to apologize. I never meant to meet Jason or fall in love with him. I never meant to meet you and fall in love with you. I cannot apologize for loving him."

Parker did not relinquish his grip on the handle of his suitcase, but nor did he reach for the door again. When he said nothing, Hadley continued.

"What would you have done if I told you? What would you have done if the girl you were falling in love with told you about her long lost love who happened to bear uncanny resemblances to you?"

Parker looked down and mumbled, "I would have stopped seeing you."

"And then we both would have missed out on the wonderful time we've shared. I wanted to be happy. I had gone most of my life—since I was six years old—searching for something I could never find, trying to reach something I would never reach. Don't I deserve some kind of happiness too? Can't you understand why, when the world gave me one last shot, I took it? And I make you happy, don't I?"

Hadley's last question ended on an elevated note of fear.

Parker looked up.

"Yes. You did."

He swiveled the suitcase around and adjusted the travel bag that hung on his shoulder.

"It doesn't matter why I love you! It just matters that I

do!"

He opened the door and went out. Instead of slamming, the heavy door slowly lumbered toward its frame. The jam clicked shut softly.

Hadley did briefly throw herself on the bed and sob hysterically, grabbing and clawing at the hotel bedding tucked so securely beneath the mattress, but after a few minutes, she flipped over on her back and stared at the ceiling, letting a few lingering tears trickle past her temples.

If Parker had not understood—if he could not understand —the effect Jason had on her... then he simply could not understand her. But if he could not understand her, how could she explain the contentment and peace she felt as he held her in his strong arms?

She could summon no other thoughts, could feel no more emotions. She was quite literally exhausted; she had expelled all the energy within her. She was empty now.

Hadley drank a couple bottles of water to wet her parched mouth and worked her way beneath the entrapping covers. She turned on the TV for the benefit of white noise.

Five years of happiness. It had been good. She should consider herself lucky. Some people never even get a day.

***

In another room, Parker stared at his cellphone. He scrolled up and down through his contacts, wondering who to call…wondering whom he could tell. He lingered over "Mom" and "Dad" and "House."

How could he tell them? How could they possibly understand? How could he confront their pity or their raging sympathy? He desperately wanted to tell someone, to relieve himself of the terrible weight, but he could not possibly admit the great love of his life had fallen apart because of…because of…

Parker could not even say the name.

And as he slid the screen of his phone up and down, he caught sight of something else: the blue lines weaving beneath the translucent skin of his wrist. He imagined a needle sliding smoothly into one, piercing the skin, sucking the precious stem cells from his blood…to give them to…him. To keep him alive.

His hand coiled into a fist. The veins on the back of his hand popped up.

He held within him, within his very body, the strings of fate. With one pulled thread, he could condemn a man to death.

For the first time in his life, Parker realized, he could make the choice—that one decision which determined destinies. He had long been the "chosen one," he thought with a smirk, the object of someone else's impulses. His biological mother had chosen one path instead of the other, his parents had chosen to love him, and Hadley…Hadley had chosen too. He had never made such a choice. Never elected to take or forgo such conclusive action.

On one trip to New Mexico to visit Hadley's family, he had traveled down to the barren badlands of the Trinity Site, where scientists—madmen, philosophers, or both—gave man the power to choose whether or not to destroy the world.

He did not have the force of the sun like those men, but as he clenched his fist, he wielded more power than he had ever known.

He would have to use it well.

***

Hadley woke with her tongue stuck to the roof of her dry mouth and to a hyper morning host yapping on the television in front of which she had fallen asleep. She heard the last few in a series of knocks at the hotel room's door. She waited for another series of knocks, and when none came, she dragged herself out from under the blankets and hobbled to the door.

Outside lay an envelope with her name written on it in Parker's handwriting. She recalled the nervous excitement and dread with which she had once looked at Jason's folded paper airplane. What would be in this missive? Divorce papers? A goodbye?

She put the envelope on the bureau to wait while she drank another bottle of water. The old habit of temporary indecision followed by total determination. She would waver and wait, popping in and out of her email window until she could steel herself to open the message, or pace a worn path outside superiors' offices before throwing open the door and boldly making her outrageous request. Now she primed herself like a professional athlete before a big race: stretching her hands, loosening her shoulders, and rotating her neck. When she could stand the anticipation no longer, she reached for the envelope, tore it open, and took out a tri-folded piece of paper, handwritten on the hotel's stationary.

> Hadley,
>
> I cannot think about you or us at the moment. I have to take this morning to decide whether or not I will still go through with the transplant. When we get back to Chicago, we can discuss what will happen to us.
>
> Parker

God he was perfect. So outrageously, aggravatingly, irritatingly perfect. He couldn't for once be the irrational, crazy one? Construction workers building skyscrapers should use him as a level, he was so even-keeled. Even on unlined paper, his careful sentences seemed written on a ruler's straight edge.

She pictured her own handwriting—childlike, her mother

had once called it, still uneven and lopsided even in her twenties. She rubbed the callused tips of her left-hand fingers together. Her vibrato was like that too: variable and inconsistent. Years of practice had never bottled it into the tight, even quavers her teachers demanded.

Fine, then, she decided. She would accept being the crazy one. She would embrace irrationality with open arms. She would finally go all the way. She was finally free, after all: she had nothing left to lose.

Hadley reached for her cell phone and dialed Jason's number.

"I need to talk to you."

## *Chapter Ten*

***Now***

Jason suggested meeting in Central Park as one last outdoor excursion before he entered the hermetically sealed clean room necessitated by the transplant. Even on this weekday morning, the generous May warmth had brought out many other New Yorkers from whatever dark cubby-holes they normally occupied into the urban pasture to stroll, frisbee, and picnic.

He told her to meet him at Central Park West and West 72nd Street. It was his favorite part of the park, he said. When Hadley arrived there, she found tourists taking snapshots of something on the ground. A small girl—six years old or so—bent down to place a daisy on the path. Hadley ignored the sightlines of the cameras and stared down at the object of fascination. Embedded in the asphalt walkway, a black and white tile mosaic swirled around one word in all caps: IMAGINE.

If it had some pedagogical purpose, it wasted its impact on Hadley. She had never needed instruction in that area. In fact, she could have used a permanent tile mosaic on her bathroom mirror reading, "Stop imagining." It was precisely this command that had propelled her into such trouble. "Believe." "Wish." "You can make it happen." Imagination always began so well. It was an exercise so full of hope, but nobody ever mentioned what happened to those dreamers once they returned from their imaginings—when they plummeted from the sky above back to the cold, hard, tiled earth.

"Don't you see a lot of irony in people taking pictures of a monument that says 'imagine,' instead of actually using their own imaginations to take a picture of something interesting?" Jason had silently approached and landed at Hadley's side.

"Perhaps you could get an exhibit commissioned of photographs of photographers taking photographs of a circle that says Imagine. It would be so wonderfully post-modern. You could even have a snappy title: Images of the Imagining Imagined."

Jason laughed and sacrilegiously stepped right in the middle of the mosaic, right on the word itself. At the other edge of the circle, he glanced back at Hadley, nodded his head in the direction of the grassy hill beyond, and moved off.

She too put her foot down on imagination as she followed him.

Jason spread a blanket on the still growing May grass and eased himself into a sitting position. Hadley pretended not to see him wince in pain as he lowered himself onto the micro-fleece. She sat as well, and they looked at each other for several seconds, but not in a turmoiled way. In fact, a half-cocked grin very much like Parker's flirted on Jason's lips. He wore a black headscarf instead of yesterday's knit hat.

"Before you even start talking, I just want to say Parker seems like a really nice guy. He's very—" Jason's eyebrows squinched toward each other. "Smooth. Not like suave or sophisticated. Not that kind of smooth. But—"

"I know what you mean." Hadley cut Jason off abruptly because he had finally supplied the adjective for which she had fumbled for years to describe Parker. This adjective also perfectly described the difference she had perceived between herself and the "normal" undergraduates of her college days—the quality every one of Them possessed but which she lacked.

Hadley continued, "He doesn't have any cracks or crevices or jagged edges. He's perfectly smooth. That comes from never having been broken and put back together again."

"Not like us."

And there it finally was: us. Just when the time had come for confrontation, so did the word that made accomplishing that task impossible. She had come to this meadow to sift through so many broken pieces. And then Jason made them whole.

"Well, I broke him last night."

"You told him?"

"Everything."

Jason nodded thoughtfully. "I realize this might not be the most tactful thing to ask right now, but you know I've never had a whole lot of tact. Does he still plan on doing the donation?"

A chuckle rose unexpectedly in Hadley's throat. "Maybe when you go back to grad school you can take a class in tact." She paused. "He said he'll decide this morning. And so I thought, why not have a pleasant chat with Jason?" She smiled broadly.

A young couple walked past where Jason and Hadley sat on their blanket. The woman pushed a stroller. Once upon a time, Hadley remembered, she would have mentally airbrushed her and Jason's faces over those of the young parents. The couple were about her age; they looked healthy, bright, content. The mother paused and knelt to tie an unlaced shoe. As she did so, the father smiled proudly down at his infant child.

Hadley turned away from the little family and back to Jason, but he was not looking at her. He also watched as the baby slept in its stroller and the father slipped his arm through the mother's and continued walking.

"Why didn't you—?"

Jason held up his hand and shook his head. He looked

calm. In fact, he smiled a small, kind, patient smile, much like the one a grandfather might wear as he fielded yet another random question from an inquisitive grandchild. Hadley might as well have asked him, "Why do brontosauruses have such long necks?"

"Hadley, you know I can't answer that."

"I destroyed my marriage last night. I deserve to at least get some answers out of this."

Jason spoke softly "I know that's what you deserve. You deserve…a lot of things. But I still can't give you an answer to that question. All I can do is try to explain…" He trailed off.

She waited with lips closed. She breathed fast through her nostrils like a caged animal.

"Hadley, I don't feel the way you do."

"I know that," she snarled. "You don't love me and I love you."

Jason patiently responded, "No, Hadley. You misunderstand me." When she opened her mouth again, Jason put up his hand once more and said, "Just let me talk for a minute. True, we don't share the same *feelings*. I'm using feeling there as a noun. But I also don't feel in the same *manner* or in the same *way* as you do. I'm using feeling there as a verb.

"I don't mean this as an insult, but you were not emotionally normal. By the time we were eight, you were feeling at a hundred miles an hour while the rest of us couldn't break fifty. You felt at one hundred decibels when everyone else was feeling at fifty decibels. And you had absolutely no idea the rest of the world didn't feel in the same way you did."

She could not stop herself from interrupting. "But I thought *you* did. I thought you were…like me. I thought you could appreciate how I felt, that you could handle going one hundred miles an hour with me. I knew the rest of the world didn't feel in the way I did, but I counted on the fact that you did."

"But I didn't." Jason's demeanor remained gentle—a word Hadley had never expected to associate with him. True, she had witnessed his gentleness on a few occasions with his younger sister during carpool trips, but he had never turned that gentle side toward her. Now his consonants melted together and his voice barely rose above the slight breeze sifting through the fresh leaves.

"Maybe I was intellectually gifted, but emotionally I was stunted. You, on the other hand—you were a prodigy, but instead of math or chess or music you were a prodigy in human emotion. Although I couldn't identify with your…affection for me, intellectually I could recognize there was absolutely nothing juvenile about you. I hate to shatter the illusion you have of me, but you should not have counted on me like that." Jason spoke with the posture and tone of an adult explaining to a child that Santa Claus, the Easter Bunny, and the Tooth Fairy do not in fact exist.

She was such a responsible person, she thought. She had always believed she had a responsibility—and with responsibility came power—to change the way Jason felt. For two decades she had willingly carried the accountability for everything which had and had not happened with Jason. Now he asked her to shed the mantle of duty she had voluntarily assumed. Now he was telling her that "the way" was immutable.

How could she have ever have tinkered with the inner mechanics of his heart? How could she have engineered it to beat at the same speed as hers, or to play at the same volume as her own? She could not have. There were no instruments or inventions capable of such adjustment.

Yet Hadley could not shed her obligations so easily. Even though she had never won the prize she so desperately sought, she had always at least drawn consolation from her pursuit of such a noble goal. Now, learning that the golden idol at which her hands feverishly clutched was a mere trick of the light cheapened and ridiculed all her old convictions.

In the midst of her analysis, Hadley hiccupped. Her stomach sent a stale, bitter taste to her tongue: self-pity and self-loathing. So stupid. So ridiculous. How could she allow herself, with all her intelligence, to actually fall for such a naive idea as love? This was the twenty-first century; such notions had long gone extinct. She had read too many books and, just as so many foolish girls did, she had believed them.

"God I'm stupid." She had not meant to say it aloud.

"No, Hadley, don't say that. You are not now and you never were stupid. You were brilliant, actually. Brilliant and funny and talented and so goddamn tenacious. You made me feel terrible, you know. Your life, your vitality, made me feel nearly dead. I couldn't even get sick in peace—you had to go try and make me feel better." He grimaced. "You were so good, and it made me feel so bad."

Hadley leaned back in shock, completely surprised and overwhelmed at Jason's lengthy explanation. "Then maybe I should have lost the district geography bee by a couple more rounds." The words flew out of her mouth as if acting by their own volition. While her conscious mind could not even form a coherent thought, her subconscious, her mouth, her tongue, or all of it at once, had assembled a joke—not necessarily a very funny one, but a joke nonetheless—completely on their own. Her eyebrows had even raised themselves into an expression of mock repentance.

Jason actually laughed. "No, you should not have. And I knew you lost on purpose." He paused and then continued, "You know, love is not always this warm and fuzzy thing everybody portrays it to be. It can create pain and expectations and it can be so strong it makes the recipient feel like shit."

"Kind of like chile peppers?" Hadley asked. When Jason look confused, she went on, "Parker says I put too much green chile on everything. He can't stand the heat. I guess you couldn't either."

"Exactly." Jason laughed again and picked up the thread of both the wordplay and the psychology. "All I wanted to do was get out of that damned kitchen, but you wouldn't let me."

He grinned, and Hadley gazed at him through her tears.

It felt so good. An almost sexual satisfaction rippled through her. How she had missed this wordplay, this tripping and twisting through language. She had not felt this same twinge of pleasure for a long time.

She loved him. She loved him so much. Free from the tensions of yesterday, under the branches of the buds of the May morning, and with the warm sun on her back, Hadley had the time and temperature to realize again how much she loved him. Not the idea of him and not the illusion of him. She loved the cluster of molecules sitting across the blanket from her. She loved his mumbling, nasal voice. She loved the way his eyebrows squiggled across his forehead. She loved those lilting hands resting lightly on his jeans.

"All I wanted was to make you feel good."

Jason's smile fell. "I know, but what we want and what happens are two very different things. Looking back on it now —" He frowned again. "You made me feel like I could never live up to the expectations you had of me. When you looked at me, I knew you didn't actually see *me*. You saw the best possible version of me. You saw all that I could be, all the potential I had."

"Yes! I believed in you! Isn't that supposed to be a good thing?" She leaned forward and pleaded, like the accused frantically trying to justify her crimes.

"It should have been, but I couldn't see it that way.

Hadley, even at eight years old, I figured out I was not the person you wanted me to be. Even at eight years old, I hated myself, my arrogance and meanness and neediness. And you just made me hate myself more, because every time you looked at me, I knew I could never match up to what you saw." By the time Jason finished his soliloquy, his tone had become bitter.

"Then why didn't you change? Why didn't you try to live up to my belief?" Hadley turned on him, transforming from accused to accuser.

"Not everyone is as brave as you!" He shouted it and then quickly looked around to check if any passing pedestrians had noticed. Being mostly Upper West Siders, they quietly avoided interfering with other people's problems.

He had called her brave. She had craved that compliment for years and years and now he finally gave it to her. Ten years too late. Still basking in the glow from the greatest compliment he had ever given her, she barely noticed as he spoke again.

Jason continued at normal volume, "You made me focus on all my flaws. It highlighted all the fear in me—the scared little coward—"

She cut him off, "But I felt like shit too, Jason. You made me feel terrible and I never cowered away. And you're also wrong about the illusions. Yes, maybe I gave you the benefit of every doubt, but I also loved all your flaws and faults. I loved you as you, warts and all. How do you explain that?"

Jason smiled warmly, affectionately, and sadly. "Because you were much braver than I was."

"You couldn't have told me that fifteen years ago?" she asked sarcastically. Then her voice became plaintive once more. "You couldn't have taken that risk? I took the risk. The fact that I loved you should have counted for something, Jason. And—and I made you laugh." She cried as she said it.

"I made you laugh and that should have mattered. I cared

about you, I helped you succeed, I was always ready to be your friend." Hadley jabbed herself in the chest with every "I." "And it didn't count or matter at all to you. Can't you see the injustice of that?"

Jason no longer smiled. He bore an expression that Hadley, having seen it so many times reflected on her own face, identified immediately as self-loathing.

"Yes, that all should have counted. And yes, you made me laugh." He said it in a voice of shame. "You made me laugh like no one else then or since could."

Hadley lunged on. "You counted other people. She—she gave you far, far less than I did. She didn't make you laugh like I did. She didn't love you like I did. And yet you wrote this." Hadley reached for her messenger bag, pulled out the clear plastic sleeve, and shoved the flattened paper airplane at him.

Jason picked it up delicately and studied the faded words.

"I thought about this so much, Jason. Every single day. I remembered everything. Whenever I unwrap a stick of gum, I think about you covering a composition book with the silver foil from gum wrappers. I still have a *Magic: The Gathering* card you once gave me. I can still hear you reading aloud from *Harry Potter* for a book report. I remember everything."

Hadley leaned forward like an elderly wife attempting to will her dementia-addled husband into recognizing her. Of course, the dedicated old spouses in nursing homes could not blame their partners for succumbing to Alzheimer's or Parkinson's or whatever had stolen away their minds, and so the ones who remained behind could take their sadness without bitterness. Hadley, though, could not take her grief without an accompanying shot of anger.

He handed the plastic sleeve back to her.

Hadley lowered her head to look at the paper airplane. A tear fell onto the clear plastic.

"Whatever happened to Katie?" he asked.

"She became hyper-religious, dropped out of college, married some guy from the church, and made a lot of babies." Hadley continued to stare down at the faded notebook paper in its protective casing.

"You know, Hadley, it's not like I didn't think about you, you know. I'm not the monster you make me out to be." At the newly defensive tone in Jason's voice, Hadley looked up.

He looked like he was concentrating hard as he said, "Just because I didn't…it didn't mean I never got a kick out of you. I enjoyed our little emails. I wasn't sending you those emails out of pity. You weren't my charity case, Hadley, and when you abruptly cut off contact, it did kind of hurt."

"Only *kind of* hurt?" Before she knew it, the words were out of her mouth, a tease instead of an endearment. Her raised eyebrows quickly fell as she erased yet another of her misplaced assumptions.

Jason managed a half smirk, and then continued "If you've come here after some kind of apology, I won't give it to you. I will not say I'm sorry for feeling the way I did. It is true that I did not treat you with the respect and civility you deserved, but I could not change how I felt back then, and I certainly cannot change it now. I have a policy of not apologizing for things I can't change."

Hadley closed her eyes and swallowed. It was not the actual substance of what Jason said that hurt. Rather, it was the way he had said it that hurt: he had said almost the exact same thing now as she had said to Parker mere hours ago. For any other couple sitting on a blanket in Central Park, riding the same linguistic wavelength would signal chemistry and compatibility and good karma.

In the topsy-turvy universe of Jason and Hadley, however, a common vocabulary was not cause for celebration.

Although they uttered the same words, they did so in service of divergent, contradictory goals. They said the same things but expressed two very different points of view.

Hadley kept her eyes closed for her next statement. She could not face him as she said it. “I just want to know that I meant something in your life.”

When no response immediately came, she finally opened her eyes. Jason sat in deep thought, eyebrows squinting together, head tilted, and invisible wheels turning in his brain.

Jason nodded several times. He then looked Hadley straight on. “You did mean something. As I look back on my life, my relationship with you does stand out as one of the formative ones. I have not met anyone else who pushes me like you, who I can laugh with like you, or who aggravates me like you. But I have met people with whom I can actually live in peace, unlike you.” He smiled ruefully.

“That was always the rub,” Hadley said tearfully. “For such similar words, ‘love’ and ‘live’ are not very interchangeable. I could love you but not live you.”

“And Parker,” Jason ventured cautiously, “Can you live him?”

“Yes,” Hadley sighed. “But he doesn’t push me like you, I can’t laugh with him like I could with you, and he certainly doesn’t aggravate me like you.”

Hadley took a long, deep, slow breath and exhaled slowly. She leaned back on her elbows and offered her face up to the sun.

“I never became as cynical as you, Jason, but after you moved away I really lost my faith in the universe. But when Parker walked into that coffee shop five years ago, I believed in God in a close, personal sense for the first time. I’ve always been an explainer, trying to figure out everything in the world. And the only explanation beyond random chance of Parker’s appearance in my life was that some benevolent universal force wanted to give me a second chance."

"Random chance is a completely legitimate explanation in and of itself." He paused, and when she did not go on, he asked curiously, "Why are you telling me this? I'm not a priest and I'm not going to prescribe ten Hail Marys to absolve you of your sins. If you want moral sanction or judgment, you'll have to go elsewhere."

"Oddly enough, you're the only one I can talk to about this. I've never talked about it with anyone else. Who else would I tell? My parents? A therapist? They'd all call me crazy. At least I haven't attempted to transform Parker into you. I'm not doing James Stewart in *Vertigo* here. I mean, I never suggested he start playing the violin or make shorts out of duct tape."

Jason chuckled. "My god, those duct tape shorts I made." Then he answered her unspoken question. "Look, people have done a lot worse things in order to feel even half-way happy. You did what you had to do."

Jason gazed off to the side, his face blank. Hadley rubbed her tired and strained eyes. This had been one of the longest conversations she had ever shared with Jason. Now it had become the longest silence she had ever shared with Jason. As usual, she gave in first.

"What you thinking?" Hadley asked.

Jason continued to stare off into space, but he answered, "I'm just thinking about the transplant and the next few months. Wondering if I made a mistake."

"A mistake how?"

"A mistake in doing the transplant at all. That is, if Parker still agrees to do it. It's so much money, so many resources that could go to other people, and for what? I have my parents and sister and that's pretty much it. I don't particularly love my job and I'm not on the verge of some great scientific breakthrough that will benefit humanity. I haven't had a worthwhile long-term romantic relationship in a while." He turned back to face her. "Why should I get the transplant?" He seemed genuinely flummoxed by the issue.

"But," Hadley asked tentatively, already knowing the unpleasant answer, "what would happen if you didn't get the transplant?"

"I would die," Jason said perfectly matter-of-factly. "And honestly, that possibility really doesn't alarm me. I'm not depressed and I don't *want* to die, but I have no guiding force or principle or person tying me down. What's keeping me here? All of the cancer books keep talking about 'hope,' but I don't know what that really means."

Hadley's immediate reaction was shock mixed with an almost perverse pride. He finally considered her shoulder worthy of crying on. At last he had opened up those elusive inner vaults to which she had desired access for so long.

"Why are you telling me this?"

"Oddly enough, you're the only one I can talk to about this." His jaw clamped in concentration. "Even though you put a lot of expectations on me, a happy face was not one of them. Everybody else expects me to be some kind of eternal optimist."

Jason looked so glum that Hadley had to open with a joke. "Have they ever met you?" Her eyebrows fell from her expression of mock questioning, and she continued, "Hope is what keeps you here. It's the expectation that in the future, you will find that guiding force or principle or person. If you have nothing binding you to the present, hope will bind you to the future."

"Yeah, the future. The doctors and my parents even—get this—even convinced me to freeze some of my sperm, because the full-body radiation destroys your sperm. For the future, they said. For when I settle down with someone and want a family.

That's all I have to get me through the transplant: a freezer full of hypothetical babies."

Hadley had to force the next words from her mouth. Of all the words she had spoken over the last hour, they were the riskiest of all.

"You could have me."

Surprise showed on every feature of Jason's face, as if Hadley had just suggested he fly to the moon on the back of a dolphin.

The shock that hung in the air between them was broken by the buzzing and beeping of a cell phone. Jason looked at his screen. "A reminder that I should probably start heading over to the hospital."

He pushed himself onto his feet, but then suddenly grabbed his forehead with both hands. He would have toppled over onto the blanket if Hadley, mid-rise herself, had not caught him. Silently she supported Jason's bent body as he let his hands fall and waited for the nausea to pass. He made no objection, physical or verbal, to Hadley's arms on his shoulders and back. He took several deep breaths and, with Hadley's hands guiding his torso, straightened up completely. Hadley also stood to her full height and looked at Jason eye-to-eye.

And then she kissed him.

She wrapped her fingers around his jaw and neck and drew his lips to hers.

He kissed her back. One of his light, long-fingered hands slipped into the hair at the back of her neck. Another slid artfully down her side to where her hip curved softly outward.

Even as Hadley pressed her fingertips into the soft skin of Jason's neck, she knew she would never be able to properly record this moment in any written language. Her muscles and nerves would have to preserve this memory in cell and tissue and fiber. She could attempt to describe the sloppy dance of their tongues, but that effort would be merely an imperfect *representation*; reading it back she could not relive it, she could only remember. And even then, how could she truly remember the sensation of Jason's knuckles tangling her hair, the weight of his fist clutching at her shorts, or his lips slipping against hers? Certainly in the future she would be able to recall that she had experienced pleasure, but the pleasure itself would disappear beyond memory or recall as soon as Jason pulled away. Every second of physical contact completed its own cycle of origin, evolution, and decay incapable of either preservation or replication. Touch lasted only as long as it lasted; it left no substantial trace of essence or honesty. Just a few microscopic skin cells and imprints that melted like footsteps in snow.

And so Hadley did not dare stop kissing him, because as soon as she let her lips fall from his, she would lose this moment forever. No matter how many words she penned or pages she typed, she would never get back to here, never truly return to this time and place and touch.

But at last Jason drew his lips away, although he did not detach his body from hers. Hadley's hands crept stealthily under the heavy cotton of his shirt and dug their nails into the bare skin of his lower back. Jason rested his head on her shoulder. He clung to her as if surrendering to a merciful foe. He did not hang on her as one would to a flotation device, but rather let her body smother him as the waves will smother a drowning man.

In the commotion Jason's head covering had shifted and exposed a few inches of bare scalp above his ear. Hadley kissed the white skin. It was the softest skin she had ever kissed.

"You were the one, Jason," she whispered in his ear. "And you turned my life into such a fucking tragedy."

They held each other for a long time, but it still was not long enough.

"I've got to get to the hospital."

Jason peeled himself away and disengaged his arms from around her shoulders. Hadley's entire body felt like her scalp did when she pulled her hair out of a tight ponytail after a long day and sensation gushed back into the restricted and tightened skin. She shivered in the sunshine.

Hadley bent to fold up the blanket and handed the neat pile to Jason. She lifted the strap of her bag over her head and settled it on her shoulder.

Jason held out his hand. Hadley took it and shook it quickly and efficiently.

"Well, have a nice life," Jason said.

"You too."

And with that Jason walked away. Hadley watched him amble back in the direction from which they had come. At last he disappeared beyond the borders of the park. He never looked back.

## *Chapter Eleven*

Parker stared at the entwined figures, their lips inches from each other's. The female form gazed rapturously up at her adoring lover, while the male's face bore the perfect Superman expression, compassion and concern mixed with pride and lust. He seemed to be saying to her, "Do not worry, my darling. I have come back." One of his pale, long-fingered hands cradled her astonished head, while the digits of his other hand cupped one of her alabaster bare breasts. The woman's own arms stretched backward, avidly extorting her lover's lips ever closer to her own.

Jealousy flickered in Parker as he gaped at them, so oblivious to the world they were, so hatefully, perfectly exemplifying the sacred love blessed and approved by the gods themselves. How unkind to flaunt their triumphant reunification before all, and how vain to not even clothe their desire. He tightened the fist upon which his chin rested.

Parker glanced again at the placard pasted onto the statue's plinth: "Cupid and Psyche" by Antonio Canova, 1794. The Neoclassical gallery of the Metropolitan Museum of Art, it seemed, would not provide him with a solution to his conundrum. He had also consulted the Egyptians, a few Japanese calligraphers on special exhibit, and George Washington himself, and even attempted to divine an answer out of the mad swirls of

Van Gogh, but after hours in the museum, he had still come no closer to a decision. What he needed—he jerked his head back around to see if a delinquent twelve-year old might have spray-painted a clue across some eighteenth-century French painting—was a sign, a signal, a lightning bolt or burning bush or shooting star pointing him in the right direction.

He wandered into another gallery. Unlike the chattering Art History groupies clustered reverently around a Mark Rothko painting, Parker could not grasp the threads of any story or extract any message out of the splotches of color hanging on the walls around him. Some plaint globs were blue, others green. The one his eyes bored into now was red. Red, like blood. Like the blood he could not figure out if he would be giving or not.

Like, like, like…All of Hadley's poetic comparisons rang in his ears, their attractiveness now marred by the realization that she had used them only to hide behind. Perhaps if he had not been no impressed, if he had questioned her talent for simile and metaphor instead of admired it— perhaps if he had dug a little deeper into her precious turns of phrase, he would have uncovered the truth sooner. The artifice of her language, Parker realized, was just like the artifice of the oils in the Cubist gallery —twisted, askew, begging to be reassembled into a cogent whole.

Parker's stomach audibly and angrily growled. An elderly couple—German by the cut of their orthopedic footwear—shot parental scowls of concern toward him. Parker glanced at his watch: 1:27. He had not eaten since the previous night's dinner. He ducked out of the gallery and consulted a museum map on the wall. He plotted out lefts and rights and staircases, then loped off toward the exit. He sprinted down a back flight of stone steps and took a wrong turn amongst some medieval tapestries. He was wandering through a room full of statues when he saw her.

There, parked in front of a sculpture of the Virgin Mary

cradling the bloody brow of her dying son, was Jason's mother.

Their mother.

His mother.

Only seconds after he spotted her, she looked over in his direction. She quickly focused on him and then smiled. Then she held out her arms, and then he was rushing toward her, burying himself in her chest, willing her to smother him and let him just sleep, sleep in her embrace.

But Linda Snyder took a firm grip on her son's shoulders and nudged him up. He brushed shamefully at the boyish tears rolling down his cheeks, but she just calmly rubbed them away. She reached into her handbag and pulled out a packet of tissues, although she conceded to his adulthood and let him wipe his own nose.

"I'm sorry," he muttered, "I don't usually just start crying like this." He blew his nose loudly and stuffed the tissue in his pocket.

To his great surprise, Linda laughed. When she saw his startled face, she rushed to explain. "Jason—he does the same thing." She nodded at his pocket. "You'd think the boy had never heard of a trashcan."

Parker forced half a smile and offered the packet of tissues back to her. She waved them away and patted her purse. "Keep it. I've got plenty more of those. They hand them out, you see, at the orientation for Your Child Has Cancer Again."

Linda too smiled grimly and turned back to the Madonna and child. She cocked her headand studied the form with an intense concentration not entirely unlike Hadley's. Parker came to her side and bent to examine a few limestone drips of blood.

"I was an art history minor in college, you know. The summer after we had you, we scraped up enough money to go to Florence. I spent hours upon hours just gazing at art, while Rick stuffed his face with gelato and pizza and wine." She laughed again, fondly and nostalgically.

Parker's tongue snagged on a sharp branch in his throat a few times before he could get out the next words: "Why did you…"

She was ready for it. "Because we were too young and too poor and way too immature and hadn't finished school. Because how could I raise someone as brilliant as you when I couldn't even spot the difference between a Raphael and a Michelangelo." She turned and smirked at him. "The painters, not the ninja turtles."

He chuckled. "You're funny," he exclaimed. "You remind me of—" but he stopped short.

Linda, though, seemed to understand. "Yep," she said in a wry voice and grinned. "Where is our Hadley anyway?"

He gripped the tissues again and fumbled for one to prophylactically stem the tide of his eyes. "She's…we…last night" he mumbled.

He heard Linda sigh: a deep, slow, resigned exhale of breath. She clicked her tongue, and for the first time her own eyes filled with tears. "She told you."

Parker's eyes swam again, and momentarily blinded, he allowed Linda to steer him over to a bench against the gallery wall. For seconds, minutes, or hours—Parker knew not how long he sat there heaving—Linda waited patiently with her arm around his shoulders and her hand softly squeezing his.

In the midst of the chaotic pain, Parker attempted to remember when his own mother—the mother who had raised him, that was—had held him in this simple way and had rubbed her thumb back and forth over the skin of his palm, numbing it to the point that the agony melted away. And then Parker realized his mother had never held him this way, not because she was cruel or callous, but simply because he had never before *needed* to be held like this. He had never need to be caught, to be saved, in the way Linda had caught him now.

"You know?" Parker hiccupped.

Linda spoke softly, almost whispering in his ear, never letting up the back-and-forth stroke of her fingers over the skin of his palm. "I don't know everything, of course, but I know enough. I know enough to appreciate how much you're hurting. I saw them grow up together. I saw her at seven years old, looking at Jason so precociously. Then I saw her at fifteen, looking at him like…You'll understand when you become a parent, how utterly strange it is to see someone look at your child and know she loves him even a fraction as much as you do."

Linda went on, and as Parker listened, her words seemed to flow in the same slow, gentle rhythm as the stroke of her fingers on his skin. "It sounds crazy to say this, but I admired Hadley. Even when she was in elementary school, I admired her. I was an adult, I was his *mother*, for God's sake, and yet I sometimes struggled with the love I felt for the difficult, impenetrable creature who was my son. But Hadley, just a child herself, bore up so well, so courageously, never looking back.

"I admit I tried to encourage Hadley. I thought she might hold the key to cracking him, to finally get him to open. To solve him. Because even though I'm his mother, Jason has always been something of a mystery to me, almost like a stranger. Not like you."

Parker twisted to gape at Linda with watery eyes. But she just smiled.

"You wouldn't think newborns have recognizable personalities, but they do. When I first met you—" Linda's eyes now filled with fond tears. "I got this unshakable sureness that you would be alright, no matter what. That you would fit in wherever it was you were going. And that's why I felt absolutely sure I had made the right decision. I still feel I made the right decision. I don't have any regrets—"

She finally removed her fingers from his palm and brushed a lock of hair away from his eyes. "Because look at what a spectacular man you've become."

Parker whipped his head around to look at her. His eyes had a pleading in them. "I'm not spectacular, though," he mumbled. Despite the near unintelligibility of his words, Linda immediately raised her eyebrows into an expression of "Why?"

"I don't even know if I can do it…tomorrow…I came here hoping something would tell me what to do. I've never not known what to do. I always knew which way to go, or someone would just tell me where to go, what to do…" He trailed off. Even his words apparently did not know where to go or what to do.

"You've never felt lost?" Linda's voice turned sharp.

Parker shook his head, without any apparent shame or sheepishness. He leaned back against the wall looking like a puppy someone had just left at the pound.

Linda did not look pleased at how well her son had been taken care of. She frowned at him, her face full of business. "Well, I am of course biased in this, but I think you should do it, do the donation and the transplant. I don't say this very often about Jason, but he *is* the innocent bystander in all of this. However angry you are with Hadley, you can't take it out on him."

"But if Jason—" Parker stuttered a few times as he searched for the right word. "If Jason is…in the picture, then how can Hadley and I… I just can't see Hadley and I together if Jason is still…"

Linda drew back upon herself—her shoulders fell down while her neck craned forward. "Oh my god," she breathed. "You still want to stay with her."

Parker simply gaped down at his hands. Hadley had focused so much on Jason's hands in her story; she had described them in such intimate detail. Parker had never thought too much about his own hands. They helped him make his living, they allowed him draw, they so sensitively slid over the skin of Hadley's body. He recalled the first time they had met, so long ago in that most generic of coffee shops. Replaying the scene in his mind, he noticed a glaring detail he had never before appreciated: Hadley's eyes drifting to his wrist, to where his sleeve had slipped down and revealed the prominent bones of his wrist.

"I don't know," Parker breathed.

"If it happens, Parker, if you do the transplant and Hadley goes chasing after Jason again, then what you do is…you go on." Linda's voice become distinctly no-nonsense. "You scrape up the broken pieces and paste them all back together. You keep living, keep waking up every day. That's what I did, that's what Hadley did, what Jason did. That's what she did," Linda nodded toward the Virgin Mary. She studied the sculpture a few more moments with her teeth gritted and brows drawn close.

"You see, Parker," and again she distinctly sounded as she had some Life Lessons to impart to him, "lots of times, doing the right thing hurts. That's the problem with the world these days: people are so afraid of pain they never do the right thing." She swallowed, and when she spoke next, her tone lost its edge and became quiet, almost a whisper. "When I had to turn you over to the social worker six hours after you'd been born, it hurt so much. But I did it, because I knew it was the right thing to do. When you go tomorrow to do the donation, it will hurt. You will be in pain. You will think of Hadley and what this means for your future, for her future, and it will hurt more. But guess what? It will be the right thing to do. It will be the brave thing to do."

Parker's head jerked up. Brave. He had called Hadley brave less than five minutes after they had met. He called her brave before he ever called her beautiful. And it was true, Parker realized. No matter the hurt of Hadley's revelations, he could not deny the deep-rooted vein of courage which ran through her story. Not the brazen fearlessness of some great warrior or the flashy gallantry of some daredevil, but the steady, unheralded fortitude required to wake up each morning and love someone. The same bravery etched in Hadley's face Parker now saw reflected in the sculpted tears of the Virgin Mary and in the very wet tears of the mother who sat beside him.

"I want to be brave," he rasped.

Linda grinned at him and helped him to his feet. He mopped himself up with a few more tissues and started for the doorway of the gallery. Halfway there, though, he paused and whirled around toward Linda. She tripped on his heels.

"How did you know I would come here? I didn't tell anyone I was coming to the museum—it couldn't be a coincidence, could it?" In his haste and anguish, Parker had skipped over the extraordinary cosmic synchronicity which had apparently led to this mother and child reunion.

Linda merely smirked, though. It was she who had passed that half-cocked grin down to her sons. She shrugged and widened her eyes in feigned incredulity. "It is a very famous and popular museum, you know. We can worry about the vagaries of fate at another time, Parker. You're late for your check in. And you still have to meet your sister."

They walked out of the gallery arm-in-arm.

# *Chapter Twelve*

The floral-patterned vinyl of the recliner squeaked as Parker took his seat. The nurse urged him back to a point at which his arms stretched out flat. To his right stood what looked like a cross between a futuristic vending machine and a circuit board. Knobs waited to be twiddled and switches to be flipped, and somewhere deep inside the machine, a centrifuge waited to spin to a blur and to filter out only the most necessary bits of him. And on another floor of this hospital, Parker knew, Jason waited.

They had not actually seen each other. Parker picked up the vibe, mostly from Linda and Rick's frequent, loaded glances at each other, and Rick's equally frequent checks to his phone, that the parents were running complex plays of interference between him and Jason.

Linda and Rick had in fact accompanied Parker through yesterday's entire pre-game walk-through, as if to prevent him from fleeing the jurisdiction. Parker had in fact attempted to cut the tension with this little joke while the hospital administrator double and triple-checked his forms, elbowing Rick and announcing, "I'm not a flight risk," but Rick had managed only a mild smile. If not for Rick's insistence that his wife return to their own hotel to get some sleep, Parker suspected Linda would have watched over him the entire night, perhaps never even closing her own eyes for fear he would disappear before the dawn.

The only time Parker dared to mention…him…was when seven p.m. came and went and neither Parker nor Linda broke to rush to the inpatient wards before visiting hours ended. Sitting in a pizza parlor gorging his stem cells on as much cheese as possible, Parker had finally, tentatively asked, "Shouldn't you guys be with… Isn't he staying overnight?"

Linda had merely exchanged yet another meaningful flash of eyes with her husband before saying, with fairly obvious breeziness, "Oh, he never wants anyone to stay with him."

Now, Parker breathed through his mouth to avoid drawing in the slightly sour hospital smell. The stench pervaded the building, even into the elevators, but it was not the sweet, putrid aroma of organic matter, nor the acidic, stringent scent of rubbing alcohols. Rather, the smell had a distinct metallic core to it, and yet also a sense of decay, almost as if the auras of lead-lined aprons drifted up from the cold x-ray vaults and if the electrons shed by the isotopes of radium or cesium carried their own odor. Parker thought he could in fact smell the radiation seeping through the vents of the hospital. It smelled like someone had just opened an attic which had been closed, not for years, but since the very origins of the universe.

Another nurse knocked irrelevantly at the open door. She carried a variety of ominously plastic-wrapped items in her arms, but more horrifying was the false cheer of the smiley-faced ribbon which held back her black braids.

"We'll just go get some coffee while you get all set up." Linda gathered up her purse and glared significantly at Rick, who had already settled himself into a vinyl-coated armchair. He rose and nodded. Linda bent over Parker and brushed her lips against his forehead in a quick kiss. Rick squeezed Parker's shoulder and followed his wife out of the room.

Parker wanted to call them back, wanted to beg them to stay with him and hold his hand, but something caught his tongue just as he was about to yell out. He put up a palm to his cheek and found he had flushed hot with shame.

The blue-scrubbed nurse prepared her instruments on the tray beside the recliner, and as Parker took in the strips of latex, the rolls of tape, and the needle feigning innocence within its neat plastic sleeve, his abdominal, pelvic, and gluteus muscles all involuntarily contracted. His testicles seemed to withdraw into his groin, while his liver scrambled to shrink itself into his rapidly tightening abdominal cavity. His buttocks clenched so tightly that a gust of coolness rose from the sticky vinyl of the chair.

Fear resides in the gut, not in the heart or the head. Sophisticated, silvery neurons may give birth to anxiety or apprehension, but it was the mucous and muscles of the intestines and the sinews of the pelvic floor which bred far more ancient and elemental terrors.

***

Three floors above, Jason splayed across a bed, defiant in jeans but compliant in a soft flannel shirt open to the waist. A nurse drew back one side of the flapping shirt and brushed alcohol in concentric circles onto a patch of skin near his armpit.

"We're just doing some extra nutrition this morning to keep your strength up. I see you're scheduled to get a central line put in tomorrow," the nurse said brightly.

"What? Oh, yeah." Jason had not been listening.

The nurse tried again. "That should make things easier." Jason merely jerked his chin down once or twice.

One small tuft of hair formed a bullseye just over Jason's sternum. He had the upper chest of a boy—thin, almost frail—but the slightly emergent paunch of a man. Two straight, inch-long scars interrupted the almost transparent white skin: one on each side, next to the armpit, above the nipple. Beneath the scar on the right side, a port-a-cath protruded out of his skin, particularly visible because of the lack of concealing muscle.

Jason's cell phone buzzed, and he maneuvered the touch screen with his left hand while the nurse proceeded to draw rusty lines of betadine over the right side of his chest.

*Parker's here. Just about to start. How are you?* his father's text message said.

He punched in *ok* and barked, "you can go" at the nurse. She gripped the port between two of her practiced fingers to hold it steady, and like some whaler harpooning his quarry, she plunged the needle through Jason's skin, through a top layer of rubber, and drove it hard all the way until it met the impenetrable floor of titanium at the very bottom of the port.

She drew the plunger of the syringe back and red flushed into to the barrel.

"Good blood return," the nurse commented, "but you've got some gnarly scar tissue there. It almost wouldn't go through."

This time Jason smiled. "Yeah, I know the scar tissue's bad. But on the plus side, I didn't feel a thing."

***

"Jesus Christ," Parker gasped. The keen point of the needle sliced into his vein. But even after it pierced his skin, it did not stop. It thrust further and further in, nicking at the interior walls of the blood vessel like some evil, animate metal snake.

Parker saw stars behind his eyelids as he screwed his eyes up tight. Through the bites of pain, he heard the nurse say, "Hold still now, almost there." And then the needle shoved in even further. Parker thought the delicate walls of his vein might collapse as he bit down hard.

"Okay, dear, we're in." Parker slowly unsealed his eyes to see the nurse sliding a board under his elbow and securing the IV with a great deal of tape. She hooked the end of the tubing to a bag of clear liquid hanging above his head.

"Now for the other arm," the nurse said, ripping open a new IV kit and again setting out and separating her various tools.

Parker must have blanched, because the nurse patted his needle-less arm with the back of one of her gloved hands. "You alright?" He nodded, but the nurse still looked skeptical. "You want me to call your mother in here?"

But Parker shook his head emphatically and clamped down his jaw. At the nurse's suggestion of calling his mother, his face had once again burned red.

He swallowed a few times and closed his eyes once more. He tried to empty his mind.

"Here we go," the nurse announced, and in the millisecond before the stainless steel penetrated Parker's body, the image of Hadley suddenly popped onto the backs of his eyelids. She wavered in and out of focus as the needle chewed deeper and deeper into his arm.

"You can relax now," the nurse said, and Hadley disappeared. Parker felt the muscles in his thighs, butt, and shoulders relax. He had not even notice they had tensed. Even his abdominal muscles had squeezed together in stress, and as Parker looked down at his belly, his stomach ballooned out with resolving tension.

"You've not had many pokes, have you?" the nurse asked. When Parker again shook his head vehemently, she went on as she taped up his arm, "Yeah, your veins are pretty delicate. They open up after some practice. They get used to it."

***

About six hours later, two nurses returned to Jason's room, one of them covered in an extra sheath of draping and gowning.

Jason looked up from the text message he had just

received from his mother, which read, "They say Parker's donation went really well. They just about have enough. Doctor said they'll probably get you started soon."

The nurse who wore enough flowing fabric to look positively medieval also carried a bag of vivid, neon yellow fluid. The liquid had the same shiny, almost phosphorescent quality as the highlighter Jason poised over the booklet open in his lap. The page he had been marking had complex graphs accompanied by thick sections of tiny text. Despite the needle residing firmly in the right side of Jason's chest, Jason's right hand moved swiftly over the page as he accented a few important sentences. He shifted against many layers of pillow with an ease belying the needle or the coils of plastic tubing snaking down from it. He barely seemed to notice the variety of medical apparatuses embedded in and connected to his body.

The nurses stood over him to perform their familiar ritual. "Name?" one of them asked.

"Jason Snyder," he answered dutifully.

"Birthdate?"

"November eighth." The nurses showed him the label on the bag of the faintly glowing liquid. The security check seemed unnecessary for chemotherapy drugs of this caustic quality. Surely no one would allow themselves to be injected by mistake with something resembling battery acid.

And indeed, this was poison, plain and simple. The "ablative" chemotherapy would drip slowly down over the next four hours, purposefully defiling the fastest-dividing cells of his body, storming in and wrestling the dividing ends of chromosomes to conclusively shut down all growth and all development in his body.

Tomorrow morning, another bag, and on the third day, an atomic scream of radiation would detonate any remaining marrow into dust. The blast would briefly render him a pale, gray, formless ghost, hovering somewhere in the ether between not quite alive and not quite dead. And then, he would rise from the almost-dead on the nourishment of his brother's blood.

The nurse had hung the bag on the IV pole next to Jason's shoulder, and she was now unscrewing the tubing from the sack of nutritional fluid in order to screw it into the chemotherapy bag.

"Wait!" Jason said it softly but sharply. The nurse held the end of the line inches away from the evil-looking sack of chemotherapy drugs.

Jason watched as his point of no return ticked slowly past. He could just say no, he thought again. He could say no and banish them from this room along with their chemo and stem cells and life-saving and hope. He could sign the refusal of medical intervention papers he had secretly had a lawyer draft, and he could be out of here forever, finally free to create whatever end he found worthiest.

He saw the nurse's gloved hand waiting next to the hanging bag of yellow liquid. Yellow liquid. Yellow…a yellow something…a yellow…And then Jason heard it—

"And we lived, beneath the waves, in our yellow submarine." The song came from a stereo boom box, and Hadley stood beside it, holding a CD cover filled with a black and white collage of photographs and drawings. She sang along happily, "Sky of blue, and sea of green, in our yellow submarine."

They could have only been seven or eight years old. One of the few times he had gone over to Hadley's house to play, she had wanted him to listen to a particular CD. Her parents had bought it for her, just for her, because she loved this song so much.

Jason never knew he carried this memory. He had never remembered it before. And yet there he was, right there beside her. And their friends were all aboard, he recalled Hadley singing. Many more of them lived next door.

None of those pamphlets or motivational speakers or inspirational books came close to adequately explaining hope, Jason decided. Hope was just a pop song, a nonsense tune for children. But it had been there all along, just waiting for him to remember. And it was enough.

"It's okay. You can start it," Jason told the nurse.

***

"This is the last one," the white-coated doctor said as she collected yet another bag of fluid from the plasmapheresis machine. "Nurse'll be in in a few minutes to take the IVs out." The doctor exited the room for the sixth time today, carrying, as always, the bag of separated blood products with her.

Parker yawned, but his arms were so strapped down he could not reach up to cover his mouth. People on TV and movies always managed to move about freely with IVs in their hands and arms and god knew where else, but every time he so much as flinched, he would feel the catheter pinch painfully. And so he had spent the day nearly immobile.

Rick had been gracious and discrete enough to help him guzzle ginger ales through a straw whenever Linda left the room, and it was only when Rick and Linda went to get their own lunch that Parker finally allowed a nurse to help him to the bathroom.

A jovial and good-humored man, Rick had also helpfully done most of the talking. Parker imagined him especially capable of mediating between the equally intense and forceful personalities of Linda and Jason. Rick filled the silences easily, questioning Parker about anything and everything and adding his own running commentary.

Jason's sister Courtney had also flitted in and out of the room, chit-chatting and running errands for what were clearly superfluous cups of coffee. Her demeanor ran closer to Rick's—

gentle, accommodating, and more aware of social niceties. Courtney had gone frequently to "check on" Jason, but never returned with much usable information. Upon one of her returns she had rolled her eyes in response to her father asking, "How's he doing," and another time, she had just shrugged and said, "You know how he is. Doesn't ever tell you what's going on in his head." And when Courtney had finally come back from one particularly long absence, Linda had asked her nervously, "Is he still there?" as if afraid her son may have escaped the hospital and gone on the lam.

In the early afternoon, with Rick's easy conversation as a lullaby, Parker finally managed something he had not done in nearly thirty-six hours: sleep. He dozed fitfully, though, never quite reaching the stage of dreams, just tottering at the edge of one and then waking to the bite of the catheters in his arm and the fleeting image of Hadley scrolling away from his sight.

She had not called or texted or sent smoke signals or even a passenger pigeon. Not that he expected her to, but, well…He started this thought several times, but he never finished it. He could not figure out what came after the "but."

Exhaustion finally overtook Parker as the nurse began to unpeel all the strips of tape from his arms. He could barely nod or grunt as the nurse prattled on about how he could treat himself to a nice, big dinner. The pulling out of the IV catheters hurt almost as much as the pushing in; the insides of his veins seemed to have their own nerve endings, and they screamed at every millimeter as the catheter snaked out. The pain seemed to come from deep inside him, from a source almost independent of himself. It was as if the pain did not belong to him, but belonged exclusively to autonomous colonies of blood vessels and nerves occupying the crooks of his arms. His brain had no apparent control over these self-governing parts of his body.

At last the nurse removed both IVs, and she wrapped

each elbow in bright yellow bandages and helped Parker bend and flex his arms several times. He stood up gingerly from his vinyl recliner.

"Can we take you out for dinner?" Linda looked up at him hopefully.

Parker thought for a moment. In truth, he would have accepted a dinner invitation from anyone at this moment, if only to save himself from the terror of being alone, but it was precisely that impulse which gave him pause.

"Thank you," he responded, "but I think I should be alone for a while." When Linda still looked worried, he added, "Plus, I'm about to crash. I would probably fall asleep in my dinner."

"Well, please keep in touch. We want to hear from you, whatever happens."

Parker noted the evenness in Linda's voice: such incredible composure. How many crises and how many tears had it taken to constrict Linda's inflection into such calm tones?

He pulled out his cellphone and entered Linda and Rick's and Courtney's various numbers, while they did the same in their own devices. They then traded hugs all around—first Rick, then Courtney, and finally Linda.

As Linda embraced him, Parker heard her whisper into his ear, "You keep going on, okay? Keep living." When Parker drew away, he expected to see Linda's face tender and concerned, but it had hardened into a tough, determined look.

As Parker walked out, he paused for a moment in the doorway and looked back at the hospital room. Something had left him while he sat in that room—something had flown out from deep inside, never to return, like a winging bird fighting and flapping its way out of a cage. And yet despite what he had left behind in that room, Parker knew he would walk away from it heavier than when he had entered. Despite losing how many millions of cells, how many gallons or pounds or cubic centimeters of blood, he would drop down on his bed tonight far more burdened than before.

Hadley had undergone the same transfiguration, Parker remembered, upon opening the wings of a paper airplane in another room in another place in another time. She had not found any release in those wings. They had only weighed her down and hung about her like the wings of a great albatross. Hadley had not flown to freedom on that flight, and neither would the rivers of blood which had flown into this room lead him to the liberty of the sea.

Into that great cavern inside him where steadfast wings had beat before, an inky tide now rushed. Parker could feel the cascade falling down, down, ever more down, where it settled and slowly sank into an immovable, immutable weight.

## *Chapter Thirteen*

Hadley gazed out into the backyard of her childhood home—the one on Paseo Sierra, off of Comanche. Just like the house itself, this yard was split-level, with flights of rough, flagstone steps separating three different stories. A great expanse of green lawn stretched across the lowest level of the yard. Surely the modern watering restrictions prohibited such a lawn, Hadley thought. Lawns like that had gone extinct in her childhood.

Suddenly, Jason appeared by her side. He looked older, much older, than he had ever been the few times he had visited this backyard. She beckoned and he followed her over to where two Italian cypresses stood at a kissing distance—in the narrow nook between them, she had once played spaceship. Then he ran after her to the overhanging branches of a huge juniper bush, which formed a dark, dry cave where she once believed a witch dwelled.

Hadley again took the lead as they climbed the flagstone stair to the uppermost level of the yard. Once she reached the top, she turned to see Jason ascend the final steps. Jason had just planted his foot on the highest one when the staircase began crumbling from underneath him. Hadley grabbed his outstretched hand and pulled him up as a cloud of dust rose from the collapsing rock. No matter, Hadley thought, as she guided Jason over to inspect cherry and apple trees. Then they looked over the mid-level of yard, where the white peach tree labored heavy with fruit. She felt Jason approach behind her.

He molded his chest gently to conform to her back, enveloping her with his body like a sleeping bag as she gazed at the summer fruit. Her hand fell to her side and grasped the air until it found Jason's. She squeezed his hand and they stood there, body-in-body.

Then, suddenly, Hadley and Jason sat in the backseat of a car with several other occupants, Jason pressed up against the window and Hadley scrunched tightly against him. The car jostled and tossed Hadley squarely onto Jason's lap. She twisted around to look at him, half laughing and half worried. But he just grinned and planted a sloppy, slobbery, goofy kiss on her mouth. As she pulled away, she grinned too…

BEEP! BEEP! BEEP!

The screeching alarm clock tore Hadley violently from her dream. For a second she thrashed frantically in her sheets, unsure of where she was or why such a violent sound would invade the sanctity of where she had been.

In a split second, she remembered: this was waking up. This was the part of the day she dreaded most. From the very moment the fascist alarm clock rang, she began yearning for the night and for the opportunity to sleep, and sleep perchance to dream. If that damned despotic timer did not ring, who knows how long she would rest there every morning. Some dawns she felt she could lay there forever. Sometimes she just wanted to press the snooze button and get a few extra years or so of slumber.

But she dutifully pressed the off button and swung her legs off the bed. There she sat for maybe a minute, maybe a century—who knew—and willed herself to stand. For the past two weeks—since New York—she seemed afflicted by a very mild paralysis. Movement no longer came naturally; she had to consciously will her body to move, even had to remind herself to breathe in and out. She had clocked her time from the subway to her office at the university, and even though the timer in her smartphone logged no more seconds than they ever had, she could have sworn she fell asleep for a split second every time she blinked.

Hadley pressed her feet into the floor and her fists into the bed. She stood slowly. She shook her arms out. The process of standing felt slightly easier this morning than it had yesterday. The first few mornings after her return from New York, she had been like a stroke victim slowly relearning how to walk, each day making slight progress as the movements etched themselves a little more deeply into her brain. Perhaps one day, she thought, she would be able to perform this routine unconsciously.

Hadley stood still for a moment and tested her balance, which had been less than steady during the past fortnight. The seismic shock she had endured had cracked open a kind of fault line within her. Every thought and every feeling tumbled down an Escher-esque series of ledges and ridges, ending up at the top of the slide to again fall down, helter skelter, to the bottom of a crevasse of numbness.

Showering, conversely, was actually easy, despite the slippery surface of the stall. She could lean into the stream of water and let it envelope her. Somehow, it reminded her of making love. She lingered in the shower, relishing the touch against her skin. The creamy fingertips of the water were the only ones which caressed her these days.

The last human hands which had whispered over her skin had belonged to Jason. After those hands had fallen way, Hadley had gone from Central Park to the hotel to the airport and was back at her overflowing University desk the very next morning. It had taken Parker three more days come back—a fact she ascertained by the magical disappearance of all of his summer clothes and shoes that Thursday. Parker had left nothing for her except next month's rent check on the mail table.

The rent check presented her with quite an interpretive dilemma. Even with all her psychological training, she could not make heads or tails of the meaning of it. Perhaps a signal that he still cared about her welfare, perhaps just concern that he not lose such a hard-to-get apartment, or perhaps a humiliating, insulting reference to her powers of self-sufficiency.

Hadley had not used the check, though. She had paid the rent out of her own account, the one filled her with meager graduate stipend. But just as she could not read the significance of Parker's gesture, Hadley could not settle on the implications of her own actions. Maybe she intended to signify her independence or maybe she wanted to show Parker that she no more wanted to be a relationship freeloader than a rent freeloader.

She had kept the little slip of paper, though, and sometimes she studied it for minutes at a time, as if it was an essay question on an art criticism examination. And indeed, Hadley briefly thought about using it as a topic for one of the discussion groups she supervised. If she could not solve the meaning of the check, perhaps ten undergraduates could.

The next question might have been too advanced for the undergraduates, though. It was more of a graduate-level question whether Parker's rent check meant he had made a stem-cell donation to his biological brother or not.

She had other means to find out, of course, but those means presented highly dangerous risks. She could wade into the black waters of social media—Jason's page set up on the transplant foundation's website, or perhaps his sister had a profile somewhere—but even in Hadley's fragile state she understood she would do better wading into a pool of heroin, so potent were the addictive effects of an unmediated internet.

Jason, therefore, existed for Hadley in a state similar to that cat of Schrodinger's splashed all over T-shirts in the university bookstore: simultaneously alive and dead, and only waiting for her to open up the box. This conceptualization proved very useful, because as long as Jason remained both alive and dead, Hadley did not have to decide which way she wanted him.

After her shower, Hadley plodded along back to the bedroom to try to dry off. The summer humidity had arrived early, and the old apartment's breakers could only handle the surge of air conditioning for a few hours each afternoon. She scrubbed and scrubbed at her skin with her towel to rub off all the remaining moisture, but a film still clung to the fine hairs on her arm and burrowed into the microscopic canyons along her legs. Even as she toweled the shower water from her hair, sweat quickly replaced it.

The irremovable stain of the almost tropical heat left her longing for the baking mountains of New Mexico. There, the mercury would bubble up to nintey degrees in the afternoons, but the night's darkness would bring a precious cool, and the hour of the dawn would still hold a chill before the afternoon sun rose again.

Hadley did not look in the mirror as she pulled back her hair. The mirror which usually hung above her shelf in the bedroom had come down a few days after she got back from New York. Hadley had caught herself staring at her own reflection for minutes a time, yet coming to no revelations, so she stowed it in the oven, which given this heat she would not be turning on for several months.

Next, she trudged along the hallway to her desk and picked up her phone. She had a new text message. She swiped across the screen.

*Still alive*. From Jason Snyder.

Hadley dropped the phone and leapt backwards from it as reflexively as she would have jumped away from the rattle of a snake in the desert. The phone thumped onto the carpet and came to rest with the screen facing up. It still displayed Jason's message of being alive. Hadley collapsed on the couch and took great gulping breaths to slow down the drum solo of her heart.

After a few minutes she reached down for the phone and held it in her hands. The metal and plastic of the device glowed warmly against her skin, as if Jason's text message of living carried with it some breath of life itself.

Hadley felt herself waking. The semi-sleep of the past two weeks abruptly lifted as swiftly as a gust of wind can blow a cloud from the sun. She looked down at the coffee table standing in front of the couch, and the edges of it came into sharp relief. The rest of the room, too, transformed from an Impressionist painting, with its bleeding lines and seeping colors, into the sharp image of a digital photograph. Hadley's ears also popped, like the popping one's ears do in an airplane descending back down to earth; through the lessening sounds of static she again heard the screech of buses down on the street below and the ticking of the watch on her wrist.

And then she waited. Except her hands moved constantly, turning the phone over and over, tapping the protective casing on the back, running her fingertips over the power port. She pushed the on button, only to pause for the ten seconds it took for the screen to go blank once more. She did this several times, over and over.

Hadley had never smoked a cigarette in her life, but she had observed some sessions with a therapist who specialized in breaking nicotine addictions. Some of the patients exhibited compulsive touching habits with their cigarette packets—the constant stroke on the box, the opening and closing, the tamping down of the tobacco with the heel of their hands. The therapist told her some of the patients even fetishized the particular sensation of pulling the little red tab and freeing the pack from its plastic sleeve. The addiction lurked not only in the lungs or the brain, but also in the fingers. That therapist was investigating manual surrogates as a psychological aid in quitting—replacing the little cigarette package with an innocuous object.

Hadley had no therapist to grab her phone away and replace it with a tennis ball. No priest or confessor and no hand of God appeared out of the sky to snatch her phone away from her. And so her thumbs flew across the touchscreen as she typed, *Are you asking me or telling me?* She hesitated for a moment over the send button, but with a rush no less satisfying than a flood of sweet nicotine, she tapped the inviting green button.

And then, all pretense of self-control gone, Hadley went to her laptop, searched Jason's name, and clicked on the blog on the transplant charity website. A quick scanning of the gushiness and the exclamation points told her Jason himself did not maintain the website; apparently his sister Courtney acted as author. No pictures of sick Jason, though. She scrolled through and then did the computer-mouse-equivalent of a double-take.

Courtney had evidently talked Parker into having his picture taken. Parker lay prone on some weird chair-thing with both arms bandaged and immobile. He smiled grimly into the camera. Courtney had accompanied the picture with a few paragraphs, but Hadley skipped over the blurb as her eyes shot to one of the comments on the post.

Someone named Katie Plaza had written, "So glad to hear Jason found a donor! Amazing to find out it's a brother!!!"

Even before Hadley had cross-checked the name through social media and search engines, she knew who Katie Plaza was. Eighth-grade Katie. Jason-kissing Katie. Paper airplane Katie.

The comedown came just as quickly as the high only seconds before. This blow was quick but shallow, like a sledgehammer hit in the cartoons—the one which left small birds winging around the head of the victim.

A short burst of sirens sang from the phone again—the notification for another delivered text message. Hadley now cautiously approached it, extending one tentative finger to make sure the phone would not burst into flames.

*Asking,* Jason's text said. *I've been thinking about you.*

Warm, buoyant air rushed from Hadley's heart into her head. She could feel the tops of her shoulders rising, and the internal breeze puffed out her cheeks into a broad smile. Her rapidly inflating and swelling heart straightened her back and deepened the breaths she drew into her lungs.

No. Not this again. Anything but this, Hadley thought, as she recognized the unmistakable symptoms of hope.

# *Chapter Fourteen*

Hadley's elbows rested on the two spaces of the desk not covered in scattered papers and textbooks and thick binders. She was not doing what she should have been doing—formatting citations in her dissertation draft. Instead, as she often did these days, she held her cellphone in her hands and scrolled up and down through the two months' worth of text messages between Jason and her. She had transcribed them into a computer document, of course, keeping a back-up log in case her phone experienced an unannounced catastrophic failure.

Hadley was undoubtedly dedicated to her job and her studies, but even the most studious of her colleagues would admit that concentrating on one's dissertation would become difficult if one's dreams suddenly came true.

Over the past three months, they had come in every one or two days, preceded each time by the siren wail she had long ago chosen for her text message notifications. For the first few weeks, she would wait several minutes before even sliding her fingertip over the touchscreen to open the message. Pricks of wariness still slithered up her spine every time she heard that siren sound. She knew what could lay beyond that wail. Each was a perfect ambush, a beautiful song concealing a maze of rocks upon which she could be dashed and flayed and wrecked.

Sometimes she held out five minutes, sometimes as long

as ten, but always, inevitably, she lightly brushed her finger against the screen to unlock Jason's words. The motion felt as significant and satisfying as the uncorking of a long-bottled message which had reached her against all odds and after years of buffeting by the waves of an indifferent sea.

And yet, for the first few weeks, they merely said "hello." Not literally "hello"—Jason would never let himself slip into such complacency. He said "hello" in German, Swahili, Portuguese, and even one time in something Hadley was pretty sure was Klingon. He phonetically spelled out greetings in Arabic and Chinese and Zulu.

Hadley would then stare at the exotic salutations while she underwent a crisis of conscience. The texts came in every other day or so, and she performed the same soul-searching soliloquy every time. To answer or not to answer.

And every day, the progress of her logic stopped short at one particular barrier: she had not yet figured out how to *not* answer. It was not really a question if she *should* answer or not; it came down to whether she could discover some method of stopping herself from doing it.

Hadley considered each mechanism on the list and tossed aside each one. She could not just toss the phone out the window; she needed it, obviously, to get work email and calls from her mother and even the occasional telemarketing call asking about her cable service. And she definitely could not change her phone number. She had given out that number to hundreds of students and put it on thousands of resumes and conference papers. Someday those students might need her and those university administrators might want to hire her. No, she definitely could not change the number. And for that very same reason, she could not turn her phone off for prolonged periods of time. Her office mate was spending the summer doing fieldwork with migrant farmworkers, so Hadley could not rely on him to police her texting. And it was unfeasible to ask one of her next-door neighbors to come in and check on her every couple of hours.

Beyond the practical considerations which kept Hadley tied to her phone, she also recognized a certain duty. Jason, after all, had chosen to dispatch these greetings to her out of his darkness and out of his doubt. He must have some reason to shout out these S.O.S-es to her.

Their frequency and faithfulness also reassured her daily of the righteousness of her response. If the first text message of life had kindled hope within her, then each day's "hello" had stoked the flame into a roaring fire. It had spread un-contained through the dry underbrush of her thirsty heart. Even when clouds gathered on the horizon—when the forty-seventh or forty-eighth hour of silence from Jason approached—the phone would emit its siren signal, and the fire would burn hot again.

And so, Hadley answered. She wrote back greetings in French, in Spanish, in Elvish. She tried to stump him with Navajo and Serbo-Croatian. And after each one, she added, *Still alive.*

Then one day in mid-July, Jason upped the ante. His text that day said, *Thinking of that time your parents got us tickets to see Itzhak Perlman's dress rehearsal with the symphony. Remember how he dropped his bow?*

Of course she remembered. After that text message, she sat at her desk for half an hour, remembering. Sixth grade, special permission to leave school for the afternoon, a handful of other kids from orchestra, and both Hadley and Jason's fathers riding up in the captain's chairs of Jason's family's minivan. Perlman so enthusiastic he lost control of his bow.

These perfect little pockets of memory arrived every other day, ranging from vague scenes of childhood to detailed recollections of adolescence. These texts gave Hadley a two-fold pleasure. The first part was the pleasure of being remembered.

The second part was the pleasure of remembering. Sometimes the pangs of joy were even so acute they hurt, like the way a particularly intense orgasm straddles the boundary between pleasure and pain.

After Jason had recalled Perlman losing his bow, Hadley lost any pretense of resistance. She no longer fumbled against her better judgment; after the siren signal from her phone, she immediately unlocked the message, knowing as she did so that finally, *finally*, she may have unlocked him.

This very morning, Jason had told her, *Suddenly recalled that time I borrowed a book from you and returned it about nine months later. I biked to your house on Memorial Day.*

Hadley stared onto the campus quad filled with orienteering freshman, as she recalled that day. She had worn a green-striped t-shirt and had been watching some random television when the knock at the door came. She had pulled the door open to reveal Jason on his bicycle. He thrust the book into her hands, nodded his helmeted head a few times, and rushed back off through the courtyard.

Hadley's landline rang twice before she even heard it through the jumble of freshman doing icebreakers on the lawn below and the whirring projector inside her own brain.

She gawked at the phone through two more rings. It had the actual phone handle, the base with the dial pad, a real-life string connecting the two, and an honest-to-god phone cord disappearing into a jack in the wall. Hadley normally received about three calls to this phone per semester. Most people just used cell numbers these days, but the department chair still demanded some connection to the twentieth century.

Hadley picked up on the fourth ring. "This is Hadley," she spoke into the strangely gigantic mouthpiece.

"Hadley Keane? Like from Albuquerque?" A vaguely familiar voice crackled on the other end of the line.

"Yes. Who is this?"

"It's Katie. You know, Katie West. Well, now it's Katie Plaza. I'm calling about Jason."

"Fuck," Hadley breathed into the phone. Then, suddenly realizing her under-the-breath profanity might have been audible on the other end of the line, she stuttered, "I, uh, sorry…Katie?" She tried to buy some time with, "Like from Franklin Middle School?"

"Yeah. I'm living up in Idaho now…" Hadley now recognized the voice and immediately recalled an image of Katie's face, plain and round and surrounded by bushy brown hair.

Katie went on, "But I stumbled on Jason's transplant site, and then I learned…"

As Katie paused over the phone line, Hadley could see Katie's thirteen-year-old face squeamishly scrunched up, her mouth twisting with a secret she was debating whether or not tell. And Hadley instinctively knew what was troubling the girl on the other end of the line.

Hadley finished the sentence for Katie, "And you learned who the donor was for the transplant. And you learned it was Jason's biological brother Parker. And you learned Parker is my husband."

Katie let out a sigh of relief over the phone. "Yes. Courtney told me. You know…Jason's sister." Again her voice faltered, as if she was unsure whether Hadley knew that Jason's sister's name was Courtney.

Hadley did not respond. Still gripping the phone against her ear, she rapidly shuffled through all the possible reasons why Katie might call her. A second-hand welfare check by Jason's family? Were they too nervous to call her themselves? An inside piece of information Jason had not shared with her? Calling to browbeat Hadley over her questionable life choices?

Hadley heard Katie breathing, but she still did not say anything. Katie had called her, after all. She had no obligation to talk.

"Hadley?" Katie asked at last.

"Yes, I'm here." Hadley grunted into the phone.

"Well, I'm calling because I thought you might…see, Jason hasn't been answering me. I've emailed him, called him, texted him. Courtney gave me his number and email. And I've tried several times, and he's never answered or written back."

"Really." Hadley's voice did not rise on the second syllable, because it was not a question. It was a gloat, a delicious smirk of triumph. If only Katie could see Hadley's face right now, see the swaggering angle of her eyebrows and her self-satisfied smile. And if only Hadley could ostentatiously pull out her phone and show Katie the entire set of text messages from Jason.

At last, Hadley was the chosen one.

Katie rambled on, "I just wanted to talk to him, you know. Let him know I've been praying for him. We all have, actually, the kids have too. I have three kids now…And I just wondered if you had seen him or talked to him at all."

Hadley cut her off, "Yes, I saw him in New York. Yes, I talked to him in New York. Quite extensively. And yes, I've been in contact with him since the transplant."

Hadley heard Katie draw breath, but she barreled on before Katie could respond. "But no, I cannot tell him you called me. I cannot tell him to call you. I cannot ask him to call you. I cannot let you—" Hadley here did not say what she really wanted to, which was "interfere with my life again," but instead she said, "disturb Jason's peace right now. If he's not responding to you, that is his choice and he has some kind of reason for it. I will not disturb his choice."

Katie was silent for several seconds. Finally, she replied,

"Oh, okay then. But the last time I talked to Courtney, last week, Courtney said Jason hadn't been doing well the last few days. He was having some skin irritation and maybe even liver problems, and I just really wanted to talk to him, and if you told him"

Hadley frowned at the news, but she nevertheless cut off Katie once again, "I'm sorry, Katie. I really can't." She bit extra hard into the last "t" to emphasize the firmness and finality of her decision.

Katie responded meekly, "I…understand. But hey, how crazy is it that you married his brother. I can't even think of the odds of that. Courtney said you guys met in Philadelphia. It sounds like it was meant to be or something. How is Parker doing now?"

Hadley swallowed in pain as tears came to her eyes. "Look, Katie, I have a class…a student…a meeting, right now. I have to go. I'll call you later."

As Hadley's hand dropped and the receiver fell away from her ear, Hadley could still hear Katie over the line. "Wait, but you don't have my number! Wait a second, I'll give it to you!"

Hadley gently placed the receiver back into its cradle.

## *Chapter Fifteen*

The pile of papers stacked next to Parker's computer screen shook from the vibration of the phone on top of it. He glanced away from his CAD drawing and toward the phone. It was her number.

He quickly slid his hand across the screen and held the phone to his ear. "Wait just a second." Then he swiveled out of his chair and approached the "window" between his office and the outer reception area. He avoided the eyes of his administrative assistant, Deborah, as he closed the window's blinds.

In the suspicious eyes and skeptical brows of Deborah, Parker saw the obvious conclusion for what had kept him closing his blinds every time his cell phone rang over the past few months: an affair. The blinds, of course, and how his wife had not come to eat lunch with him in over three months. However, he had not removed the pictures of her from his desk and had not asked HR to take his wife off his insurance. So it had to be an affair.

That seemed to be the gossip of the entire office as well. Indeed, several times after he reopened the blinds on his window, he had seen his boss try to compose himself and find a plausible reason why he should be hovering at Deborah's desk. Still, Parker had not failed to complete any assignments, nor had he begun charging romantic candlelit dinners on the company credit card, and so surreptitious cell phone conversations would go unremarked for a little while longer.

In truth, however, Parker was cheating. At least, that was how he felt about it. It was why he had never added her name as one of his contacts and why he closed the blinds every time she called. Something illicit, some feeling that they should not have grown so close, compelled his secrecy. It also compelled him to never answer when she happened to call when he was out at his parents' house.

Still, he continued their regular conversations, because much stronger than the slight queasiness was his overwhelming need to break. He could not shatter in front of his parents the way he yearned to do; somehow he could not reveal his most intimate breaking points to the people who had known him his entire life. It would embarrass and shame their endless love and support to fall apart before their feet. An almost chivalric desire to protect them from his desolation perked up his smile and pitched his lilting summer tone. He was their son, after all, and had always stood proud and strong. He would not turn from that role now.

So he lied. He told them Hadley had decided to spend the summer in New Mexico working on her dissertation and waiting at the bed of her dying grandfather. He lied and said the transplant had gone off without a hitch. He lied and said his biological brother would visit as soon as he was well.

But *she*—she offered the ideal combination of perfect strangeness and haunting intimacy. She knew him and yet she did not. He could dissemble before her without any worry of disappointment and could unmask his weakness without fear of rebuke. And of course, she knew all the characters of this strange scene and could discuss their movements with a facility his parents could never hope to do. Sometimes he even called her deep in the evening, just before he turned in for another restless night, to have someone to say "goodnight" to. And she would simply say "goodnight" in return and then lightly, lovingly, hang up the phone.

Parker settled himself back into his chair, took a deep breath, and returned the phone to his ear. "Yes, I'm here."

"He left. No one knows where he is. He just left the hospital this morning." The voice on the other end was frantic and shaky. He had never heard her like this.

"Whoa, whoa, whoa, Linda, calm down. Just take a deep breath and calm down."

Parker heard Linda inhale and exhale several times before she spoke again, "I checked on him last night, you know, to see if his liver function had improved at all. And then this morning, the hospital called to say he had just left. No one knows where he is. One of the nurses said he asked her to take out his IV for one night."

"Let's just think through this, Linda. I'm sure there's an explanation. Where would he have gone?"

After a few seconds, Linda's voice returned, level now. "I checked his apartment, his office, we called his old girlfriend. No one had seen him or heard from him. And the credit card company won't give us his records until he's officially been missing for forty-eight hours."

"But what happened in the last few days that would have made him disappear? Last time I talked to you nothing had really changed. His symptoms hadn't gotten any worse."

"I last talked to you four days ago, right?" Parker nodded, even though Linda could not see him over the phone. "Well, two days ago a post-transplant specialist came down and said that it was definitely the early signs of graft-versus-host disease, but he couldn't tell right away whether it would be acute or chronic GVH."

"What's the difference? And what the hell is graft versus

host disease?"

"It's basically rejection." Linda paused. "The new donor cells reject the body they've been put in."

Parker noted how carefully Linda had phrased it, but even her words could not hide the real import of what she said. "You mean my cells. My cells are rejecting him."

"God, when you put it like that…"

"I'm sorry," Parker breathed. "Is there—" He paused before he finished his question, suddenly aware that he did not know what he wanted the answer to be. "Is there a treatment?"

"Yes, there's lots of treatments. It's usually very treatable."

"Oh," Parker responded. He could not tell whether he felt relief or fresh terror at Linda's answer.

"But yesterday he was already pretty sick. He broke out in a rash and his liver function is down, and the nurse told me he had diarrhea. He should not be out on his own in the middle of New York City. His immune system is still depressed, and the GVH makes him even more susceptible…" She ran out of breath.

"Parker," Linda began again, "I thought that Jason might…might try to contact Hadley, and I thought you could…I know it's a long shot, but we have to try everything."

Parker gripped the handle of his ergonomic office chair with the hand not holding the phone. Then he put his palm up to his cheek, which had flushed red hot with fear.

"You want me to…Hadley…you know I haven't…in months…I can't…not yet…"

The phone slipped from Parker's grasp as he reached for the trash can and dry heaved into it. He heard Linda's voice still emitting from the phone, "Parker, I can't believe I'm asking you to do this, but I'm frantic. I'm at the end of my rope and I don't know what to do anymore."

"Okay, Linda. I'll go over tonight. But if you find Jason,

let me know right away, because I don't want to have to go…and it be for nothing."

"Good. I'm going to keep looking and calling. Call me if you hear anything."

Parker nodded.

"Parker, are you there? Will you call me?"

"Of course I will."

"Good." Again Linda paused. "Hey Parker? I love you."

Parker clenched his eyes shut as he said, "I love you too." He ended the call and sat for several minutes with his head between his knees, fighting back tears so he could at least walk through the office to the elevator with a modicum of dignity.

At last Parker stood up and walked back to his office "window." He twiddled the knob that controlled the slant of the shades, and then he pulled them up entirely.

What he saw next made his stomach heave again. In the small reception area, a man sat on a couch. He had an extremely short layer of brownish-grayish hair and glasses. Though jeans and a red fleece covered him from the neck down and all the way to his wrists, Parker could see the man was clearly underweight. Blue eyes stared at him through glasses and above sunken cheeks.

It was Jason.

## *Chapter Sixteen*

Parker scanned the office layout like a cornered spy trying to determine the safest egress. Jason stood between him and both the elevator and the stairs. Even a path to the service stairs would take him past Jason. Of course, he did have fifty pounds on Jason, and probably could move much more quickly and easily. He could do it if he ran.

"Goddammit," Parker said aloud. He was actually plotting how to do a James Bond-style escape from his office… as if his own brother was a sniper. Good lord, what would his boss have to say about it tomorrow?

And so Parker opened the door to his office and then retreated back to the guarded position behind his desk. He waited with his eyes closed and fingertips pressed together. About a minute later, he heard the door click shut and a body sink into one of the chairs on the other side of his desk.

Parker opened his eyes.

"You look like shit," Parker said. Indeed, up close Jason's skin had an eerily green tinge beneath the ghostly white veneer. The bones of his hands and wrist, which showed below the rolled up sleeves of his sweatshirt, jutted out like those of a prisoner of war.

But still, Jason laughed. "Thanks. It's good to see you too." He smiled, but the effect was more frightening than reassuring, since his gums had receded from his teeth.

"Shouldn't you be wearing a mask or something?" Parker asked.

"Probably," Jason sighed. "But I didn't want to scare your office mates. Of course, I probably already did scare them quite a bit, walking in here like the zombie apocalypse version of you."

Parker did not say anything in reply, but picked up his cell phone. He was swiping his way to the last call when Jason spoke up again.

"Please don't. Can we just talk a little before you tattle on me to our mother? I thought big brothers were supposed to do that."

Parker looked up sharply. Jason was smirking; the left side of his mouth had risen lopsided over the right side, his eyebrows playfully arched. If not for the fact that Jason was about forty pounds underweight, Parker would have felt he was looking in a rather blurry mirror.

Curiosity got the better of him. "How did you know I would have called Linda? And how did you know she had called me?"

Jason shrugged. "I know my mother well enough that I knew she would call everyone when I left this morning. And I know that her everyone includes you. I know she's been talking to you all summer."

Parker flushed, suddenly ashamed that he had so foolishly believed his conversations with Linda to be privileged. Here he was, yet again, on the outside and out of the loop, clueless to information everybody else seemed to know.

"And from there, I know you are not living with Hadley right now. Actually, I know you haven't spoken to Hadley since New York."

The mention of her name had an instantaneous effect. "Why are you here?" Parker shouted.

Although Jason had barely enough bulk left to sink into his chair, he managed to sink just a little bit further in. He closed his eyes for a few seconds, apparently marshaling the energy he needed to summon an answer.

Jason opened his eyes. "Because the questions I need to ask you are really not appropriate for a phone call. They really need to be discussed face to face."

"For my birthday I'd really like a new set of golf clubs, thanks very much," Parker spat sarcastically.

Jason just sat calmly. "Actually, my first question was going to be, do you still love Hadley?"

Parker leaped from his chair and loomed forward across his desk. "What the fuck? Where the hell do you get off asking me that?"

Jason did not retreat, but rather he too leaned forward, elbows on knees, hands in a fist wedged against his forehead, as if using that fist to absorb any anger which would otherwise leak out of his brow.

"Parker, please spare me your indignation. I don't have much time." Jason lowered his hands. His blue eyes looked up into the blue eyes of his brother.

Parker met Jason's gaze. A shiver ran down his back which had nothing to do with the central air cooling. Jason did not look scared or angry or even pleading. He looked…at peace —at peace with his life and with his death. Jason's blue eyes were those of an old man resigned to fate, who has already placed his destiny into the hands of others, and has placed it there willingly. He stared out at the world with the particular impatience of age; waiting so longingly for an end which cannot be hastened and frustrated with the youth which will not listen.

Parker grasped in the air behind him until he caught the arm of his chair. He gingerly sat down in it, never unlocking his eyes from Jason's.

"As you may have heard, I have been diagnosed with graft-versus-host disease. My new immune system—" here Jason doffed his head toward Parker—"has decided that it does not particularly like the accommodations of my body. Therefore, it is asking for its money back."

Jason swallowed oddly, as if trying to stuff a sob deep down into his throat.

Parker had known Jason only very, very briefly, and yet he understood—he knew instinctively—that Jason let such an obvious sign of human emotion pass from his body only extremely rarely. Parker had never met someone who so obviously and so strenuously guarded the vaults of his heart.

"And I therefore have to decide whether I want to treat the graft-versus-host. Or whether I just want to let it take its course and…you know."

Now it was Parker's turn to lean in to the leathered padding of his chair. He let the ergonomic foam lining absorb the shock which Jason's words had sent through him. The words had ripped through his chest like a bullet, and Parker drew back in physical pain.

Parker felt his lips move with the automatic logic that was his shelter in every storm. "I would assume most people would choose to get the treatment."

Jason nodded calmly. Calmly like he was agreeing to most people choosing to get the lobster bisque. "Yes, most people get the treatment."

"But you're not most people."

As Parker processed the thought and let it fall from his lips, he found the answer—or at least half an answer—to one of the questions he had tossed and turned over for the last three months: what did Hadley see in Jason? What had captured her so long and so deeply?

"No, I'm not." Jason smiled again, although this time

almost ruefully, like he wished for a moment that he could be most people.

"There are a lot of factors that go into this decision," Jason went on. "My parents, of course. And Courtney my sister. But there's also Hadley." Jason rubbed his palms together a few times and then looked down into them, perhaps searching for a life line. "You see, I've thought a lot about Hadley this summer. I've been in contact with her, you know." He looked up at Parker.

Parker, though, sat silent. He was not a confessor and would not give sanction to what Jason obviously believed were impure thoughts.

Jason nevertheless went on. Perhaps he understood that he would get no absolution from Parker. "I've gone over so many memories of her. I've remembered so much. Hours and hours I just lay in my bed in that goddamn hospital, just remembering. And I don't know what it was, maybe the morphine or the specter of imminent death, but it made me realize a few things I should have realized a long time ago. She's extraordinary, you know. She gave…so much to me."

Jason again gazed up into the eyes which so imperfectly mirrored his own. "And I don't deserve her. I never did."

His tone had remained calm, his voice steady. He evidently had come to this conclusion after much careful study. He had made peace with it, just as he had made peace with his own life and his own death. It seemed almost a law of the universe: mass is conserved, light is both particle and wave, and Jason never deserved Hadley.

And indeed, Jason's conversation turned to relativity. "Time's such a bizarre thing. In three months of sitting on my ass in the hospital I relived what it had taken Hadley and I almost twenty years to live. The past looked a lot different from up in the nosebleed section of the future."

Parker angled back on the spring of his chair. He clasped

his fingers behind his head. He had all the time in the world, he tried to convey to Jason. This was just a leisurely conversation and he had no urgent need to come to the heart of the matter.

"I'm really happy that you've had some revelations, Jason, but what does this have to do with me? I'm sure with your newfound sensitivity you can understand that I'm feeling a bit selfish at this point. I've got to look out for myself right now."

Jason smirked, pointed his right index finger at Parker, and shook it several times. "Selfish. That's exactly what I'm talking about. See, I have two options right now. I can do an absolutely selfish thing and walk out of this office, go back to New York, and start a course of high-dose corticosteroids. Or I can walk out of this office and do an incredibly stupid, incredibly selfless thing. And the only thing standing between me and that door—" he gestured with his thumb backward over his shoulder at Parker's closed office door, "is not knowing whether you still love Hadley."

Parker's hands fell from his head. "Jesus," he breathed.

"It's times like this when I wished I believed in Jesus," Jason cracked. "So do you? Love her?"

Jason's eyes bore into the side of Parker's head; Parker had swiveled his chair to look out over the great mountain range of downtown, each peak constructed of steel and glass and light. He recalled one part of Hadley and Jason's story—where Hadley purposefully gave the wrong answer to a geography bee question because she wanted Jason to have the honor of giving the right answer. Hadley believed a wrong answer would produce the right result, but here Parker knew neither the right answer nor the most desirable result.

Parker did not have to look into Jason's eyes to know that they would pass no judgment on the answer. There was no implied "should" in Jason's question, no suggestion of the response he *should* give. It was unlike so many questions which so dogmatically demanded the answer which should be given. "Do you take this woman?" Of course I do. "Do you want a hit of this?" No, just say no. "Do you want cheese on that?" Yes, why do you even have to ask?

For the first time in his life, Parker felt the absolute freedom of absolute honesty. And he could not deal with it.

"I don't know."

Jason jumped in immediately, with no evidence of disappointment or annoyance at Parker's indecision. "Well, let me ask it to you this way. Imagine your future five years, ten years, fifty years down the line. Imagine it right now. Is Hadley there? Can you imagine your life without her?"

Parker obediently closed his eyes. At this point he would take direction from anyone or anything, even the devil himself, if only to give up the power and obligation of determination.

Birthdays. A puppy bounding after a tennis ball in a backyard and straight back into Hadley's arms. A backyard. A backyard to a house. A house to which Hadley had a key and opened the door and sang out, "I'm home." Hadley studying so intently—the way she always did—the ceiling of the Sistine Chapel on the trip to Italy they had been planning for next spring. Burying his parents, as he knew he one day must, but having Hadley's hand next to him to squeeze. A party celebrating his retirement; a party celebrating her dissertation. Discussing whether or not to start a family. A family. A family portrait. With Hadley.

"She's there. And no, I cannot imagine anything without her." Parker turned back around to face Jason.

The way Jason smiled instantly reminded Parker of Linda —of the way she had almost gleefully grinned at him back in the museum, in New York. He had been blubbering, pondering profound questions about his future and whether to save Jason's life. And Linda had come back at him with a wide-mouthed beam. And here he was with Jason, discussing life and death and love, and Jason just sat there wearing his best cocky smirk. Laughing at the world. That was Jason.

"Good," Jason said. "Now, one more question. Can you forgive her?"

This question had crossed Parker's mind often over the last three months, but he could never come to a decision, because first he had to figure out the answer to a predicate question—the first logical step implicit in the issue. He approached it like an engineering project: before devising a solution, one had to first define the problem and sketch out the exact parameters of that problem. Normally, of course, he would discuss these matters with colleagues, but this one of course required absolute secrecy. Now, with the chance to finally get a second opinion, he tossed the question back to Jason.

"Forgive her for what?"

Jason cocked his head and frowned; he had not expected this volley. After a few seconds, he began, "For her past. For loving me. For putting all of that energy into me. And for not telling you about it, obviously."

Jason's mouth remained open and his brow remained tightened. He leaned forward once more, looking more at a spot above Parker's shoulder than at Parker himself.

"But it's more than that. Can you forgive her for the future? Can you forgive knowing that she will still love me, even if I'm…when I'm…gone?"

Jason's last syllable seemed to echo in Parker's office. Gone, gone, gone. Growing fainter and fainter to the point where it was—gone.

Parker reached out one hand into the space above his desk, trying to grasp this enigmatic, inscrutable quality of goneness. It was absence—a sense of nothingness, of a perfect void of space. And yet the goneness also sank straight to his bottom like a dumbbell hurled into a swimming pool. And it hurt; the goneness hurt like the inadequacies of hunger.

And then the goneness took form. It swirled into a shape and a specific set of circumstances: Jason was proposing to die and leave Hadley to Parker. To live together again. To go on. And this course of action all depended on whether Parker could forgive a fraudulent past and a compromised future.

Parker swiveled again toward the window. The question had once again grown entirely too large; he had to once more break it down to basic principles. In his debate over whether or not he could forgive Hadley, he had compiled a list of the crimes she committed against him. Chief among those was concealment and secrecy, of course. But Jason's answer pointed to the motive at the heart of each of Hadley's wrongdoings.

How could he consider love a crime? Yes, Hadley had been foolish, even blind; she had loved Jason so recklessly, so unwisely. She had dived headlong into an ants' nest, unaware of or just unconcerned for the consequences. She never asked how it affected anyone else. She never questioned her feelings. She was just like—

She was just like him.

He had acted much the same way, after all. He had taken her at face value, no questions asked. He never probed why she looked so sad sometimes, never dug into why she seemed so afraid every time they parted. She had told him, though. The very first day they met, she said a sad thing had happened to her.

And that night they first made love—she had told him everything in those few words spoken to the dark. She had once known someone like him. She had waited for him. He could still hear her voice: "he never wanted me." And he had disregarded it, tossed aside her entire life as just one offhand comment from an inexperienced girl.

Parker remembered the other words they said that night.

She had said, "I love you." He had not even paused to imagine how many other times she had said it or wanted to say it. And he had responded, "I love you too," not even contemplating the colossal significance of those little words. He had said them many times—even, he now realized, when they were not deserved.

Parker had grown up with constant promises and exhortations of love. Not only had his own parents professed it many times, but when his mother explained adoption to him, she always said that his biological mother and father loved him enough to let him go. Friends had said it, past girlfriends. Extended family, even his mentor at his first job had said it.

He had grown up privileged; not privileged because of his skin color or chromosomes or birthplace or zip code, but privileged because he had never known the ultimate deprivation which Hadley had known all too well.

He had loved her carelessly. So arrogant he was, that he just assumed she would love him. How entitled to her he had felt. So used to affection, he had never even questioned why she had chosen him.

Parker swallowed his newly realized shame several times. He did not want to face Jason yet, did not want Jason to see the guilt which must be written all over his face. And so he spoke to the window and the greater Chicago metropolitan area: "Yes, I can forgive her. For everything."

Parker wiped the tears from his cheeks, took several deep breaths, set his jaw, and whirled around to look at his brother. "So there you have it. I've answered all your questions. What now?"

Jason sat zen-like in his chair. "Now I go and do that incredibly stupid, incredibly selfless thing. Now, I've asked far too much of you already, but I have two more requests."

Parker just nodded.

"First, also forgive Hadley for what I am about to make her do. Please understand that it is only for her, only my terribly insufficient attempt to make things up to her. I have to try to give her just a few moments of what she always wanted. Of what she always deserved."

"What?" Parker shot up from his chair.

But Jason merely put up a hand, like with just this signal he could magically force Parker back into his seat. "And second, give me a head start. Don't go after her for a couple of hours, okay?" Jason began rising awkwardly from his chair.

Jason held out his hand over the desk. Parker shook it, but his jaw was still dropped as he did so.

"Thank you," Jason said, and walked out of Parker's office.

## *Chapter Seventeen*

Hadley screwed the knob at the end of her bow until it stuck. She gripped it in her fingers and tried to tighten it further, but the summer humidity had swelled all the twisty spots of her instrument. The pegs, too, had become immovable, lodged firmly in their little box with the brightly woven end of the strings curled around them like boa constrictors around tree branches.

Anything she played in the swelter of August would be slightly out of tune, but out of tune would have to be good enough right now. After the surprise phone call from Katie this morning, Hadley had dumped her books into a bag, slapped her out-of-office sign on her door, and heeled it back to the apartment. Geysers of sweat gurgled down her back and thoughts spluttered out of her brain no matter how hard she pressed back against them.

Was he sick? Why was he sick? Why did he not tell her? How many people knew? How serious was it? Was there treatment? Was this normal? What should she do? Should she ask him or pretend not to know? Call Courtney? What if they needed to do the transplant again? What would happen with Parker?

Only one thing would shut off the flow and circumvent the endless piping of her brain, and so she brought out her poor violin from the cool, dark cabinet where it spent its summer days, hiding away from the swelter of high noon. Hadley buried her head beneath the covers of Tchaikovsky, distracting herself with octaves and thirty-second notes and harmonics so that she would not think about Jason.

The violin had given her salvation from silence all summer. Only its gently sloping curves, the still sharp edges of its f-holes, and the cold metal sheaths of its strings could fill up the void which the apartment had become. She returned each evening from the noisy, teeming campus to the silent hole of her home, and then she played herself to exhaustion, until her fingertips split and flaked, until she had a dent in her neck, and until she could go two minutes without thinking of him. Or him.

Hadley was working through a tough passage of arpeggios when the string-crossings began to take on an oddly ringing, shimmery sound. She slowed down, but still the ringing persisted. She finally took the bow off the string. There it came again: a loud jangling sound.

Hadley set her violin down on the couch as quickly as she could and sprinted over to her desk to where her phone sat ringing. She experienced an infinitesimally time-compressed panic attack as she registered the name Jason on the phone's screen, but then answered and put it up to her ear.

"Hello?" Inside Hadley's own head, her voice sounded magnified to the level of a stadium concert, yet outside her own head, she heard only a whisper.

"Hadley? Hadley? Are you there?"

"Yes," she said more loudly. "Yes I'm here."

"Where is here? I need to talk with you and you can't be distracted." Jason's voice on the end of the line carried the quiet urgency of a terrorist in a bad action movie.

"I'm at home. At my apartment. No one else is here." Hadley inched over to the couch as she talked and lowered herself to the edge of it.

"Hadley, listen to me very carefully." Jason again sounded

like he was about to deliver a ransom for an atomic bomb.

Hadley nodded and then hastily added, "I'm listening."

"I'm at the airport right now waiting to get on a plane to Albuquerque. You need to come with me to New Mexico right away. As in, you need to leave as immediately as possible. Just throw some clothes in a bag and buy whatever ticket there is. I'll pay you back."

The gag reflex in Hadley's throat ricocheted violently, but she breathed through the spasm. It was the reaction of sheer shock which sent the taste of bile into her mouth, but after the harsh metallic of the bombshell passed, a sweet, milky aroma washed over her tongue. Its center steamed with beery nuttiness and then wafted into flowery sheets: keen, joyful awe. It swirled up and she breathed in the scent of wonder itself.

"For how long? I mean, I need to tell the university. I have to give them some warning. This isn't like the movies. I can't just up and—"

"There is no time for that, Hadley. I'm serious. I know when I've said that in the past, I have not been serious at all, but this time, I really mean it. I've never been more serious about anything. Just—act like your life is a movie, for god's sake. It is literally now or never, Hadley."

Now sat on Hadley's left shoulder, while Never sat on her right shoulder, arguing like the cartoon angel and devil from old television shows. It was a short argument; Now shouted so rambunctiously that it completely drowned out the doubtful strains of Never.

"Alright. I'm coming. I'm throwing clothes into a bag."

"Good. Text me when you leave your apartment, and then text me when you get to the airport and get a flight. I'll be waiting at the airport in Albuquerque."

"Okay. I'll let you know what flight I get."

"I'll see you soon."

Hadley sat on the couch with the phone still pressed to her ear. She stared intently at a small smudge on the coffee table. It appeared at the end of a very, very long tunnel—as if Hadley looked at it through a kind of interstellar straw. It was… incomprehensible.

But then she felt the twisty folds of her brain rearranging themselves. First, they untangled and unbunched themselves like a cosmic yarn ball and lay stretched out on the floor of the universe. Then the strands began weaving themselves back together again in a new pattern—a new picture. Sumptuous strings spliced and snaked until they had tightened into a sharp, clean, origami-esque sphere.

Now it was all perfectly comprehensible.

She rose from the couch, retrieved her suitcase from the hall closet, carried it to the bedroom, and began throwing clothes into it. She went online and bought a ticket for the first available route that would get her to Albuquerque, then she slid her laptop and a few notebooks into her messenger bag, tossed her phone charger in, and stood the bags against the door to wait. She had just hooked her bow into its slot in her violin case when she heard the front door open.

"Hadley?"

She rushed to the foyer.

Parker stood in the doorway of the apartment, keys still dangling from his hand, staring at the clearly packed and waiting suitcase.

He looked up from the suitcase and at Hadley with wide, dry eyes. "What did he ask you to do?" he demanded hoarsely.

"He asked me to go to New Mexico with him." When the horror on Parker's face did not dissipate, Hadley added, "He didn't ask me to drown puppies." She crossed her arms defensively.

Parker continued to gape. He closed and opened his mouth

several times before he finally forced out, "Hadley, you cannot go. You cannot go. He's…he's…"

"Sick. He's sick." Hadley smirked defiantly and threw up her hands. "And so what? It makes no difference whatsoever. I'm going and you can't stop me."

Parker's voice became louder, faster, more urgent. "Did he tell you how sick he is? Did he tell you what he plans to do?" When Hadley did not respond, he blustered on. "Hadley, you obviously don't know everything. You don't know what he just told me. You don't know how bad it is or what he's going to do —"

"I don't want to know," Hadley screamed. "I don't care anymore about knowing everything. I know the most important thing, which is that Jason just asked me to run away with him. You know how people act in movies? When they just get up and make wildly irrational decision with no worries or cares for practicalities? I want to do that for once in my life. I want to make one decision purely for myself. I want to smash the world down. I want to disappear with him."

Hadley paused for a moment and panted through her nose. "And I don't want to hear how bad it is or what evil plan he has in store. I don't want to hear it. You can't stop me; do you understand? You can't stop me."

Parker maneuvered around the suitcase and grabbed Hadley's arm before she could dart away. He held both of her wrists tight. She responded by smashing her eyes shut.

"I'm trying to help you, Hadley. I'm trying to save you. He is going to hurt you, Hadley. He is just going to hurt you again. Do you remember what you told me the very first day we met? You told me the definition of insanity is doing the same thing over and over and expecting a different result. You're doing the same thing over and over with Jason and you expect a different result. It's insane."

Hadley opened her eyes. She was not crying, but her eyes had a bright sheen, as if they reflected the glare from the armor of the army against which she battled.

"Sometimes people change, Parker. And then the results can change. And I've never been afraid of getting hurt. I'm scared of a hell of a lot of things, but getting hurt never scared me. What does scare me is waking up one day, twenty years from now, and asking myself, 'What if I had gone to Jason?' The 'what if' scares me to death."

Parker dropped Hadley's wrists, but she did not move away.

Hadley moved in closer, her own lips coming close enough to Parker's that, in another time and place, he would have met her mouth for a kiss.

"I know it's hard to understand, but this is not a choice. I don't have a choice here. I have to go. I guess you don't understand because you've never wanted or needed anybody the way I need Jason. You've never felt like there is a hole inside of you. No," Hadley said, now reaching out to stroke Parker's temple, "You were perfectly whole. I haven't felt whole since I was six years old."

Parker had started crying, but Hadley continued. "I remember, that night we were first together, in bed, you said you never contacted your biological parents because you didn't need to, because you never felt like you lacked anything. You never had that hole inside of you. You said you'd never trade in the certainty of your parents' love to go off and chase the mere possibility of love from your biological parents. You said you would never take that risk."

Hadley wrapped her long fingers around Parker's jaw and pulled him close. She kissed him, at first violently, and then tenderly and sadly.

"I'm not like you."

She slung her messenger bag over one shoulder and grabbed the handle of the suitcase. She walked out of the apartment and closed the door softly behind her.

# PART FOUR

## *Chapter Eighteen*

Through the double-planed plastic of the tiny window, Hadley got her first glimpse of the Sandia Mountains as the plane circled down to the Albuquerque Sunport. Hadley smiled at the big, friendly mountains guarding the city. On the west-facing side, the one she now greeted fondly, the foothills started out welcoming, their piñon and cactus-covered ridges sloping softly. Then the mountains' disposition turned nasty, with a precipitous and severe rise through multiple geologic areas. A thick block of pinkish-purple granite acted like a great "Keep Out" sign to those intrepid enough to challenge the summit before finally, the last five hundred vertical feet or so mellowed out again in groves of aspen.

As the early afternoon light hit the mountains directly, the great mass seemed only two-dimensional, like a great paper-doll of a mountain set against the sky. But Hadley knew that if she woke in time for sunrise or waited until sunset, the slanting sunlight would roll slowly over the wild rocks and uncover hidden valleys, twisting canyons, and dark green pockets, including some that, it was still possible, no human foot had touched.

The mountains stood their post at the eastern edge of the city, defending the Burquenos from the onslaught of those oriental barbarians who came up from the flatlands to steal sun and sky. Hadley had always felt a child-like affection and gratitude for those mountains. They protected her of course—they held up the dome of the sky, they prevented it from falling on her, and they held her back from falling off of the eastern edge of the world. But like the best childhood guardians, they also lifted her up; they drew her eye and her imagination far up into the clouds and promised that if she just climbed higher and stretched out her arms further, she could reach the sky.

Out to the west was a different story. The mesa which stretched off to the west belonged to the ancient world of a flat Earth—it just continued on like a perfect plane, untroubled and undisturbed by the curvature of earth or the curvature of space-time. The plugs of seven extinct volcanoes slithered along the western vista like the spine of one of the sea monsters which decorated the edges of antique atlases. From a high enough vantage point in the city, one could watch the sun set over the mesa and disappear into a limitless horizon which stretched, like the sea, forever.

As the plane rattled with the usual turbulence of the updrafts created by the mountains, Hadley imagined the Spanish explorers' first reactions to this dramatic scene. Thirst, of course, but not just literal thirst. As their horses' hooves stepped over the chalky rocks of what would become the Camino Real, they must have looked with thirsty eyes on the Rio Grande Valley. Beckoned by tales of the seven cities of Cibola that had come down to them out of the north, they had already projected onto the dusty, rough earth a magic and majesty. This would be the country of golden cities.

Plenty of blood had soaked the soil of this land. So many larger-than-life legends had occupied the mountains and plains: cowboys and Indians, lawmen and outlaws, revolts and rockets and bombs. And yet it—the sky, the ground, and everything in between—could accommodate more. So much sky there was; so much room for so many gods.

Gazing out on the endless expanses of space on car trips in her childhood, Hadley wondered why anyone would want to conquer these lands. They had few visible resources, and the Native Americans who eked out a society from the hard clay relentlessly resisted the invaders. The Pueblo Revolt even effectively repulsed the Spanish imperial apparatus, driving the conquistadores all the way down to Mexico City and unleashing herds of wild horses into the sympathetic hills.

But still the settlers returned, unable to take the hint of both the natives and the droughts that they were not welcome. Why, a ten-year-old Hadley had wondered, as her car window looked out at arid deserts and jagged peaks, did they keep trying? Were the Spaniards simply stubborn or were they actually stupid?

Now, looking out of her airplane window, she decided they had not been stupid at all. They may have even been genius. In a country of little arable soil and even less water, they had discovered a different kind of precious resource: space—space they could fill with their dreams. They had already filled their home country to the brim with their ambition and faith and cruelty. They had run out of values to defend and wealth to pursue. They simply needed space, space for their lungs to breath and hearts to beat and minds to wander, a space for imagination. It was the Land of Enchantment, after all, a land in which one's dreams might actually come true and materialize in the unclaimed air.

Hadley had interpreted the state's nickname to mean that the land itself enchanted its inhabitants, but perhaps it really worked the other way around. So many dreams had been dreamed here. Seekers of extraterrestrials found proof of their quarries here, countless artists sought inspiration in the motes of dust hanging in the unapologetic sunlight, and scientists conjured explosions out of the barest of atoms. And of course, before all of that, strange shape-shifting demons rambled the desert, visible to only the holiest of the Ancient Ones.

Viewed in this way, the barbarism of the conquerors diminished. They became knights errant to that other Spanish nobleman, Don Quixote de la Mancha, chaser of windmills and dreamer of impossible dreams.

A flight attendant's voice carried over the plane's PA system, "We'd like to welcome you home to Albuquerque or wherever your final destination may be."

This was not a coming home. It was an expedition, an exploration, a discovery.

***

Hadley approached the glass gateway between the secure terminal and the free area beyond. She paused just before making her way through the revolving door; she had seen Jason, recognizable even with his back toward her. Even though he had lost weight, even though the bare scruff of his hair was now gray, and even though loose clothes concealed most of his frame, she immediately recognized all the whorls on the back of his head, the way his slightly hunched posture gave him an arrogant air, and the tendons in his wrist as he rested his hand on his hip. His other hand gripped a cell phone to his ear.

And then Jason did something Hadley had never seen him do before: he turned around with the quick, unconscious motion of someone who senses surveillance. He stood twenty feet from Hadley, separated now only by the glass security door.

Hadley held up her hand in a still wave, like the kind aliens give to humans as they step off their spaceships. Jason raised his own hand in similar fashion, although his lack of blinking made his gesture look more distinctly alien. He spoke a few more words into his phone and then lowered it from his ear.

When Hadley still did move, Jason nodded a few times

and smiled, as if beckoning a nervous puppy to him. At Jason's reassurances, Hadley dragged her suitcase through the revolving door and walked calmly to him.

"I'm glad you didn't run and try to leap into my arms." He rubbed his chest. "I'm still a bit too fragile for that."

Hadley nodded. "Are you too fragile for…" She raised one fingertip to his chapped lips.

"No." Jason grinned. "I'm sure all of your germs are perfectly lovely."

Hadley dropped her messenger bag softly at her side and kissed him gently. Then she slowly, gingerly wrapped her arms around him. "I'm glad you asked me to come," she whispered in his ear.

"I'm glad you came," Jason responded.

Hadley disengaged herself and then reached down and pinched her thigh, hard.

"What are you doing?" Jason asked.

Hadley smiled simply at him, her eyes glossy. "Making sure this is not all a dream."

Jason's eyes clouded and he bit his lip. "Hadley, I should —"

"No," Hadley broke in, still smiling but now rather wistfully. "You don't have to. Just let me live this for a few minutes."

Jason swallowed several times, cleared his throat, and grinned again. "I already rented a car. My stuff's already there. You have to drive though. I don't think being post-transplant would get me off for speeding."

Hadley nodded. Jason turned around, slipped his hand through Hadley's and started off toward the escalators. After only a few steps, however, he winced, cried out, and pressed against his abdomen with his free hand. Hadley saw it, heard it, and registered it all, but she did not ask any questions. She squeezed his hand and waited for Jason to begin walking again.

After a couple of escalators, they finally stepped out from the terminal into the oven of hot summer air. Those accustomed to the stickiness and thickness of other summers—of atmospheres so textured that one waded or swam through the air —marveled at this species of thin, standoffish heat. This dry heat did not invade you and did not get down into the tiny crevices of skin. It stood at a respectful distance, undamming rivers of sweat but retreating back into the stars at night, leaving skin and cement equally cool at sunrise.

They made their way to the rental car parking area. Jason popped the trunk and Hadley deposited her bags inside. She closed the trunk and turned to see Jason standing patiently a few feet away, his black, long-sleeved t-shirt contrasting sharply against a swath of the cloudless, cornflower blue sky. He held the car keys up between two fingers.

Hadley reached out for the keys. She slowly closed her entire fist around the plastic of the clicker-remote and the cheap rental car company key fob. Once she had secured the key in her own grip, Jason's fingertips fell away.

Hadley lowered her hand and opened her fist. She stared at the remote, with its symbols for locking, unlocking, and alarms, and the thick, shiny metal of the key itself. She smiled up at Jason, who waited patiently.

"I finally found it," she said.

"Found what?" Jason asked.

Hadley tilted her head back and laughed. It pealed around the baking cement barriers of the parking lot.

"The key," she answered. When Jason continued to frown, she added, "to you."

Jason smiled back, but Hadley glimpsed something old in his smile which had never been there before—some quality of age unmistakable in the eyes.

"Then let's hit the road." Jason moved off and opened the passenger door. Again Hadley noticed but did not note how carefully and slowly Jason maneuvered himself into the car.

Hadley got in and put on her seat belt. Then she turned to Jason. "So where are we going? Don't tell me you brought me all the way here just to enjoy the views from the airport parking lot."

Jason widened his eyes and stared with mocking intensity into Hadley's. "I'll give you a clue. You have such hot eyes." He broke off his gaze and grinned.

Hadley snickered. "Ojo Caliente it is." She turned the key in the ignition.

Jason pulled out a small travel pillow from the bag at his feet and settled it behind his head. "I hope you don't mind, but I need a bit of a nap. It's been a rather…eventful day."

Hadley nodded. Jason leaned back and closed his eyes, but his left hand wafted over the gear shift, knocked against Hadley's forearm, and then found her right hand. He gave it a squeeze and then lifted it to his lips for a light kiss.

Hadley sat in the rental car in the airport parking lot, her hand grasping Jason's. She held on to his hand for a full five minutes and brushed tears away with her other wrist, afraid that if she let go, the whole thing—the car, the sky, the mountains, and him—would evaporate like a mirage in the flashing waves of summer heat.

At last, she carefully untangled her hand from Jason's. She held her breath. It did not disappear.

The stop-and-go rush hour traffic on the way to Santa Fe led them past several reservation casinos—the mythical golden cities become real—and monuments to the courageous crusaders who braved the deathly journey all the way up from Mexico City.

Next, she drove through Santa Fe, the city of holy faith, on a meandering street named for a saint. Over one hundred years ago, a mysterious carpenter had appeared in the town and built a miraculous staircase—a stairway, the local nuns claimed, to heaven.

Like everything else in Santa Fe, traffic moved about ten minutes behind schedule. The sluggish flow gave time for Hadley to consider her own salvation. She was a sinner, obviously—no, she was a pilgrim in this holy land seeking absolution, no different from those penitentes who walked along I-25 on Good Friday to the chapel in Chimayo and its legendary healing soil. This sojourn would cure her and restore her. She had already proven the following part of faith: she had followed him for most of her life now. And she had already confirmed her devotion over those years with so many offerings and atonements. But beneath the mountains dubbed Sangre de Cristo and daubed with the blood of Christ, her purification would perfect with a communal ritual baptism in the warm waters of the springs.

Finally, the street turned to open road, and beyond the casinos north of Santa Fe, the mesas divided and branched like the tributaries of some great river system. Hadley chose the exit for Espanola and glanced at the plateau to which the other tong of the fork wound, to the secret fingers of Los Alamos.

From there the influence of the supernatural also declared itself. Up there, in the whimsical town at the end of such a windy road, magicians and sorcerers discovered and developed forces so strong, so elemental, they led their first harnesser to proclaim himself Shiva, Destroyer of Worlds.

Hadley briefly stopped in Espanola to pick up food at the Blake's Lotaburger and a six pack at the Allsup's. Jason momentarily stirred as the scent of green chile and beef wafted up from the paper bag, but he did not wake. By the time Hadley guided them back onto the now two-lane highway, Jason had slipped back into a deep, restful slumber.

As the sun began its odyssey through the night and under

the earth, a few drops of rain splashed the windshield. Hadley slowed her speed to better appreciate the vast thunderhead gathering over the rusty mesas. Enough summer rains had already fallen to carpet the southern slopes of each ridge with plucky green bushes of juniper and sage and to fatten up the skeletons of ponderosa pines with fresh new fronds of growth. The roots of those brave little plants dug into clay while above them loomed great cliffs of sedimentary rock formations, their stripes like Neapolitan ice cream sandwiches. Each layer of this vast geological cake represented the cycle of life writ large; births and deaths of millions of creatures, mass extinction and mass creation. Most recently, a vast inland sea had bathed these canyons and left behind fossils in the sandy rocks and rich reserves of natural gas beneath them.

At last, Hadley pulled off the road into the tiny village of Ojo Caliente. She parked in front of the inn, now busy with the quiet hum of tourists shuffling along in bathrobes and flip-flops.

Hadley reached over and took one of Jason's hands. She stretched out his palm and tapped the middle of it several times. Jason's eyes fluttered open, and he turned sleepily to Hadley. He maneuvered fingers behind his glasses to rub his eyes.

"Does wearing your glasses while you sleep help you see more clearly in your dreams?" Hadley asked as a greeting.

Jason sleepily grinned and then yawned. He turned to Hadley. "Actually, I think my vision has improved for the first time since I was six." When Hadley's forehead furrowed, Jason added, "Must have been all those stem cells. Better than a wheatgrass and kale smoothie, and tastier too."

"No kale here." Hadley held up the bag of fabulously greasy Blake's.

"Great. I'll go check in."

Hadley stayed silent as Jason slowly unencumbered himself from the car. Instead of watching his slow saunter into the main building of the historic hacienda, she focused on the purple-black thunderheads marshaling themselves in the valley below. Soon they would begin their assault on the higher ridges —thin, bright slivers of lightning and faint groans of thunder already sounded from the clouds like warning cannon shots.

At last, Jason stepped out from the shadow of the vigas ringing the main house, waved, and pointed at a gazebo in the courtyard garden, beneath which a picnic table and benches waited. Hadley had already spread out the food and popped open the beer by the time Jason slowly lowered himself to one of the benches.

"Jesus, that's good," Jason said after he swallowed his first bite.

"Green chile hard to come by in the hospital?" Hadley asked.

"The therapeutic benefits of green chile cheeseburgers have unfortunately not been yet peer reviewed," Jason responded. Then, dabbing at his streaming nose and sweating, flushed cheeks, he added, "God, look at what a mess I am!"

Hadley laughed, and the sound echoed around the courtyard so gleefully that the hollyhocks and black-eyed susans seemed to perk up and laugh along with her.

They did not talk for the rest of dinner, instead just grinning at each other through mouthfuls of cheeseburger and curly fries. After Hadley had finally gathered up all the lardy wrappers, Jason said, "We're in number twenty-four. Meet you there." He tossed a key at Hadley, which she deftly caught.

## *Chapter Nineteen*

Hadley had returned to the car, driven it over to casita twenty-four, and moved all the suitcases into the room by the time Jason arrived. At the creak of footsteps on aged floorboards, Hadley's head jerked up from where she had been settling suitcases into various corners. Jason stood in the doorway, framed in glistening gold by the late afternoon, late summer sun.

From far off, Hadley heard the round, rhythmic tolling of a bell. Simultaneously, a gust of wind whistled through the open door, ruffling the bedclothes and raising goosebumps on Hadley's sweet, sweat-stained arms.

A ray of slanting sunlight struck the tin crucifix which hung over the bed and showered shimmery sparks through the room. Hadley raised her arm to her eyes to shield them from the bright light. She was still blinking away the shine when she heard Jason move into the room and close the door. By the time the stars had stopped spinning in her eyes, she felt Jason's hands on her shoulders.

Hadley reached out and gently removed Jason's steel-framed glasses from his blue eyes and placed them on a table. Then she grasped the zipper of his faded red sweatshirt. Jason remained motionless as Hadley slowly led the zipper all the way down and then gently pushed the sweatshirt from his shoulders. Next, she grasped the hem of his white cotton undershirt. Jason cooperatively stretched his arms up and Hadley gingerly lifted the shirt over and off.

She looked at his now bare chest. Below his collarbones on both sides, almost near the armpits, were neat, straight surgical scars, each half an inch long. Just beneath the scar on the right side, a bump arose out of the skin, about the size of a quarter in circumference. In the very middle of his chest, equidistant between his nipples, was another round scar which looked almost like a bullet hole.

Hadley swallowed hard in order to keep her eyes from smashing shut. Although a shiver ran up her back, she reached out and brushed her fingertips over each scar. Jason never flinched.

"What…what are all of these?" she asked quietly.

"The top two are from port placements. And this—" he did not look down at his chest but instead ran his own fingertips over the protuberance on the right side, "is the port itself. It's very helpful for chemotherapy. And the hole right here—" his fingers moved down to somewhere in the vicinity of his heart, "is from a Hickman line they placed for the transplant and recovery."

Hadley kissed his mouth again and then she bent her head over his chest, her hair falling like a curtain. She kissed the scar on his left side, and then the right. She kissed the places where he had been broken and stitched back together. And finally, she bent and kissed the scar right near his heart, where a plastic tube had filled him with blood and cells and fluids: the hole that had made him whole.

She led him to the bed, eased him onto his back, straddled his torso, and bent to kiss him once more.

"Hadley," Jason whispered, and she sat back up. "I know where you want this to go, but I don't think I can, and I mean that purely physically."

"It's fine," Hadley said, and she meant it for once. "I just want to…be…with you."

To prove her point, she leaned back against the headboard and let Jason's head rest against her own chest. She stroked his thin, scruffy layer of gray hair. His hands wandered down to her thigh.

"Your fingertips aren't callused anymore," Hadley commented sleepily.

Jason did not lift his head as he responded, "The hospital is a screech-free zone, so it was not conducive to practicing." After a few sheepish seconds, he went on, "Actually, I haven't played in years. I really should've kept up with it."

Hadley's chest sunk with a contended sigh. "You were really good. Your left hand especially. Your fingers were so fast."

Jason's hand moved further and further up Hadley's thigh as he said, "Well I'm glad I can still be of some use." He reached inside her khaki shorts.

Hadley lay back and felt him touch her, watched him touch her, even heard and smelled him touch her. The small hairs on the back of her neck picked up the sonic vibrations of him tugging off her shorts and lifting off her shorts, but it was some other sense entirely which reacted to his first taste of her.

The earth began to move beneath her, and then a tunnel opened up before her, lined with racing stars like some great wormhole through space. Hadley hesitated for a second, and then she lost herself within that spinning, glittering spiral. She abandoned her name and history and language and concentrated into pure nerve and muscle. She was a supernova collapsing into itself, all the particles of her compacted so tightly together that all gaps disappeared into each other. She had no more empty spaces; everything finally fit perfectly together.

Jason's voice slowly brought her back from wherever she had traveled, gladly beyond any experience, enclosed in precious silence.

"Hadley." Slowly he came into focus. "Hadley, what's wrong?"

She reached up to her cheek and discovered that she was crying.

Through the still hazy curtain, she murmured, "Nothing. Nothing at all is wrong. I've never felt that way."

She did not know how long they lay there, but she knew that Jason became cold and she wrapped him in her arms to warm him. And she knew his heart beat against hers as the August breeze drifted in through the open window.

And then with the breeze, through the window came the smell of rain and the sound of thunder. Hadley gently lifted Jason's head from where it rested on her chest, rose, and collected his glasses. Without speaking, they dressed and pulled on sturdy sandals. Jason retrieved the key and a pillow, and they exited the room. Jason took Hadley's hand and guided her away from the casita, around the spa, and down through the sand to a small arroyo which ran at the foot of the ridge. They found a flat rock and Jason sat on his pillow. Hadley climbed behind and wrapped her legs around him.

The sun had already set but still suffused the horizon with golden and pink light. The soft, warm rays of the dying day purpled the gray rain clouds with strokes of violet, and diffuse lightning lit from within the bellies of the fat and bloated thunderheads. There beside the arroyo they silently watched the far off rain billows and listened to the moaning thunder. Although the sky directly overhead was still the gentle blue of sunset, plump raindrops began to fall on the entwined figures: rain from a sunny sky, a uniquely New Mexican phenomenon.

A gust blew the scent of falling water to her nostrils. The smell of rain carried a mythic, supernatural air; it seemed to her eternal and timeless—this falling water had run down rivers to the sea, fell on places far away and long ago, traveled on waves and in clouds, had come from great distances to fall now upon her own skin. The smell of this rain woke in Hadley memories not her own—memories of epics and adventures and love stories of ages past. What people in long-gone eras had smelled this same scent and held their lovers close? Who had stood on wind-swept towers and watched through sheets of cold rain for a returning figure?

Out there, exposed to the elements of wind, rain, and thunder, Hadley and Jason had also become somehow elemental. They had left their cities of concrete and steel and brick; they had left their analyses and statistics to come to this high desert mountainside to partake of some other kind of existence, primordial and pure. Here, stripped of all modern associations and worries and free to communicate with the ancient earth, they at last left behind their histories and languages and became instead, like the rain now gathering momentum, wild and fluid and free.

Jason shivered as the clouds drifted directly overhead and raindrops began falling with serious purpose.

"Let's get you inside." Hadley uncoiled her legs from around Jason and they walked back to the room.

***

Jason closed his eyes and said, "Good night, Hadley."

"Good night, Jason."

She closed her own eyes and listened to him breathe. Her own breath dancing with his amid the soft nightsounds of the desert was as perfect as a Beethoven symphony. Hadley thought back to all the hours she and Jason spent making music together; they had even sat side by side and played actual Beethoven symphonies together, and yet those moments had never achieved the same feeling of unification and harmony. Perhaps, she thought, because she never played honestly in his presence. Ever fearful of doing something slightly wrong that would lessen her in his eyes, even her violin had not sung out at full volume.

Practicing alone or playing at lessons, Hadley had a sizable volume and a rich, concentrated tone. Her teacher, a salt-and-pepper haired man from Austria, demanded she use one hundred percent of the hair in her bow, rather than play on the side of the hair in accordance with common and accepted violin technique. In her solo playing she willingly complied, rejoicing in the depth and breadth of the sound she produced and reveling in the luscious and exuberant tone she herself generated. During her daily hour of practicing at home, she dreamed of Jason one day watching her in Carnegie Hall as she brought the audience to tears with her Tchaikovsky or Mendelssohn. She performed for him those many afternoons, imagining him listening all the way in the back row, until her chin ached and her fingertips flaked with torn skin. Picturing him at the edge of the balcony in the cavernous auditorium encouraged her to play louder, pressing all the hair down into the string so that even at his great distance he would hear every detail.

But in her orchestral playing she pulled back, restrained her voluminous sound, and played on the side of the hair. She did it out of respect for the group's dynamics, but perhaps she also did it because she had to hide something from Jason. She could not reveal herself in that way, could not play freely and openly in his presence. When she sat next to him in orchestra, she sought to dazzle him with technical perfection and impeccable attention to execution. While she dutifully watched the conductor and followed all expressive markings to a T, she never selfishly—or even selflessly—lost herself in the music. Her violin that in solitude was her greatest microphone in Jason's company never laughed, never screamed, never wept.

Tonight, though, she had finally lost herself in her own music. She had finally learned to live on the full hair of her bow and let the sound ring out all the way to the back row. She had become herself melody, harmony, and rhythm. Dynamics swelled and receded within her and tempi raced forward and pulled back. She had transformed into glistening tremolos, thrilling trills, and powerful sustained chords. She vibrated, and her vibrations separated and joined again to create something living and vivid, strings and bells, wood and brass all vibrating in perfect harmony as she looked down at Jason's sleeping face.

Hadley turned out the light, and rested her head on the soft pillow, feeling as light as the clouds floating past her doorway and as light as the sun that would illuminate the world tomorrow.

## *Chapter Twenty*

In the morning she woke slowly. The waves of sleep waned back and forth, each one receding just a few inches beyond the last one as they surely took her dreams back to sea. The shadows of clouds swam on the underside of her eyelids.

With eyes still closed, she listened to the birds chirping in their trees and children's footsteps bumping along the uneven wooden slats outside. She separated out each sound as if peeling away the layers of an artichoke: she grabbed hold of each leaf and gently tore it away. Each sound removed took her closer to the soft, warm heart which lay at the center.

The birds fell away, then the children, then the unmuffled engine of an old pickup, then the hum of the generator, and finally she heard it. In and out, in and out. A slight snortle on the ins, and an almost imperceptible hesitation on the outs. Steady, although a little bit slow for her comfort. Perhaps labored, but perhaps merely the feathers of the pillow.

Hadley listened to Jason breathe beside her.

Finally she opened her eyes to the old, unpainted vigas of the ceiling. She listened for several more minutes before raising herself and leaning over to look at him.

He was so much smaller than she remembered. He slept on his side, with his knees tucked up and his arms held tight against his chest. Snuggled underneath the covers, he could have been a boy clutching his teddy. Even with his gray hair he somehow looked young and untroubled. He looked…peaceful.

Hadley leaned over him and kissed his still sleeping mouth.

Jason's various limbs unbent. He flopped onto his back, let out a few deep sighs through his mouth, and then opened his eyes.

"Good morning sunshine. The earth says hello."

Jason blinked several times. "Hadley, is that you?"

"Of course it's Hadley."

Jason turned toward her, but his eyes swam without focusing. "Is this the morning?"

The world rushed back in; all the various sounds outside the room snapped back into place like a sped-up, backwards video of a rose shedding all its petals. The birds returned, the kids started yelling again, the engine roared, and the generator fired back again.

"Yes, this is the morning."

"Oh," Jason said, and smirked.

"What? You act surprised to have woken up alive."

"I am surprised. I'm surprised every morning to wake up alive."

Hadley's stomach twisted with pity. Over the years, and especially over the past several months, Jason had loomed so much larger than life in her mind that she forgot that he, too, was painfully alive—that he was made of flesh and blood and that that blood threatened his life every day. She had forgotten how sick he had been…how sick he might still be, and how much pain he must have hiding beneath his scaly exterior. Admitting to being surprised by life must have cost him a lot today; it must have concealed a much deeper fatigue.

Hadley rubbed his thin chest. Even through his T-shirt she could feel the bumps of the scars which criss-crossed his skin.

"Did you have nice dreams at least?" she asked.

"I never remember my dreams, actually." Immediately after he said it, Jason opened his mouth again as if to add a disclaimer or explanation, but he closed it again when he could not seem to find the words.

"I remember mine. Because, you know, a lot of them had…" Hadley stopped short.

Hadley reached out and ran one fingertip down Jason's temple. None of those dreams really had him. He had never visited her in the night, never fluttered into her ear to whisper to her under the stars. He had remained in his own bed all those nights, without his own dreams, his knees tucked to his elbows, right cheek pressed deep into the pillow.

No, it was not him in her dreams. This was him, here in this bed, the one who never expected the morning, the one whose pain and myopia made him do a double take, the one with a relief-map chest of scars.

"I didn't dream last night, though." And she kissed him again and took his hands in hers and held them against her chest, because now she had him. She had him and his hands and his everything here in this bed.

***

After breakfast in the hotel restaurant, they headed to the pools. Between the bare rock of the ridge and the green leaves which bordered the stream, in a courtyard ringed by coyote fences, a dozen or so pools bubbled and boiled with the fire of the earth. Steam even rose from some, still visible in the cool of the early summer morning and against the waterless, thin atmosphere of the high mesas. A mineral smell forged in the air, somewhat like the salt air of the sea, but heavier and more metallic, as if invisible gold rings hung suspended from the sky.

Jason had surprisingly sprung for one of the private pools —surprisingly, Hadley thought, because she had always considered him slightly cheap. Although now that she thought about it, she had no basis to believe him cheap and no experience of him being cheap.

Behind the latilla gate and the prying eyes and candid mouths of inquisitive children, Jason slipped off his T-shirt. He stepped into the pool and rested gingerly against its stone side.

As Hadley descended into the hot water, she imagined herself descending down through the earth's crust to the roaring core at the center of the world. It was from there, the burning heart of the planet, which came the fires which heated this water. These naturally flamed springs sat atop an open conduit to the depths below; they revealed a passageway down to the pulsating, throbbing sphere of iron in the middle of the planet. It was that red mass at the center that magnetized the earth and provoked schoolchildren's peals of delight at their ability to magically manipulate iron shavings.

Hadley waded ephemerally through the pool, her legs magnified and distorted by the swirling water. She stood before a seated Jason and again touched her fingertips to the scar where the central line had once emerged from his chest. The catheter would have started in a large vein in the neck, and from there it would have twisted and snaked through the waterways of his body until plunging out of the skin of his breast. It would have skirted the beating red mass at the center of him, though.

It was to that center of the world that she had searched so hard for an opening. It was that mass inside of him—not the iron ore of the earth—which turned her about like the needle of a compass. It was that to which she would always turn.

Jason sighed a long, long sigh, and his shoulders dropped into the thick water, which felt almost slippery to the touch from the metal suspended within it. The bells of the old missionary church just down the road struck nine. Hadley grasped Jason's hands and stood him up in the middle of the pool. Then, she gently dipped him backwards until the scruff of his hair bloomed in the water and only his face hovered above. As Jason floated, a hawk launched itself with a cry from the top of the ridge which bordered the pools.

Jason backed himself to the stone rim of the pool once more. He looked up at Hadley with unclouded, steady eyes. And even without his glasses on, he focused right on her. His blue eyes were as translucent and clear as the spring in which he sat. Hadley saw shimmering pillars of light stand strong and firm in those eyes, like the cathedrals of light the sun constructed beneath the sea. Behind him, the bright blue ocean of New Mexican sky beckoned.

"I'm glad you're here," Jason said.

The bottom half of Hadley's body was bathed in steaming water, while the summer sun baked the top half of her body. And yet she felt a different, distinct heat diffuse through her body. This warmth had the quality of the blue center of a candle's flame: deep, concentrated, and pure.

Hadley grinned. "I'm glad I'm here too."

"Do you think this really works? These springs? Do you think they really have any healing capability at all?"

The question made Hadley double take. He had always been—or at least he had always been with her—supremely evidence-based, to the point of cynicism. No touchy-feely nonsense for Jason. Hot springs were not quite therapeutic crystals, but it was as New Age-y a statement as she had ever heard him make.

"Really?" She raised her eyebrows at him. "Do you want the rational answer or the romantic answer?"

Jason smiled. "Try me with the romantic answer, just for the novelty."

Hadley started to think, but no grand romantic answers came to her. No poetic pronouncements of life and death or sage advice. She thought back to all those pages and pages of journals she had written, all those words she once dreamed of saying to him. And then she thought about the exchanges of the past summer—the simple hellos and the memories condensed into text messages. And then she thought of the kiss in Central Park and of the touches of last night.

All of those words, both rational and romantic, now seemed old and excessive. Precocious in language, even at six years old she had spoken so much because she could not experience him any other way. She read to reach him in the pages when she could not reach him in body. She wrote to find in a pen what she could not find in his touch. She built him out of letters and figures. But now, now she had no words. Because she needed no words.

"You never know. Maybe there are still things we don't understand, forces beyond our comprehension. Maybe folks in the olden days had it all right."

Jason nodded and sighed again. As Hadley rested against the rough stone next to him, she briefly wondered how much healing Jason needed, but he took her hand and with that pushed the thought out of her mind.

## *Chapter Twenty-One*

They stayed several more nights at Ojo Caliente and then drove up to the old hunting lodge in Chama. To get there, they dropped back down to the bluffs above Espanola, wound up through the exposed canyons of Abiquiu, and finally climbed again into the wild San Juan forests. Here the northern-facing slopes of the peaks shone with snow, and the elk bulls they watched from the porch wore thick tufts of fur on their chests like sweaters.

The September sky still sparkled blue as ever, but the world seemed to darken on the approach to Chama. The evergreens here grew black and sturdy against the bitter winters, and the purple ridges hid themselves in alpine shadow. The valley spread so green and ancient that Hadley could easily imagine dinosaurs roaming on the primeval plain.

On the drive there Hadley and Jason spoke little. The single-lane highway was windy enough that she had to concentrate on driving, but at every flat mile her attention turned to Jason. He had fidgeted for the first few miles out of Ojo and kept checking his phone. As the terrain grew wilder, he grew calmer, and when he finally lost all cell phone signals, he relaxed back into his seat and smiled at the wild black-eyed susans which grew around the guard rails.

When Jason stepped from the car in Chama and drew his

first lungful, he clutched at the door, heaving. Hadley rushed to him and began shouting toward the lodge for help, but Jason waved her pleas away. When his coughing subsided, he finally got out, "It's fine. It's good, actually. It's just the altitude—it's so thin." He paused and took several more gulps. "But it feels good. It tastes good."

And indeed, this air had the constant quality of cold which all true mountain air does. Even in the height of summer, it retains a sharp edge, as if the winds themselves carry the memory of winters and never forget the mournful chill of lonely summits.

The two days soaking in the springs had strengthened Jason. He proclaimed he would wrestle one of the ten-point elk which came at dusk to graze in the meadow, and also proclaimed that he would win. When they took the narrow gauge railroad through hills and over passes, his cheeks reddened and his wasted muscles expanded as if the growing summer thunderstorm crackled with steroids as well as lightning.

They talked leisurely, although not much. They discussed and argued the merits of Beethoven versus Bach, indulged in small morsels of memory of their past, and joked about how the designer, upscale frito pie at the lodge rivaled the "corn chip pie" of the school cafeteria.

One day Jason even had the energy to accompany Hadley on her morning hike. They did not venture too far from the lodge, but far enough to reach the groves of aspen. Here the slender white trunks were permanently bent from quaking in the winds. Their green leaves were already rimmed in palest gold and rustled and whispered to each other at the slightest breath of air.

Hadley and Jason sat against a fallen log trying to decipher the mysterious language of the trees. Birds also chitter-chattered to each other, and Hadley pressed her palm deep into a fragrant bed of spongy moss.

"Hadley," Jason said. She turned away from the moss and toward him. He looked serene and peaceful, smiling up at the sky and not even cursing the tree root he had tripped over earlier.

"You've been happy these past few days with me, haven't you?"

Hadley's intellect and her sense of logic rose as pointedly and quickly as the hair on a threatened dog's back. Alarms sounded inside her; shields went up, armories opened, missiles waited ready to launch.

It was the first time her guard had woken since she had landed in Albuquerque. They had talked about anything and everything over the past week, except they had never talked about their…relationship…affair…whatever it was. They had acted like characters in a film unaware of the eyes of an audience. Now Jason was breaking the fourth wall—he was talking to the camera itself.

Hadley's heart quickened as the felt that old, familiar panic stir in her stomach. A bitter lurch of adrenaline shot into her throat and sunk through her gut. She began grabbing at her old defenses—readying for persuasion by mentally listing all the reasons he should not just get back in the car and drive away and leave her all alone, compiling all the "pros" and positive factors in her favor. She readied herself for argument and for defense of her position. If she could not keep him by pleasure she could still try to keep him by skill.

"Hadley, I'm not leaving. I'm just asking."

Still Hadley did not lower her weapons against the intruding insecurity. Sure, he could say he would not leave. But the trail stretched back toward the hotel, and he had left so many times before.

"I'm not leaving." He reached out and took her hand. "And even if I wanted to leave, which I don't, I don't have a valid driver's license. I can't even drive out of here."

Hadley still could not believe him. She still could not take such a leap of faith. In a remote New Mexico town with all the sky before them and all the roads open to them, she could not venture blindly down that path with him.

But what she could do, what she could make herself do by grit and effort and the determination which for so long had been her only weapon, was tell him how she felt. She had come this far—crossed rivers and climbed mountains and traversed deserts—to be with him, and she would finally tell him and maybe—just maybe—he would finally stay.

"Of course I've been happy with you. Happier than I've ever been. It's not like a dream, because it's real. I wish we could stay here forever. I don't know what will happen when we—" Jason nodded at her to go on. "When we have to go back to the big, scary, real world waiting out there."

Hadley watched Jason, her sixth, detective sense searching for any clues in his breathing, his posture, the tiniest shifts in facial muscle. He was thinking, computing, calculating.

"Were you happy with him?" Hadley narrowed her brows in confusion. "With Parker?"

Hadley grabbed at a few twigs in surprise. They had not mentioned his name in days, and she had not thought—well, she could not say she had not thought of Parker in days, but if he had entered her thoughts it had been momentary and accidental.

"Happiness is fleeting. Happiness is never permanent. But I had many moments of happiness with him." Hadley paused. She had so much practice at describing her pain, but nobody had ever asked her to describe her happiness.

"The more important part is that he wanted me to be happy. He thought I deserved to be happy. He tried every day to make my life better. No one had ever done that for me before. No one had cared about my well-being in that way. And that's what made me happy with him. It made me…better. He made me think I could actually achieve that happiness. And because he thought I could, I did. I became…better…with him."

"Even in the big scary world?"

"Yes. Well, the world has always been big and scary for me. This is my first time in a small, non-scary world."

Jason got up from the fallen log. "We should head on out to Abiquiu tomorrow." He began walking back down the trail toward the lodge.

# *Chapter Twenty-Two*

"Were you happy with her?" Linda sat on the couch in the living room of the Chicago apartment. Rick had decided to busy himself replacing the hinges on the bathroom door—a project which had been on Parker's list for months but which he had never completed.

After Jason and Hadley had fled to New Mexico, Parker had of course immediately told Linda and Rick. Linda yelled forcefully enough at the credit card company that she was able to verify charges at a hotel in Ojo Caliente. That had already been weeks ago, though, and Jason had not answered any calls.

As soon as Linda and Rick confirmed that their immunocompromised, graft-versus-host-afflicted son had lit on out for New Mexico, they jumped in their car and headed west. Parker immediately offered his apartment—recently vacated by Hadley, of course—as a stop-over, even before he considered whether they would be taking the northern or southern route.

Right after promising a bed for the night to his biological parents, Parker finally spilled everything to his own parents. It had been a very awkward revelation, made tense by Parker's embarrassment at being cuckolded and by his inability to truly relate the enormity and history of the situation. Parker's parents had been textbook sympathetic and had offered open hearts and open ears, but they simply did not know what to say.

And as Parker confessed everything to them, he sensed that as much as his parents tried, they just didn't get it. They could not believe, they said, that Hadley would do something like that or keep a secret like that. They also could not believe, they said, that someone would turn down life-saving treatment.

Having seen those very things with his own eyes, Parker could believe it all, and his parents' disbelief preserved an unbridgeable distance between them. If they could not believe it, how could they understand, and if they could not understand, how could they help him? Somehow they seemed too fortunate—they apparently had never seen or felt the desperation Hadley had revealed or the desperation Jason had shown only days ago in Parker's office. They related to it only as if Jason, Hadley, and even Parker were characters in a movie, rather than living, breathing people.

And apparently they had never seen or felt the desperation Parker himself had felt so keenly the past several months, from the desperation he felt in response to Hadley's story to the desperation of choosing whether to do the donation, or the desperation at Jason's do-or-die questions. Perhaps his parents had once been desperate for a child to love, but it had not left an imprint upon them which was recognizable to Parker.

So Parker retreated back to Linda and Rick and their far more specific sympathy. Their understanding was shaped by the desperation of a sick child, but also, Parker realized, by the desperation of raising such a child as Jason. The other advantage to Linda and Rick was that they could definitely believe that Hadley would do a thing like that. Linda and Rick knew a Hadley which Parker's parents did not, and they had recognized early on in Hadley all the things which Parker had not.

Parker felt guilty, of course, at feeling more comfortable with these biologically related strangers rather than with the parents who had raised him his entire life. But the comfort Parker felt with Linda and Rick had nothing to do with how well they knew him, but rather came from how well Linda and Rick knew Jason, and ultimately, Hadley.

The first night Linda and Rick stayed at Parker's apartment, the spouses had a knock-down, drag-out fight about whether to immediately go on the search for Jason or whether they should respect his wishes, however inexplicable and devastating those wishes obviously were.

Perhaps it was sexist, but Parker saw the parental gender roles reversed in Linda and Rick. It was Rick who wanted to drive all night long and search all the canyons and valleys of New Mexico for his son. Rick had what Parker identified as a raw maternal instinct which would stop only when Jason was handcuffed to a hospital bed and force-fed…whatever was the treatment for graft-versus-host disease.

It was Linda who held back, who debated with fierce logic that Jason had to have a plan and had to have some profound meaning or message. She advocated for ideas and that Jason must have some big ones. And it was Linda who dared to ask, "What about Hadley?"

Parker sat right on the couch as Linda and Rick fought, but Linda's voice dropped noticeably on "Hadley" as if trying to protect a young child from a dirty word.

"What about Hadley?" Rick retorted.

"She deserves something in all of this. She was there too, from the very beginning. She should get her time, too," Linda responded.

Parker had just sat silent. On the one hand, these people were mere acquaintances to him, and he felt he was intruding on a very private argument. On the other hand, these people were his mother and father and they were arguing about his wife.

Linda eventually won out. For several weeks they had maintained a quite bizarre domestic arrangement. Parker went to the office and pretended to work, Linda went to museums, and Rick repaired and polished every last fixture in the apartment. A few weeks after Linda and Rick arrived in Chicago, Rick was scraping hinges and muttering about Phillips head screwdrivers and Linda and Parker were mindlessly flipping channels.

That was when Linda asked, "Were you happy with her?"

Parker had thought about it, of course. He had spent a lot of the summer thinking about it, in the moments when he needed a distraction from actually thinking *about* her.

"That's a hard question. I remember going to a couple weddings in the years before I met Hadley, the weddings of my best friends from college. And at a couple of weddings they had these terribly sappy vows where both the brides and grooms would say, 'I'm strong because you love me.' 'I'm powerful because you love me.' 'I'm better because you love me.'"

"And Hadley did that for you?" Linda asked.

"No, not at all," Parker answered with a laugh. "I wasn't better because she loved me. I was better because I loved her."

He took a swig of the chamomile tea Linda made him drink. "My world was already fine when I met her. I was happy. I had plenty of friends. My parents told me all the time I could accomplish anything. Plenty of people had told me I was amazing. I was loved and I knew it."

"But Hadley never got any of that before she met me. When I first met her, she was very brittle. So strong, but so fragile. It seemed like no one had ever believed in her. Nobody had ever told her she was the best person in the world. On the outside she was perfectly fine, but on the inside she was like a lost puppy in the rain.

"I fell in love with her, with her intelligence and humor and ambition. But I also felt that I *had* to love her. She needed to be loved. She needed someone who would try to make her happy. And I had to do it. I felt so compelled to do that for her." Parker stared down into his mug.

"And I realize now, that it made me…better. It was fulfilling, to do that for her."

"So the answer is…?" Linda pressed.

"The answer is that yes, sometimes I was happy with her. But more importantly, I was better with her. She made me feel so special. Not like there was anything inherently special about me, but that I had a special purpose, a unique and specific reason for getting up every day. And I needed that."

"And do you still feel that way?" Linda drank from her own mug, which held something much stronger than tea.

"I don't know. I mean, what is Hadley going to do, when…"

Parker got up from the couch. "Why do you ask if I was happy with her?"

"Parker, you know what's coming. I want you to be prepared for that, to know what you are going to do when it happens."

Parker walked away from the sitting area and toward his bedroom. After a few steps, though, he stopped. Without turning around and without even knowing exactly what he was sorry for, he told her, "I'm so sorry."

***

Parker lay on his side of their bed. Back in his single days, Parker's fastidiousness compelled him to alternate which side of a double bed he slept on. Since he had moved back in the apartment, however, he had remained on his side of their bed, and the covers remained neatly folded on her side.

Rick's hammer still echoed through the walls, and the television still hummed in the den, but the world was silent to Parker. More than anything he missed her sounds—her throaty huskiness in the morning, her giggles audible from the other room of the apartment when she watched TV, the little snorts as she shifted position in her sleep, the deep moans when he made love to her, the old hippy songs she played while grading papers. During the long summer months he spent in various hotel rooms, tramping footsteps from the hall sometimes led him rushing to the door to say hello to her. A few times he had even opened the door expecting to find her back again. He peered into the gloom of the corridor and found nothing.

His parents did not understand and he did not dare tell friends or work mates. And even in person with Rick and Linda, he could not cry openly like he wanted to, like he needed to. This had been how Hadley lived most of her life, carrying such a terrible and yet beautiful secret.

He still loved her, he had told Jason. And he still dreamed of her. He lay in his bed not knowing whether or not he wanted to fall asleep, because he did not know which was less painful: seeing her in his dreams or waking without her.

And over the past days, since Jason had come to see him, Parker had accidentally started doing something Hadley had described to him. He did it over several nights before he realized what he was doing, and he did it several more nights before he realized that Hadley had done the same thing so many nights herself.

Parker closed his eyes and began imagining. Seeing her again, of course, but then also after that. He imagined next Christmas and that trip to Japan he always wanted to take. He pictured the houses he had secretly begun scouting that spring, before everything happened. Her kneeling in the garden. Her playing with children.

It was not so easy, this letting go. He could not just toss her off like a backpack at the end of a long school day. He would carry her forever.

## *Chapter Twenty-Three*

From the lush green valleys of Chama, Hadley and Jason descended back again into the stony tunnels and gorges around Abiquiu. Here purples and pinks predominated: the deep eggplant of the thunderheads, the amethyst flowers which had blossomed in the monsoons, and the rose-colored rocks which bloomed in their own way along the canyon walls.

They talked less and less. Jason preferred to sit on the porch and just look out in the sky. Summer was still deep here, but Jason could not seem to get warm enough. Hadley held him for long periods of time, and she laid him against her in bed trying to heat him, but he remained chilly no matter the strength of the sun.

Hadley did not cry when she held him. She was concerned, of course, but tears seemed superfluous now. Tears were the overt signals used by strangers, little better than words themselves. Hadley had passed into a language beyond words; she said all she needed to say to Jason with her breath on his neck or her lips on his. And Jason, somehow, beyond her wildest hopes, told her everything, written out in his hands as they grasped her own and as he tasted her and as his nimble fingertips played her like a violin.

There was desire in him, and deep affection. He liked her now, he thought she was funny and smart, and he actually was grateful for and contented by her presence. He had transitory moments of genuine joy, usually sparked by laughter. But then the fear would return. He was scared, oh yes he was scared, he told her. But he did not fear the future; his fear was concentrated on the past. That was what regret was—fear of the past, of all the actions taken and not taken, coming back again and again to be relived and refeared.

At dusk the ombre of the sunset matched the ombre of the rock formations—purple flowing to pink melting into salmon and then deepening to orange and gold. In those moments they shared memories. Hadley and Jason had read *The Giver* together in their seventh grade class, and like in that novel, Jason's memories flowed steadily from him, as if he was giving them to Hadley for safekeeping.

Hadley had dreamed often of hearing Jason say so many things—all the things she wished to hear. However, this different intimacy surpassed her dreams. It proved she had not been wrong all those years; the channel really existed. She really could understand him; there really was some connection between them. She had known all along. She had believed it and felt it, and now it was finally real. She had gazed upon a star and now it had fallen into her arms.

Once upon a time, waiting for Jason to write a message on a paper airplane, Hadley had seen something, a perspective of the world. She saw herself from the outside, just her and Jason. But she saw only those two, a world with only two occupants. The regular world existed as it always had, but a parallel world existed alongside it. She and Jason revolved around each other in this place, facing each other, oblivious to all other matters or people.

Up in the high desert, her vision had become real. Hadley's world had been reduced to just her and Jason. Perhaps the regular world still existed outside, but Hadley and Jason existed in a parallel world alongside it. There, in that world, were only Hadley and Jason, and they were oblivious to all other matters and people.

Sometimes Hadley would wake as if from sleep to find that hours had passed, and yet she had not thought of anything at all. She had not worried, had not considered or judged or concluded. There was nothing to think about, after all. Jason was beside her, and that was all.

One morning Hadley woke early and slipped softly away from Jason. She headed out toward the mesa to watch the sun rise over the far mountains. She tossed aside her jacket despite the morning frost, so warm was her heart. And she breathed in the cool desert air, and as she exhaled it, she felt it—fullness. She was full. She was complete.

Hadley had solved the great puzzle of the world, and now all the pieces popped themselves together. She looked out on the morning world and say them all fitting perfectly together, all aligned and with not a single piece missing. She had finally become whole.

Jason found her an hour later. He kissed her and then said, "We should go back to Albuquerque in the next couple days."

Hadley nodded and turned back to the sky.

***

It was a hot afternoon toward the end of September when they rolled into Albuquerque. Jason had fallen asleep as Hadley drove and did not wake when the car came to a stop.

Hadley nudged Jason awake. He opened his eyes and frowned in confusion. They had come to rest in a half-filled parking lot. Pre-teens strolled and screeched around them and several school buses waited at a curb. A low brick building stood at the end of the parking lot, and several portable buildings sprawled off to the side.

"What? Where are we—" Jason stammered.

"Franklin Middle School," Hadley answered, pointing to the sign and seal on the side of the brick building. "I thought you might like to see it."

Of course, it was Hadley who wanted to see it. This was the final step in the plan. She would come to this place with him, full and whole and together, and this place would become clean again; she would exorcise all the ghosts which haunted this innocuous middle school campus. So many memories lived here; she needed to add one more beautiful one. It seemed an important corrective measure.

Hadley led Jason out of the car and through the throngs of students just released from their classroom prisons. They skirted the main building and instead headed to one of the courtyards ringed by portable barracks. Hadley stopped in front of the barracks classroom labeled B-5. They had spent two periods of each eighth grade day in this portable building, for language arts and literature. They had scuffed dents into the stoop and ramp as they lounged there during lunch periods or waited for their teacher to unlock the door and herd them inside for class.

Hadley planned to start here and then go inside the main building to the deeper chambers of secrets—the orchestra room and its storage closet—but she wanted to begin with a happier place: the barrack on whose ramp they had occupied many lunch periods, sitting on the bars, arguing, and joking. The door had changed from a dark brown to an attractive turquoise and had a shiny new doorknob, but everything else, including the few patches of native plantings, appeared just as it had over a decade ago. She lovingly remembered the smell inside, a mixture of sharpened pencils, swamp cooling, and musty textbooks.

Hadley had come back to this spot several times over the years and had grown misty-eyed as she watched the kids—or were they teenagers—nonchalantly drift past B-5. They walked past it without a second thought, and why would they? It had absolutely no distinction, no atmosphere, no decoration. It could have stood on any school grounds in any city in the country. The vast majority never went inside it, and even the ones who lived within it for an hour and a half every day for one school year would most likely never give it another thought after they departed from Franklin Middle School.

To Hadley, though, the door of B-5 looked as magical as the door of the enchanted wardrobe that transported human children to the fantastic land of Narnia. In Hadley's mind the little prefabricated structure deserved Historical Landmark status and some kind of plaque commemorating, "Here is where Hadley and Jason once stood." And now stood again.

Hadley pulled Jason to her side and then asked, "What do you think?"

"It's really weird." Jason loosened Hadley's arms from around his waist and slowly, deliberately climbed the two steps up to the door. He put his hand on the doorknob carefully, like someone taking one last moment of contemplation before opening the door into another dimension.

"God." Jason looked over at Hadley with wet eyes. "It takes me back."

"In a good or bad way?" For Hadley, it would always be in a good way simply because she had stood there with him.

"Hadley, I—" He gazed at her with those blue eyes widened in an expression of discovery: as if he had just glimpsed a new planet or established the one unified theory. As if he saw the whole world at once. Hadley was sure he had never looked at her like that, yet she knew the expression was familiar.

Then she saw it; she remembered. It was Parker. Parker's eyes had opened to her exactly the same way on that first day they had met. She remembered them perfectly, because no one had ever looked at her like that. She remembered how Parker's eyes had expanded, had deepened, had erupted as he watched her.

Now Hadley watched Jason; Jason gazed right back with those blue eyes. They exploded and burst and whirled like the swirling storms which once gave birth to the very earth itself.

"Yes?" She waited. The entire world, too, seemed to hold its breath.

Jason grimaced, lunged for the railings on the stoop, and vomited over the edge.

The world rapidly exhaled, and Hadley rushed over to him and supported him as he heaved. She was calm, cool, collected. No worry or panic came over her. Every single brain cell not occupied with running her body had turned its attention to helping Jason.

After only a minute or two, he stopped and clung to the metal railings, gasping for breath.

"I have to go the hospital," Jason muttered.

Hadley supported him back toward the car, still as efficient and single-minded as she had ever been. She settled him in his seat, where he sat gritting his teeth and concentrating on not throwing up again.

"To the emergency room?" Hadley asked as she got behind the wheel.

"No. The University Cancer Center. There's a doctor…I called him this morning."

Hadley got on the road. A few minutes later she saw Jason pull his cellphone from his jacket and send a short text message. They did not speak once on the entire journey, and the first fingers of panic began grabbing at Hadley as the car edged nearer and nearer to the hospital. She reached the Cancer Center and parked illegally, entirely oblivious to the postings and warnings.

She supported Jason past the fountain and the healing Zen

garden and into the building. A slight man in green scrubs jumped up from a chair in the waiting area and rushed over.

"Jason Snyder?" he asked. Jason nodded. "Good to meet you finally."

The man, barely in his thirties, gripped Jason's arm with one hand and stuck the other out toward Hadley. "I'm Dr. Chavez," he said, as if this explained everything.

Hadley would not relinquish her hold on Jason in order to shake the man's hand. She just glared at him coldly.

"You can let go. I'll take him from here," this Dr. Chavez said, but Hadley did not move a muscle. She gave no indication that she would be letting go: certainly not now, and certainly not ever, and certainly not because someone who claimed to be a doctor said so.

Jason just stood grimacing, eyes closed, trying to stop the world from spinning.

"Or don't," Dr. Chavez conceded. "We're going up to the third floor. I commandeered a room." And so they moved off through the lobby like a strange entrant in a four-legged race, both Hadley and Dr. Chavez supporting one side of Jason. Hadley glanced over to the admissions cubicles, but none of the clerks even looked up.

They took the elevator to the third floor and shuffled down the hall to an empty room. Two hospital beds stood on either side of a not-at-all-calming pastel curtain.

Jason lay back on one of the beds and unzipped his jacket. Dr. Chavez donned latex gloves, stuck his stethoscope in his ears, and slipped the other end of the scope under Jason's t-shirt.

Dr. Chavez steadily moved the stethoscope around Jason's chest. He then hung the scope around his neck and began probing around Jason's abdomen.

The second hand of the clock grew louder and louder as

more and more time ticked by without a word from anyone. Each click of the clock ratcheted up Hadley's panic, and the growth was exponential; each move doubled the dread, confusion, and dismay.

At last she burst out, "What's going on here? Jason?"

Dr. Chavez looked up abruptly and sharply at Hadley and then back down to Jason. Dr. Chavez asked Jason a question with just his eyebrows, a question Hadley could not decipher. Jason nodded ever so slightly.

"Jason has graft-versus-host disease. Acute. It's a reaction to the transplant. The transplanted immune cells attack the host. It can affect the liver, kidneys, cause infection…" He trailed off.

The panic broke through. Hadley had to clutch at a chair as the frenzy raged within her. She shook, she could not breathe, her face flushed hot and her knees buckled. And she, too, had to clamp her eyes shut to beat back the nausea.

Hadley concentrated on her breathing, focused on slowing it down, on in and out, in and out. At last, she could draw enough breath to say, "And you can treat it, right? It's treatable. Fixable. You can fix it. You can give him the medicine to fix it."

"I…can, but…" Dr. Chavez frowned and shrugged. He looked down at Jason.

"But I don't want it," Jason finished. He spoke flatly and without looking at Hadley.

Something broke inside Hadley. Towers fell within her and windows shattered. This time she could not suppress it; she ran into the bathroom attached to the room and vomited.

And then she stood up and swallowed the sour taste. Her body slowly screwed itself back together and tightened all the screws. She stood tense and rigid in the doorway between the bathroom and main room. Jason still lay on the bed but would not look at her. Dr. Chavez was nowhere to be seen.

Hadley closed her eyes and found herself back on the mesa above Abiquiu; she felt once again the cool morning air, saw once again the pink of the sunrise rainbowing into the blue of the sky. The calmness she had felt that morning fluttered down into her as softly as the wings of a butterfly. She remembered the sensation she had of wholeness and completion. She drew a breath, filling herself more and more. She was full; she was whole; she was the center around which all other things orbited; she was the one to which all else gravitated.

Hadley opened her eyes and stalked to the side of the bed and looked down at him. She raised her right hand and above his cowardly and craven face and clenched her fist.

"If you do it, Hadley, I won't blame you," Jason said.

Hadley let out a guttural cry and her fist landed in the pillow right next to Jason's cheek. She toppled over onto the bed and sobbed into the loosely woven cotton of the hospital bed sheets. It could not be happening…this must be all just a dream…a nightmare. Through her ears one phrase kept repeating itself over and over on a loop: "He is going to hurt you." It was one of the last things Parker had said before she left. And she said she was not scared of it. She had been so brave, so fearless.

"Hadley, I made this decision a long time ago. Parker's immune system apparently does not like me."

Hadley hauled herself up and snarled back at Jason, "Don't you dare make this about him. Don't you even dare." She pulled herself to a full standing position and gripped the railings of the hospital bed so hard her knuckles turned white. "You… you…"

"Hadley, I cannot fight anymore. What am I fighting against? I'm fighting against something *inside* me." Jason's voice was measured and practiced, like he had rehearsed the speech many times.

"So am I!" Hadley screamed. "You know what I have

inside me? I have you. You inside me. And I've been fighting, fighting so long and so hard, but I don't get to give up. I'll have to live with it forever. And you get to just waste away. You get to give up."

Jason had not expected this response, because he raised himself to his elbows and shouted back, "I am not giving up!" He sunk back down again and said, at a normal volume, "When the graft-versus-host started, it hurt. It hurt a lot. The only thing that kept me from withholding treatment right then and there was the thought that you never—that *I* never—that we never had…what you wanted…what you…deserved."

"A month? That's what I deserved?" Hadley punched her fist against her chest.

"No!" Jason sat up so quickly that he yelped in pain and clutched his ribcage. "No, that's not what you deserve. You deserve so much more than that. You deserve so much more than I could ever give you. And so does…" Jason gritted his teeth in pain. "I can't explain it."

Hadley laughed, but her laugh had no mirth in it. It had sarcasm and bitterness and anger, and it came through Hadley's joyless grin.

"You know, I always thought you were intelligent. You always used fancy words and read all the impressive books and went to the most prestigious college and had such a glittering job in New York. And yet now, you cannot explain why you are refusing life-saving treatment and why you called me to come out here with you. You can't explain what I deserve and why I am standing next to your hospital bed."

She laughed again. "You must be pretty stupid if you cannot explain that." She waited with her arms crossed and eyebrows raised like a teacher challenging the know-it-all student.

Jason swallowed in shame, gritted his teeth, and frowned.

"I can explain it, Hadley," he said resentfully. Obviously she had touched a nerve. "Do you even have any idea what I've gone through the past few months? Since I saw you in New York? Hours and hours just lying in bed, and all I could think about was you. I tried to work, I tried to read, but I just kept remembering you, remembering all the things we did."

Hadley flinched—the first movement toward embracing him, because finally, finally he had thought of her. It was what she had always wanted: for him just to think of her, to remember her. The desire had lurked so long within her that her reaction was involuntary. Her nervous system had built itself and twisted itself so tightly around this wish that the urge to forgive everything was as automatic as a heartbeat.

But just as soon as she sprang forward, she fell back. No, she would not—she could not—accept any more half-answers. She wanted the truth—she was entitled to it was she not? And she could certainly handle it now.

When Jason saw that Hadley would not react to him, he continued, "There were some nice memories, Hadley, but for the most part, it wasn't fun, all that remembering. I discovered that I…regret so much. I was just sitting in the hospital, and instead of looking forward to life and feeling grateful that I could survive, I just sat there regretting so many things I did, that I said…that I didn't say."

"So?" Hadley purposefully concentrated on a spot just above Jason's head to avoid looking at his watering eyes. "You have regrets? Everybody does. What makes you so special?"

"So it made me want to make things right with you. And then the graft-versus-host started, and I knew I had to fix things with you, before… I didn't want to be lying in another hospital bed, dying, and regretting that I never did anything to make things right. I didn't want to be lying here like I am now and regret never fixing things with you."

Perhaps it was just a trick of the light reflecting off of Jason's glasses lens, but Hadley thought she saw a tear escape Jason's blue eye. She turned away so she would not have to see it.

Hadley's cheek flushed and she put her palm to it as if she had been slapped. He wanted to fix things and make things right. Was that not a sign of affection, of loyalty, of—? It was such a tempting thought. She could feel a part of her mind slipping under the possibility like a warm blanket. She turned away from him and glimpsed herself in a mirror which hung over the sink next to the bed.

Back when she had seen herself in a mirror in a high school orchestra room long ago, after Jason had responded to her love with sorrow, she had thought she had looked old. Apparently that had been nothing. The ancient face which stared back at her from this mirror looked exhausted and burdened, like she had just emerged from a forced march through the wilderness carrying a heavy load on her back, as if she had crossed continents and oceans without a rest carrying precious cargo and pursued by villains both mortal and immortal. Her eyes flirted back and forth between focus and wandering.

She did not turn around to look at him. "So you tried to fix things with me by asking me out here and spending one fucking month with me. But the dying? How does the dying fit into that? How does you dying fix anything?"

This time Jason was ready with the answer; this was a question he had anticipated and for which he had prepared. "Because maybe then you can finally move on. You can go back to…him. You won't constantly be wondering 'what if?'"

The words fell anticlimactically into the spare hospital room. The cinderblock-and-plaster walls did not ring or echo like the stone walls of some great hall. The sounds of beeping, overhead pages, and nurses came from the corridor outside instead of harpers and song and battle. He had proclaimed that he would die for her, that he would sacrifice his own life for her. And yet it sounded not brave, not heroic as in epic songs of old. It did not roar out clear and cold, did not inspire memories of gallantry or valor. It was only a hollow whisper.

"That fixes you, Jason. That makes things right for you, because you won't have to face all of this anymore. You won't have to wake up tomorrow, and tomorrow, and tomorrow. But it doesn't fix anything for me. I'll still be carrying you. I'll still be dreaming of you.

"You're dying for me. For Parker. You think you're doing the brave thing. But it's not brave. Dying is not brave. What's brave is living. Dying for someone is so much easier than living for someone."

The room was silent for several moments as Hadley stared back at her reflection which just several mornings ago had seemed so full. At last, Jason said, "Come on Hadley, look at me. I know that you're just shocked and you'll realize that it's all… you won't leave—"

Hadley whirled around. His words had sparked an old fire, one which used to quicken so much in the old days. "Really? You know that? You think you know everything, don't you? But I knew more than you. I let you win. I let you win all the time—that spelling bee, class competitions, chair auditions. You were never better than me. And sometimes you were wrong. And what if you're wrong now? What if—"

Hadley consciously told her leg to move, to walk out the door just to prove him wrong, to leave and never come back. She pushed her palms against the shelf and willed her shoulders forward. But nothing happened. She wanted to leave so badly, but she felt like she had a whole ship attached to her back—like in those strong-man competitions where huge men harness themselves to semi-trucks. Jason had framed it as a question of whether she *would* leave, but it was really a question of whether she *could.* Could she even walk out the door; could she possibly carry both herself and all that weight: Jason, the past month, the next month he'd spend dying, the possibility that she'd never see him again if she walked out the door this minute.

"I know he still loves you. I asked him." Jason's tone was almost petulant.

It caught her so off guard that Hadley asked, in spite of herself, "What?"

"Parker still loves you. I thought I could give you something, give him something…a future…whatever."

Something lifted in Hadley. It was small, very small, almost imperceptible, but the weight had lessened. Her heart was not nearly as heavy as it had been only moments ago. Hadley bended her knee—yes, the resistance was less. She took one step toward the door.

Hadley took a deep breath, and her shoulders lifted. Then she walked out of the hospital room without looking back.

## *Chapter Twenty-Four*

The call came around six p.m. Parker had wandered home and shared a desultory dinner with Linda and Rick. They had rather absurdly decided to play Scrabble. It was an appropriate choice, Parker decided. Trying to make words out of random tiles seemed a fitting metaphor for trying to make a life out of the random set of facts the world had chosen out of its infinite bag.

It was Linda's cell phone which rang. She grabbed it, shouted, "It's him," and Rick flung all the tiles and the board away. Linda placed the phone in the center of the table like an idol.

"Jason?" Linda spoke with the urgent tone of a hostage negotiator or someone reciting nuclear launch codes. "You're on speaker."

"Jason? It's dad. Where are you?" Rick jumped in.

"I'm in Albuquerque. I'm at the UNM Cancer Center. I'm with a doctor who will help me, who accepts my choice about treatment. He'll help me get to the right places, get me help for the next few days."

Rick stifled a sob with his fist, but Linda just sat there steely-faced as ever. "Well, what's your blood count? Have they looked at your liver function?"

"Mom, none of that stuff matters now."

Linda just unfolded and refolded her hands and leaned

further into the phone. "Jason, you have to stop with this ridiculousness. You're obviously not feeling well and not thinking rationally."

There was silence for a few seconds and then Jason's voice came again from the phone. "Hadley left."

The heads of both Linda and Rick swiveled to look at Parker. His eyes flickered guiltily between them, as if they had turned on him in accusation. Parker shook his head rapidly and shrugged; he would not be the one doing the talking here. Linda raised her eyebrows at him, silently asking him what to say about Hadley.

"Mom? Dad? Are you still there?"

"Yes, we're still here. Um, what do you mean Hadley left?"

"Well, we were together the past few weeks. Today I knew it was time to get back into a hospital, and just after we got here, she…left."

Linda asked Parker again what he wanted to do by bugging out her eyes, holding up her hands, and thrusting out her chin.

Parker's mouth quickly grew dry as seconds ticked by his open jaw. He looked back and forth at the phone and at Linda's waiting concern. He could not decide if he wanted to know. He could not decide if he needed to ask. He saw Linda mouth, "Parker" but did not know whether she actually said it aloud. He suddenly could not hear much of anything besides the whirring of his own brain.

"Where is she?" At first he was not sure if he had actually spoken it or merely thought it, but Linda looked back down at the phone, so he must have found his voice.

"I don't know where she is." Jason's voice was flat and affectless. "She left and she had the car keys."

Linda rubbed the back of her neck. "Jason, you have to

stay right where you are. We are getting in the car in ten minutes. We're in Chicago. We'll be there tomorrow night."

"Alright," Jason responded, which made Linda's eyes bug out again, in what Parker assumed was surprise. "I'll text you the address of the hospice place." Linda's cell phone went blank; the call had ended.

Rick sat with his face in his hands; small moans escaped his tight grip. Linda stood up and announced to no one in particular, "Be ready in ten minutes." She headed off to the guest bedroom, but paused in the doorway. Parker had not moved an inch.

"Parker?" He looked over at her. Light streamed in through the kitchen and illuminated Linda's form in the doorway. "You're coming—" His ears were still muffled, and he could not tell whether she was asking or telling. And he did not know whether he would answer or obey.

He felt a hand slip into his and raise him to his feet. Without exactly understanding whether he wanted to or not, he let himself be led into his bedroom, where he filled up a suitcase. And then they drove through the night.

***

Parker had never driven into Albuquerque before. When going to visit Hadley's family, they had always flown. And in fact, he realized, he had never driven very many places at all. His family were not road-trippers; their vacations had been to theme parks and coastal cities. He had never sat in the back of a car and stared out into the vastness—the emptiness—of the American interior. He fell asleep somewhere in Missouri, where the lights of small towns still promised civilization, but when he woke up in north Texas, he was not entirely sure he had not awoken on the moon. The only sign of civilization for many miles at a time was the asphalt of the highway itself. It was an impossibly lonely landscape: brown fields as far as the eye could stretch, as monotonous as the sea, and only the wind to speak of. Out in the middle of it Parker could not help feeling like the tumbleweeds piled up against the cattle fences: blown about by the whim of the world, never coming to rest except when tangled against the cruel barbs of those endless wires.

He had never asked Linda and Rick when exactly they had moved to New Mexico, whether it was before or after Jason had been born. He imagined them making this journey long ago, perhaps with a baby Jason sleeping in the back, or with a toddler Jason ogling the endlessness through the window.

And he thought of those pioneers in their covered wagons coming to take a piece of the American west, and why not—there was so much to take out here. It all could be yours, if you just survived the journey. Go west, young man, and grow up with the country.

Parker wondered if he would have gone west, if he would have lit out for the territories. Would he have taken what was promised? Would he have believed that it was his? He guessed not. After all, even playing the old MS-DOS version of Oregon Trail on the Macintosh at school, his oxen had always died fording the river. He did not seem to possess that pioneer spirit, that belief that destiny itself was manifest. The future was not his to take by force or will.

He was not like Hadley, that quintessential child of the west. For her, desire alone was enough to mandate possession. She believed—she knew—her destiny was fully manifested. Her treasure had already been formed; it lay before her like these vast open plains, waiting to be taken, to be held, by sheer force of will.

***

The hospice center was called La Manera, which according to Parker's cell phone translation, meant "the way" in Spanish, another example of what Parker thought was the

Albuquerque tendency of excessively naming things in Spanish to give them extra cache. This one seemed particularly obnoxious; calling a hospice center "The Way" would be universally criticized as corny and cloying, but hiding it in Spanish gave it an undeserved refinement.

He walked in with Linda and Rick, feeling younger than he ever had in his life. He trailed behind them like a kid, and he still felt surprised, maybe even embarrassed, at Rick's frequent crying spells. Seeing your father cry is always a world-shattering occasion, but seeing Rick cry left Parker particularly foundering. He had known Rick only a few months, and had only considered him anything close to a father for a few days, and yet he had already seen him cry. It made Parker feel impossibly young, like a seven-year-old glimpsing hidden paternal tears through a crack in a door.

His own father had never been a crier. In fact, Parker was nearly twenty when he first saw his father cry. It was at Parker's grandfather's funeral. That had been Parker's first experience of death, and it had been a distant one. Parker had been away at college and received the news that grandpa had a massive, fatal heart attack. By the time Parker got back home, the only evidence of death was the urn next to the tasteful orchid arrangement.

The evidence of death at this hospice center was there, but sanitized: a parking space reserved for "funeral transport," free tissue packets at the reception desk, and the aggressive scent of air freshener. For a reason he did not know, Parker had expected the place would be chilly, but he detected almost no difference between the inside of the building and outside, where the late September afternoon still blazed into the eighties.

Jason was sitting in a chair next to a window, still in jeans and a hooded sweatshirt. Linda and Rick swarmed around him, while Parker hung back. He pretended to study all the outlets behind the bed.

"Did you see the name of this place?" Parker heard Jason say. "La Manera. It means 'the way.' What a bunch of bull." Parker turned around and stepped closer to Jason. Did Jason really have the same views on Spanish translations of cloying English phrases?

"Of course," Jason went on, "at least it's not 'the journey.' That's so fucking saccharine I would die of diabetes instead of cancer if I had to stay at a place called 'the journey.'"

Parker snorted in laughter. Jason swiveled toward Parker, and their eyes met. Jason tilted his head to the left and continued to stare into Parker's eyes. Jason's gaze was too intense; it made Parker want to look away almost immediately, yet he held his line.

Jason's eyes had recognition in them; he had spotted something familiar, like the brief glimpse of an acquaintance's face in a crowd, and was now trying to place the connection. It was not just the physical resemblance, Parker knew. It was not just Parker's eyes, jawline, or nose which was familiar. Jason had spotted a deeper resemblance. Parker had laughed at a sarcastic remark, and Jason had realized, for perhaps the first time, that they were brothers.

At last, Parker looked away and turned to Linda and Rick. They evidently had not noticed the spell between Parker and Jason. They concentrated more on the pallor of Jason's cheeks.

Parker cleared his throat and announced, "I'm just going to go to the bathroom."

Instead, he sank into an armchair in the "family solarium." He pulled his cell phone from his pocket. He slid his finger up and down his contacts, but he fell asleep before he could decide whether to stop on Hadley's name.

***

It was dark outside when Linda came to him, woke him gently, and told him that Jason had asked for him. She told him softly, as if it was a secret that Jason had made the request. Parker got up and waited for Linda to proceed with him down the hall, but she shook her head. "Just you," she murmured.

Parker made his way down the darkened corridor. The light bulbs in their soft-focus sconces had been lowered, so that they shone like muted candles in some dark stone hall. Perhaps like in a medieval dungeon hall, Parker thought.

Jason lay in bed, still wearing the same ratty red hoodie, although he had consented to cover his legs with a blanket. Only an incandescent lamp lit the room from a nightstand next to the bed. It made the room smaller, more mysterious, even secretive. The soft orange glow reminded Parker of the glow of the prayer candles so ubiquitous in the windows of every Mexican and Salvadoran restaurant in Rogers Park.

"I couldn't sleep," Jason spoke from out of the twilight.

Parker just stood in the doorway.

"There's a chair here. Sit down." Jason raised a hand and pointed, his white finger almost ghostly in the murky light.

Parker crossed to the chair and sat down. He did not pull it closer to Jason's bed.

"Do you ever have trouble sleeping?" Jason asked.

The question seemed innocuous enough, and Parker was not quite sure what kind of hostage situation he had gotten himself into, so he decided to answer. "Not often. At least, not before…before, I almost never had trouble sleeping. The past few months, though…"

"Yeah, the past few months…" Between the little light of the lamp and some rays from a streetlight bleeding through the curtains, Parker could see only half of Jason's face. It seemed pained. Parker saw Jason's Adam's apple move up and down several times before he spoke again.

"Look, Parker, I don't know how to do this."

"Do what?" Parker responded. His wariness had dropped once he realized that Jason was defenseless and weaponless there in his bed.

"Talk, apparently. I don't know how to talk about what I feel. And I don't even know if really know how to feel. Some people, and I think you realize who I'm referring to, they know how to feel, almost like it's a skill they've perfected. And they can identify it all and express it in words I've never even considered."

Parker peered toward Jason, but he could not see the details of Jason's face in the darkness. Jason was venturing into territory with which Parker was certainly unfamiliar, and before they traveled too far, Parker wanted to know what kind of land mines lay ahead.

"Maybe I should go get your mother…our…Linda, I mean." Parker started to rise, but Jason held out a ghostly white hand.

"No, don't get her. Oddly enough, you are the only person I can talk to about this. You are the only person who might understand." Jason coughed, and Parker could hear fluid rattling around in Jason's lungs. It was a sound Parker had heard described in books, but it was the first time he actually heard it—the uneven, slow vibrations like the blowing of a winter wind through the hollow of a rotting tree. Parker sat back down, suddenly aware that he might be the audience to a deathbed confession.

"What is it?" he whispered.

"I think I love Hadley."

Parker certainly heard the words, but they took a very long time to register in his brain. He watched the clock that stood just below the lamp on the nightstand. Eleven fifty-eight became twelve-o-one, today became tomorrow, before he could even attempt to answer.

"Why do you think I would understand this?" The very idea that Jason would—could—love Hadley seemed utterly foreign to Parker. Jason might as well have implied that he would understand particle physics or the United States tax code. It was an idea Parker simply could not touch; it floated somewhere above his brain, just out of reach.

Jason answered as if the entire thing were perfectly logical, "Well, because you love her. This has never happened to me before. I don't have anything to compare this to."

"When? How?" Parker's brain still processed Jason's confession as a discrete event, like the breaking of a vase or a three-car pileup; he had not yet grasped it as an abstract concept.

Jason's response now was less measured, more pensive. "I don't know, exactly. Maybe it was always there and I just didn't recognize it. But something was different about her when she came to New York, when she walked in on me in that coffee shop. Something I never saw in her before—or maybe it had never been in her before.

"Maybe—"Jason coughed again and Parker heard once more that terrible flapping, like a flag in a strong wind. "Maybe it was you."

"Me?" Parker leaned forward toward the bed.

"She was better. After being with you. She was so much better. When she came in that day, and then when we met in the park the next day…"Jason's voice became almost wistful. "And the past few weeks, she was amazing. It finally hit me when she took me back to our old school. And then—"

Parker slowly exhaled the breath he did not realize he had been holding. "And then what?"

"And then it was too late. Then I had to go to the hospital and then she left." Jason was silent for so long Parker thought he might have to check his breathing, but just as he prepared to rise from the chair, Jason spoke again.

"Do you know why I came to visit your office a few weeks ago? Why I asked if you still loved her?"

Here at last was a question to which Parker coud offer answer, even if that answer was only his own solid uncertainty. "Actually, I'm still working that one out. I've gone over it and over it and just cannot figure it out," Parker said.

Apparently the question had been rhetorical, because Jason continued on without acknowledging Parker's answer. "At the time, I didn't even really know myself. But I had this vague notion that I wanted Hadley to be—not happy, that's not the right word—I wanted her to be better. I didn't want her to be like she was back in the day with me. God, she can be so great. And she could grow so great in the future. She can be amazing, but it won't happen with me in the picture. I saw it. She would never be as good with me as she became with you. She could be so great, but it wouldn't happen with me in the picture. Isn't there some saying, 'if you love someone, let them go?'"

"I think it's a bit more complicated than that," Parker interrupted.

"I told you that day that I didn't deserve her. I asked if you could forgive her. I had this plan in my head—that I would make things right with her and then quietly depart the stage for you to come sweeping in."

Parker had gotten to his feet before Jason finished his sentence, but he stood rooted to the floor, unable to take a step either way.

"At the time it was just a plan; one of my stupid intellectual analyses. It was just pieces on a chessboard. But now —dude, please sit down, you're making me nervous."

Parker could now see Jason's entire face as Jason looked up at him and he looked down. Jason looked as calm as ever. He had lost weight and the bones of his eye sockets cast shadows over his cheeks, but if not for the pallor and the thinness, Jason might have been any other man talking about any other topic.

Parker did not sit down, shocked as he was not just by Jason's revelations, but by the fact that Jason viewed his own life —and Parker's life and Hadley's too—as dispassionate pieces on a chessboard. The moment seemed so…momentous…that it called for wild outbursts and crying and screaming and yelling. It needed something like Rick's effluent tears to make Jason's dry analysis grow into a living being.

"I'm serious, man, you need to sit down. You're freaking me out." Jason hoisted himself up against his pillows. He stretched his hands out, palms downward, and motioned for Parker to lower himself back into the chair. The modernness of his words, his gestures, and the worn red hoodie he wore tore into the almost ancient incandescent light cast by the bulb on the nightstand and the streetlamp in the parking lot beyond the window.

"Back then it was all academic, like I was writing a script for a movie. I moved us all around, anticipating moves and planning out the sequence. And it made sense, at the time. All that time, even if I hadn't loved her, I still respected the hell out of her. I knew she had to be better. I knew she had to get rid of me."

Despite himself, Parker whispered, "That was back then. But now?"

Jason's voice in response sounded both flat and thin and also unbearably full and thick with regret. "Now none of that matters. Now I love her and now she's gone and now I'm a twenty-eight-year-old dying man who regrets every day of his life since the first day of first grade."

Jason's right hand fell limply onto the bed, palm up, fingers half-curled towards his palm. Parker barely saw it, it was so subtle, but it happened. Jason's long, white, elegant fingers opened, reached out, stretched toward Parker like the unfurling fronds of a fern.

Parker did not even have to decide. It was not a question, and he did not have to answer. Without seeing any other options, Parker slid his fingers across Jason's cold palm, wrapped them around, and squeezed. Though it was weak, Jason squeezed back. Jason turned his head away and covered his face with his left hand.

"I need to see her. You have to get her. Make her come back. Just for a few minutes."

"I will," Parker murmured. "I will. I will," he kept murmuring. And as he repeated the words, they grew louder in his heart. The crusade, the great quest grew bolder and more urgent in his mind. No more equivocating or drawing back, as he had done before he donated for the transplant. That was simply saving a life; this was saving a soul, and he shouldered this burden much more easily.

"But Parker—" Jason turned back and his eyes were dry as ever. "Don't tell her. Please don't tell her. She can't regret anything; not like I do. She shouldn't have to ask 'what if' or wonder what she should have done differently. She did everything right."

Parker nodded. It made sense. He heard the terrible hole in Jason's throat, at once hollow and yet achingly, excruciatingly full, and knew that he could not bear to hear that regret in Hadley's voice.

***

Pigs were flying. Cows too. Well, technically just one pig and one cow, plus several beer bottles, soda cans, and even a stagecoach and Noah's Ark. It was Thursday morning Special Shapes Rodeo Day at the Balloon Fiesta. Beneath each billowing collection of silk scraps a gondola carried pilots who pumped bursts of hot air from pressurized tanks into the cavernous dome of fabric, that hot air lifted the ingeniously crafted flying machines into the altitudinous air.

Parker looked out tiredly over the western horizon at the suspended shapes. Although his dedication had not flagged over the last hours, he had to admit that questing was much harder than he expected. Hadley had not turned the rental car back in, she had not bought any airplane tickets (at least not on their shared credit cards, the accounts of which he could access remotely), and she was not at her parents' house (boy, that had been an awkward and hurried conversation). Jason had suggested searching at their old schools, but Parker had not found Hadley among any of the streams of commuting students.

Now Parker leaned on the hood of Linda and Rick's car, sipping tepid coffee and watching the balloons drift. He once again pulled his phone from his pocket and slid his finger back and forth. He looked down and his eye caught an icon in the shape of a space satellite. Parker snapped to attention and focused down on the screen once more. He shoved his coffee to the side and pressed his finger to the satellite icon.

"Please work, please work," he begged. She had once made him download a GPS tracker app one finals season when she had misplaced her phone. He could track her device from his. They had used it only once, as a test, and he did not quite understand how it worked, whether her phone had to be on or updated or…whatever.

He sighed in relief as the app went to work "searching." A grid appeared on the screen, and then a field of green beneath it. An arrow pointed to a spot in the middle of the green, far from any street or identifiable landmark. Next to the arrow, the GPS grid said "Sandia Crest."

Parker stepped away from the car and turned three-hundred-and-sixty degrees, from west to east. The great slab of mountain occupied the entire eastern view. It rose steeply and squarely from the foothills below, as if the earth had just plopped down a gigantic Lego brick onto the plain. The morning sunlight glinted off the few buildings and radio towers up at the top, 10,000 feet high and 5,000 feet above the city.

Somewhere up there was Hadley.

Parker had never quite understood exactly what constituted irony, but this seemed like it would fit the bill. Every single time he had visited Hadley's hometown, she had begged him to go with her to the top of the mountain, to get into a cable car and ascend to the gasping height—on nineteenth century technology, no less. And every single time he had resisted, freely admitting to a terror of heights. No—it was not just a fear of heights. It was the fear of falling from those heights. Or falling thousands of feet from a glorified phone booth held up only by some bundles of cable.

Of course it would come to this. He could protest no more. The mountain would not come to him, so he would have to go to the mountain.

***

Parker lined up behind excited tourists for the next scheduled "flight" from the tram's base, a small building tucked into the foothills at the edge of the mountain. Fresh from the balloon fiesta, the tourists seemed way too excited about experiencing two technological dinosaurs in one day. Hot air balloons and cable cars—this was why airplanes had been invented, for God's sake.

The descending gondola slid into its resting berth, and Parker could have sworn he saw it dangle precariously on its cables. After the returning passengers disembarked, a teenager in an official-looking polo shirt opened the gates to allow the next group in. Parker followed the chattering groups of camera-toting tourists, and although he would have much preferred a spot in the center of the car, he got pressed up against one of the plexiglass windows right at the side of the car.

With an ominous crunching sound, like boots pulverizing gravel, the tram started upward. As soon as the car cleared the dock, Parker felt a separation between his stomach and the rest of his body. His stomach obviously wanted to stay down there, but the rest of his body decided to go along with the tram. The cable stretched far ahead, both vertically and horizontally, with a terrifyingly long span between the last tower and the top.

The tram car bumped over the first tower and Parker clutched at his stomach in nausea. He closed his eyes and counted to thirty.

When he opened his eyes, he found he was flying. Not the soaring flight of an eagle, with its grand swoops, but the slow, steady glide of, say, a wandering albatross. The tram car flew over the mountain, with only a thin aluminum floor separating him from the thousand feet drop below. The wilderness coursing past the windows seemed so close he could reach out and touch it; hardscrabble cactus and sagebrush, pine trees clinging stubbornly to sheer rocks like mountain goats, and boulders which from here looked like they could be pebbles in the palm of his hand, but as the tram operator explained, were actually the size of school buses. Groves of aspen, their leaves already yellow at 10,000 feet, divided the endless pines like yellow traffic lanes dividing blacktop.

Indeed, maybe it was the height, the weightlessness, or the sensation of suspension, but Parker seemed to have lost his sense of perspective, maybe even of depth perception. The trees and rocks looked so close, so small, that he could easily grasp them. Blinking and refocusing, however, he knew they must be thousands of feet away, thousands of feet higher or lower, and they must be huge, immovable even. Distance meant nothing up here in the clouds; size was meaningless in the ether. It was so different from the terrestrial world he knew, where reality proved his senses correct, where the flat plains gave everything a healthy sense of proportion.

Hadley had grown up in the shadow of this mountain. Her eyes—her sense of perspective—had developed beneath a massive optical illusion: the mountain viewed from the city looked sheer, square, almost two-dimensional. Viewed from above, however, the mountain cautiously, gradually rose, and deep canyons furrowed for many miles into the bedrock. The cable car actually covered more distance horizontally than it did vertically. How odd it must have been for Hadley to grow up in a place where flying was the only way to see the real truth of things.

At last he saw the tram's upper dock. The buildings at the top stood out, sharply red against a sky as vast and blue as the sea. Parker did not look backward toward the city as the car slid softly into its berth. He darted around the tourists to be the first one out as the teenaged pilot threw open the doors. He stepped out and gasped in the 10,378-foot air. Not just thin—it was crisp and cold and fresh and tasted untouched by the hand of man. Like breathing in a lungful of some high mountain stream.

Parker scanned the groups taking pictures on the decks and gazing out through those ancient view finder machines. On the farthest deck, he saw a lone figure leaning against the fences which ran along the very edge of the mountain. He took several deep breaths and made his way over various staircases toward her.

About fifteen feet from her, he stopped and watched. He did not know how long he stood there—time also seemed to lose its effect up here—but she never turned around. She seemed to have stood there for so long that she had become a permanent fixture, like the picnic tables welded down to the decks and the weathered signs explaining the landmarks visible hundreds of miles away. She seemed to have lived forever on top of this mountain where time stopped and where the seconds were marked only by the clicks of the tourists' cameras.

It was strange of her not to turn around. He remembered the very first time they ever met. He had looked at her for only a few seconds when she snapped up. She had felt his eyes that quickly; he had barely had time to get a good look before she had noticed his gaze. And in the years since, her sixth sense had not diminished at all. He would try to sneak some ogles at her, to catch her in a few moments when she was unfocused, when she was not "on." She always felt it, though, and switched on instantaneously.

Now, though, she either did not feel his eyes or did not care to face them. And so he watched her in "off" mode, perhaps for the first time since that very first moment so long ago. The late morning sun enclosed her warmly in a pleasant halo, so that she looked fuller and wider than she had the last time he saw her. The profile of her face slipped downwards, as if the constant gravity of sadness had a permanent effect. She had her hair tied back, and even in repose, he saw tension in her neck muscles, in her shoulders beneath her light jacket. Had it always been there? Had he passed over it when he touched her? Had he mistaken strength for the constant clenching of grief?

He lowered his gaze to her hands, which she held remarkably still. As long as he had known her, her hands moved constantly: grasping and un-grasping, reaching to replace a wisp of hair into its correct place, index finger drawing on a palm, nails pressing, nails picking at a stray fleck of skin. She had loved Jason's hands so much, she said, had watched them and waited for them. And her own hands—with their own long fingers and their own close-cut nails, a holdover from violin days—had searched and fumbled so much, trying desperately to make their way into his. Now, though, they lay still against the red laminate of the fencing.

She looked sad and exhausted, but also peacefully alone. Not one of those lonesome people at tourist sites hiding their jealousy of smiling couples and families, those who take surreptitious glances away from their books or meditation or expensive cameras. She looked genuinely at peace with her isolation.

And no doubt, she was still beautiful. Although her beauty had obviously changed. She no longer had that beauty of youthful potential. That was what had first held him, when she seemed just on the edge of coming to a rolling boil, bubbling and popping everywhere. Now she bore the beauty of afterwards, of subsidence—of the calm that remained after the storm.

At last he walked the last dozen feet, stood beside her, and rested his elbows on the fence. The country spread far and wide from the base of the mountain. The city glinted in the morning, the river gleamed silver like the skin of a great snake slithering through the city, and at the edge of a far expanse of mesa, another mountain stood at the end of the eastern horizon.

"Hadley." She turned. Her eyes were tired and wan, like she had stared too much at the sun. The skin around her eyes had the puffiness he knew evidenced long spells of weeping. Stray hairs fluttered around her face in the breeze. Despite all that, she looked quite lovely.

She did not say anything, nor did she raise her eyebrows quizzically at him. She just looked at him with a waiting expression. Parker was on the verge of losing his nerve, of mumbling some stupid pleasantry like, "how are you?" when he remembered the horrible rattle in Jason's throat, remembered Hadley begging him to hit her, remembered Linda's arm around him in the museum. Compared to these memories, his own hurt shrank and diminished to nothing. And he knew what he had to do—what he should have done the very first time he met her.

Parker wrapped his arms around this cold, hurt, injured

little thing. He embraced her and held her unequivocally. And then he felt her let down; her shoulders relaxed, as did all the other muscles and nerves in her body. She let herself be held, let his arms support her as she had never done before. This was so different; she must never have completely softened, never totally loosened herself, in all their times together. Her body had kept her vigilance and her secret for all those years.

"He asked for you. He wants to see you," he spoke into her ear as he held her. When she did not respond, he spoke again. "He really did ask for you. He begged me to find you."

Although he could not see her face from where it was buried in his shoulder, he heard the surprise in her voice as she said, "And you came. You found me." Her surprised statements implied the questions, "Why? Don't you hate me forever? Won't you leave?"

The answer which immediately came to mind was, of course, "Because he loves you." The rest of the answer unspooled in his mind. 'Because he loves you. And that is such a profound thing, such an unmissable and impressive fact, that I could not possibly disregard it. Because I cannot bear the thought that you may bear a terrible regret one day. That you would regret not going to him.' But Parker remembered his promise to Jason and said nothing for a few moments.

"And you came up here," Hadley murmured.

Parker's eyes drifted out over the ledge of the mountain, to the long expanse of cable stretching down and down and down, to the highways that ran in all four directions through the city, to where he had come from, to where he might go. He had come up here, thousands of feet, against all his fears. He had scrunched in a car for thousands of miles, not stopping, just to get there in time. He had dreamed about her all summer, had not stopped thinking of her. And why? What had driven him back to her, driven her back to him?

Back in the hospice center, Jason had said he thought Parker would understand, but in truth, Parker did not understand Jason. Parker did not understand how anyone could know Hadley for ten minutes, let alone ten years, and not love her. He did not understand how Jason could not have rushed headlong into loving this brilliant, troubled, brittle, steely, courageous, scared girl he held in his arms. No, it was not Jason whom Parker understood.

Parker unhooked his arms and pulled Hadley away so he could look at her.

"I came up here because I think I understand now. I understand that sometimes, you cannot let go. Some people, you love no matter what, and you cannot stop loving them. You know you'll carry them forever. I get it now. That's why I'm standing here."

***

It felt so different this time. That first time he had embraced her, those years ago in Philadelphia out on the city street, it had felt only temporary, only superficial. He had not held all of her; his arms could not wrap all the way around her and her sadness, her history, all the weights she carried. There was appreciation, but not understanding.

Now his arms seemed as wide as the sky above them, as deep and tall as the mountain upon which they stood. He held all of her. He reached all the way around to embrace all she was and all she had been. He understood now, and she collapsed gratefully into his understanding.

Hadley looked up into Parker's face, and there she also saw his understanding. He looked older, definitely. His face was not any wrinklier, and she knew the bags under his eyes were likely just from the sleepiness of the past few days, but his temples had gained edges of stately grace and his jaw sloped with maturity. He had the grizzled tan of the young soldier already worn of battle.

"Parker—" She coughed, her voice hoarse from two days of silence. "Parker, I don't think I can go back down there. I can't see him," she said, finally unafraid to be honest with him.

"I know it'll be hard, but someday down the line, you don't want to regret not seeing him again. You'll regret not saying goodbye. When you miss him, and I know you will, you don't want to regret the last thing you said to him."

When you miss him, Parker had said, but Hadley could not see any whens. There was only now, only the heavy, heavy pain of now. No more fantasies to be had, no more dreams to distract. There were no more futures with Jason, and so there were no futures at all. Time stretched only across the mesa to the mountain which stood symmetrically on the western horizon. There it stopped, and Hadley could see nothing beyond it.

"Hadley, he's changed." Strangely, Parker's voice sounded almost proud, as if he could not wait to show off a son in a graduation cap and gown.

A breeze shifted overhead and the yellow leaves of the aspens quaked and fluttered, carrying a faint whisper on the wind. It spoke again of hope, of that ineffable belief in change, of that faith that once the leaves were fallen and once a thousand feet had trod them into the earth, that they would return again and would grow green again.

The yellow leaves of aspen saw a future beyond their fall and beyond their oblivion. Others would grow in their place and others would still sing that whispering song, still rustle restlessly in summer winds, long after they had drifted down the mountain, after they had been buried like a treasure of golden coins.

"Besides, unless you plan to hang-glide out of here, you're going to have to come down with me." Parker nodded toward the gliders drifting on the currents below the crest.

Hadley nodded. She had no more tears left, so she did not

cry.

Hand-in-hand they made their way back to the tram dock and waited for the next take-off.

***

The sun was setting when she came to him that evening. Only one faint light shone from his room, and yet to that light she moved like a moth to the flame, the attraction so simple and fundamental as to merit only the careworn, overused saying.

She paused in the doorway and gazed at him. His eyes were only half-closed beneath his glasses, but he did not look up. Even though she knew this would one of, if not the very, last time she gazed at him this way, she could not help but think—was it only with her that he never looked up? Or did he never feel anybody's eyes on him? Again she asked herself whether it was her or him—did she watch too intensely, or did he resist the notice of everyone?

But then Jason opened his eyes and turned his head toward her.

He raised his right hand. He held something in it—something pale was all Hadley could see in the semi-darkness—and snapped his wrist swiftly. The pale something flew through the air. Hadley could see its entire arc, as if it moved in slow motion. She saw its pointed nose, its fluttering wings; it was a perfectly aerodynamic paper airplane. She tracked it as it rose from the bed, as it peaked, and as it began to descend in a perfect trajectory toward her. She opened her hands and waited. It landed as smoothly in her palm as one of the supersonic spacecraft of science fiction movies.

She held the paper airplane in her hands as delicately and preciously as if she held a butterfly. And indeed, she could not be sure that it would not fly away from her like some mercurial insect, that it too would leave her as soon as it had come. She looked over at Jason, who was now fully awake.

He smiled, more broadly and genuinely and warmly than she had seen him smile in…years. It was the smile of a child, the grin of youth, the welcoming sign of adolescent affection for which she had waited so long. Jason's teeth were as straight as the day he had gotten his braces off, but Hadley could also see the slightly bucked front teeth he had in first grade. Jason smiled at her across the ages; he grinned at her like no time had passed at all.

Jason made a gesture with his hands like the opening of a book, indicating that Hadley should open the paper airplane. Hadley nodded and gripped the wings with her fingertips. She tugged, and the airplane opened it. The writing was shaky and faint, but it was undeniably Jason's.

Hadley,

When I am gone, please let him in. Let him make it better. Let him make you better. I know it will hurt, but you do not have to carry the world on your shoulders. You do not have to carry me anymore. Be happy and smile and play the violin again. And don't be afraid. I know you will make it.

Jason

"Oh god," Hadley said. "No." It was all she could say. Hadley carried the page in her quivering hands and walked to the edge of Jason's bed. He looked up at her with dry blue eyes.

She wanted to say so many things and wanted to shout out thousands of questions, but it was late and dark and she was so tired and so sad. The end was so near. She should be fighting harder than ever, here at the end, but she could muster no molecule of strength. The point had finally come when she just wanted to surrender. Let the world take what course it would. Let him die, and let the winds blow her where they would.

"Jason." She could go no further and broke down weeping.

"Hadley." His voice sounded raspy and painful. When she uncovered her face and looked at him, he shook his head and put a finger—a long, white, graceful finger—to his lips. He lowered his hand and touched the creased paper she held in her hands.

"Promise me."

"I will," she whispered. She could barely hear her own voice, but Jason had seemed to hear her, because he patted the blanket beside him. She crawled into the narrow bed beside him.

"I love you." She whispered it into his ear and then took his hand in hers.

***

Jason looked down at her as she nestled in the crook of his arm. She felt warm, and her hair was soft as he ran his fingertips along her brow. After a few moments she closed her eyes, and within a few minutes her breathing had slowed down to the regular, easy pattern of sleep. He peered down at his left hand, which was entwined and covered with Hadley's hands. Her hands were beautiful—long-fingered but strong, with freckles on each knuckle. Like his own, her wrists were slim and elegant. He remembered her hands embracing her violin and bow, her fingertips flying over the fingerboard as her right hand held the bow so delicately it seemed bonded by magic only.

He wondered again if he should say it back to her, if he should disturb her sleep. But she looked so peaceful, finally, in his arms. He did not want to wake her. And anyway, it was a very hard thing to say.

But he thought it, and he felt it. He kissed her sleeping head and held her hand and thought, "I love you."

***

Jason stood at the bottom of an old-fashioned staircase

leading up and into an airplane. He carried no luggage. He looked tan and healthy, dressed in shorts and sandals and a T-shirt. He reached out and hugged her for a very long time. Then he kissed her, turned, and climbed the staircase into the airplane. Hadley remained standing on the tarmac as the plane's engines started up. She stayed as the plane taxied to a nearby runway. She watched as it took off and climbed out of sight into the sky.

When Hadley awoke the sky outside was pitch black. Dark figures hovered around Jason's bed. One held a clipboard, another had her fingers on Jason's throat, and yet another spoke quietly into a telephone in the corner of the room.

Hadley propped herself up on one elbow to look at Jason. Someone had removed his glasses, and his eyes were closed. His mouth was also closed.

It took several seconds for her slumbering brain to connect all the dots: the closed eyes, the nurse feeling for a pulse, the officials noting the time. She knew it…it was a very simple word, only a few letters.

"Honey, let's get you off the bed." A young nurse in purple scrubs took hold of her arm, but Hadley jerked away. She could not leave. She could not leave him all alone. He would get cold, and she had to keep him warm. She squeezed his hand to reassure him.

He did not squeeze back. She lifted her own hand, and as it rose through the air, so did Jason's. She unlocked each of his fingers from her own and then held his wrist in both of her palms. She tried to picture this hand—it was his left—around the neck of his violin. In her mind she tried to make it move, but it would not. His fingers would not stay on the ebony fingerboard. He would not play anymore.

She kissed the back of his hand and then laid it back on the blanket beside his body.

She looked up at the waiting nurse.

And then she was slipping and sliding all over the place. She tried to stand up but slid back down again. She tried grasping for some wall or railing, anything to get her bearings, but she could not find anything to steady herself. Even as she felt herself get to the bottom of the slide, she started back up at the top and slipped down again. Or maybe she really started at the bottom and slid upwards—she could not tell east from west, up from down, right from wrong, or light from dark. The hospital room had dissolved, the building had dissolved, maybe the earth had even dissolved. Maybe she had slid through some hole in the ground. Maybe the hole had swallowed her up. Perhaps she would slip all the way down to the center of the world.

It was utterly empty down in that hole. Nothing, no words, no feeling, no tears.

And then something pulled her out. Something took her hands. It guided her to a chair and sat her down. When the world briefly stopped slipping and sliding around—it was like an ancient wooden ship weathering hurricane seas—she thought it would be safe to open her eyes without vomiting.

A face swam up before her eyes.

Jason! She tried to move her leaden arms to swim toward him, but waves of sorrow drowned her again and again.

He had lost his glasses…he couldn't see her…he didn't know she was looking for him.

"Hadley." He called to her! She had to go to him! She had to reach him before the waves carried him away.

"Hadley, it's Parker. Look at me."

Some force placed itself on either side of her head and held it steady. She opened her eyes. No glasses, longer hair, bushier eyebrows. The pressure left her temples and her head dropped. She saw two hands, but the third finger of the left one had a gold band around it.

"Parker?"

Her stomach spasmed and heaved, but nothing came out. Several more times her diaphragm muscles contracted and worked to expel something through her mouth, but nothing would come up. She was empty.

Her eyes rose to the eastward facing window. Lights flickered in the pitch sky. Hadley hauled herself up from the chair and moved to the window. A line of lights shone in the middle of the sky like the lights of some great extraterrestrial vehicle hovering over the city. Just below the row of lights, a darker-than-dark mass began. One light twinkled at the top of this darkness, but instead of blinking on and off, its light shone steadily as it moved diagonally—upper right to lower left—over the blacker-than-blackness.

Hadley watched the lights of the tram car from where it left its berth at 11,000 feet to where it disappeared into the residential lights of the foothills at 6,000 feet. She watched the line of lights at the top of the mountain as they shone on and on through the night and through the darkness. They never fell. The mountains held strong, the towers still stood, and the tram descended on its thick cables.

Hadley never bothered to find out when exactly Jason died, so she did not know how long she stood looking to the east for the coming dawn, how long she stood looking at those beacons on the crest, how long she waited for the mountain to collapse.

But she would not see the dawn rise from that window. Long before the earliest flickers of day, Parker took her hand and led her away.

She let herself be buckled into the front seat of a car and be driven through the dark streets. The car stopped in an expansive parking lot, and with Parker's hand still firmly guiding her, Hadley boarded a school bus. The old bus threaded its way through the city, and after it came to rest and someone up at the front shouted instructions, Parker led her out and away into the cold, thin, pre-dawn air.

Carnival lights and the smell of frying dough swirled around her. Masses of people crowded before a long line of food vendors' booths. The growling of Hadley's stomach briefly awoke her out of her haze, but Parker steered her away from the makeshift food court. The hard asphalt beneath her feet became grass. They finally stopped.

Giant lightbulbs hovered over the black sky, and some invisible hand was turning them on and off. They did not all turn on and off at the same time and did not remain lit for the same duration, but they did all shine with the same wavelength of color: a soft orange glow reminiscent of sunset. The invisible fingertips flicked a switch and the lightbulb instantly glimmered gold for a few seconds. Then, just as abruptly, it went dark again.

Parker whispered in Hadley's ear, "Aren't they beautiful? Do you remember the first time we came to this together? I asked you to marry me."

Yes. She remembered. They were not lightbulbs. They were hot air balloons still anchored to the ground and inflating their sails with the air that would carry them into the morning.

As they waited to lift off, the glowing orbs drew thick packs of people around them. Children sat atop their fathers' shoulders to get a better view of the fire that briefly flamed within the dome of fabric. Cameras snapped away as their owners squealed in delight. Quick bursts of heat from a propane tank diffused hot air through the billowing nylon like a beating heart propelling oxygenated blood into arteries for carriage to the far reaches of the body.

Hadley dropped her hand from Parker's and wandered to the nearest balloon. She wormed her way through the crowd right up to the inner edge of the gathered circle. Each squeeze from the propane tank not only illuminated the balloon but also shot warm air over the heads of the congregation. The waves of hot air slowly thawed Hadley's frozen body.

Two hefty men dressed in the black-and-white striped shirts of sports referees approached the balloon and consulted with the passengers packed into the basket. The referees blew whistles and cleared a path through the swarm of observers. Then the ropes cast off, the ground crew pushed against the basket, the pilot pumped his propane tank, and the dawn carried the balloon away as gracefully as the sea embraces a sailboat. The cold mountain drew the flying machine to its breast, and the balloon flew off into the bluing sky.

Hadley followed its course as it soared into the black. Other balloons had also launched—perhaps fifteen or so—and fought against the dark curtain that still hung over the new day's stage. They twinkled like stars, flickered like flames, and turned on and off like man-made lightbulbs installed against the sky by humans desperate for illumination both physical and otherwise.

A blue light had snuck up on the watchers. Hadley tore her eyes away from the west and turned to face the blue light rising in the east. Parker waited patiently a few feet from her. She went to him and looked up into his blue eyes, pale as the dawn.

"He's gone."

"Yes, he is."

He took her hand and led her away again. The Mass Ascension had really begun in earnest. The first full row of balloons was already laid out on the grass and preparing to inflate. It was like—actually, no appropriate metaphor existed to describe the line of huffing and puffing color. Perhaps it was like a rainbow become three dimensional and tangible, or maybe like a tropical fish tank made breathable.

Hadley and Parker passed under a tunnel composed of the fabric of two adjacent balloons. When they emerged on the other side, Hadley dropped Parker's hand and stopped beside one balloon still resting on its side. The huge canopy—more than thirty feet in length—lay prone on the ground. If one faced east, as Hadley did, the huge volume of the balloon obstructed the view of the mountains. Hadley could not see the monumental gates at the rim of the world; she saw only billowing yards of yellow, blue, red, and green.

The balloon was already inflated but still remained horizontal. The next puffs of air would right the balloon and set it correctly vertical. Slowly the balloon tilted upwards as if pulled by invisible strings. As it moved, it uncovered the lower slopes of the Sandias, purple in the emerging morning. Inch by inch, foot by foot, as the balloon righted itself, the mountains reappeared. And finally, just as it reached its perfect vertical axis, the motley colors of the balloon uncovered the first flaming rays of the sun as it came over the crest of the mountain.

Hadley automatically and involuntarily raised her hand to her eyes. The suddenness of the sun, after looking into opaque color for ten minutes, momentarily blinded her. Another zebra-striped air traffic controller motioned her away from the righted balloon. She backed away but continued to look in the vague direction of the sun that relentlessly struggled against the boulders of the mountain. The dawn lit the peaks from behind, encasing them in shimmering gold.

There it was: the balloon drifting up to heaven on a soft breeze, the cold light of the rising sun, and the great bulk of the mountains.

He loved me.

It came to her as inevitably as the fact of the sun's rising. No argument, no analysis, no need for second-guessing. That was how it was, plain and simple. The balloons rose because the air within them was hotter than the air outside. The hotter air was less dense, so it rose, and as it rose it carried along the balloon, the basket, and the people inside it. These were physical laws and principles. And just as inviolable as the laws of physics was the truth that Jason had loved Hadley.

"Gorgeous, isn't it?" Parker sidled up to her.

Without taking her eyes off of the balloon and the sun and the mountain, Hadley said, "Yes, it is."

She stared for a few more minutes, but the feeling did not dissipate. It did not float away as the balloons did. The wind did not bear it away as it bore the baskets. The morning did not carry it off on the air.

"Jason loved me."

"He told you?"

Still Hadley did not turn her head away from the sun. It now hung in the sky just over the summit of the mountain range. Its cast rays warmed the worshiping mass.

"No, he didn't tell me, but I know he did. I feel it. I believe it. He loved me. I know it as I know the sun is rising. I feel it as I feel the warmth of the dawn. I believe it. I loved him and he loved me. For whatever reason, he didn't say it, but I know it is true."

Parker smiled. He smiled like the day she had first met him. This smile had joy and pride and hope. "And no regrets?" he asked.

"None. If I had to do it all again, I would do it. I won't lie. It hurts, it really does. It will hurt for a long time, but what can I regret? I did everything perfectly this time. I took my chance. I took the risk. And I will never regret that."

Parker said nothing, but he took hold of her shoulders, turned her toward him, and wrapped her in his arms. She reciprocated, and they held each other close and tight. He kissed her. This kiss was unlike any they had shared. As they kissed now under blue skies, he felt like one of the tanks under the balloons' canopies. He filled her and inflated her with his breath. She became hot, light, and expansive under his arms. His touch, he knew, would heal her and make her whole once more.

A cool breeze blew back her hair; if Parker had not held fast to her, she might have been carried away just like the balloons.

"Hadley, I love you too."

She remembered Jason's final flight and his last words to her.

"I love you too," she said.

They finally broke apart and stood facing each other with hands clasped. She was crying, but did not bother to wipe away her tears.

"You hungry?" he asked.

"Starving." She put her hand to her stomach.

"I'll go get us something. Stay right here, okay?"

She nodded and watched him walk off toward the food stalls. He would return. She did not have to worry about that.

THE END

## *About The Title*

The title of this book derives from the lyrics of songs by several bands I love: "Carry That Weight," by The Beatles, "One," by U2, and "We Got a Hit," by The Who. Due to copyright laws, I could not include the lyrics to these songs as an epigraph. I invite and encourage readers to listen to these songs to better understand the title of this book.

--Kristina Caffrey

## *Acknowledgements*

I would like to thank Evelyn Moore, Kathy Richter-Sand, Karen Glinksi, Khit Harding, and Desiree Perriguey for their encouragement, insight, and support. I would not have reached the point of sharing my writing with the world without your help, and I am forever grateful for both your feedback and your friendship. I would also like to thank Jonathan Livingston Terry, Jason Rogers, and Sheila Bednarski for reading early drafts and providing encouraging feedback.

## *About The Author*

Kristina Caffrey lives in Albuquerque, New Mexico, where she works by day as an attorney. In addition to writing, she acts in community theater and plays the cello. She is a past *Jeopardy* champion and a noted rock and roll fan.

Made in the USA
Columbia, SC
20 July 2020

14239060R00205